THE WINTER LAIRD

MISTS OF FATE - BOOK ONE

NANCY SCANLON

This is a work of fiction. Names, characters, places and incidents either are the product of the author's imagination or are used fictitiously. Any resemblance to actual persons (living or dead), events, or locales is entirely coincidental.

THE WINTER LAIRD. Copyright © 2020 by Nancy Scanlon. All rights reserved. Printed in the United States of America. No part of this book may be used or reproduced in any manner without written permission from the author, excepting only brief quotations embodied in critical articles or reviews.

Print Edition ISBN: 978-1-7349671-0-4

Cover photo and design: Kim Killion, The Killion Group

www.nancyscanlonbooks.com
Sign up for Nancy's newsletter:
https://www.nancyscanlonbooks.com/contact

If you purchased this book without a cover, you should be aware that this book is stolen property. It was reported as "unsold and destroyed" to the publisher, and neither the publisher nor the author has received any payment for this "stripped book."

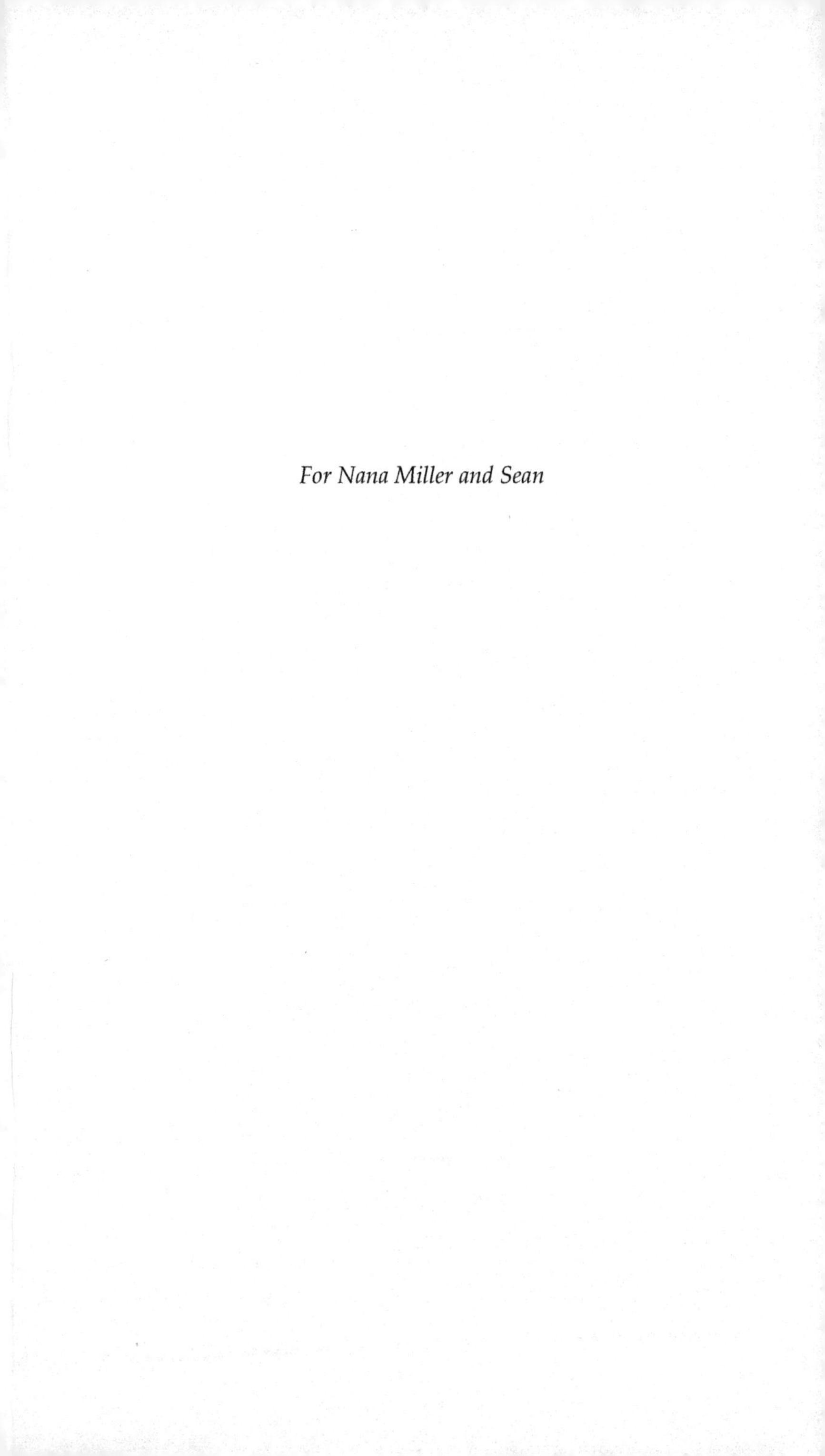

For Nana Miller and Sean

PROLOGUE

Brianagh O'Rourke carefully adjusted the elbow-length veil. She smoothed the ribbon-lined edges into place, then blew out a shaky breath.

Taking a final, critical look in the mirror, Bri felt a flash of triumph overcome her nerves. This moment was almost two years in the making. A difficult courtship almost failed at the last moment, mostly because of one partner's inability to commit, threatening their happily-ever-after. Brianagh redoubled her efforts, giving the relationship the lion's share of her time. Late nights, early mornings, frantic phone calls… and in the end, it worked out.

It always did, she thought proudly.

She met Kristen's clear gaze in the mirror. "You made it."

"I did," her client said dreamily.

"You look lovely." Brianagh smoothed her hand over the veil again, drawing a smile from Kristen Bouchement, her most difficult client to date.

"I hope Justin thinks so. I can't believe I found my soul mate…and it's all thanks to you," Kristen said softly. "I wish I listened to you sooner. I would've been married a year already."

"Justin would wait an eternity for you." Brianagh infused just the right amount of happiness before switching back to professionalism. "But let's not make him wait any longer, okay?"

Kristen laughed, a sound Bri was more than happy to hear after the panicked phone calls just the week before, when Kristen decided she couldn't possibly love Justin as much as he did her, and how did one go about breaking off an engagement as high-profile as theirs?

Two years ago, Boston's most talked-about socialite—and only daughter of the state senator—waltzed into Bri's then up-and-coming matchmaking service, Celtic Connections. Kristen presented Brianagh with a massive challenge: take a list of must-have "husband qualities" and find Kristen the perfect husband…before her father ran in the next presidential election.

The "husband qualities" included old wealth, politics, good looks, more than two estates—preferably on both coasts—no false teeth, limited use of hair product, and family ties to oil.

"Well, I think it's safe to say that your company's one hundred percent success rate holds true."

Brianagh stepped back to let the wedding planner fuss with Kristen's earrings and allowed herself a true smile. "I'm happy to agree with you."

Celtic Connections was now Boston's most selective and successful matchmaking service. As they took on only a few select clients per year, they could dedicate a significant amount of time and resources to finding the perfect match. And Brianagh O'Rourke always found the perfect match.

Kristen's match, Justin, had exactly what Bri knew she needed—a level-headed, easygoing personality and the patience of a saint. Kristen resisted, as his money was "new" and he hadn't any ties to politics, but in the end, love and common sense prevailed, and Justin, the CFO of a local banking chain without any ties to oil—but with a full set of natural teeth—stood ready for his bride.

Brianagh checked on him earlier in the afternoon, when he was pacing and damning the fact that he agreed to a three o'clock wedding, wishing he had pushed for a brunch.

"Because we'd be married already, and I can't wait a minute longer!" he burst out in frustration.

Bri gave him her usual speech about how long he'd waited, that another two hours wasn't going to kill him, that Kristen was also dying to see him in the church…it was the same song and dance she played at each wedding she attended.

Kristen and Justin were her sixteenth match—her eighth high profile match—in four years.

"It's your turn now, Brianagh," Kristen said suddenly, breaking into her thoughts.

Bri smiled, a touch of practiced understanding in her gaze. "It's every bride's wish to see everyone around them happy." *Every* happy *bride's wish,* she amended silently.

This part of the job, she recognized, was possibly the worst. Her unmarried state didn't deter any of her clients, but, when she stood with them in their dressing room before the nuptials, most of them made a statement similar to Kristen's. And it wasn't as though she didn't believe in happily-ever-afters. She most certainly did, and refused to match anyone whom she believed wouldn't be a true and loving spouse to someone.

She just didn't believe in her own happily-ever-after. It wasn't for a lack of trying, but she was too busy ensuring everyone else got their fairytale ending.

"Matthew simply fawns over you. I think he might be the one," Kristen added conspiratorially. "I wish you the same kind of happiness you found for me!"

Bri forced a smile. *Fawning* was a gross overstatement. She was lucky if she garnered her boyfriend's attention for more than it took for the next phone call to come in.

Matthew de Burgh moved in the same circles as Kristen. He was a huge supporter of Senator Bouchement, and when Kristen introduced him to Bri…well, if sparks didn't exactly fly, she felt more for Matthew than she had for anyone else, and that was enough for her. As the founder of a matchmaking service, she knew there was a lot to be said for a comfortable relationship. All-consuming lust wasn't on *her* must-have list of husband qualities.

Her Director of Registration strongly disagreed with her line of thinking, but as he was also her cousin, Brianagh ignored his opinions of her life as often as possible.

"That is so sweet of you to say, Kristen. All I did was introduce you to each other. You and Justin followed your hearts…and now, it's time to follow that heart down the aisle."

The wedding planner, whom Brianagh recommended to Kristen, seamlessly took over the interaction and directed Kristen out of the room, into her teary-eyed father's arms. A moment later, the bride, her father, and her wedding planner were gone.

Brianagh tiptoed down the hall of the enormous church and peeked in, where Kristen was nearly to the end of the aisle. Justin's face was alight with wonder, and his eyes were only for his bride. Bri let out a little sigh of happiness for the couple.

Her phone buzzed discreetly, and she fumbled through her purse. Pulling it out, her shoulders dropped at the message.

Dinner tonight at seven. Semi-formal, wear heels. Xoxo

She tamped down an annoyed sigh. Lately, Matthew had been offering her suggestions as to what she ought to wear when they were out in public together.

"I have a reputation to consider," he'd said, slipping her

the business card of a personal shopper at Neiman Marcus. "You know how we're always being photographed."

Actually, she didn't—she only saw photographers at the philanthropic events they attended together—but she'd taken the card. She hadn't made use of the service yet, though.

Brianagh glanced again into the church, unable to ignore the small pang in her chest when she again caught sight of Justin, unable to remove his eyes from his bride who, even from here, was blushing.

Just once I'd like someone to look at me like that, Brianagh thought. She squared her shoulders and pushed away the thought. She was twenty-nine years old; the time for starry-eyed fairy tales was over. Passion and swept-off-her-feet love didn't exist for her, and she had made her peace with it.

Almost.

BRIANAGH REMINDED HERSELF THAT SHE WHOLE-HEARTEDLY believed in happily-ever-afters, despite the sparkling engagement ring at which she was currently gaping.

The night started innocently enough. Matthew surprised her with reservations at Top of the Hub, one of Boston's most impressive restaurants because of its unparalleled, 360-degree views of the city's skyline.

Matthew excelled at saying romantic things, so when he claimed that he wanted nothing more than to watch the sunset together from their sky-high vantage point, she didn't blink.

When he turned his phone off, Brianagh felt a prickle of nervousness descend upon her spine.

When he kept it off for longer than it took to restart it, she began to feel faint. And not in the way her clients claimed to feel when their significant others were near.

Glancing again at the obscenely large diamond in front of

her, Bri swallowed hard. Apparently, he had more than just the sunset on his mind.

"Say yes," Matthew murmured from his knee in the middle of the very crowded, uncomfortably silent restaurant. "Make me the happiest man alive, Bri. Marry me."

Tapping her fingers on the white tablecloth, she tried to breathe but found that simple task beyond her. She glanced out the floor-to-ceiling glass wall overlooking the harbor; the reflection of Boston's city skyline, while beautiful, didn't ease the tightness in her chest. The incoherent thoughts in her head buzzed with the answer he certainly did not want to hear, so she gave him the answer he did.

"Okay," she managed to say. Not a ringing endorsement of said happily-ever-after, but Matthew's eyes lit up as if she had declared her undying love.

Maybe she had; she didn't know. She was in uncharted territory, no one had ever proposed to her. He gently slid the diamond onto her finger as the entire restaurant erupted into cheers.

She thought she might be sick and wondered briefly if this was a normal response.

She didn't think so.

He kissed her, and Bri fervently hoped he didn't notice her lack of enthusiasm. When his mouth opened, she wished that, just once, she could feel the surge of desire she'd heard about. She read enough romance novels and listened to her clients wax lyrical after a particularly successful date. But logically she knew, and Matthew knew, that lust simply wasn't for them.

"I'm so happy," Matthew said, pulling back suddenly and signaling for the check.

She blinked, feeling as though that kiss was more of a handshake to seal the deal. And, as she usually did, she began to rationalize her feelings. Intellectually, she knew she and Matthew worked well as a couple. She had relationships down to a science. She knew the formulas behind the hows and whys of happily-ever-afters. On paper, she and Matthew were a perfect fit.

Spark was a fleeting thing, in her opinion. Bri believed companionship, common backgrounds, and intellect kept a relationship stronger than a spark, but her coworkers argued that it took more than a formula laid out in a database. They claimed that for some, the spark was the deciding factor.

Somehow, she'd never really gotten to the point of a deciding factor when it came to Matthew.

Probably a moot point now, she thought as he led her out of the restaurant. Matthew called for his driver, and he gave a quick nod to a passing acquaintance as he herded her into the car.

"You did very well," he said as he powered on his phone. He handed her a glass of champagne. "I wasn't sure how you would react when I put you on the spot like that... But what I did know, from our very first date, was that you'd be my wife."

Bri tossed back the drink as the driver pulled away from the curb. She stared at her empty flute, saying nothing for a long moment.

"What makes you so sure we'll work, Matthew?"

His phone immediately began to ping with incoming messages, texts, and missed call notifications. "Why wouldn't we?"

She raised an eyebrow but remained silent.

He looked up at her briefly, his eyes already distant. "We connect on a deeper level, Brianagh. Think of it as an acquisition." He looked back at his phone, and his thumbs began to move as he answered a text. "Both parties already complement each other in some way. And together, they'll be a force to be reckoned with. We have all the right things to make the other better, and that's what you always say makes a match successful."

As he spoke, Bri studied him. Matthew was so handsome—his blond highlights stood out in deep contrast to his dark brown eyes. He could've been a model for high-end clothing. *Why can I not be more attracted to this man?*

It was a question she'd been asking herself for a long time. The only conclusion she'd drawn was depressing, and after seeing Kristen—who, by all accounts, was possibly the most difficult-to-please woman in all of Boston, and perhaps in New England—find someone perfectly wonderful to love forever, Brianagh accepted the truth. She was incapable of love. Not the kind of love she had for her family—she had that in spades—but the kind of breath-stealing, mind-blowing, passionate love she found in her dreams.

She sighed to herself and poured another glass of champagne, half-listening to Matthew's phone call about an upcoming acquisition of some sort. He flicked his eyes toward her, and she offered a wan smile. He gave her the thumbs-up, then reached into his pocket and absent-mindedly handed her the empty ring box. She accepted it and placed it in her purse wordlessly before looking out her window, catching sight of the moon's reflection on the Charles.

It reminded her of the novel she just finished last night, where the hero climbed a tower in the moonlight to see his love one last time before she married another. A smile curved Bri's lips as she remembered how it ended—the hero and heroine managed to be together, despite the evil fiancé, stalwart father, and society's expectations.

Bri groaned silently, cursing books for her predicament. If only she hadn't picked up that romance novel on that library cart all those years ago, enticed by, of all things, its cover, she wouldn't be so stuck in her fantasy world. She loved and hated that she dreamed of the same man every night. Rationally, she knew her dream lover was a figment of her imagination, made up with various pieces of all the characters she grew to love from the myriad of novels lining her bookshelves at home. But she could picture him clearly, even here, with her boyfriend—well, now her fiancé—clasping her hand and looking every bit the charming millionaire from one of those very books. Here she was, dreaming of her fictional romance hero, when she had a real-life Prince Charming in the flesh.

"Let me conference in Jimmy, then you two can work this out. I'll be at the office in less than an hour." Matthew pulled the phone away from his ear. "Brianagh, I'll drop you at your house, okay? This merger is getting sticky, and I really don't want it to wait until morning."

We just became engaged, she felt like screaming. *Shouldn't there be more to this than a ring, a glass of champagne, and a business call?*

Instead of voicing any of those thoughts, she merely stated, "Of course."

She knew better than to dream of the perfect man. Such a creature didn't exist. She made it her *business* to know better than that.

Matthew brought her back to the present by taking her glass out of her hand and ending his call. "I should meet your family. Other than your director…what's his name again?"

"Colin."

"Yes. Colin. Right."

"My family is very important to me. You know that."

"You can still see them, Bri. It's not like I'll try to keep them away from you."

"What about children?" she asked suddenly. "Do you want children, Matthew?"

"Bri, there's plenty of time for that discussion. Let's just enjoy being engaged." Matthew held his phone up to see who was calling him. He rolled his eyes. "*Boston Globe* already. They know to call my PR department."

"Why would *The Globe* be calling you?" Brianagh asked hesitantly.

He gave a look that spoke volumes. "I'm engaged. To you." He said it as though she should be thanking him for choosing her. An icy tendril of dread snaked up her back.

"Right," she managed.

"I should probably take this," Matthew said apologetically. "I don't trust my new assistant and my PR staff won't be in until tomorrow. The driver will walk you to your door, though." He leaned over and bussed her cheek, then took the call.

~

INSIDE HER BROWNSTONE, BRIANAGH SLID THE LOCKS INTO PLACE and slipped her shoes off. She leaned her forehead against the door. "What have I done?"

"Found my soul mate?" a hopeful voice asked.

Brianagh flipped on the light and threw one of the shoes at her cousin. "Oh, shut up, Colin. Why are you on my couch again?"

"Argh!" he cried out, dramatically flinging his arm across his eyes. He tossed the blanket aside and rose from the couch. "I locked myself out of my apartment," he explained, running his hand through his dark-blond hair with a shrug.

"Really. And you just happened to have *un*locked yourself out of mine?"

"Yep." He stretched languorously, his T-shirt pulling tight over his large chest and flat stomach. Rolling his shoulders, he grinned at her. "I prefer to sleep on a couch rather than the floor."

She rolled her eyes as she deposited her purse on the table. "I pay you a ridiculously large salary. Maybe you should invest in some furniture instead of a weekly female conquest. And why not crash at your mother's house?" she demanded.

Colin gave her a mock-pout, which did nothing to detract from his all-American good looks. He swept her shoe off the floor and assessed her with knowing, chocolate-brown eyes.

"Her couch isn't as comfy as yours. You seem grumpy, which is weird given that our dear Kristen Bouchement is now quite definitively Kristen Millings. Which, I might add, you would have witnessed, if you ever sat all the way through a wedding instead of skipping out before the vows." He dangled her shoe from his finger and tapped his chin mock-thoughtfully. "Let me guess…bad night with the millionaire?" He dangled her shoe from his finger.

She just barely managed to not roll her eyes. "I'm going to bed."

"I was *in* bed before you tromped through the front door," Colin replied. He plopped back on the couch, her shoe falling to the floor, and reached for the remote.

Brianagh snorted with disgust. "Technically, you were *in* couch. Wait. Were your shoes on my couch?" she exclaimed, noting the mud-splattered boots on his feet as he propped them onto her coffee table. "Colin! Get your shoes off my table! Those boots are filthy!"

"Filthy or not, I love my Docs." Colin smiled fondly at the well-worn boots, but he began to unlace them. "They can do more damage than those strappy things you're wearing."

"Shut *up*, Colin."

"Nice ring. You know, smart as you are, you are damn stupid when it comes to guys," he replied. He kicked off his boots and tossed her shoe back to her.

She whacked him with her other shoe as she walked by, aggravated that she loved him enough not to shove him onto the street. She hated when he was right—both about the ring and the strappy shoes.

"You're not *really* serious about marrying that guy, are

you?" His pitying laughter followed her into her bedroom, where she fell onto her bed and looked out the window. She twisted the ring on her finger. It felt heavy, foreign, and oddly constricting.

Soul mate. Ha.

She could love Matthew. She was sure of it. Love—*well, love based in reality,* she amended as she studiously avoided looking at her crammed bookshelf—was comfortable, and easy. That's what she had with Matthew. She could talk to him about almost anything. Not many men would understand her driven nature—she was pretty ruthless when she had to be. Maybe that's why she was initially drawn to Matthew. He was the first man, other than her smart-mouthed cousins, to respect her without making her work so hard to prove she was just as savvy, if not savvier, than he. He simply accepted that they were equals, and that was…nice.

But shouldn't there be more than nice? That crazy desire—the need to touch, to feel, to be with that person every waking moment? A part of her longed for that connection, but she knew it wasn't rational. She'd never felt that connection with anyone, so she sympathized for the tiny part of her that still believed in the happily-ever-after. Late at night, she would think about the kind of epic love she read about, when, even at eighty years old, a woman would still be pulled into darkened corners and kissed as though she was the most beautiful woman in the world.

So what if she didn't have that? She couldn't have everything. She had everything else—a thriving, successful business, a wonderful family, and now, Boston's most eligible bachelor as a fiancé. Pining over the idea of love was childish and naïve.

Soul mates didn't exist. Passion was fleeting, and her marriage would be built on something much more robust than that. Things like…

She paused.

Well, she would think of something. Even if his casual dismissal of her tonight made her feel more like a business acquisition than an engagement, he did still ask her to marry him. He must feel something more than friendship toward her if he was willing to pop the question. She was pleasantly surprised he did it in person, too, instead of via text.

That should've given her pause. The fact that it didn't concerned her, but her phone buzzed, pulling her from her thoughts.

I miss your smile already. Dream of me.

She tossed the phone on her nightstand and nodded purposefully. Passion didn't exist. *Nice* existed. Passion was great for her dreams; it was even something that made for good reading, but really—who would want that every day? It was probably exhausting.

She was almost sure of it.

THE WOMAN SAT ON A SMALL WOODEN STOOL NEAR A BLAZING FIRE set in a large hearth. She hummed tunelessly as she dug around a basket, pulling out one pouch at a time and tossing the contents into the flames, creating a quick burst of red with each addition.

"Come."

Brianagh crossed the cold flooring and sat next to her, waiting.

The woman looked down at her and smiled. "A gift." She took Brianagh's hand and placed a dusting of pale-yellow powder in it. "Go on," she whispered, her eyes reflecting the light.

Brianagh tossed the handful of powder into the fire and jumped when the flames caught it. They danced wildly, and the bright-orange burst made her eyes burn and water. She blinked quickly, not sure what she was about to see but desperate not to miss it.

She saw an outline begin to take shape—she recognized him immediately. He wasn't as he had always been in her dreams, though; usually, he was smiling, or laughing, or there was a heat in his captivating eyes. Now his head was bowed. His hand rested lightly on his enormous sword, which held but a single sapphire in its hilt. He'd shown it proudly to Brianagh the day his clan leaders had presented it to him. He looked older than he'd ever appeared to her before, and she could feel the tension radiating from him.

"What's wrong?" she asked the woman, her eyes never leaving the vision. "Why is he standing like that? What's happening?" Everything felt so wrong. His mouth was moving, as if he was talking, but Brianagh couldn't hear him or make out what his lips were saying.

"You didn't come," the woman replied. "It may be too late. It may all be for naught."

"What's for naught? Go where?" Brianagh watched, realizing something was very wrong. He was stoic. Serious. The last time she had dreamed of him, he had loved her sweetly. He'd been relaxed, happy.

She watched as he nodded once, and it was done…but she wasn't sure what it *was. "What's happening?" she asked again, her voice rising in desperation. She had never seen this side of him.*

"You didn't come for him," the woman replied, watching the scene unfold. "So now, he agrees to marry another."

Brianagh was beyond confused. He was just a dream—her dream. But she was losing him to another? How is it possible to lose a dream?

"No," Brianagh said suddenly, leaning forward. "No, he is mine. My dream. Mine." She sounded like a three-year-old on the verge of a tantrum, but she didn't care. She couldn't lose him. He was the only one she loved.

"You didn't come. So he never claimed you…and now, it may all be for naught." The woman shook her head sadly. "You will unite with one other than your predestined mate…and he will do the same. The hawk shall fly no more."

Years of dreaming, just to watch her love in a silent discussion that made her heart ache for reasons she didn't understand. He nodded, in deep discussion…then a woman appeared. He grasped her hand and placed…

Was that a ring? And then she saw the flash of a sword, swinging in an arc from behind him…

"No!" Brianagh screamed into the fire. "No, no! Behind— "

Brianagh bolted upright in bed, her heart pounding and her breathing ragged. Her face was hot, but she was freezing everywhere else.

Without bothering to check the time, she grabbed her phone and hit speed dial. "I had a dream."

The Irish brogue was thicker than normal. "Jesus, Bri, it's two in the morning. You gave me a heart attack." Reilly O'Malley, her closest cousin and dearest friend, yawned loudly.

"I agreed to marry Matthew."

"You dreamed you agreed to marry that bastard? That would frighten me, too."

"No, no. I mean, I actually did agree. The dream was something else entirely," she explained, exasperated. Reilly loathed Matthew; he believed him to be a pompous ass with little to recommend him. Matthew thought Reilly was a backwoods hick from Ireland who was too overprotective of his cousin. It was a mess, and Bri hated being in the middle of it.

Reilly swore, sounding much more awake all of a sudden.

"Save it," she cut him off before he could start in on Matthew's faults. "I have to get away for a while."

To anyone else, she knew she would sound like a raving lunatic. But Ry knew her better than she knew herself. He was used to her need for constant movement; he had, after all, appointed himself her guardian when she was too little to remember, and had been her travel companion each time she hopped on a plane.

His sigh almost blew her off the phone. "Let me guess. Ireland?"

The one place Matthew was sure not to follow her. He disliked everything about the country—mostly because Reilly hailed from it.

She laughed in relief. "I knew you'd be up for this, Ry. I'll make the arrangements."

"And I'll play bodyguard," he replied dryly. "You know I have to break a date for this?"

"You know, if you went through Celtic Connections, I'd feel worse about it," she teased, then added seriously, "Think we can leave tomorrow?"

"Your wish is my command," he muttered good-naturedly. "I was actually planning to go there next week. I don't mind pushing up my plans; I miss home."

"Me, too. Thanks, Ry."

"What are cousins for?"

"Yeah," she replied, a smile in her voice.

"I'll meet you at Evelyn's in the morning," he said, then let out a big yawn. Her heartbeat slowed and the tightness in her chest eased fractionally. "Are you okay?"

"I don't really know," she admitted.

A long pause followed, and Reilly finally replied, "Don't worry, Bri. I'm with you."

She smiled, relieved. She knew he would be.

CHAPTER 1

"James!"

Evelyn Sullivan shot her eldest son a look only a mother could, and he reluctantly let go of his brother's neck. She turned her attention to her younger son. "Colin, where's your cousin?"

"She'll be here in a second. She was on the phone. She's traveling again." He rubbed his hands together as he sat down at the breakfast table. "I love Sundays, I love pancakes, and I love eggs!"

"Wash your hands," she chided just as Brianagh joined them.

"How old does one have to be in order to remember to wash up before a meal?" Brianagh wondered aloud, grabbing a plate.

James smirked. "Well, seeing as Colin is twenty-six—"

"And you are almost thirty. I didn't see you at the kitchen sink, young man," Evelyn cut in, taking the serving spoon out of his hand. "Honestly, boys. I thought I raised you better than this."

"You know, if you keep feeding them, they'll keep coming back," her uncle Connor boomed as he entered the kitchen.

He caught a glance of the large mound of pancakes on Colin's plate. "I thought we weren't supposed to feed the animals at the zoo, anyway."

Brianagh laughed. Sunday mornings were the same almost every week—no matter what their schedules were, it was ritual to show up around ten, eat pancakes and eggs, and tease each other until either James or Colin tackled the other to the floor. She loved it.

"Reilly's coming, too," she said, placing her phone on the table. "We're heading to his cottage tonight."

"You're going to Ireland?" Evelyn exclaimed, almost dropping her coffee. "Whatever for?"

"She's running," Colin cut in, pouring syrup all over his food. "I think she should invest in a good pair of Docs, personally. Those heels she's wearing won't last much past a mile before she breaks one of her ankles." He shoved pancakes into his mouth, then mumbled around them, "Go on, Bri. Tell her why you're running this time."

She glared at him. "Don't be a jerk."

"Jerk? What are we, in high school?" Colin swallowed, then turned to his mother. "Matthew popped the question, and Bri can't handle it so she's convinced Ry to go with her to Ireland. She's itchy. Don't even try to deny it," he added as Brianagh opened her mouth to protest. "You're tapping your foot."

"Marriage?" Evelyn asked, shock evident in her voice. "But you've only been dating, what? Three months?"

"Six," she replied, holding out her hand.

"You said yes?" Connor asked. "He didn't ask for my blessing…but, I suppose times have changed."

Brianagh sighed. "Uncle, I'm sure he meant no insult. And while I did say yes, I'm still thinking on it. There's a lot to consider."

Evelyn was gazing at the large diamond, biting her lip.

"This is a very, er, *large* ring, honey. I thought your style was a bit more understated."

She snatched her hand back. "I like it. Can you please pass the orange juice?"

"Morning." Reilly strode in, filling the kitchen with his presence. He grinned at Bri. "Hello, cousin. I hope you're ready for why you can't marry that prig. I made a list. We'll go over it on the plane."

"I made one, too," Colin added unhelpfully.

"Give me a few minutes and I'll come up with one as well," James piped in.

Brianagh groaned and dropped her head in her hands. Sometimes her family was overwhelming.

"You'd best tell me everything."

Brianagh zipped her suitcase and rolled her eyes as Reilly dropped onto her bed, his large frame dwarfing its size. She gingerly moved his booted feet off her comforter. "It's simple. Matthew proposed and I said yes. I need some time to process it, and Ireland is a good place to process things."

Reilly shook his head. He folded his arms over his chest and stared silently at her, waiting for her to explain further.

She rolled her eyes. "Oh, don't pull that strong-but-silent thing with me," she said. "You know that when you cross your arms like that, all your muscles bunch up. It's revolting."

Reilly grinned. "The lasses don't agree with you there." He flexed and wagged his eyebrows at her.

"Ew, Ry." She hauled the suitcase off the end of the bed and the zipper split. She gave it a glare and kicked it for good measure.

"Everything, Brianagh."

She huffed out a groan. "Fine. The truth is I need to think this out logically. You know, weigh the pros and cons."

"I've never heard a lass so recently engaged looking to make a list of pros and cons." Reilly raised an eyebrow. "Do you really have such deep affection for him, that you're willing to tie yourself to him for life?"

Bri frowned. *Life* sounded so…long, when put that way.

"Whatever happened to romance? Finding someone who makes your pulse race?"

She snorted. "Reilly, come on. I'm twenty-nine. I've had exactly two relationships. The first one—"

"He wasn't a man, Brianagh. The boy wet himself when James, Colin and I had a little chat with him. You need a real man."

She threw him a slitty-eyed look. "You bullied him. I don't care that he, um…wait. He really wet himself?"

Reilly nodded gravely.

"Oh. Well." She cleared her throat. "Anyway, the fact is, I have so much in my life already. I can't expect to have everything handed to me on a silver platter. My lot in life is business. I'm probably not even cut out for all that pulse-racing nonsense."

"What if you were fated for something different?"

Brianagh cocked her head. "If fate had anything to do with marriage, I wouldn't have a business."

"Sounds like excuses to me," Reilly replied dubiously.

The doorbell rang, interrupting them. Reilly held a hand out. "Sit. I'll answer it."

After years of arguing with him, Bri decided to fight the battle with her suitcase instead. Reilly had been in her life since before she could remember—and he hadn't any parents either. Perhaps that was why their bond was so strong; they were more brother and sister than cousins. He had been to every school play, dried her tears, and applauded her accomplishments. She adored him…but he could get incredibly annoying, incredibly fast. He was a throwback to another time—she never could place her finger on it, but whenever she said something to him, Reilly would grin at her and proclaim that as long as he lived, chivalry wasn't dead.

The smile on her face only grew as he walked back into her room with her aunt at his side.

"What are you doing here?" Bri asked, hugging Evelyn tightly.

Evelyn smiled. "It's pouring outside, and I thought you two may not want to walk to the subway with all your bags."

"I had planned to call us a cab," she replied, "but I'll take a ride, since you came into the city for us!"

Evelyn shook her head, amused. "Well, I also have this to give you. It's something that's been handed down on my side —our side—of the family when a woman is engaged." Evelyn smiled, a bit sadly, as she handed Brianagh a box. "It's very old," she warned. "Something we O'Rourkes have always worn on our wedding day."

Bri tore off the wrapping and opened the box, and her breath left her in a whoosh.

She pulled out a circular silver brooch about the size of her hand. The image on the front was worn, but the elaborately etched hawk was still glorious. Peering closer, she noticed the small shield in the middle of the hawk's chest: the letter *M* with tiny leaves of ivy snaking their way around each line of the letter…and a sword slicing across the *M* and all its foliage. Everything, down to the last feather on the hawk, was etched in fine detail, at least it had been at one point.

"Amazing. How old is it?" she asked, running her fingers over it. A shiver traveled down her spine, and she pulled her hand away as if burned. "It almost feels as though it's humming."

Reilly's face turned ashen.

Alarmed, she asked him, "Do you know what this is?"

"Aye," he finally said. "'Tis the brooch." He wordlessly held out his hand, and she reluctantly placed it in his palm. He turned it over, and then she saw him shiver as well.

The brooch? She turned to her aunt, the question in her eyes.

Evelyn smiled. "You rub it for good luck and a blessed marriage as you walk down the aisle—or run, in the case of some of our ancestors. That's why it's so smooth. It's our family legacy."

"Ah. So that's why Reilly looks so ill. It's meant for weddings," she joked as Reilly continued to stare at it.

His eyes met hers, and she immediately stopped her joking. He looked stricken.

"Reilly—" she said.

He shook his head once, then looked at Evelyn. "Tell her the story. The legacy."

Evelyn frowned at him, but then smiled at Brianagh. "It's one that we pass down to each generation, and I do love this story. Until you came into my life, I didn't think I'd ever get to tell anyone, as you know the boys would never care to hear it." Both she and Bri rolled their eyes together, then burst into a fit of giggles.

"Evelyn!" Reilly barked. "The story."

"Relax!" Brianagh exclaimed. "We don't have to leave until tonight. There's plenty of time. Don't be so grumpy, you big oaf."

"Thank you," Evelyn replied with a regal nod of her head. Reilly just scowled, gave the brooch back to Brianagh, and then sat back down on the bed and glowered.

Brianagh returned her attention to her aunt. "So…family legacy. I'm all ears. You know how I love happy endings."

~

As she poured herself and Evelyn a cup of tea, Brianagh felt the weight of the brooch in her pocket. It was pretty heavy for its size, but it wasn't uncomfortable—it was quite the opposite. It gave her a feeling of security.

Odd.

She sat down and slid the cup to her aunt, then leaned forward, her eyes sparkling. "Okay. Spill."

"Where's mine?" Reilly asked.

Evelyn and Bri didn't even acknowledge him.

"It's been said that once, a very long time ago, a curse was put on the O'Rourkes."

Brianagh nearly rubbed her hands in glee. She loved this tale already.

"However, being as we're Irish, things are never as they seem. Our clan at the time—"

"When was this?" Bri interrupted.

"Oh, before recorded history, I'm sure. No one knows exactly when. The Fates—you know, like the ones in history, the three old women—decreed that the O'Rourke clan would be the time passage keepers. One family member from each generation is given the ability to move time itself, but only for the greater good."

"Obviously," Brianagh agreed. "But what's the 'greater good' entail?"

"Do you never stop asking questions?" Reilly asked, joining them with his own cup.

"Something not for personal gain, I'd assume," Evelyn replied with a shrug. "Let me get through the story. You'll miss your flight if you keep asking questions."

"Sorry."

"So, the family has this legacy of time-traveling. The O'Rourkes whispered it, ensuring that it was more feared than revered. The clan, you can imagine, had a very difficult time securing husbands for the women, but this only strengthened us, as was intentional. Only the bravest warriors married an O'Rourke."

"Bravest or daftest, depending which side of the O'Rourke border you're on," Reilly muttered.

"*Anyway,*" Evelyn continued, "the O'Rourkes started time-traveling only at a specified point in the future. Well, our past. But the Fates' future."

"Huh?" Brianagh asked.

"It's complicated," Reilly cut in. "But the bottom line is that when the O'Rourkes were handed this curse, blessing, legacy, whatever—it was determined at the time of the decree that the clan would not begin their time travels immediately. It was only at an undetermined point in the future, once the clan had proven itself capable and good and all the rest of it that the time-traveling could begin."

"But then history took a dark turn," Evelyn said dramatically, lowering her voice. "The child suspected of being the first time traveler disappeared!" At Brianagh's predicted gasp, Evelyn nodded authoritatively. "True. The O'Rourke woman—her name, we believe, was Kathryne—was visited by the Fates one night and was told the daughter she carried was the one who could move time. Kathryne, of course, told her husband, who somehow let it slip to another clan."

"How does one let that kind of thing slip?" Bri asked incredulously. "I mean, if the baby wasn't kidnapped, it'd be a miracle, right? I could see people wanting a power like time travel."

"That's exactly right. The baby's very life was put into danger before she was even born…so time twisted on itself." Evelyn took a breath. "The story goes that within minutes of the baby's birth, she was taken away by a future relative and brought to a time where none would find her. She was to be brought back at the hour of her wedding, where she would marry the fiercest of warriors, with a clan so loyal that they would lay down their lives for her and all children she and their lord would create." Evelyn waved at the brooch. "The only way to know if she was truly the chosen daughter would be that she was wearing this brooch—and something else, but I forget—and that she would unite two very powerful clans." Grinning, she added, "And, of course, live happily ever after."

"Well…if a relative from the future takes her away, then obviously she ends up safe. And, of course, madly in love with the lucky guy." Bri smiled wistfully and let out a sigh. "I see why women wear the brooch on their wedding day. They want that kind of happy ending."

Well, you can't always get what you want, she reminded herself, ignoring the tightness of her chest.

Evelyn nodded sagely. "I hope you find yours, Brianagh. I think it's a good sign that the brooch has an M on it."

"Oh, yes! For Matthew!" She laughed uncomfortably. "That does seem like a good omen."

"Don't count on it," Reilly grumbled.

CHAPTER 2

Brianagh woke up with a start. She'd had her dream again—she'd lost her love. She used to feel ridiculous when she woke up, realizing she had only her dreams to keep her company, but after so many years, she figured if she couldn't be honest with herself, then she'd simply make herself feel even more foolish.

It was a minor revelation as far as revelations went, but she took what she could get.

Her dream followed the same pattern. She was dressed in strange clothing and her hair was loose and long. Her warrior—she really didn't know what else to call him, as he wore a sword, some sort of kilt, and clearly medieval trappings—always opened his arms, and she would run to him. They would talk about his daily life—she felt as though she knew more about medieval times than was normal—and kiss, and as she got older, they had some pretty incredible sex, usually in a meadow, but sometimes inside his massive castle.

Dream, indeed.

She had been in fairy-tale love with her dream for as long as she could remember, and she was fairly certain if she let that little piece of knowledge out, she'd be ruined as a matchmaker.

But in last night's dream she was sitting with the old woman again and nothing had changed. The dream ended right before the sword came down upon his head. The depth of pain in her chest at the thought of losing her imaginary boyfriend frightened her.

She really needed to get out more.

Brianagh stood up and stretched, pulling her T-shirt down as it inched up her belly, and checked the time. She sighed when she saw it was only five a.m.; jet lag was the only downside of traveling. They'd arrived at Reilly's charming little cottage outside of Dublin only a few hours earlier. She padded downstairs silently, avoiding the creaky stair, and entered the kitchen for some water. As she filled her glass, she saw a movement in the back garden and froze. Slowly, she put the glass on the counter and pressed her nose to the window above the sink, her eyes widening as she watched a man hack at the air with—*was that a sword*?

She almost screamed, but then her eyes locked on his chest, and the magnificence of *that* stopped her in her tracks. In the predawn light, she could see the muscles bunching and flexing as he swung the sword at frightening speed. He was half-naked and sweating, and his arms were huge. His left arm had a tattoo wrapped around the top of his bicep—

Her mouth dropped open in shock and a little bit of healthy disgust for her thoughts a moment ago when she realized whom she was ogling.

Reilly. In the back garden, at five a.m.

With a sword.

And where the hell did he get all those muscles? she thought indignantly. He hid them underneath his shirts. He had leashed power in spades…how had she never noticed it?

Because he is like a brother to me, she admitted. *And the last time I saw him without his shirt, I was probably in elementary school.* She couldn't wait to tease him about his pecs—she loved nothing more than to make him blush, and that hadn't happened in much too long. Years, even. She looked one last time out the window—he really *was* trying to kill a particular bit of air—and chuckled, then grabbed her glass and went back to a blissful, dreamless sleep.

"WE NEED TO GET THERE BY SUNSET."

Brianagh glanced over at Reilly. He was tucked into the small driver's seat of his little Renault, concentration lining his face as he urged the little car to go faster. "I'm not a fan of sunsets lately. And we should've taken the Range Rover," she replied.

"It's with my mechanic," Reilly muttered, "and don't worry about it."

"It's not me who's worried. Relax, Ry. We can't even go in —the waiting list for this is years long," Brianagh flipped through the brochure. "Newgrange predates Stonehenge? Why have we never been there before?" Reilly's tense muscles were the only response she got. Furrowing her brow, she asked, "What's with you?"

He rolled his shoulders. "I—"

"If it's about Cory and the pub last night, I'm just glad that we weren't forever banned for the black eye you gave him."

"He told everyone he was going to get you in his bed!"

"I didn't say he didn't deserve it," she replied calmly, turning the page. "Wow. The pictures of the inside of this cave-thing—"

"Monolithic structure," Reilly corrected tightly.

"Right. The inside of this *monolithic structure* is beautiful."

"What does it say about Dowth?" he asked.

She flipped a couple more pages, then shrugged. "Not much. Looks like it's a good place to go for the solstice sunset and it doesn't have a waiting period, since you can't go inside it—no opening available to the public after dark. The northern side is locked to tourists, but the western side reacts the same way that Newgrange does when the sunrise happens. The entire ancient tomb—sorry, *monolithic structure* —is filled with light." She glanced up at him, taking in his set jaw and the five o'clock shadow. "Sounds pretty mystical. I wonder what it was originally used for."

Expertly navigating the car around a small herd of sheep in the road, Reilly risked a glance at her. "What does your little book tell you?"

She read for a minute, then replied, "Says here that no one really knows. Apparently, it has lots of little passageways and rooms. It's thought to be a tomb for the dead."

"It's not."

She grinned. "But it says in the next sentence there are those that believe it had some other purpose. Astronomical, perhaps? Or something magical?" She clapped her hands together. "Ooh, I bet there were sacrifices!"

"There weren't any sacrifices."

"You say that with such authority," Bri teased.

He glanced at her again. "There were never any sacrifices."

"You asked," she pointed out. "No need to get your knickers in a twist. No sacrifices, then." She glanced at the sky out her window. "It looks like snow. We're going to freeze our behinds off."

Reilly took a deep breath and released it slowly. "Brianagh, I…" He rubbed his temple. "I need you to trust me."

She looked at him curiously. "I always have. Why?" He pulled the car off the road and cut the engine, staring straight ahead for almost a full minute. "Reilly?"

He reached for a bag on the floor behind his seat. He held it in his hand for another long minute before finally handing it over to her. She pulled out a long, woolen dress, followed by some sort of gauzy thing and a pair of very ineffective, rustic-looking shoes. *Actually,* she thought as she held them up, *more like two pieces of leather roughly sewn together.*

Weird.

"What are these?"

"I have a, er, matching set in the trunk," was his reply. "Will you put it on?"

She looked at him in silence until he finally met her gaze. "Reilly, there's no need to be embarrassed about this." She bit her lip. "I've seen you playing with your sword in the mornings. I've kind of figured out that you're into reenacting the Middle Ages. I get it. That's fine. And if you want me to be involved, I can give it a shot. I didn't even know reenactment groups met at Newgrange."

"*Dowth.* We're going to Dowth."

"Fine. Dowth, whatever, although the brochure says it's closed to visitors until Easter. I do want to see Newgrange at some point, though. Other than sunrise," she added, her brow furrowing as she glanced down at the brochure, now lying on the floor at her feet. "There's a lottery just to get into the lottery to attend the solstice sunrise. Crazy."

"So you'll wear it?" He glossed over everything else she'd said.

"Sure. Are there any leggings or tights? I'm really going to freeze if I don't get something else under it, though."

"Nay," he replied, unbuckling his seatbelt. "Nothing but the dress. We have less than thirty minutes to get to where we're going, so I'll hop out and watch the road to give you privacy to change."

She took another look at the dress in her hands and raised an eyebrow. Well, no matter what he said…she was keeping her underwear firmly in place.

~

Twenty minutes later, Brianagh huffed over to Reilly. "Is this the place?"

He nodded once. Dressed as he was, Brianagh felt slightly intimidated. His dark, shoulder-length hair hung freely, framing his serious, beautiful face. The dark green kilt—okay, a *léine*, as Reilly told her when she first caught sight of him—had golden threads laced within it and hung to his knees. The fabric crisscrossed over his chest and back in a complicated swath. His sword, tucked into the folds of the fabric, rested securely against his back, and his boots were sturdier than her flimsy leather scraps. She had a fleeting moment of medieval-replica-shoe envy until she noticed he stuffed them full of small knives. *Dirks*, she corrected herself. She really had to get into character. She didn't want to inadvertently insult anyone.

Blowing her hair out of her face, she looked around, wondering when the rest of the troupe would show. Brianagh walked around the site, marveling at the beauty of the circle. It was so peaceful and seemed to hum with energy as sunset drew closer.

"Brianagh—we haven't much time. I have to tell you who I am."

"Ah," she replied, smiling. "Of course."

"This isn't a reenactment," he said, closing his eyes briefly. "I've known you since the day you were born. Your own mother placed you into my arms, and your father charged me with your care until you were once again united."

She nodded sagely. "Of course. Will my name remain Brianagh? Or can I be a different character?"

"This isn't a reenactment," he repeated patiently.

"Oh, right. Sorry. I didn't realize we were already in character. Okay. My mother handed me over, my father charged you with my care. I'm with you. What happens next?" Bri strove to appropriate an acceptable level of seriousness to her tone.

"Your parents are far from dead, Brianagh." He slipped a

leather belt around her waist as he spoke, then looped it around in a series of patterns, much like his own, except hers wasn't as tight. He adjusted it slightly and stepped back.

She glanced down and touched the brooch attached to it by her right shoulder. "Why this?" she asked, running her fingers over it. She felt the same shiver caress her, and she dropped her hand. "Oh, the legacy! Of course. What will my parents' names be, again?"

"Please, Brianagh—for once in your life, stop questioning and just listen." Reilly took a deep breath and drew himself up to his full six-feet-four-inches. "I am an O'Rourke protector. I bend time to protect the prophecy, and I have sworn my loyalty to ensuring the secret remains just that—secret. I speak the truth when I say you are not from here. You are the O'Rourke daughter who will save our clan. And your destiny has come for you." He ran his hand over the brooch. He led her to the north side of the passage and pointed to a slim opening. "We go through there and wait for sunset."

Brianagh didn't know what to make of him. She didn't want to laugh at him, but...*Bend time?* "Um, quick time out, please. First of all, this area is locked to us. And, you can't fit through there with all your gear."

Reilly didn't answer. He had placed his hands on either side of the opening and stood, silent. He spoke in a voice that shook her soul: "*De réir an cumhacht ag an gods, ordaímse duit a oscailt le haghaidh dom, an Protector.*"

"By the power of the gods, I command you to open for me, the Protector."

The rock widened, and Reilly grabbed her hand and dragged her inside even as it began to close up again. She was immediately enveloped in the darkness, and her heart began to beat harder, though she took a moment to appreciate the special effects. She wondered if Ry had some movie connections, and reminded herself to ask him about it when the reenactment was over.

He led her away from the north wall, the small passageway veering to their left.

As her eyes adjusted to the darkness, she saw he was using his hands to trace something on the wall as they walked. He was murmuring in that strange voice again, and she clutched her skirt in an effort to not get too swept up in the moment.

He turned to her suddenly and flashed a reassuring smile. "You are the future of our clan. You must trust me."

She didn't say a word, just watched him silently as he finished whatever he was doing and then braced himself against the wall.

He pulled her to him and slipped a dagger into her belt. "It might make you feel safer," he said by way of explanation. "Keep it close to hand. This is your fate." He gripped her chin, then gently placed a kiss on her forehead. "If I forget to tell you later, it's been an honor. Hold on to me, as tightly as you can."

The tiny cave was growing brighter as the light moved into it from a partially-covered window she hadn't noticed. *Sunset.*

She looked up at Reilly, amazed at the beauty of the tomb.

He wrapped his arms around her, and as the cave flooded with the full light of the setting sun, the beams hit them. She gripped Reilly's leather belt, her arms tightly coiled around him, as the world around her suddenly exploded into shards of light and space and a million other things she couldn't identify. Shock blanked her mind; the only thing that anchored her to her body was Reilly, whose arms never moved from her. The shards of light were pelting her, bruising her skin, and she cried out as Reilly covered her body with his own, shielding her.

Her heart pounded in her ears for long minutes before she realized whatever had happened was over. She let out a shuddering breath, and Reilly slowly lifted off her, leaning back on his haunches.

"What the hell?" she finally managed, her eyes wide. "That was…" She trailed off, unable to find any words.

Reilly laughed, relief on his features. "Imagine that. I've finally found a way to shut you up!"

She snorted. "Yeah, you only had to 'shift time' to get me there." She laughed, rolling her eyes. "So it's over? That was pretty incredible. How did you make that vortex or wind tunnel or whatever it was? That thing was powerful! I bet that if time travel could happen, that's what it'd feel like. Although I'd leave out the pelty-things next time. But otherwise—very realistic, Ry."

He frowned. "Brianagh, we really did shift time. I bent it to my will to bring you back."

"Oh, sorry. Just let me know when we're done. I'll stay in character until you say it's over. So, back where?" she asked, looking around. "Where are we?"

Reilly spun around with lightning speed, bringing his arm up as his sword clashed with another, cutting off any other words.

CHAPTER 3

Brianagh scrambled backward, belatedly realizing she wasn't inside the cave anymore, and tripped over the hem of her skirt. Reilly spewed Gaelic at the man who seemingly appeared from nowhere, and who now swung a sword at Reilly's head. Reilly deftly avoided the violent hacking and returned parry for parry.

Historical actors were a crazy bunch, it seemed. Especially this one—his clothes were fashioned the same as Reilly's, although not nearly as nice. His tunic was torn in various places, and his bushy beard looked to be full of last night's dinner.

Gross.

She became aware of their conversation—taking place completely in Gaelic—and was grateful to Reilly for teaching her his native tongue. Although, after a moment of really listening to what they were saying, she rather wished to be a bit more ignorant. Her opinion of them was quickly firming—crazy seemed a mild term.

"There is no one here to save you, O'Malley, so give up now. The rest will come—oof!—from their posts soon!" the half-deranged man snarled as he dodged a swing. "We've been expecting you, with MacWilliam marrying."

"You want to be the one who took what is MacWilliam's? You would die a painful death by his hand!" Reilly growled.

"I think not," the man shot back as he narrowly avoided the business end of Reilly's sword.

Brianagh tried not to gag as Dirty Beard's smell wafted past her. She scanned her surroundings and saw nothing but trees. She wondered if they were going off-script; no one else had arrived. She certainly hoped they weren't discussing her; Reilly hadn't mentioned that he told his group anything about her, and he didn't inform her that she was cast to play some sort of major role.

"Dagger in hand!" Reilly barked to her, in English. "No screaming. We don't want the attention."

She fumbled for the blade and pulled it out, ready. For what, though, she had no idea. In her opinion, this took reenactment too far—the swords were most definitely real; the clash of metal-on-metal was too loud to deny that. They also looked pretty sharp. One false move and either could be skewered. She shuddered at that unpleasantry, then refocused as Dirty Beard sliced Reilly's arm. The sight of blood alarmed her. She took a step forward but froze at the look on Reilly's face.

Brianagh watched, open-mouthed. She'd never seen such fury.

"Your body will be proof enough that Burke will not have her," Reilly said as he thrust the sword into the man's belly.

Brianagh stifled her scream, then turned and retched as Reilly quickly cleaned his sword on the dead man's tunic.

Holy mother of God; Reilly just killed a man, she thought hysterically. She looked up at him, panicked.

Reilly wasted no time. He dragged the man into the trees and his eyes scanned the forest. He whistled sharply as he returned to her side and grabbed her hand. "We have to get out of here before the others arrive," he said grimly. "It was us or him, Brianagh. I promise to explain later." She heard the pounding of hooves before she saw it. The most enormous black horse she'd ever seen skidded to a halt in front of Reilly, snorting and shaking its head in greeting.

Reilly wrapped an arm around her waist, and in one ridiculously Hollywood move, swung onto the beast and pulled her up with him. He placed her in front of him, squeezed the horse with his thighs, and gave a "Yah!" as an arrow whizzed past her head.

Her last coherent thought before slipping into a dead faint was that this wasn't how she expected her day to go when Reilly suggested they take a drive to a *monolithic structure* this morning.

BRIANAGH'S HEAD POUNDED AS SHE SLOWLY WOKE. SHE WAS lying on something cold and unyielding. She felt around gingerly.

Dirt.

"Brianagh, open your eyes."

Although Reilly's voice seemed close by, when her eyes adjusted to the twilight around her, she didn't see him. She sat up and her head spun. "What happened?" she asked in a shaky voice. "How did we get out of the cave?"

Reilly squatted in front of her and offered what looked to be a cup made out of tree bark. She peered at the water inside suspiciously. "It's from a creek just up the way," he explained. "We are on Burke's land. We have at least two more hours of fast riding before we get to safety. He's a cruel laird, and unfortunately, a smart one too. But once we get to the O'Rourke side—"

"O'Rourke side of what?"

"Ireland. O'Rourke—your clan—is a safe place." He took

the cup from her and helped her stand. "I'll tell you more later, but we have to stay ahead of Burke's men."

"They really don't like trespassers," she said as she brushed off her skirts.

"Actually," Reilly replied as he hoisted her onto the stallion, "he'd love nothing more than for you to stay."

"Then why were his thick-skulled men shooting arrows at us and trying to hack you with a sword?"

"I didn't say they wanted *me* to stay. They'd much prefer me dead. You're the one they want, Bri." He glanced meaningfully at the brooch on her chest.

She twisted around to stare at him, and Evelyn's words from yesterday came back to her in a rush: *The only way to know if she was truly the chosen daughter would be that she was wearing this brooch… One family member from each generation is given the ability to move time itself, but only for the greater good.* He shrugged and kicked the horse into a gallop. They only traveled a few hundred paces when the horse reared, almost throwing them. He reared again, and Brianagh screamed. They toppled off the horse, Reilly twisting in midair so she landed almost fully on top of him. She snapped her head up to see the horse take off with a very bloodied back leg. Trying to catch her breath, she frantically searched Reilly's face. His eyes were closed, and he had blood on his tunic, although she couldn't tell if it was old or new.

"Reilly!" she screamed as she scrambled off him. She shook him. "Reilly! Wake up!" He didn't move, and her throat constricted. She put her head on his chest, but she couldn't tell if he was breathing over the sounds of her choked sobs.

Without warning, she was grabbed underneath her arms and hauled roughly to her feet. She screamed again, but someone quickly stuffed a gag into her mouth and secured it around her head. Even as she struggled to get away, her arms were bound behind her and her ankles tied together.

Once she was trussed, she was hefted onto a mount. She glanced back and saw Reilly, still lying on the ground—dead or unconscious—and wished with everything she had that she hit the ground first.

Her rider wrenched her back around, and as fear clouded her mind, Brianagh started to shake. Apparently, that annoyed her kidnapper. He barked something unintelligible at her, then clunked her on the head with something solid.

"AIDAN, IT'S BEEN TWENTY-TWO YEARS." NIOCLAS MacWilliam, laird of the clan MacWilliam, stood in front of the large hearth in his great hall.

The laird's younger brother, Aidan, was his most trusted—and most bothersome—clansman. Aidan's green eyes danced as he tried to contain his mirth; there was little else he enjoyed more than irritating his brother, despite their advanced ages of thirty-four and thirty.

"The O'Rourke sent his messenger just this morning. Care you to hear what he says, or shall I just send him to the kitchen, pat him on his head, then send him home? The man did travel an awful long way just to see your pretty face. The least you could do is feed him and hear his claims of a vow you made."

Nioclas tried to unclench his jaw. His brother's humor was, as usual, unwelcome. He had waited years for his missing betrothed to appear. He'd honored his promise to wait for her for as long as possible. But his clan needed him to choose a wife; news of skirmishes was increasing with each passing month.

A fortnight ago, two lesser lairds to the north sent their best daughters to him. This time, one of the lasses, aged only ten, carried a note that promised full clan allegiance to the

MacWilliams if he married her, and the promise of retaliation if he chose the other lass.

Nioclas was tired of entertaining unwanted guests and sidestepping threats of warfare. He sent them both back to their sires, then doubled the guards at his gate.

The MacWilliams clan was strong, and though many threatened, few dared to engage them in battle. Nioclas knew he couldn't hold off from his duty forever. If he didn't marry soon, the veiled—and not so veiled—threats would arrive at his castle.

All his clansmen wanted was peace. By the saints, he wanted peace as well.

Just last week, Nioclas quietly agreed to marry a lass from the Kildare clan in the east. Her father assured him she was tractable, that she was more than happy to marry, and, most importantly, came from a long line of fecund women. The O'Rourkes hadn't sent back their official word that they accepted the troth-break, but once he was married, there was little they could do. He looked forward to the day when the O'Rourkes had nothing more to hold over him and his clan.

Aidan shrugged. "Let the messenger have his say, then release him. O'Rourke is daft if he seeks our alliance."

"Laird O'Rourke is not daft," Nioclas grumbled. "I made a foolish vow when I was a lad, and he's held me to it."

Aidan frowned. "What vow?"

Nioclas shuffled a stack of parchment and capped the inkwell. "Shortly after I took control of our clan, I met with Kiernan. To keep his alliance, I agreed to marry his daughter."

"The O'Rourke has a daughter?"

Nioclas's steel gray eyes held his brother's emerald green ones pointedly. "Aye. He does."

Aidan choked as realization suddenly dawned. "You can't be serious. You agreed to marry *the O'Rourke lass*? The one who can walk into the future?"

He snorted. "She cannot walk into next month, brother.

She's not a sorceress. The whispers of her supposed powers are merely mystical stories the O'Rourkes bandied about to encourage clans to keep their distance." Nioclas sighed. "And it worked for all but me."

"You're a powerful ally," Aidan supplied helpfully. "If I were a laird, and I had a daughter, I'd want to secure your hand."

"If you had a daughter, I'd best know about her posthaste," Nioclas replied with a long-suffering sigh. He rubbed his hand over his eyes as if to erase the last few hours from memory.

"No daughters. Although the MacDermott lass won't give up."

"Stay away from the MacDermotts," Nioclas commanded. "That clan is troublesome. They're bloodthirsty and poor."

Aidan held his hands up in surrender. "Aye, brother, I'm aware. She follows me like a hound."

Nioclas snorted. "I wouldn't say that to any other, Aidan. If MacDermott hears that his daughter's true love thinks her to be a hound, the only price he'll accept is your head on a stake. And then I'll be honor-bound to marry the lass, which, thank you anyway, is something I'd rather avoid."

"How can you marry a lass that doesn't exist?" Aidan asked. "We've all heard the tales of the powerful O'Rourke woman who can move time, but O'Rourke only has sons."

"I met with Kiernan a few weeks after I took control of our clan, as I needed a strong ally and the O'Rourkes were willing to talk. No one would give us alliance, Aidan. Even with the backing of our clan leaders, other clans saw us as weak, to allow a twelve-year-old to take control."

"You were a brilliant strategist then, as you are now," Aidan said fiercely. "Any who doubt are fools."

Nioclas nodded in agreement. "Aye, and your loyalty—like that of the rest of our clansmen—was well appreciated. But without another clan, we were susceptible to attack. I realized this, as did the leaders. For his alliance, Kiernan's price was high. Perhaps too high. He claimed he had a seven-year-old daughter, who was sent to live with guardians on the mainland when she was but an infant. He secured my hand for her, and offered a marriage to her when she came of age."

"Came of age?" Aidan repeated incredulously. He did the numbers in his head quickly. "She would be nine-and-twenty now, Nick! What age did Kiernan say she must be when she was to marry you?"

Nioclas frowned. "That was the hole in my agreement. We never specified, and Daniel, our clan elder, realized it the day after we agreed to the match. Kiernan said he would present her when he felt she was ready. And, with my upcoming nuptials, I know not what they plan, but with each missive O'Rourke sends me, the more desperate he seems. The O'Rourkes lost their chance by not presenting their daughter, and I will ally with the Kildares now. I cannot wait any longer, and to break the marriage with the Kildares will invite war."

"The Kildares bring nothing to our clan," Aidan hesitated to point out. "I see no value in this marriage, Nick."

"The Kildares aren't the most loyal of men, but having an ally in a part of the country where we haven't any is a boon I cannot overlook," Nioclas divulged.

"We're a large clan, too."

"Aye. But very few lairds will attack us if our numbers are doubled. All I want is peace," Nioclas reiterated. "A show of force is, sometimes, more effective than the force itself."

"What if the O'Rourke lass really is here?"

"Then it would be a miracle indeed, as there's been neither sight nor sound of her since the supposed day of her birth," Nioclas replied dryly. "Bring the messenger so I can eat my supper in peace." Nioclas didn't interact with the O'Rourkes much. They were far from him, and although they were a strong clan, they were a peaceful one.

Nioclas wanted to keep it that way, even if Kiernan sent him annual missives to remind him of a promise made when he was a foolish lad of ten-and-two.

It grated on his nerves that with each reminder sent, the unspoken threat of war loomed if he dared marry another. Yet the O'Rourkes continued to refuse his request to see her. He had but little choice now.

"Laird MacWilliam, I bring a message from Laird O'Rourke," the messenger said, shifting from foot to foot. At Nioclas's nod, he continued. "The laird is on his way here and should arrive before nightfall. He brings news of his daughter, Lady Brianagh." At MacWilliam's continued, ominous silence, the messenger cleared his throat again. "I, ah, am also to inform you that he travels not alone and brings with him three men."

"They bring news? They don't even have her? What are they going to do, lock you in a tower until this mythical daughter appears?" Aidan asked incredulously. He guffawed. "I don't envy you, brother."

"Is there aught else?" Nioclas asked tersely.

The messenger cast his eyes heavenward, as if sending up a prayer, and squeaked, "Um, aye." Clearing his throat, he said, "Lady Brianagh shall be presented for the wedding held here tomorrow."

"Oh, well, if that's all," Nioclas replied, his patience snapping, "then I best get my rest tonight. Be off to the kitchens with you to find your repast." The messenger's head snapped up in surprise and he scurried off to the kitchens in haste.

"Before nightfall?" Aidan grinned, scratching his chin with his dirk. "I suspect they'll be riding up to our gates within the hour."

"To no end," Nioclas replied sourly, stalking across the great room toward the staircase. He threw a look over his shoulder. "When they arrive, you may send only Kiernan to my solar. The rest can go to hell."

Aidan watched his brother stomp up the solid stone steps, then turned and winked at the maid hovering nearby. She blushed to the tips of her toes, bobbed a curtsy, and asked what he needed.

"Ensure a strong dinner is sent to the laird's solar tonight. Make it for six."

CHAPTER 4

If Nioclas thought he could kill his brother without overly mourning his loss, Aidan would most certainly be dead.

Said brother ushered the menacing-looking travelers into the laird's solar, maids following them with stools and food. The smell of roasted beef with bread assaulted the senses. If Nioclas weren't so angry that his brother allowed the men up, he'd be angry about the elaborate food now being placed in front of them.

What a waste.

"Leave us," Nioclas barked to the servants, who scurried out of the room. He glared at Aidan, but said in a measured tone, "Enjoy that meal, O'Rourke, for once it's done, you'll be leaving my castle."

Kiernan O'Rourke ignored him, digging into his meal with a single-mindedness mirrored by the other travelers in his party.

Nioclas took stock as they ate. He did not recognize the travelers Kiernan brought. Two he could guess solely by the stories he knew of the clan. The largest one, with long, midnight-black hair and ice-blue eyes, must be the eldest O'Rourke offspring, Brody. Nioclas approved of him by sight —he was brawny and his eyes held a sharp intelligence. According to Kiernan, the man looked just like his mother, Kathryne. Brody was respected in battle—he was merciful but lethal—and he put his clan above himself. Nioclas could respect a man with those values.

The lad with the shorter, lighter-brown hair also had blue eyes, but his nose was fashioned more like his sire's, as were his mannerisms. His body had not quite filled out yet. He still looked young, perhaps not quite twenty. He must be Reeve. Kiernan didn't speak overmuch about him, except to sigh and wish he'd get his head out of the herbs and into the battles.

The last one Nioclas did not recognize. He looked nothing like an O'Rourke. He was as tall as Brody, with dark eyes and hair. He entered the room behind the O'Rourkes, standing straight with a small effort. His garb was finer than most, and a dark bruise marred his right cheek. His right arm appeared stiff, and although he was eating, it was clearly difficult for him to manage with his left. But his presence was more defined than even Kiernan's. Nioclas wondered if he was a laird in his own right, perhaps from the mainland.

Finally, the men finished their suppers and the trenches were carried away. Nioclas sat back and waited silently.

"I expect my messenger arrived this morning?" Kiernan asked, his eyebrow raised. "I did warn him you might be all day about getting to him, though. I hope you didn't throw him in your dungeon while he waited. He's a nervous sort."

Nioclas folded his arms. "What do you want?"

"Never one for small talk," Kiernan noted, nodding his head to Brody. "This is Brody, my eldest son, and Reeve, my youngest. And over there is Reilly O'Malley."

"What happened to you?" Aidan asked without preamble. "Fall off a horse?"

O'Malley turned his attention to Nioclas. "I was riding for the O'Rourke castle when my horse's leg was shot with an arrow. He reared, throwing us to the ground."

"Us?" Aidan asked.

"I twisted so I would take the fall, and she fell on me. I woke up in the forest alone, but I found this on the ground." He reached into the folds of his léine and withdrew a small silver brooch. He handed it to Nioclas with a nod. "I put it on her before we left. Somehow, it came off when she was taken by Burke's clansmen."

Nioclas held the brooch in his hand and his gut tightened.

"Where did you get this?" Nioclas demanded.

He'd fashioned it after a dream came upon him many nights in a row—a beautiful woman, a lake, and a flying hawk. Not even Aidan understood why he'd chosen the bird for their crest. His fingers constricted around it.

Reilly's eyes held Nioclas's steadily, but he didn't answer.

Kiernan glanced between the two men before speaking. "We gave the care and keeping of our daughter to O'Malley when she was born and hid her in a place no one could get to her. We trusted in the Fates that she would be brought back to us at the right time."

"A day before my wedding to Kildare's daughter seems to be more *convenient* than *right*." Nioclas's tension radiated. He ignored the small shot of energy from the brooch. "You say she is in Burke's hands now?"

Reilly jerked his head in affirmation. "Aye."

"Willing to risk your life on it?"

Reilly met his eyes. "Tá mé Protector mhionn."

I am a sworn Protector.

Nioclas didn't blink, but his jaw clenched and he swore.

Kiernan nodded briskly. "We knew you'd see it our way. Now, we need a plan to get her back."

~

Brianagh tried to stop shivering, but it was a useless endeavor. She had been in this hole for an interminable amount of time. The dim light filtered through the gate above her, and she heard the whinny and soft stamping of horses.

She woke up in the underground dungeon hours ago. When she realized the floor was soft and moving, she jumped up faster than she ever thought possible and hadn't sat since. She was filthy and her wrist hurt—perhaps she fell on it when they put her in this place? From when she fell off the horse? She had no idea.

At one point, she gathered enough courage to call out and hope someone above her would have a kind heart and let her out. Her reward was a slew of Gaelic curses, and she became a moving target for the guards above to relieve themselves.

Terrified didn't do her current state justice.

Night surrounded her, and she felt the darkness close in. She became accustomed to the smell after the first few hours, after retching until her stomach hurt. Occasionally, she found a patch of floor that didn't have a creature of some sort slithering along the bottom, and she stayed in that spot for a while. She dreaded the next thing that would try to climb up her leg.

At some point during the night, she began to bargain with herself. When she got out, she wouldn't complain about wearing pantyhose ever again. In fact, she would gladly take a pair now as an extra layer between her and the slithery creatures any day of the week, and twice on Sundays. Never again would she complain about having to wear them to meet a client, or during the postdate wrap-up, or—

The bargaining didn't last too long. As she thought of her life just a day ago, she had a sinking feeling she had lost her mind, mostly because she believed Reilly had spoken the truth when he said he had moved time.

She suspected that Reilly believed her to be the daughter

in her family legacy. But her parents died in a car crash. She'd seen the news article.

Distracted again by yet another *something* trying to make friends with her leg, Brianagh bit back a scream. She screwed her eyes shut, kicked the offending creature off, and tried to breathe normally.

In the hours since her captors tossed her into the dark, stinky hell, she gleaned few details about her whereabouts. The men tasked to guard her dropped the name *Burke* a lot and whoever he was, he seemed intent on kidnapping and keeping her. Apparently, he'd been searching for her for years because he believed, like Reilly, that she was the O'Rourke legacy.

She also learned a couple of fun facts about the men who stomped around above her. The first was that her holding cell doubled as a toilet. If she didn't move, they weren't going to aim around her.

Lesson learned.

Another fun fact was their inability to get along. They didn't seem particularly fond of each other, judging by the name-calling and swearing. Some insults led to sword fights, and by her estimation, the death count was two, possibly three, people.

One of the men seemed to have celebrity status, as he claimed to be the one who killed her protector. No one taunted him, as far as she could tell.

Her throat caught at the thought of Reilly. Once again, she sent a prayer flying that he was okay and made it back home for help. James would know what to do—he was an ER doctor, for crying out loud. He was a resident at the best trauma unit in the country. He'd be able to fix Reilly.

Firelight crept into the space, and calls from the guards were cut suspiciously short. She craned her neck to see what was going on, but as she could only see the faint outline of wooden beams and some thatch, she gave up and instead pressed herself against the nearest wall. She hoped she wouldn't die in a fiery blaze, but at the moment, it seemed like her best option.

She began to cry softly.

CHAPTER 5

"Brianagh!"

Bri's eyes snapped up and locked on Reilly, who pushed a ladder into the hole.

"Ry?" Her eyes had trouble adjusting to the bright torchlight coming from above. She scrambled for the ladder, tripping over the slime and sludge, and desperately grasped it. She clumsily made it up two rungs when Reilly reached down, grabbed her arms, and hoisted her up, then pushed her ahead of him toward the open door at the end of a line of horse stalls.

They skidded to a halt when three men stepped into their path. Reilly drew his sword and placed Brianagh behind him.

"One at a time, lads, or all at once?" Reilly asked pleasantly. Two charged him at the same time, and the other went straight for her. Her would-be attacker got a swift sword in the belly from somewhere to Brianagh's right, and then she was being pulled away from Reilly again.

"Let go!" she cried out.

"Go with him!" was all Reilly managed before swinging his sword again.

She obeyed immediately—after all, whoever had her arm

headed toward the door and not the dungeon. She couldn't see around the warrior, as he was at least a foot taller than her and his shoulders were enormous. He barely paused when they reached the horse; he swung her into the saddle, leapt and landed behind her, and kicked the horse into a gallop before he was fully seated.

He spurred the beast on as a bevy of others surrounded them. Fear choked Brianagh, but the man spoke close to her ear. "The rest will follow. These are my guardsmen and will keep us safe until we get to my castle. Take your ease. O'Malley will meet with us there."

She stopped breathing. She knew that voice. Half-fearfully, she glanced back into hard, gray eyes, and promptly fainted for the second time in her life.

When she came to, Brianagh couldn't see anything in front of her except a horse's head. And if that wasn't disconcerting enough, she felt an arm around her waist securing her to a broad, hard chest.

She forced herself to concentrate on staying atop the racing horse instead of thinking about how disconcertingly familiar she was with that chest.

In the fog ahead, she glimpsed a light, then another. Voices called out and torches flared around them as the horses slowed.

Something creaked loudly, and the horses pranced as the sound continued. Awed, Brianagh watched a drawbridge hit the ground in front of them with a dull thud. Her rescue squad crossed and silently entered a long tunnel. The sound of horses' hooves echoed off the tall, arched, moss-covered stone visible in the flickering torchlight. She peered ahead and saw a courtyard of sorts at the end of the tunnel. Once there, her rescuer dismounted, then held up his arms. She refused to look at his face for fear that her insanity would somehow materialize, so she reached blindly and grasped his forearms.

Recognition shot through her, and her gaze involuntarily snapped to his. Familiar eyes, as gray as the mist that surrounded them in the courtyard of the castle, searched hers.

"It *is* you," she breathed.

He didn't say a word, just looked at her intensely, his eyes reflecting the light from the torches. Easing her away from the horse, he slowly released her and stepped back. Recognition flitted across his face before his expression shuttered.

Brianagh stared. The man from her dreams had become very real, and even more handsome in person. She surreptitiously fanned herself, then choked on her own stink. It occurred to her that he'd been downwind of that same stink as they rode.

Her face flamed. Her dream man saved her from a fate worse than death, only to breathe in her toxic fumes.

At no point in her dreams did Brianagh ever stink, or be anything less than perfect for him. The fact that she stood within arm's length, covered in slime, urine, and who knew what else, was a brutal slap to her reality.

"Riders approach!" someone called out from high above her.

"Let them through," the warrior called out. He turned to her. "You are safe now, Lady Brianagh. You may take your ease."

She nodded numbly, and he walked away without looking back.

"Brianagh!" Reilly called out. He threw himself off his horse and swept her off her feet. "Thank the saints! Are you all right?"

She blinked up at him. "Well…I did just spend a fair bit of time in hell, Reilly. I'll let you draw your own conclusions."

He laughed, then swung her around again. "Conclusion drawn. I'm so sorry I let them take you."

"I'm so grateful you're alive," she choked out before bursting into tears. "I thought…you were lying there…"

"I knew I was outnumbered." He pulled her into a hug. "There were more around us. I would've pulled my sword if I thought it would do any good, but I knew they would overpower me. So I played dead. I knew Burke wouldn't want you killed. Just hidden." He pulled back and winked at her. "But don't tell MacWilliam that. I left out the playing dead bit."

She absorbed all of that for a moment, then decided she couldn't do any more today.

"I smell," she announced.

"I believe you have a bath waiting for you in your room." Reilly smiled. "Shall we?"

"I don't think there's really any other choice," she replied, looking around her in consternation. "Care to fill me in on what's *really* going on?"

"You said it yourself." Reilly gave a nonchalant shrug as he guided her to the castle steps. "Just a bit of reenactment."

"You're an ass," she replied succinctly.

"And you're just about ready to hear what I was trying to tell you before we left."

She didn't feel at all bad when she *accidentally* tripped him on the last step.

~

"YOU'RE WEARING A TRENCH IN YOUR STONES," AIDAN SAID THE next morning. "Stop pacing. The battle's done. I even managed to take one of their cattle."

Nioclas, while grateful for the extra food his brother had stolen for the clan, ignored him.

The woman from his dreams finally had a name.

She recognized him, and if he had it right, it was the same way he recognized her. But knowing someone from a dream was not possible. And though Nioclas wouldn't cast aside any form of magic—he did, after all, live in Ireland, where his clan still followed the old ways—seeing someone materialize from his dreams was a bit much for his mind to absorb.

When he woke that morning, he resolutely decided his dream occurred only because he had ridden three hours with her lithe form pressed against him last night.

Shaking his thoughts free, Nioclas turned his thoughts to his sire. Burke would seek revenge when he found the O'Rourke lass gone. Nioclas had sent the Kildare lass home to her own sire with a promise of alliance in apology for breaking the troth. The child had cried in relief, but Nioclas knew Kildare would come banging on his door with threats of retribution.

He also knew they would be empty threats unless someone paid the Kildares for their time. They weren't the most loyal of clansmen.

Someone knocked on the solar door. Nioclas turned and shot an expectant look to Aidan, but the only response was a shrug.

"I'm eating."

"And I'm laird," Nioclas reminded him. "So get off your arse, show some respect, and open the door."

"I respect you enough to point out that you're closer." He took a drink from his cup.

Nioclas grit his teeth and shot Aidan a glare that inspired fear…in others. Aidan wagged his eyebrows and continued to shove food into his mouth.

Nioclas flung open the door with a barked, "Aye?"

"Lovely to see you as well, MacWilliam," Kiernan said cheerfully. "I always love the morning after a skirmish. Nothing makes you feel more alive!"

"I can think of a few things, starting with that feisty maid downstairs—" Aidan started.

"We've a lady present," Kiernan cut in quickly.

"Care to explain that?" Aidan replied, looking him up and down.

Kiernan laughed. "MacWilliam, you and I shall meet in the lists over that. I meant Lady O'Rourke, my wife. She arrived just this morning."

"My lady." Nioclas bowed as she entered behind her husband. "I do hope your travels were uneventful."

"Oh, aye," she replied with a smile. "But 'tis my understanding that my next few days will be just the opposite."

Nioclas repressed his sigh and inclined his head. "That is my understanding as well. Shall we discuss the betrothal terms?"

"Certainly. Once we know for sure she's my daughter."

"You mean…" Nioclas trailed off as he realized Kiernan wasn't certain the woman they rescued last night was his true daughter.

"There's only one way for us to know," Lady O'Rourke said gently. "We must see the mark."

CHAPTER 6

Brianagh was not one to give in to hysterics. She never was—a fact of which she was absurdly proud. When her first matched couple decided to get married and the best man was caught with not one but two bridesmaids the night before— neither of which were his wife — she managed to calm the bride and groom, remove the offending parties from the ceremony, and save the reputation of her business before the snake could even put his pants on.

However, as she looked around the barren room, with its stone walls, hard floor, and prickly bed, she accepted that everyone had their limits.

The frustrating thing about it was that Bri wasn't quite sure *how* to have a hysterical fit. *Perhaps*, she thought, I *ought to review the issues.*

The first thing on her list had to be the time travel itself. Bri couldn't fully piece together the logistics of it—it was a sensation she never really wanted to go through again, and she hoped Reilly had a different way to get her home.

Speaking of Reilly, he was high on the list of issues, too. He wasn't who he claimed he was, and although she was angry with him, she understood why he never told her about his little superpower. She would have laughed herself into a fit of tears, then teased him mercilessly for the rest of his days. But he was the only person she knew here, so she'd reserve the teasing for after they got back. She vowed she wouldn't speak to him for a good six months, at least, though.

And he killed a man. It was, she understood, to save their lives. But he should've at least given her a briefing on the situation of this place.

She also didn't know exactly what *this place* was—Ireland, but when? She understood the language. Gaelic was taught to all the O'Rourkes at an early age. Her aunt ensured it. Reilly had finessed her language skills by spending almost five straight years only speaking Gaelic. He knew she was curious —or stubborn—enough to learn it just so she wouldn't miss out on what he was saying. But Bri was completely unaware as to how the language may have changed from this point in time—again, wherever this time is; the lack of knowledge was really bothering her—to her time. Modern times.

Her list further proved she needed answers, and she needed them now.

Unfortunately, she had no idea where her dress went, and the long white nightgown she wore covered her from the bottom of her chin to the tips of her toes.

She needed some clothes.

She flicked the covers off herself and immediately pulled them back on. The air was bitingly cold, and she was fairly certain if she dared to place her feet onto the floor, they'd stick like a tongue to cold metal.

Her door creaked, and Bri sat up, clutching the covers to her chest. When Reilly poked his head in, she narrowed her eyes. "I have some questions for you."

He sighed. "I figured you did. You always have questions." He closed the door behind him and withdrew something from his tunic. "But I also have questions. Such as…what's this, Brianagh?" He tossed her purse to her.

Her face lit up. "I thought someone stole this from me!"

Reilly sat on the edge of her bed, his expression grave. "If I hadn't felt it on you when we were in Dowth, you'd be in some serious straits right now. I told you in the car, *nothing but the dress.*"

She unzipped the pouch and dumped the contents onto the bed. "My phone! License, credit card, cash…"

"None of it will do you any good here."

She turned her phone on. "About that," she said in what she hoped was an even voice. "Where is *here*?"

His gaze never wavered. "The MacWilliam castle, in what will be County Mayo, Ireland, in the future."

A breath whooshed out of her before she could stop it. Collecting herself, she asked, "The date, Reilly?"

"Sometime in November of fourteen fifty-seven."

Her mouth opened, then closed, then opened again, but no sound came out.

"What are you doing?" Reilly asked curiously.

"Well, if you're really interested," she said with a sniff, "I'm attempting to go into hysterics."

"How's it going?"

"Not well," she grumbled, flopping back on the straw mattress. "I don't think I'm capable. But I suspect it would be a good release of all the emotions I have rolling around in my head right now."

He cleared his throat. "Well, if you're done with that, give me your things and I'll lock them in my trunk. If anyone discovers you with them, you'll be burned at the stake for witchcraft. If anyone finds them on me, I can get away easily. Oh. I've brought you a maid," he suddenly remembered. "She has clothes and will help you dress and do all kinds of, um, womanly things."

Brianagh slanted a glance at him as she gathered her things, then handed them back to him. "Define *womanly things.*"

"By the saints, I don't know, Bri. Your hair and shoes and lacings and stuff." He fidgeted uncomfortably for a moment. "You and I can talk more once you're properly dressed. I want to speak with you before...um..." He coughed. "Before Kathryne does."

"Who's Kathryne?" Bri asked as a young woman popped into her room, arms laden with clothing, ribbons, and shoes.

Reilly shot up from the bed. "Your birth mother. See you in a bit," he said as he shut the door behind him.

Brianagh couldn't have responded even if he had stayed. She was speechless.

BRIANAGH SMOOTHED THE SKIRTS OF HER DRESS AND TRIED NOT to fiddle with whatever it was Darby, her thirteen-year-old maid, did to her hair.

It was rather alarming how the girl simply walked over, stripped Bri naked before she knew what was happening, then just as quickly tugged a warm dress over her. With an authority Bri had never seen in any teenager before, Darby sat her on a stool near the fire, opened a wooden box that had been somewhere in the pile of clothing she'd carried in, and proceeded to wrangle Brianagh's hair into a fashion "befitting her station."

She reached up and touched her thick, dark hair. She had a feeling it was brushed to a gloss that a shampoo model would envy. It was pinned back on the sides with silver ribbons to match her dress, and cascaded over her shoulders in perfectly behaved waves.

The dress was simple but soft. Bri wondered what it was made from; tags didn't exist yet, but she couldn't think of another textile available other than wool. But she'd always known will to be rather scratchy. The deep blue fell in a soft fold all the way to the floor, and her leather slippers peeked out at the hemline.

They were effective in keeping the chill off her feet, and for that, she loved them. They also weren't twisting her arches into uncomfortable positions like her heels back home.

"If you care for a wimple, I can procure one," Darby offered, gathering the nightclothes in her arms. "Our laird doesn't require one of the women in the clan, but as Sir O'Reilly said you're from the continent…"

"No, I don't like wimples," Bri hastened to assure her. Darby nodded and dropped a quick curtsy, but paused when her eyes caught on something near the bed.

"I see the chamber pot is empty," Darby noted.

Bri glanced with alarm at the large pot on the floor. She hadn't even noticed it, much less considered using it. The thought of it was enough to make her feel ill; she didn't want anyone emptying anything out of her window.

She made a mental note to keep an eye to the sky when she went outdoors.

"We have garderobes in this castle, my lady, if you prefer those. They're marvelous things; they empty right into the moat, and the water carries everything right out to the fields in an underground trench. You know it's good for the crops, aye? Truly, the laird is brilliant for thinking of such things."

Bri managed a smile, and as Darby left, Reilly walked in and nodded his approval.

Brianagh swallowed. "The castle has garderobes."

He blinked. "Aye. Many do."

She nodded, biting the inside of her lip. "Tell me again who you are."

He closed his eyes as if in pain. "Reilly O'Malley, O'Rourke protector." His eyes opened and searched hers. "But I'm still the same Reilly you've known your entire life."

Unwilling to discuss that, she folded her hands in front of her. "Why on Earth did you bring me here?"

He shot her an incredulous look, but she waited silently for his answer. After a moment, he realized she was serious. He sighed again, then closed the door. "Because, Brianagh, you are the chosen O'Rourke daughter who is the first in our line of time-travelers. You were given to me right after you were born, and I took you to the future, to Evelyn and Connor."

"Do they know who I am?" she asked.

His eyes shifted to a spot on the wall somewhere behind her left shoulder. "Aye, Evelyn does. And Colin, too."

"Colin?" she gasped. She couldn't believe she'd been deceived by everyone around her since her infancy. "How does Colin know?"

"We couldn't tell you, Brianagh. The Fates decided long ago, before you and me, that you couldn't know until the proper time. For generations, the O'Rourkes held this secret. When your aunt realized she was the one charged with your upbringing, she knew the stakes. If she told you, the threat of what you might do would alter history."

"Like what?" Brianagh exclaimed, angry. "Do you think I would jump off a bridge because my family thought I was some sort of fantastical legacy-holder? Maybe try to go back in time myself?"

She paused. *Damn*. That's exactly what she would have done, if for no other reason than to prove their insane story false.

"You know you would have," Reilly said, crossing his arms. "While it was my job to protect you, it was Evelyn's to raise you."

"This is unbelievable," Brianagh whispered. It was no use trying to deny any of it; she stood in the middle of a castle, lived through a medieval dungeon of sorts, and watched the man in front of her kill to protect her. "I want to go home."

"You are home," he replied gently.

"No!" she snapped. "No, home is where my life is. My business, for God—"

"You really want to discuss your business? Colin has it in hand. You've spent years training him for this."

"Colin? He's not ready to take over an entire business!" she nearly shrieked, her self-control slipping another notch. "He can't even find himself a date that sticks around for more than a week!"

Reilly grabbed her shoulders and shook her once, hard. "Brianagh, Celtic Connections isn't your destiny! Your destiny is here, to have children and to pass on the ability to time-travel—"

"You don't have a say in my destiny!" she cried, wrenching from his grasp.

They stared silently at each other, her breathing labored, his arms folded.

Finally, she spoke in a low voice. "You're telling me that I am responsible for an entire line of O'Rourkes, and that if I don't start having these magical kids, that line will simply cease to exist?" He took a step toward her, but she threw out her arms. "That's a hell of a lot of pressure you didn't bother to prepare me for! I don't even *want* children!"

"If you do not do this today, history will be changed in ways even I can't comprehend," Reilly replied, his voice haunted.

"Wait—do what today?" Brianagh suddenly felt ill-at-ease. She rubbed her arms to ward off the chill that stole over her.

Reilly dropped his head. "Marry the MacWilliam."

She cocked her head to the side. "I'm sorry. Come again?"

~

A KNOCK INTERRUPTED THEM.

"My lady?" A servant stood at the doorway, looking as if

she wished she were somewhere else. "You've been requested to join the laird and company in his solar to break your fast."

Brianagh looked at Reilly, panic flaring in her chest. She'd never felt more like running, but she was trapped. She had no idea how to get home, nor even where was safe within the walls of the castle.

"Relax," he said immediately, sensing her urge to flee. "You will be fine. A solar is just the laird's private room, where he conducts most of his business. Your birth mother and father expect nothing from you—"

"Except for me to marry a stranger and have a boatload of ankle biters," she cut in angrily.

"Your brothers will not be there, though they are in the castle."

"I have brothers?"

"Aye. They, alongside your father, the MacWilliam, and I, helped rescue you." Reilly led her down the hall, then down another. As they walked, he told her of the battle and of her brothers.

Reilly stopped outside a door that looked like all other doors, but this one gave Brianagh a terrifying sense of déjà vu.

"Chin up," Reilly murmured. "I will bring you in, but if asked to leave, I must. This isn't part of my journey, but I won't be far, Bri."

"Reilly, I'm not the woman in this legacy," Bri said desperately. "You're bringing me to people who think I'm their long-lost daughter, and I'm not. I'm just a woman from Boston, looking to get back."

Reilly put his arm around her and rubbed her shoulders in support. "Bri, I've known you your entire life. I've known you because the woman behind this door placed you into my hands when you were a babe. I held you and carried you and kept you safe."

"This isn't fair," she said, fighting the sting of tears. "You claim that you gave me a life, and now you've taken it away, as if you own me."

"I don't own you, Bri. The Fates do. You must understand, if I didn't do my part, I would be erasing thousands of people from history. Your descendants. Family."

Her mind balked at the enormity of that, and she grabbed his arm. "One more question."

He smiled down at her, his eyes twinkling. "Unsurprising."

"When are you from?"

The amusement fled his eyes, and he gave her a self-deprecating smile. "Brianagh, there isn't enough time in the day for me to answer that. Let's just say that I'm from all time." He knocked on the door. "Good luck. I won't be far."

"Come in, lass. O'Malley, make yourself useful in the lists."

Reilly winked at her, then walked down the hallway. She stepped into the room and closed the door. The soft sound of a latch echoed.

"Brianagh." A woman stood, clasping her hands in front of her. Bri studied the woman's face; they had the same blue eyes. The sunlight filtered through the window at the far end of the room brightly enough so Brianagh could see they were both brunettes, but that's where the physical similarities ended.

"Yes," she said cautiously. Despite Reilly's insistence that all these people were here to protect her, she couldn't fully believe it. Aside from the fact that they didn't know her from a hole in the wall, he claimed they were trying to marry her off—as if they could do such a thing.

Ridiculous.

"I'm Kathryne. Your mother. And this is Kiernan, my husband, your sire. I am grateful you've returned to us." She walked over to Bri and clasped her hands in her own, searching her face. "You are well?"

Well, this was awkward. Bri bit her lip. "Um, yes. I'm well. I'd feel more comfortable if Reilly returned, though."

"I understand. He is the only one who knows you, aye?" Kathryne continued. "This must be so sudden for you. Come, eat. I know you were held below the stables. Were you fed?"

Brianagh shook her head, sitting down on a proffered stool. "I did eat last night after I returned."

"Well, at least Nick's servants are doing something to earn their keep." One of the men grinned at her, his green eyes flashing with good humor. "Aidan MacWilliam," he said with a bow. "Brother to the laird over there. Known throughout the land as the better-looking one, as well."

She reflexively smiled at Aidan.

Her eyes fell on the commanding figure who halted his pacing and openly stared at her.

A shiver of awareness passed through her. Bri felt naked under his intense gaze. His eyes raked her from top to bottom, appraising her, then slowly reassessed. His leisurely perusal heated her in unfamiliar ways; she felt the blush begin on her neck, and a flash of irritation that she reacted at all. His eyes met hers, and she sucked in a breath as desire lanced through her.

Wholly inappropriate! she chided herself. Then, as she remembered him in a particularly compromising position during one of her more recent dreams, she blushed even more furiously.

Get a grip!

She couldn't help but sneak another look at his perfectly carved face, though.

He was smirking at her, as if he could read her thoughts. She narrowed her eyes. Whatever game he was playing, she was sure she didn't want any part in it.

Nioclas spoke. "I am the MacWilliam. Welcome. We asked you here because Lady O'Rourke thought it wise for you, being of advanced age, to listen to the betrothal agreement we've set."

Brianagh choked. "Advanced age?"

"Aye. You are nine-and-twenty, are you not?"

"That's not advanced age!"

He ignored her and turned to Kiernan. "Recite her dowry, O'Rourke."

As Kiernan listed off a whole bunch of animals, gold coins, and other nonsense, Brianagh's jaw slid farther and farther south.

She was being *sold*?

"Um, excuse me," she tried, but neither man heard her. "Hey. HEY!"

All eyes landed on her, expressions ranging from surprised, amused, slightly taken aback, and completely void of expression.

She got the feeling Nioclas MacWilliam was a master of the poker face.

"What happens if I don't agree to this wedding?" she asked, rather bravely, in her opinion.

Kiernan's eyebrows nearly shot off his head. "What?"

"Why would you not?" Aidan asked, amused.

Too many reasons, she thought. "Well, to start, I really don't think I am who *you* think I am."

Kathryne smiled gently at her. "Easily proven."

Oh, now *that* was interesting. "How?"

"Well, you'll have the mark," Kathryne explained. "The Fates promised to leave an unmistakable marking on the chosen O'Rourke daughter."

"I don't have any marks," Brianagh replied with an apologetic shrug, but inside, she was dancing an Irish reel. "Sorry. I should probably get going, so you can find the woman you're looking for..." Her voice trailed off as Kathryne shook her head.

"No, you must have the mark." She gestured. "It should be somewhere on your arm."

Bri sighed. "I haven't anything there but a small scar. But I wasn't born with it. I tripped on some rocks when I was a child. I remember it well."

"Ah, but I didn't say you'd be born with it." Kathryne turned to Nioclas and Kiernan. "Perhaps we ought to tell her what we're looking for before she shows us."

After a beat of silence, Nioclas finally said, "A hawk."

"Like this one," Aidan said, walking over and handing Brianagh something smooth, round, and heavy.

"My brooch!" she exclaimed. "Wait. How did you get it?"

"My lady, I ask that you show me the mark on your arm," Kiernan said, his voice brooking no argument.

Bri immediately disliked him. Commanding, intimidating, overly loud men didn't rank very high in her book, and she gave him a frown. But she grit her teeth and began to roll the sleeve of her dress.

She just wanted to go home, but they weren't going to let her go without a fight. Fine.

She yanked up the last of the material. There, no larger than a quarter, was the only mark on her, aside from a smattering of freckles across her lower back. And she certainly wasn't going to bare any more of herself than she was at present.

Kathryne's sigh of relief likely carried to the next village over, it was so loud. "Aye. You are the chosen one."

Wordlessly, Brianagh looked at her in shock and a little bit of pity. The woman was so desperate to believe she was her daughter, Bri almost felt guilty. There was no way that small scar was the shape of a hawk. She glanced at it. It was the same scar she'd always had. She remembered how she'd fallen, but she hadn't needed any stitches or even a trip to the doctor. But the scrape had scarred, and despite every type of cream Evelyn put on it, it never faded.

She looked at the brooch in her hand, then froze. Her gaze flew to the scar, then back to the brooch. Then back to the scar. Surprised, she looked up into the grimly determined face of Nioclas. Her scar was a near-perfect outline of the hawk on the brooch she held.

Nioclas spoke, his voice ringing with finality. "We marry tonight, before Burke has a chance to strike."

She shook her head, but no sound emitted. This was absolutely not how her day was going to go.

CHAPTER 7

Somehow Brianagh found her way back to her chamber, where she spent an hour trying to calm herself. She couldn't be expected to marry someone she'd only just met on the basis of a childhood scar.

She had to figure out a way to get back home, and Reilly clearly wasn't going to help her. She had to convince him he had the wrong person. She was not a time-traveler—well, not by choice, anyway.

Bri knew if she tried to leave the castle, she'd be stopped. She doubted she'd get past the front door, much less the huge portcullis she spied out her window. She stepped closer to the alcove in her room, watching the bustle of people outside. Her room appeared to be located in the keep, as she was higher than any other building, maybe the fourth floor from the ground. She saw three walls outside: one to her left that seemed connected to the keep, one in front of her that contained the wicked-looking portcullis, and the wall to the right. The courtyard—bailey, as Reilly referred to it—was expansive; people were everywhere. A few women were hanging laundry, children were playing with wooden swords, and horses were being led toward the wall on the right. She watched as the men leading the beasts walked through an archway she hadn't noticed. Apparently there was more down there than she could see.

Beyond the front wall was another, smaller building of some sort. The portcullis was up and so was the drawbridge. Outside the castle walls was a barbican, and from her vantage point, she could make out helmets and weaponry glinting in the sunlight as guards walked its parapets.

Her shoulders slumped as a feeling of desolation swept over her. There was no way she could make it across the bailey, over the drawbridge, and out of the barbican without someone noticing her.

She couldn't give up; she had to at least *try*. Brianagh straightened and gave herself a good shake. Someone in this castle had to know where Newgrange was, and once she found out, she'd make her way there. She could find Dowth from what she remembered in her brochure; she couldn't be too far.

With renewed purpose, Brianagh flung open her door and ran smack into a hard chest. Arms grasped hers, and the touch traveled like lightening up her arms. Bri looked up… and up…and up.

Nioclas MacWilliam was one very, very big man.

The top of her head didn't quite reach his shoulders. He wore no adornment on the léine wrapped about his chest, and his lower legs were bare except for his boots and the assortment of knives tucked into them. His hair was restrained with a strip of leather, and his eyes were still the intense gray she remembered from her dreams. His hands—big, strong, and calloused—held her arms gently.

The gesture was at odds with his fierce appearance.

He released her, then gave a swift bow. "Perhaps, my lady, you would humor me with a walk in my gardens."

That wasn't at all what she expected to hear coming out of

his mouth. She stood there, trying to assimilate what he wanted, when he raised an eyebrow at her.

"I won't bite, I assure you."

When he offered her a smile, her knees weakened and she repeated to herself, *Not going to get involved. At all.*

He still stood, his arm outstretched. Really, what else was she going to do? Slam the door in his face and hide in her room? At least this way, she could gauge her best attempt at fleeing.

Finally, she gave a slight nod. "Okay."

"Okay?" he repeated as they walked down the hallway. "I'm unfamiliar with that word."

"Sorry. I meant, I agree."

"Ah. Then I won't complain." He led her down the circular stairway, then, at the bottom, signaled to a servant. "Bring me a woolen cloak for Lady Brianagh." He glanced at her. "Rather cold out today. November in Ireland tends to be much colder, but we're in a warm spell."

The servant bobbed a curtsey, and a few minutes later, returned with a heavy, light-blue cloak lined with fur. Brianagh allowed Nioclas to fasten it about her shoulders.

The cold blasted Brianagh and she shivered as they stepped outside the castle walls. "This is a warm spell?"

He chuckled. "Oh, aye. In January, sometimes 'tis so bitter I have my clansfolk sleep in the great hall instead of their cottages in the village."

She had nothing to say to that. Instead she walked next to him, silently observing the hustle and bustle around them. He walked her to the archway she'd noticed earlier. It led to another bailey containing the stables, a blacksmith, and a small building with smoke rising. "The kitchens," he explained, noticing her concern. "It connects to the main castle in the back. There's a garden on the other side of it."

"I had no idea castles were so big," she murmured.

"Some are. This one is only so large because my

grandfather, and his before him, created it and added on to it. I added this bailey when I realized moving the kitchens out of the main building lessened the risk of fire." He led her around the side of the kitchen to the mostly walled-in garden. Alcoves with small benches carved into them were built into the walls, He led her to one and she was surprised to see the walls were hollow, creating a passageway.

"They don't go anywhere," Nioclas said as she peered into the wall. "In summer, we store food and supplies for the castle in them."

"How many castles are there in Ireland?" she asked.

He shrugged. "A handful. None as large as this, though. My clan is a prosperous one—we have the sea at our back and fertile lands through our borders." He nodded once to a guardsman standing near the wall, and the man nodded back before leaving.

"I will not attempt to tell you how you are feeling, but perhaps I can imagine it."

Bri jerked her head towards him, surprised. Before she could respond, he continued.

"O'Malley has led me to believe you have a full life where you've been living, on the continent."

She swallowed hard when she realized that the America she knew hadn't even been discovered yet.

"Were it me in your position, I would be concerned that my freedoms, whatever those may have been, would be taken from me. In Ireland, we do not force marriages, but I have no cause to think you'd know our ways, so you must know that you may decline the marriage if you choose to. You may walk from this castle and these lands without fear of recourse, for I've no interest in a battle with your clan."

"I don't have to marry you?" Why he would tell her this was beyond her comprehension. Did he not want to marry her? Did he want to marry someone else?

"Nay. And I feel it important that my wife enter into this

union willingly. My suspicion is that you weren't told about me, whereas I have known for a score of years about you."

Brianagh's head started to hurt.

"In order to ensure we are both equal at the start of this, I wanted you to know that your choices are not me or death."

"Death?" she gasped.

Did his eyes twinkle when he glanced down at her?

Yes. They were definitely twinkling.

"Many a lady has contemplated a jump from the battlements over an unwelcome marriage," he noted dryly.

"Ah. That hadn't yet crossed my mind," she faltered.

They walked along the passageway in silence for a moment before he took a deep breath and fully turned to her. "I have an idea that would benefit us both," he said carefully. "I was betrothed to another as of yesterday. She is unsuitable. Many other clan lairds want my alliance and wish to use their daughters as a way to secure it. My clan elders wish for me to marry to avoid any unhappy lairds knocking on my door." He slanted his eyes at her. "If I wed a lass outside my clan, our clans are allied, and my clansmen will battle alongside that clan, as they would for us. If I marry you, I'm already in alliance with the O'Rourkes, who are a peaceful clan. I will not have to involve my clansfolk in any other battles for yet another clan."

"I'm sorry, but—" she started, but he held up a hand, effectively silencing her.

"For me, this is a perfect match. But perhaps you see nothing of value for you, were you to wed me."

She searched his eyes. "Laird MacWilliam, that's not really the problem. Aye, I don't know you, but I want to go back home, to my life there. I'm not meant to be here."

His eyebrows drew together. "Tell me about your home."

Uh oh. He showed curiosity instead of irritation, and the last thing she wanted was to invite questions. She scanned her brain and blurted out, "What I mean is, I want to marry for love."

She flinched. Of all the things to say! A warrior laird wouldn't care about love. She must sound like a naive, ridiculous—

"In my clan," he said softly, running his hand down her arm to gently clasp her hand, "when you marry for love—or fall in love with your wife, if you weren't so lucky to find love before marriage—you are not expected to marry once she's dead." At her gasp, he shook his head. "No, do not misunderstand me. I have no reason to hurt you. You wish to return to the life you've built in your country, and I need to marry, if only to stop ambitious sires with very young girls whom I have no interest in taking as a lover or a wife. If you agree to stay for three months, which is enough time for other clans to hear of our nuptials, and enough time for my clan to perceive us in love, I will return you to your home, unscathed. And I will arrange travel with men who will verify your status as a clan widow."

She considered that; he would believe that she'd need the protection of widowhood to get along in the world, and she appreciated his kindness in thinking of it. She nodded, then asked, "Do you know of Newgrange?"

Obviously not the answer he expected. "I cannot say that I am familiar with it."

Brianagh flashed back to the brochure in the car and remembered reading it was "rediscovered" in 1699. She wasn't sure about Dowth, though. "How far are we from Dublin?"

His impassive mask stayed firmly in place. "Four, perhaps five days' ride."

Brianagh hadn't built a thriving company based on indecision. She had a great aptitude for assessing a situation and making executive decisions as fast as she could gather all pertinent information. And in this situation, she knew she couldn't get anywhere near Newgrange if they were that far from Dublin.

She would need this man's help to get home. He was clearly thoughtful, but he was also smart. She had no money, no transportation, and no sense of direction, as James repeatedly pointed out to her whenever she called him, lost on some back road in the suburbs of the city.

She let out a sigh, then nodded. "If you promise to bring me to Dublin, I will agree to this marriage."

She could see he didn't understand why she wanted to go there, but all he responded with was, "As you will. And, as we're to be married…you may call me Nioclas."

She inclined her head. "I'm Brianagh. But my friends call me Bri."

"Those closest to me call me Nick."

"Shall I call you Nick?"

"I prefer Nioclas," he replied dryly, "but I suppose, as you've accepted my hand for the next three months, you may call me whatever you wish, as long as it remains 'my laird' in front of any clansmen. Shall I call you Bri?"

"I prefer 'my lady,'" she said, fighting a smile, "but you may call me 'my lady Brianagh.'"

"You're quite spirited," Nioclas said, fighting his own smile. "I do think we'll get along quite well."

"Talk to Reilly," she suggested as they headed back to the main building. "He'll tell you all about how spirited I am." Brianagh cautioned herself not to let her guard down, but she already felt her heart lighten. She just prayed he was true to his word, for she fully realized she needed someone's help to get home.

A fake wedding and marriage for three months?

She was a matchmaker by trade. She knew all the signs to look for in a match. She could certainly pretend most of them to uphold her end of the bargain. It seemed a small price to pay to get back to her life.

A long price to pay, but she hadn't any other choice.

~

THAT AFTERNOON, BRIANAGH WAS BACK IN HER CHAMBER AND surrounded by at least ten women, all convinced they were the best to help her dress for the wedding. She was getting a headache listening to them talk over each other. There was no clear hierarchy that gave one person management capabilities over another.

The businesswoman in her was tearing her hair out.

"Ladies," she said, holding up her hand. The arguments continued, so she raised her voice. "LADIES!"

"Aye, my lady?" ten voices asked at once.

Brianagh zeroed in on the oldest woman. "How many brides have you aided?"

"Well, there was me own daughters, there's four right there, and a right mess, too, with the last."

"Does anyone else have more than four weddings under her belt?" Bri asked. At the confused, blank expressions, she clarified. "Has anyone aided in more than four weddings?"

One woman stepped forward, bobbing a curtsey. "Aye, my lady, I have had a hand in fourteen."

"Oh, I did so love Regan's wedding," one of the other women exclaimed. "Getting her ready in just an hour, and rushing her to the abbey before Cormac's family arrived! 'Twas nicely done!"

"All right. You—" Brianagh motioned to the woman with the most experience. "—are in charge. Determine what needs to be done, then give half of the tasks to her." She indicated the first woman who stepped forward. "Then, the two of you can tell the others what they need to do—smaller tasks, such as fetching ribbons or…" She faltered, not sure what else was needed for a medieval wedding. She just matched people and *attended* weddings. The only involvement she had in planning was to hand the happy couple a business card of her most-used wedding planner.

"I see what you need, my lady," the woman with the most experience said, saving her from thinking about it anymore. "My name is Sheila, and this is Iona. We'll take it in hand from here."

"Wonderful."

Two hours later, Brianagh was bathed, dressed, coiffed, and ready to head to the abbey.

"My lady, a word?" The others had left, and Iona stood alone near the door.

"Of course."

Iona fidgeted, then smiled. "I wanted to thank you. The way you put Sheila at the front of it and all…it made a difference. The last big wedding we had in the bailey, it took us all day to get the bride ready. The groom thought she'd run off, but really, we just spent so much time arguing over whose way was best…well, I thank you for sparing us womenfolk the weeks of arguing that usually happens between us after the blessed event."

Bri smiled back. "You're welcome. Thanks for telling me."

Iona curtsied, then added quickly, "The MacWilliam's a good man, takes care of all of us. Your sire chose well."

Bri offered another smile, and Iona closed the door behind her.

Bri's smile disappeared. *I don't have a sire. But, perhaps I just might find a purpose while I'm here.*

BRIANAGH MANAGED TO NOT GRIND HER TEETH IN FRUSTRATION, but she was nearing the end of her patience.

How long was a medieval wedding ceremony supposed to take?

She felt as though she'd been standing for hours, listening

to Latin—and of course, she couldn't understand a word. Nioclas was listening attentively, as was Kiernan, Kathryne, Reilly, Aidan…and the entire MacWilliam clan. There had to be over five hundred people standing in the bailey, watching the laird take his wedding vows. Bri hoped she wasn't the only one who had no idea what was going on during the ceremony.

"I will," Nioclas said solemnly.

Oh, that she recognized. She let out a little sigh of relief. At least she didn't have to answer anything in Latin and put her ignorance on display. She realized Nioclas was looking at her expectantly, and she quickly said, "Oh. I will too."

He slid a gold band onto her finger, and the entire clan burst into wild cheers that melded into a chant of some sort. She couldn't make out what they were yelling, but she turned and smiled at the crowd anyway.

"They're saying, 'Kiss,'" Nioclas murmured as he smiled at his people and gave a wave. "Let the game begin, aye?"

And then, in front of everyone, Nioclas pulled her close, bent her backward, and, cradling her in his arms, covered her mouth with his own. When she let out a surprised gasp, he slid his tongue between her teeth, where it tangled in a heated battle with hers…a battle to which she quickly surrendered.

As far as kisses go, Brianagh thought, her mind fuzzy as he righted her and reluctantly ended the kiss, *I just had my socks blown off.*

CHAPTER 8

Nioclas didn't bother cursing himself for giving in to his temptation. Brianagh was standing on the step of his castle and she had agreed to be his wife. He told himself it was his duty to make the marriage seem realistic. It didn't hurt that her crystal-blue eyes held intelligence, or that her mouth—the color of raspberries in summer—was shaped just for kissing. Or that the strange words that came out of that mouth showed a keen wit, sharp intelligence, and a sense of humor. He let himself have just a taste, and he was certain he would regret it. Eventually.

Leading her up the castle steps, he turned, waved one last time, then entered the great hall. It was blessedly empty, save his normally-stationed guardsmen. Once they were inside, Nioclas looked at his bride, who looked as though she still hadn't fully recovered from his kiss.

He grinned and led her over to the stairway. Two steps up he backed her against the wall, dug his hands into her hair, and lowered his mouth to hers again. He felt her resistance, but as his skillful tongue and lips worked their magic, she melted against him, her arms coming to rest lightly on his shoulders as she allowed him in.

He toyed with the fine hair at the back of her neck and felt the gooseflesh rise as she shivered. Kissing down her neck, then back up to her ear, his hand slid farther and he began to knead her backside—

"MacWilliam!" a voice boomed into the great hall.

"Damn him," Nioclas growled as Brianagh dropped her head onto his neck, her breathing ragged.

"Who is that?" Brianagh asked, licking her lips.

"Maguire." Irritation laced the word.

"Remind me to thank him," she said as she pulled back, regaining her equilibrium. "We almost made a very bad mistake there."

"MacWilliam! There you are! I heard tell you just got yourself married!" A man with dark-blond hair and brown eyes, dressed in a blue-and-red léine, rounded the corner of the stairs. "Oh ho! And apparently 'just' is exactly when!" His laughter boomed as loudly as his voice, echoing off the stone.

"Donovan!" a female voice exclaimed. "Let them be! Come back down here!" A woman appeared and grabbed his hand. "Congratulations, Nick. We shall speak soon. Donovan, leave them be." She looked back up at Brianagh and grinned. "We'll see you at the feast."

"Feast?" Brianagh asked Nioclas, her belly rumbling at the thought.

"I can make you forget about food," Nioclas said in a husky voice, his eyes darkening.

"That's probably not a good idea." She slipped out of his arms and headed downstairs. "I really am hungry."

And skittish, Nioclas thought as he watched her hasty retreat.

When attempting to convince her to become his wife, he didn't think to mention the marriage bed.

Damned oversight on his part, but one he hoped to rectify soon.

He followed into the great hall, where Erin Maguire was

clasping Brianagh's hands as if they were long-lost friends, looking apologetic and shooting her husband, Donovan Maguire, looks that would kill any other.

"She doesn't look like a Kildare," Donovan noted, joining him.

"No, I don't think she would, being as she's an O'Rourke," Nioclas replied.

"What?" Donovan's mouth dropped open. "She's not—"

"Her family seems to think so," Nioclas cut him off quickly. "But I don't. She is beautiful, was raised on the continent, and can hold an intelligent conversation…but I don't think we can add 'power over time' to her list of attributes."

"And what a fine list she seems to have," Donovan replied appreciatively. At Nioclas's glare, he laughed. "Oh, you know I've got more than enough with my Erin. But I'm not dead, Nick. I can appreciate a beautiful woman."

Nioclas watched Brianagh chatting with Erin. She was animated and full of life. Her dark hair was slightly mussed from his hands, and she was flushed. Her eyes were sparkling and her laugh, albeit nervous, carried clear across the room.

Beauty was a fitting description.

BRIANAGH HAD NO IDEA WHAT ERIN MAGUIRE WAS SAYING to her.

She suspected the woman was apologizing for her husband, but as Bri couldn't shake her mind from that kiss, she really couldn't say with certainty.

She had never felt like that before, where her insides turned to mush and all rational thought fled. All that existed was feeling; a feeling that, even now, had her just the slightest bit shaky. Never before had a man kissed her as if he wished to devour her. The intensity was mind-blowing and every other experience she'd ever had with a man was nearly erased.

And with just a kiss.

Bri reconsidered. She had felt something like this, but it was only in her dreams. And it was never this intense or this unfamiliar. Even now, she longed to be back in his arms.

Which was frightening in and of itself. Brianagh didn't *long* for anything. Yet she could feel his eyes on her, and she felt a pull.

It was inconvenient and confusing and so very not what she needed right now.

"…to the north. We spend most of our time there and always make it a point to stay here when we travel between our lands," Lady Maguire was saying, then paused and looked at Brianagh again. "Lady MacWilliam, are you all right?"

"Oh," Bri nodded. "Yes, of course. I just…ah, I just…"

"Say no more," Erin said with a knowing smile. "I've seen that look before. All the maids at my castle get the same look in their eyes when Nick deigns to grace us with his presence." She sighed. "I vow, he never gives me enough notice so that I can get the maids out before he arrives. Once he does, you see, they forget about everything except him. Makes Donovan crazy. He is forever grumbling about how Nick must have more baths drawn than a body needs when he's in residence."

Brianagh smiled at Erin's obvious irritation. "Well, I apologize on his behalf, then."

"Oh, you mustn't!" Erin exclaimed with a laugh. "If you start, you'll never stop. Nick has more things to apologize for than you have time, trust me. I'm a MacWilliam by birth and we grew up together. Believe me when I say his penchant for insects in my dress was a lamentable one."

"I would think that would've been the laird's brother, Aidan."

"Oh, I've no doubt they worked together," Erin replied

darkly. "But I'm convinced it was Nick. He always gave the air of a somber lad, but then he'd throw me a wink, and I just *knew*."

Brianagh did laugh then. She was getting the same impression.

"You must call me Erin," Erin exclaimed suddenly, "and I shall call you Brianagh. There's something about you I like."

"Call me Bri, and I feel just the same. I hear there's a feast in this marriage's honor?"

"And I'm starved. Shall we get your husband?"

Bri looked over at Nioclas, who hadn't taken his eyes off of her. His lips curved into a smile, and she felt her stomach flip. *Stop that!* she demanded, but of course her stomach ignored her. Then he winked.

She bit her lip to keep from smiling. "No, I think the men have catching up to do. They'll join us when they're ready, I'm sure."

"I have a new opinion of you, Bri. I'm going to truly, truly like you," Erin declared with a grin. "You are just what Nick needs."

Bri beamed at her. She really needed a girlfriend right about now.

NIOCLAS WATCHED HIS NEW WIFE SAUNTER TO THE HIGH TABLE arm-in-arm with Erin, and inwardly groaned. Erin was one of the very few who knew him well, like a sister. She usually couldn't keep her opinions to herself and was the most outspoken lass he knew, although most of the women in his clan took no issue airing their grievances. He didn't care to know how other clans worked, but in his, he found out early that the women knew what they were about. His mother was a prime example. Although his sire thought her useless, she had taught both him and Aidan how to read and write when that sire banished each tutor for one reason or another. His mother had taught them sums, too, and how to manage a large clan and the castle he currently resided in while navigating the delicate feelings of many people at once.

Women also tended to know everything that was happening in and around the castle, and on more than one occasion he'd heeded the warnings of feuding clans from his clanswomen.

Nioclas well understood the value of a good woman.

"Is Kildare angry?"

Nioclas rubbed the back of his neck. "I don't know, Donovan. I sent the lass home yesterday. She probably hasn't arrived yet. But I did send a messenger on one of the faster mounts in the stables." He shook his head in disgust. "His daughter is but twelve. I couldn't marry a child."

"It would do you well to remember that at that same age, you had mounted a battle against your sire for killing your mother," Donovan said quietly. "And, if you recall, you won. Your clan—well, most of them, anyway—stayed true to you and accepted you as a laird at that age."

"'Twas not me who won, despite them calling me laird. I had strong clan leaders," Nioclas felt compelled to point out.

"Aye, you did. And still do. But these men and women here." Donovan nodded to the clan as they began pouring into the great hall. "They believed in a child."

"Nay," Nioclas said quietly. "They believed in my mother."

DONOVAN HOPPED UP TO THE TABLE AND GAVE BRI A QUICK KISS on the lips. "That's Irish luck, there!"

She blinked in surprise.

Erin rolled her eyes. "Bri, this is my husband, Donovan. Donovan, try not to upset Nick today."

"I make no vows," he replied jauntily. He winked at Bri. "MacWilliam's a moody sort. If I can get some sort of reaction out of him, it's a good day."

"Is that why you left him to the mercy of all those people?" Bri asked, watching in fascination as members of the clan continued to congratulate him. She felt a twinge of regret for fooling them into believing the marriage was a real one, but quickly reminded herself it was Nioclas who was doing that. She was just trying to get home.

"He's a fair laird," Erin said thoughtfully. "His people respect him, and other clans fear him."

"His battles are legendary," Donovan noted, "and I'd want no other at my back."

"Save me?" Aidan asked, leaning over and giving Bri a smacking kiss on the mouth before making himself comfortable on the other side of Donovan. "I'm a helpful sort in a fight."

Taken aback, Brianagh didn't reply. She'd never been kissed by so many men in one day, and she wondered if this was a clan custom, or if everyone enjoyed teasing her new husband.

Would every man in the room expect to kiss her by the day's end?

"Aye," Donovan agreed, serving his wife some of the food from the large trencher on the table. "But your name doesn't inspire the same kind of fear in other clansmen's hearts."

"'Tis true." Aidan sighed, then smirked. "But it does inspire all manner of other emotions from the women of those clans."

"You're incorrigible!" Erin laughed, swatting Aidan's arm. "You should be looking for a wife. You're next, you know."

Aidan's horror showed on his face. "Lass, I will tie your braids into knots if you ever so much as mention such a thing again!"

"I don't wear braids anymore," Erin replied, supremely

unconcerned, as one of the servants filled her cup with wine. "Besides, you'll have a slew of daughters as payback for all the lasses whom you've left heartbroken."

Bri looked at the feast laid out in front of her and took a sip of the wine. She had a wooden trencher, big enough for two, and she wasn't quite sure where to begin. She wasn't even sure what some of the offerings were; she'd never seen most of what was served. It looked like meat in a whole lot of unidentifiable sauces.

"I appreciate you waiting for me," Nioclas said as he sat next to her. "I see that the others hadn't any patience."

"No." Bri noted the other three hadn't even acknowledged his presence yet. "I don't think they did."

"I am laird here," Nioclas said, filling the trencher. "I do have some who respect me."

"And some that fear you," Brianagh added with a slight laugh. "I've heard. Lady Maguire filled me in." At his furrowed brow, she clarified, "Erin told me."

"Ah." He finished filling the tray and signaled for his own wine. "Listen not to what she says. 'Twas all Aidan's fault."

"You can't blame it on me forever," Aidan said around a mouthful of food.

"Blame what on you?" Erin wondered aloud.

"Everything," Donovan replied, heaping more food onto their trencher.

Brianagh felt a laugh bubble up inside of her, and with it, a glimmer of hope. Perhaps these people were ones she could trust.

She took a large sip of wine, allowing herself to relax a small bit. She'd get home. It was just going to take some time to get there.

CHAPTER 9

Brianagh leaned into Nioclas. "I need to stop drinking the wine."

His brows lifted. "Oh?"

"It's making me hot, and this dress is, I think, made of wool."

He kept his expression neutral, but she could tell he was amused. "I am not one to follow fashions, my lady, but I believe that most of your clothing is made from wool."

"Even my summer ones?" Fanning herself, she shook her head. "That's insane. These things are hot. And restrictive."

"I wonder what the women wear in your country. Does it not get hot?"

"Oh, it does," she replied with a slightly off-balance nod. "But we wear less clothing than this. I'm pretty sure I'd die if I had to wear this in the middle of the summer."

Nioclas took in her dark hair, curling madly about her face as some of the locks escaped the knot on top of her head, her blue eyes luminous. The dress she spoke of pushed her chest upward; the expanse of skin looked unmarred and softer than his own. Cinched about her waist, the dress flared out over her hips and thighs. Nioclas drank in the sight of her, his breath catching as he thought of her in less clothing.

She was laughing at something Erin had said. He caught the sound and held onto it a minute longer than was wise. She was different from the other women he had been with. She was artless in the sweep of her arm as she discussed something, but graceful in step as she walked. Her presence was a strange mix of confidence and vulnerability.

Intriguing.

He hadn't been intrigued by a woman in years. And especially not as intrigued as he was currently, his eyes narrowing when his brother gave his bride yet another kiss.

The only man kissing those lips will be me.

The thought took him by surprise. He had never been a jealous man, especially with women. He was content to have them while they were willing, then walk away when either was done. But there was something about Brianagh. Maybe it was because she so strongly resembled the woman from his dreams all those years ago, before the weight of the clan became so difficult to bear. Or maybe it was her beauty. Her radiance almost hurt his eyes, and he desired it more than he'd ever desired anything before.

Or maybe, he wondered, *it was because she is now my wife.*

As he watched her take another sip of the wine, then bestow a sweet smile on one of the clan elders, he allowed himself a small smile of his own. She would do her part, and in three months, he would do his.

All would be well.

BRIANAGH WATCHED WHAT SHE SUSPECTED WAS SOMETHING Nioclas rarely allowed himself: he seemed relaxed with his friends and family. When she added in the pretty fantastic kissing and all that it evoked, she could lose herself very quickly if she didn't remind herself that it was all a ruse.

The room quieted as one of the clan leaders stood from his seat. "Clansmen. 'Tis a very great time to be a MacWilliam. Our clan is strong and prosperous. We are at peace, and we have the MacWilliam—the most powerful laird in Eire—to thank for that." Cheers erupted.

Brianagh sneaked a look at Nioclas. His face was serious.

Erin leaned over and murmured into her ear, "That's Daniel, the clan elder. He's the oldest in the clan, and Nick's closest advisor."

Daniel continued. "He rescued us from evil, a man who would destroy us if it suited his purpose. When we stood with MacWilliam, we stood together, and we haven't sat down. For twenty-two years, we've been waiting for the day when we would welcome a Lady MacWilliam, and we now have her. Clan MacWilliam, I present to you Lady Brianagh MacWilliam, formerly Lady Brianagh O'Rourke!"

The silence was deafening while everyone digested that their laird had just married an O'Rourke—clearly they hadn't expected that. Then Aidan started to applaud and was quickly joined by Erin and Donovan. The rest of the clan followed suit.

The whispers were almost as loud as the clapping.

"Now, 'tis time for the standing up," Aidan called out.

Nioclas shot his brother a look of death that made even Erin squirm. The crowd began to cheer again. The rowdy suggestions tossed about made Brianagh blush from head to toe.

Nioclas stood, and the entire room quieted immediately. "There will be no standing up," he said, his voice ringing clearly throughout the hall. "I thank you all for coming and for attending my wedding. You are all welcome to stay at the castle tonight." He held his hand down to Bri, who quickly realized she was supposed to follow his lead and took it. She followed him out of the hall and up the stairs.

"I think we'll let them talk for a while yet about your former surname," Nioclas said as they walked. "It will take them a few weeks to forget you're an O'Rourke, but once they choose to, the tale your family has spread will not be mentioned again."

Brianagh didn't really hear all of what he was saying—that wine was stronger than she thought—but she did hear *former surname*? "What do you mean by that? The former surname part?"

He opened the door and brought her into a chamber much more luxuriously appointed than hers. Whereas she had only a small stool, straw mattress, and washstand, his chamber had two stools, a large washstand, an ornately carved dresser, and a huge bed, which was the focal point of the room. Complete with posts, an ornamented canopy, and richly embroidered hangings, the bed was laden with coverlets, pillows, and fur blankets.

She would've bet her leather slippers the bed was not made out of straw.

"This is your chamber?" she asked in wonder.

"Absolutely not," Nioclas replied. "My chamber mirrors your own. This is the guest chamber."

"It seems overly fancy for a guest." She touched one of the tapestries on the wall.

"My sire, when he controlled the clan, believed it best to make one of the rooms fit for royalty. No one was allowed to sleep in it, but it was displayed to all." Nioclas snorted. "He simply wanted to prove that he had the gold to own such a chamber."

"Did he have the gold?"

"My mother did," Nioclas replied, "and once it was gone, he killed her."

Brianagh covered her mouth with her hand. "I'm so sorry."

"It was a long time ago, lass."

"Why are we in here now?"

"Because the laird would be expected to spend his wedding night in the best chamber with his chosen lady," Nioclas replied softly.

"Which brings me back to the question I asked. What did you mean by former surname?"

Surprised, he responded, "Where you're from, do the women not take the man's surname as her own once the vows are spoken?"

"Well…sometimes," she replied, careful in her wording. "Most times, actually. I suppose my question is, are we really married?"

"Aye." He looked at her curiously, but his expression changed to wary. "That was our agreement."

"I thought we were just going to pretend to get married! How do I explain this when I get back?" Realizing what she said, she snapped her mouth closed and shut her eyes.

She really, really didn't mean to say that.

Nioclas's face went carefully blank. "Are you betrothed to another?"

"Um—"

He sighed and pinched the bridge of his nose. "Will he come for you?"

She rolled her eyes. "No."

He glanced at her curiously. "You say that with such certainty, I'm led to believe the match is not a love match. It must be arranged, then?"

"No, it's a love match." She almost choked on the words. "He asked me, and I said yes. But he won't come for me. He doesn't know where I am. I don't know why I'm explaining this to you; it doesn't really matter anyway."

He frowned. "Is he a laird?"

"No. He's in trade."

Nioclas scoffed. "Trade! You, the daughter of a powerful Irish clan, agreed to marry a *tradesman*? 'Tis laughable. You're worth more than that."

She bristled. "Apparently so. *You* bought me."

He immediately sobered. "Aye, I did. Will he wait for you, if he receives word that you are to return in three months?"

"Are you offering to send word?" she asked cautiously.

"Nay, and you know why. I simply wonder if he would wait that long for you." Nioclas paused. "Three months is not long, to be sure, but some men have different priorities in a marriage. Often, time is important."

Brianagh shrugged. "I would like to believe he'll wait for me." *But I wonder if he would.*

Her unspoken thought hung in the air between them.

"Your parents—"

"Who haven't known me since the moment I was born—"

"—assured me you were unattached—"

"—and had no idea what my life was like before I was *sold* to the highest bidder—"

"—and I married you to avoid war, not bring it to my doorstep—"

"Well, maybe you should've asked Reilly, seeing as he was with me from the minute my mother gave me up!" Brianagh snapped.

"O'Malley? You were betrothed to O'Malley?"

"No! I was betrothed to Matthew de Burgh!"

"A *Frenchman*?" Nioclas exclaimed in disgust. "And probably a distant relation to the Burkes—an entire side of the clan left Ireland years ago to get away from my sire's rule. I had heard tell they changed their name. Cowards."

"Oh, now you want to insult an entire family based on the fact they changed their names?"

"Are you always this argumentative?" Nioclas countered angrily.

"Absolutely not. I'm usually quite agreeable!" she shouted. With effort, she lowered her voice. "Well, again, Matthew doesn't know where I am. So I'm fairly certain he won't come banging on your gates in the middle of the night."

"Are you so desperate to get back to him that you'd give up your honor?" Nioclas spat. "Surely, if he thinks you're ruined, he'll want no more of you."

"That's not how he thinks," she replied hotly. "He won't care about that."

"The man won't *care* if his love marries another?" Nioclas raised an arrogant brow. "If the lass I loved married another, I would ride to the ends of the world to find her. Then I would slay the fool who thought to steal her from me." He lowered his voice. "And I wouldn't wait to do either."

"We have different visions of love," Bri said, her voice unsure.

His eyes, full of questions, locked on hers for a long moment. "I don't think we do, lass."

She laughed nervously. "Your words are quite romantic, Nioclas. I hope that when you find your own love, you can say them with the same finesse."

His eyes clouded. "You know me not, Brianagh. Tread carefully with your tone. You may be able to speak with your *Frenchman*"—he uttered the word angrily, as though it were an insult upon his person—"like that, but you will not do so to me."

"Why are you so angry about this?" she demanded. "This isn't even a real marriage, and he's not going to come looking for me!"

"How are you so certain?" Nioclas demanded back, closing the distance between them. "Are you not important enough to fight for? Is he too busy with his trade to be bothered by this?"

The truth of his questions slammed into her, and she sucked in a breath.

Nioclas's expression immediately softened. "By the saints, Brianagh. 'Tis the truth, isn't it?"

Brianagh could feel his warm breath caress her face. Stiffening her spine, she tried to ignore the hot, intense flash of lust, and remained silent.

"That isn't love. When I kissed you, I felt your surprise." Nioclas pressed closer.

Bri stepped back, but he followed. "Well, you did kiss me in front of all those people. I wasn't expecting that."

"I'm talking about the kiss inside the castle walls, Brianagh. When it was just you and me. Tell me, did your de Burgh ever kiss you like I did?"

Her eyes widened.

"I wonder…" His voice was barely above a whisper and Bri leaned involuntarily toward him, drawn by a force she couldn't control. "I wonder if he's ever made you feel this?" Nioclas's lips met hers in the barest of kisses.

Somewhere, someone whimpered.

That couldn't have been her. She was angry with Nioclas, not burning for him. And she didn't whimper.

And then his lips were on hers, hungry for her taste. Instinctively Bri wrapped her arms around his neck as her heart pounded in her ears. He tasted like fine wine, intoxicating her. His mouth was making love to hers in a sweet tangle of tongues and teeth. Her knees buckled, and he swept her up without breaking the kiss.

Carrying her to the bed, Nioclas carefully laid her down, feasting on her lips, coaxing her response to a fevered pitch. Bri knew she should stop it before things spiraled out of control, but she couldn't find it in her to push him away. She'd dreamed of this for years; having it here, now, was surreal and wonderful and confusing. She was so hot she was going to combust, and she couldn't—didn't want to—do anything to stop it.

Nioclas's hand reached for the ties to her dress and gave them a quick yank. The knots fell away, as if they, too, really thought this was a good idea.

She dimly realized his tunic was off, and she caught a glimpse of bicep. A tattoo wound its way around the large, corded muscle. Fascinated, she gently traced it with her finger, curious as to where it led.

"You're worth something, Brianagh." He trailed kisses down her neck. "You're worth fighting for. Don't allow anyone to say otherwise."

Her mind was wrapped in a sensual fog, but she wasn't so far gone that she couldn't stop. She couldn't sleep with Nioclas; she wasn't the kind of woman who had flings. She had never flung before and she really didn't want to start in the Middle Ages.

"Have you ever been kissed here?" Nioclas continued, trailing kisses down her neck. "Or here?" Over her collarbone. "Or…here?" The top of her breast.

Oh, God, it was just like in her dreams. His lips were so familiar to her; she was drowning in her desire, and she had a sinking suspicion that were she to give into him, their game would become a whole lot more dangerous than either of them realized.

She drew a deep breath. "This isn't love, Nioclas. It's lust. And I can't give myself to a man who doesn't love me. And you're right. I am worth something; after all, *you* bought me. If I sleep with you, I'm no better than a common whore."

Nioclas reared back, as if struck. The anger on his face sent a frisson of fear cascading over her.

Wordlessly, he glared at her, and then withdrew from the chamber completely, leaving her cold and aching.

It was nothing less than she deserved.

Much later, when Nioclas finally returned, he wrapped himself in a blanket and laid himself on the floor next to the bed where Brianagh slept.

Kiernan certainly had played him well. He found Nioclas at his weakest point when he was a desperate lad. Extracting a promise for something so far into the future was cunning, even Nioclas admitted that. But to encourage the marriage when the lass was already betrothed?

He had no idea what betrothals meant in France. In England, to which he'd traveled once and hoped never to return, betrothals were as binding as marriage, and the only way to break it was to have both sides agree, then involve the church. It was a long process, and by the time it was done, the lass was thought too old to be married.

Brianagh was about that age. He supposed if they were to annul their marriage, it would take her until she died to get all the necessary approvals from the continent. Ireland wasn't nearly so difficult—all she needed was clan approval.

Considering how much pressure he had been under to get married in the first place, however, approval might be more difficult than obtaining the proper documents from France.

Grudgingly, he admitted that she fascinated him. She was different than other women of his acquaintance. Intelligent, bold, saucy…and beautiful. He couldn't deny the pleasure her face brought him when he looked upon it.

His head began to pound and his body surged again, seeking relief from its earlier…hopes.

Growing up, Nioclas always had dreams of a woman he ached for; one whose love was so unconditional, so fulfilling, that he felt uncompelled to marry. When those dreams faded to a distant memory and reality intruded, he understood his duty. Marry, produce heirs, protect the clan. He was mere hours away from doing all of that…

The Fates must be women, he decided abruptly. Fickle, mean-spirited creatures who enjoyed torturing unsuspecting men in their dreams.

Brianagh's blue eyes, looking at him with love. Her sweat-soaked body after their lovemaking in the forest, in the meadow, by the sea. Her laugh, her smile, even her hair, haunted his dreams.

He recognized her when they dismounted from his horse, but refused to believe it. What kind of woman could come to him in his dreams, then be brought to his doorstep?

The irony that he himself had carried her there was not lost on him.

Nioclas knew before he kissed her how her lips would taste. His heart settled somewhere deep in his chest, and for a brief moment, his entire world shifted, then righted itself into its proper place.

He never was one to let opportunities sneak by, so when she responded, he allowed hope to enter his hardened heart. But damn him if the lass claimed to love another. Now that he had her in the flesh, he wasn't sure he wanted to let her go.

He loathed how insignificant it made him feel.

Brianagh murmured something in her dreams, and Nioclas paused. It was curious how he'd dreamed of her face —and her body, if he were truthful—for years. And 'twas also strange how she came into possession of the brooch; he'd lost it in the ocean almost a year prior, and while the one O'Malley handed him wasn't as pristine as the one he'd created, there was no mistaking it.

Nioclas only fashioned the one brooch, and that was after one of his more vivid dreams. He entwined his initial with the leaves of ivy that grew along the walls of his castle. The hawk, which adorned his clan's crest, was an obvious choice, and he'd carved his own sword through the initial. He wanted to have his smithy replicate it. Though it took him months to create the brooch, within days, Nioclas lost it. And with it, dreams of the woman he now recognized, who was snoring softly on the feather mattress.

BRIANAGH WAS EXHAUSTED THE NEXT MORNING, AND WHEN SHE woke from a particularly fitful bit of sleep, Nioclas wasn't anywhere in sight. He had been angry; when she woke up during the night, she could feel the tension radiating off him as he lay on the floor. Bri wasn't sure what to expect. She'd let her guard down last night and it didn't feel like the outcome was going to be any good.

It didn't help at all that when she did sleep, she dreamed of his lips on hers.

She turned her thoughts away from that. Stretching, she noticed the bed wasn't made out of straw—it was feathers, as she suspected. She wondered if she could move in to this room instead of going back to the other one. At least she woke up warm, with a fire in the little hearth she hadn't noticed the night before.

A dress was laid out at the end of the bed, and Brianagh grudgingly got up. She changed, performed her morning ablutions, then sat back down on the bed.

She had no idea what to do next.

Bri was never one to sit around and wait for life to happen to her. The fact was she was stuck in medieval Ireland for three months; perhaps she could do something to help the castle. Her decision made, she hopped off the bed with renewed purpose.

Pulling the heavy door open, Bri slipped into the hallway and tried to determine which was the correct way. There were too many hallways in the castle for her to attempt to keep them straight. Maybe she'd ask Nioclas for a map. *Then again,* she thought, her heart sinking as he strode towards her, *maybe not.*

His face was devoid of all emotion. She tried a greeting, but he wasn't in the mood for pleasantries and cut her off mid-sentence as he led her back into the chamber and closed the door.

"I've sent messengers out to determine what de Burgh's plans are. If his goal is to steal you away in the night, I've no stomach to send my men into battle for you, and if they find out I've deceived them in this, they will not trust me."

She blinked, taken aback. "I told you, he won't come."

Nioclas's pitying gaze seared her. "Then he's a fool, as are you, to be so blind to his lack of affections."

She frowned. "I'm not blind to it. I know his faults."

"I've no wish to argue the point when we've already thoroughly done so. Today, I'll be in the lists. You may stay with Lady Maguire, in your solar. Meals are served three times per day, and you will take them with her. She will instruct you on how the castle runs and your expected duties as my wife. Your family has departed, and you should be aware that I strongly dislike your father, though your mother seems tolerable. Do not expect many visits."

Her heart sank as his commands rattled from his tongue.

Yesterday, he spoke of starting off as equals, of choices. But now that she was tied to him, he was dictating her days?

Brianagh couldn't believe she fell for it. He gave her sweet words and a possibly empty promise. Her chest felt hollow.

She drew her chin up. "I only just met them yesterday, and they didn't seem like the warm, loving type," she snapped. "I'll probably see Reilly more."

"Nay. He took his leave with your sire."

Brianagh felt a moment of panic as she stared at his impassive face. Reilly was *gone*? "Nioclas, I need Reilly to get back. You'll bring me back to him, right?"

He looked more through her than at her. "I honor my vows. If O'Malley is the one to return you to your love, then O'Reilly you shall have. In three months."

"I'm sorry for what I said last night," Bri offered, feeling a bit shaken at his cool countenance.

"You stated nothing more than the truth. I did purchase you, but you did not come away without something as well, my lady."

Her heart sank even more at the clipped words. She hated when her temper got the best of her, and she knew an apology wouldn't be enough.

"You're right, and I'll do exactly as we agreed."

"We never agreed to a marriage in name only."

She paused. "We didn't?"

"Nay. If you recall, you are to be returned with widow status."

She chewed her lip. She wasn't a fool, contrary to Nioclas's earlier assessment. She had many clients fall into just such a place; keep it casual, keep it distant, keep it fun.

Well, at some point, one party started to want more. It was a dangerous game to play, and Bri knew her heart wouldn't recover. It was already breaking with the acceptance that the man of her dreams lived in a time not her own, in a life far different than what she loved. And with his change in demeanor from yesterday…

"Is this something you'll force from me?"

He frowned. "Nay! I don't take unwilling lasses to my bed, Brianagh. Lady Maguire will be along to take you to your solar. If you need anything, my clan will attend to you." He bowed stiffly and walked away.

Brianagh's stomach fell even further, then twisted upon itself. She had the distinct impression that she'd insulted him, but wasn't sure how. She didn't know him, nor he her. Last night, she threw cold water on a hot situation. Today, he showed her his true colors.

She tried valiantly to convince herself that the pain in her chest was relief, not disappointment. The Nioclas she knew from her dreams was exactly that—dreams. The real

MacWilliam was someone completely different, and rationally, she knew she couldn't hold him to a standard she'd created in her mind.

Brianagh swallowed past the dry lump in her throat.

Three months suddenly seemed like an eternity.

CHAPTER 10

In the shelter of the trees, a man slid a bag of gold into his boot. Rain soaked his blue-and-silver léine and his tunic clung to his chest. The sword strapped to his back was slick with mud but held fast to its position, belted into place with leather straps.

"MacWilliam has married."

Burke's obsidian eyes flashed in the gloom. "Her name?"

"Lady Brianagh. She was brought here two nights past. She was pulled from your pit by MacWilliam, his brother, and the O'Rourke clan." The man hunched his shoulders against the wind.

Burke scratched his beard. "Brianagh O'Rourke. Did the O'Rourke claim her as a daughter?"

"His only daughter," the man confirmed.

Burke felt a flash of rage. Years ago, after he was banished from his clan, Burke began to formulate his eldest son's demise. Every attempt at killing Nioclas proved unsuccessful as each man Burke managed to get into the castle proved inept, and was either killed or languished in the man's dungeon until death claimed him.

He resisted the urge to smash his fist into the nearest tree.

He had his men on the lookout for the Kildare lass, as stealing Nioclas's bride would've brought Nioclas directly to him. However, they unknowingly captured something infinitely more important.

Everyone in Ireland heard the whispers of the O'Rourke child who had powers greater than that of a witch. The legacy, they whispered, would be fulfilled only by one who was worthy enough to respect it. Burke hadn't paid much attention to the rumors, but he always suspected the lass would bring ransom enough for him to hire the best assassins in the country.

His mind spun. There were other ways to destroy the MacWilliam. "What do your clansmen think of your laird marrying an O'Rourke?"

"They're superstitious fools," the man replied with a scoff. "No person can control time. 'Tis the only way O'Rourke instills fear, as his battle skills leave much to be desired."

"And you desire battle?" Burke asked, not caring about the answer.

"Aye." The man cracked his knuckles. "I don't agree with MacWilliam. He thinks speech is best. I believe in killing the laird, taking their women, and eating their cattle."

I didn't ask you what you believed in, Burke almost said, but quickly controlled himself. "I agree. Action gains power. Speech gains nothing."

"Aye. MacWilliam broke a betrothal with the Kildare lass. I thought we should keep her and demand ransom, but MacWilliam sent her back with an apology and some gold. Wasted opportunity."

"I do think Kildare will want…satisfaction. His daughter was rejected, and MacWilliam refused a clan alliance." A plan began to form in Burke's mind. "The MacWilliam has shown weakness. That cannot be tolerated for a clan as powerful as yours."

The man nodded quickly. "Aye, 'tis a mistake, no doubt.

MacWilliam is firm in his disapproval of the O'Rourke clan; they left this morn as soon as their horses were readied, unwilling to stay in the castle any longer than necessary."

"Tell me of Kildare. Is he vengeful?"

The man snorted. "Perhaps. Kildare is boastful and weak. He'll believe the gold and apology is enough. He bows to MacWilliam in the hopes that one day he'll pay him some attention and promise alliance."

"How long have you served the MacWilliam?" Burke inquired. The man was young, blood-thirsty, and without loyalty. Burke could understand a man like that.

"The whole of my life. Two score years, and I've only been in four battles. Four! It's a waste of my talent. I can cleave a man in half with just a flick of my wrist! I tried to join with Kildare but found him lacking. I need a clan that—" He stopped abruptly as riders approached.

"I'll need more information," Burke said as they watched the horses disappear into the forest from a hidden vantage point. "I want to know if his fair lady-wife is indeed who she says she is. Watch them and see if they are well-matched. I want to know what they do with their days and with each other. We will meet back here in a fortnight…if, that is, you care for more gold."

The man's eyes glittered. "All I want is your gold."

"Then go earn it," Burke snapped, finally losing his patience. MacWilliams were known for their fearless fighting and intelligence. Why then, Burke wondered, was he talking with surely the most dim-witted among that clan?

The man hurried away, and Burke fought the urge to throw his dirk into the man's back. The lad thought he was so brave and battle-worthy. If that were true, he'd know never to turn his back to any man—friend or enemy.

Burke sincerely hoped the rest of the clan was as ignorant as his informant, despite their reputations otherwise. When his time came to kill their laird, Burke fully intended to make certain they knew a laird's position was won and not given.

He should've killed Nioclas and his brother when he killed their mother. Then he wouldn't have been caught off-guard when the bastard went to the clan elders and mounted his attack. He'd been having a very nice time with a particularly unwilling maiden—always a favorite—when Nioclas had launched himself at him and knocked him off the lass. That act alone warranted Nioclas's death, but Nioclas had almost the entire clan at his back when he claimed Burke as exiled.

Exiled. As if a mere twelve-year-old could exile the most powerful ruler in Ireland. Burke allowed a smile to curve his lips. It was the number of men the child had with him that forced him off his own land. It was the number of men that had closed ranks around the boy that prevented him from getting too close.

Nioclas had changed the name of the clan from Burke to MacWilliam in honor of his murdered mother. Burke, once he realized his wife brought nothing more to the marriage than alliance with a weak clan, had set fire to all their homes and stables. He even killed their cattle, just because he could.

He was powerful. Her father had been weak and had suffered for it.

I will rule again, Burke thought as he slipped through the forest, away from the MacWilliam castle. The lass would ensure that…hopefully unwillingly.

"DO WE *REALLY* HAVE TO DO THIS ALL DAY AGAIN?"

Erin looked up from her sewing, a perfectly serene look gracing her features. They had been mending for hours already, and Brianagh—who hadn't picked up a needle since the Home Ec Disaster of '08—wasn't sure her fingers could take any more abuse. She rolled her shoulders and sent Erin a pleading look. "It's been three days of nonstop sewing. I don't think I can handle this anymore."

"Bri." Erin sighed and placed the tunic she was working on in her lap. "There's really not much to do. Yet."

The twinkle in Erin's eye had Bri leaning forward slightly. "Yet?"

"Yes, yet. Once the rain stops, and once lunch is done, we'll stroll."

Brianagh actually felt her entire being deflate. She couldn't possibly take three months of this. Erin continued smoothly threading the needle through her tunic, which resembled an actual shirt. Brianagh had no idea what hers looked like, but as her job was to mend the holes…well, she wasn't sure what happened, but it now only had one sleeve and the bottom right was quite a bit higher than the bottom left.

"Stroll," Bri finally said, her gaze not leaving the window. The mist that enveloped the castle earlier had turned into a steady rain, and she wasn't so certain she wanted any first-hand knowledge of medieval healers when she came down with some sort of cold.

"In the morning, the guards train with each other. The MacWilliam guard is made up of the strongest and most loyal clansmen," Erin said, snipping a piece of thread with deadly-looking scissors. Erin smiled at her progress, then picked another piece of clothing out of the basket at her feet. "After the midday meal, the laird—and any visiting laird—trains with his guests and personal guard." She looked up and a hint of a smile played around her lips. "It's my most favorite time of day." Brianagh looked at her blankly, and Erin laughed. "Oh, you'll see, Brianagh. It makes this wait so much more enjoyable."

Brianagh eyed the full basket of mended clothes at Erin's feet, then her own with the one and only tunic she'd touched —and really, one could consider it a new fashion. She figured catching a cold was better than sewing for the next couple months of her life.

After the last few days of silence from Nioclas, she wasn't sure she could uphold her end of their deal. Her time was dragging endlessly and she'd been stuck in the castle. At least she'd been able to really watch how the clan interacted. Seeing them, she had crafted a pretty solid plan to present to Nioclas.

If she could ever find him. His avoidance was the stuff of legends. And, if she were to believe the tales around the castle, so were his skills in the bedroom.

Her cheeks flamed at that memory. She'd been innocently wandering around one of the hallways, trying to find her way back to the main hall, when she overheard two women gossiping about the rumors surrounding her husband and his female conquests. Legendary, indeed. No man could possibly do what they described for the length of time they claimed he did it. Although, when he had kissed her the night of their wedding, he wasn't exactly in any hurry…

"Are you feeling all right, Bri? You look feverish," Erin asked, pulling Bri back into the present.

"Oh. Um, no, I'm fine. I was noticing that the castle seems a bit…um…disorganized." Bri picked up a pair of hose and wrinkled her nose. Holy cow, they were almost completely ripped at the knee. She gritted her teeth and set to the task, sending a silent apology to whomever had to wear these when she was finished with them.

"Disorganized?" Erin asked, confused.

Bri was momentarily jealous of Erin's blood-free fingertips and peaceful countenance. The woman could probably out-sew Vera Wang the day before a royal wedding and keep that tranquility wrapped around her like a cloak.

"I mean that there's no order. No leader among the non-warriors of the clan. It's kind of a free-for-all."

"I can't say I've heard that term before, but it's the way

clans work. As you didn't grow up in Ireland, I could see how it looks rather muddled." She looked up and smiled a little dreamily. "Donovan took me to England once. It was beautiful. We were welcomed into an enormous castle, with turrets and flags and more furniture and tapestries than I ever thought were made. There wasn't a clan, of course, as we were in England, and they do things quite differently. But there was a definitive order to the household. The lady of that castle certainly wasn't doing the watchman's mending—just her husband's. And it had been washed before she mended it."

Bri made a face. She was mending a watchman's dirty leggings? As inconspicuously as possible, she dropped the hose back into the basket and grabbed another tunic.

"I saw that," Erin said without taking her eyes off her thread. "Here, the laird gives his sword in protection and the people work for the castle. Some have land they farm, others have small ships and fish. Still others have neither and they spend their days here at the castle, trying to do something to earn their keep. If they don't work, they aren't guaranteed the laird's protection."

Well, that was news.

"Do you think it would be well-received if I suggest a few changes?" Bri asked. "I just think we could run this so much better if people had duties they could really excel at. You know, like Sheila, the woman can sew really well and really fast. And, for whatever reason, she claims that it soothes her soul." Bri couldn't imagine that statement ever ringing true for her. "Darby is competent as a ladies' maid, but she's so young. I'd much prefer Iona. The way she styled my hair was incredible." Bri touched the dark mass of tresses tied in a neat knot at the nape of her neck. "She kept it off my neck when she last did it."

"It invites kissing," Erin said matter-of-factly. "Darby may not know of that."

Bri stared.

"What? Of course you want to invite kissing, especially from Nioclas. It leads to other activities...*wedding night* activities." Erin placed another completed léine in her overflowing basket with a satisfied smile. At Bri's open-mouthed stare, Erin laughed. "Oh, never with me! He's like a brother! I'm talking about before you. He has quite the reputation as a skilled lov—"

The midday meal bell rang, saving Bri from having to go down that road.

"They'll bring the meal in here," Erin said, pushing the baskets away from her. Bri hastily followed suit. "I think your ideas are worth talking to Nioclas about. He very much appreciates efficiency in battle. Seeing the same applied to his household may appeal to him. You just have to be careful about who is assigned to what within the clan. You don't want to upset any elders."

"Elders?"

"Aye. Clan leaders. You see, we're all family, though some more distant than others. MacWilliams are a strong lot, especially after Nioclas led the revolution against his father—oh, I can't even remember how long ago. Two-score years, maybe? No, it was slightly longer than that. But he became laird at such a young age, and all the elders supported him. Nick became a master at avoiding the expected clashes of putting one elder in front of another. You should talk with him about who's going to have his léine in a twist if he's not leading whatever job he wants to lead."

Bri hadn't considered the politics behind a clan. Not that she knew what those were—she was thought to be from the continent, after all. *Which technically, I am,* she reminded herself. Just not the continent everyone thought.

Since Erin was in her usual chatty mood, Bri encouraged her. "Well, as you were part of this clan until you married

Donovan, who do you think would be best for heading up the washing and hanging of clothes?"

Erin thought about it for a minute, then nodded. "You'll want Maggie on that. She's got three daughters, and they already do most of the washing. They live here, usually sleep in the great hall, sometimes the stables if there's another clan staying—"

"We have women and children sleeping in the great hall?" Brianagh interrupted, shocked. She hadn't been to the main floor after dinner. "But there are unused chambers everywhere!"

"Yes, but they're used for other lairds when they come to see Nick." Erin shrugged.

As they ate their meal—a very strange concoction of tough, chewy meat slathered in some sort of heavily herbed sauce—Brianagh's wheels were spinning so fast, she almost couldn't keep up. She knew next to nothing about medieval servitude—which, she acknowledged, was actually distant relations working for a safe place to sleep—but she wondered if it would strengthen the clan if they were treated better than sleeping on a stone floor or with the horses.

She had to tread carefully when she brought her plan to Nioclas.

"You may want to think about installing a new cook here," Erin said as she swallowed with difficulty. "Being from the continent, I'm sure you've had better food than this. Nioclas is not one to notice such things, but as his wife, you must ensure his comfort."

Brianagh managed a sickly kind of smile that Erin misinterpreted as a sign that the food really was that bad and announced, "I believe it's time for our stroll. I'll have someone fetch our cloaks."

A few moments later, they headed across the bailey. No one even gave them a second look.

"Where are we going?" Bri asked, pulling the hood closer around her head to ward off the chill.

"The lists."

"But Nioclas was quite clear when he said we aren't allowed in them," she said, remembering how a few days ago, he'd sent his brother to her solar to deliver the castle rules.

Ridiculous.

"Oh, they won't know we're there," Erin scoffed. "We'll be hidden. If you remember, I grew up here." She flashed a mischievous grin at Bri. "I know just where to watch, without anyone being any wiser."

Bri followed, fully planning to blame the entire thing on Erin if they were caught. She was the new kid in town; she didn't know anything. They did things differently on the continent. Her list of plausible excuses was lengthy, so she smiled at the thought of no more mending and scurried against the wall separating the two courtyards she'd seen this morning. Nodding at the men they passed, Bri tried to look like she was just out for an afternoon stroll.

Against a wall.

"Here we are," Erin said, her voice low as they crept into the small archway separating the two baileys.

Bri stopped in her tracks, her jaw slack. Men were everywhere. Some were on horses, running at each other down a track and ramming long poles into each other in what looked like an attempt to force the opponent from his horse. Others were fighting with a wooden machine with extensions, each with something dangling from it—Bri fervently hoped that wasn't a dead pig she thought she saw tied to one of them. The machine was wound back by two men, then released in a frenzy of flying objects at a guardsman. The reaction time of the current guard was impressive until he was taken off his feet by the pig.

But the most interesting was the hand-to-hand combat

happening at the far end. There, only two men were engaged —swords, by the look and sound of it—and a large cluster of guards stood to the side and watched, calling out to the opponents. Bri couldn't make out the words because they were too far away. She couldn't even see who was fighting—not that she'd recognize anyone, anyway.

"Come on," Erin said, grabbing her hand and tugging her into the wall.

Bri laughed a little. The wall was a slim archway with openings on either end and was clearly a well-used passageway between the baileys.

"The wall is built out, with benches for people to watch our tournaments when we hold them," Erin explained as they walked. "We're underneath the top level of those benches."

"Oh, yes, Erin. This is super-secret."

Erin gave her a mock glare. "Trust me. The men get so involved in their training, they don't notice anyone in this thing. Well, he does," she amended as they squeezed by a guard standing in the middle of the tunnel, "but he won't breathe a word. Right, Ambrose?"

"I see nothing, my lady."

"Great answer. My mother and his were sisters. He knows nothing."

"Nothing," Ambrose agreed with a wink before sauntering back the way the women had just come.

"Now…look at that," Erin said triumphantly. The large cracks in the walls facing the lists made it easy to see the men using swords, and the guardsmen calling out insults and slurs were somewhere to the left. "Stay back in the shadows and no one will be any wiser."

Bri and Erin peered out…and Bri's mouth went dry as a shot of pure lust lanced straight to her core.

Nioclas had his tunic off. Dressed in just a léine and boots, his chest shone with sweat, and his muscles tightened as he crossed swords with Donovan. His hair was tied back, but some strands escaped the leather band and plastered themselves to his neck. Pushing aside her irrational reaction, Bri's eyes drank in the sight of him. The tattoo she spied on their wedding night was just the tip of the iceberg. It wound itself all the way around the top of his bicep and to his shoulder, each arm mirroring the other. The intricacies of the Celtic knots looked fascinating, although she was too far away to make out any real detail. With each clang of the swords, Nioclas's calves flexed, strength underscoring his every move. Bri's body tightened in response.

Nioclas laughed suddenly at something Donovan said, and Brianagh thought she might expire on the spot.

"He rarely does that," Erin murmured.

"Train?"

"No. Laugh." She slanted a glance at Bri. "Mayhap marriage agrees with him."

Brianagh bit her lip, a sense of guilt invading her. She had no idea what agreed with him. She hadn't even caught sight of him since the morning after their wedding.

Nioclas finished with Donovan, sending his sword flying. It landed about five feet from where the women were, and they both jumped back quickly, hands over their mouths. Once the sword was retrieved, they burst out into a fit of quiet giggles.

"See?" Erin whispered, leaning forward as Aidan took up with Nioclas. "Best part of the day."

Still ogling Nioclas, Bri had to agree.

"THE WOMEN ARE UNDER THE BENCHES," AIDAN SAID QUIETLY AS he bounced on the balls of his feet, waiting for Nioclas to finish his drink. Admiring his sword, he added, "Been there for about ten minutes or so. I give them another twenty before they get cold and head back into the castle."

Nioclas sighed. "I'm unsurprised. Does Erin still think no one knows about her forays into the lists?"

Aidan shrugged and quickly crossed swords with his brother. "Of course. I'm certainly not going to tell her. She'll skewer me on the end of her sewing needle whilst I sleep."

"Are you that afraid of a wee lass?" Nioclas mocked, jumping back and just avoiding the tip of Aidan's blade. He grinned. "I don't think Donovan has much trouble with her."

"Oh, I'm sure Donovan has complete control over his wife," Aidan replied, and they both grinned as they hacked away at each other. "I don't think he's ever been privy to the full extent of Erin's talents, though."

Nioclas ducked and rolled out of Aidan's path, springing back up and crossing blades once more. "I—oof—doubt he would've agreed to marry her, had he known."

"Marriage. I don't envy you, brother. Shackled for life. I hope she is worth it." Aidan narrowly avoided the flat of Nioclas's blade, then spun to avoid it again. "Saints, Nick, I was only jest—oof—is there something you care to talk about?" he asked sardonically as Nioclas's attack intensified.

"Nay," Nioclas replied curtly, swinging his arm relentlessly.

"Hmm. There's a tale there." Aidan plunged his sword toward his brother, who leapt backward.

"None I care to tell you," Nioclas replied, wiping the sweat off his forehead with the back of his hand.

"Well, you're putting on quite a show for her." They circled each other. "Mayhap this will be a love match yet—" Aidan's sword went flying. He watched, open-mouthed, as it soared through the air. Someone called out, and men scattered as the blade went hilt-over-tip, landing about twenty feet from where they stood.

He looked at his brother in alarm. Nioclas had never bested him by forcing his sword from his hand. That was something they'd agreed long ago was unnecessary between them. War was never far, and neither wanted the other without his sword if it broke.

"Love is for fools," Nioclas growled before stalking off.

It was a rare thing for Nioclas to lose his temper, especially in the lists. Bemused, Aidan watched him go, then threw a wink over to the source of his brother's obvious discomfort.

Smirking at the feminine gasps, Aidan collected his sword and sauntered off.

CHAPTER 11

"Is it so bad, then?"

Nioclas rubbed his temples as Aidan entered, unbidden, into his solar. "Truly, brother, you've no wish to know."

Aidan furrowed a brow. "Contrary. I very *much* wish to know. You've never thrown my sword, nor walked off a field before training was done for the day. That's the third time this week. I vow my lips are sealed with whatever you choose to tell me."

Nioclas swallowed his ale and sighed, rubbing his hand over his jaw.

"Is it so bad, then?" Aidan repeated.

"Aye." Nioclas stood from his seat and paced the solar, then slammed his fists on the table. Aidan didn't flinch. "I made a bargain with her."

"What kind?"

"A fool's kind. If she married me, thus relieving me of having to marry the Kildare lass, I'd ensure she got back to her home in three months."

"Nick!" Aidan exclaimed. "O'Rourke will have your head

spiked on his gates! Sending a wife back to her clan rescinds clan alliance. You're asking for battle!"

"Nay." Nioclas shook his head. "Nay, I mean her real home. She isn't from Ireland. I believe her to be from France."

"She's not an O'Rourke?"

"She is. She looks just like Kathryne did when she was younger. But she lived somewhere else, with O'Malley, for the whole of her life. Her accent is…odd."

"She doesn't sound French," Aidan replied skeptically.

"You would know, as you've been there more often than I," Nioclas agreed. "France seems the most likely. If she were from Italy, her skin would be darkened from the sun."

"She sounds nothing like the Italian woman you entertained last year," Aidan replied with a small smile. "Although I doubt you did much talking with her."

Nioclas ignored him. "She's Irish by birth, but that's all."

"Something else about her?"

Nioclas gave a small laugh. "Aye, there's more. Unbelievable, really."

"Nothing's unbelievable in Ireland," Aidan quipped.

Nioclas met his brother's eyes. "Remember the dreams?"

Aidan froze.

"Aye. *Those* dreams…the ones I had for years." Nioclas ran his hands through his hair and blew out a breath. "Brianagh is *that* woman."

"Saints above," Aidan whispered. "Truly?"

"I wouldn't be saying it if it weren't true," Nioclas snapped, then immediately relented. "I sound daft enough when I say it in my mind—saying it aloud only makes it worse."

"When did you know?"

"Almost immediately." Nioclas picked up a quill from the table and examined it. "When I saw her face in our bailey, the night we pulled her from Burke's land, I suspected. But I confirmed when, after the O'Rourke told her she was to marry me, I asked her for a walk. I was going to allow her to stay on as part of the clan, as O'Rourke was adamant she remain here to fulfill their damn legacy. When she spoke… There was no doubt. 'Twas that odd accent." Nioclas's eyes were tortured. "I knew her voice, Aidan. I saw her in my dreams for years, but until I heard her voice, I wasn't certain. I don't know if that means she's cursed…or I am."

"You don't believe in curses," Aidan pointed out.

"I didn't," Nioclas agreed. "Until this past week, which has given me nothing but an ache in my head. I thought I could avoid her, then send her on her way, but I suspect that won't be enough for the elders to believe I love her." He set his jaw. "It doesn't help that she is—was—betrothed."

Aidan raised a brow. "Betrothed."

"She wants to return to him and has agreed to give me three months."

"And you agreed."

"Aye."

"To give her back to another man, after making her your wife."

Nioclas rubbed the back of his neck. "In a sense."

"In a sense?" Aidan repeated. "Do you not plan to send her back after all?"

"Nay. I just married her in a sense, 'tis all."

Aidan let out a low whistle. "Ah…you're not married in the truest sense, then. Not the consummated sense."

"Nay," Nioclas muttered.

"You agreed to this? To return her to her beloved, untouched?"

"Not exactly."

Aidan fought a smile as he processed this. "Do you want her to be your wife, in all ways?"

"It matters not what I want. I will not force her. I find myself at a loss," Nioclas finally admitted. "Our mother…she came to me in that dream the day she died."

Aidan nodded. "She told you how to succeed over Burke. She gave you the words you needed to convince the elders you were different—no boy can come up with those thoughts himself." Aidan joined him at the fire and placed a hand on Nioclas's arm. "You always believed she sent you the woman in those dreams, and you now have that woman in your castle. She's here for a reason."

"You always did believe her tales."

"And yet you're the one she sent the dreams to. I find humor in that."

"You always have."

"I know." Aidan slapped his brother on the back. "Donovan and I will keep an eye on your lady-wife while you figure out your plan of attack."

"I don't even know where to start," Nioclas grumbled.

A slow grin crept over Aidan's face. "The MacWilliam. *The* MacWilliam, who can have any woman with a crook of his finger, can't get his wife to look his way."

Nioclas fisted his hand, and Aidan held up both of his.

"Easy, brother. I merely meant to say that, if you want the woman, then woo her. You have everything you need to do so. Make her forget about the other man. Your reputation precedes you—'tis easily done."

"Your reputation is much the same," Nioclas shot back.

"'Tis true." Aidan fell silent as Nioclas stared into the fire. After a moment, he clapped his hand on Nioclas's shoulder. "Don't take too long. She's a beauty, and an O'Rourke, rumored to be the key piece to the O'Rourke legacy. There are many in the clan who would try to woo her from you if it's believed you're not interested."

"I'm aware. She's not the key to a legacy," Nioclas warned.

"Perhaps not," Aidan agreed. "But she's the key to something."

~

After hours of searching for Nioclas, Brianagh finally gave up. He didn't want to be found. So, executive decision time. She approached Donovan as sweetly as she could and asked for an escort into the village.

"Why would you want to go into the village?" he asked incredulously. "It's outside the castle walls. I beg you to think about this, Lady Brianagh."

"I wonder if your teeth ache?"

He blinked. "Sorry?"

"Your teeth. Do they ache after you've eaten your bread here?"

Donovan tried not to smile but failed. "They did, until my own cook was brought over. He arrived yesterday."

"That's exactly why I need to go into the village," Brianagh replied triumphantly. "Your cook and the MacWilliam cook do not get along. But there is a woman in the village who, according to clanswomen in the castle, can make any food palatable. And her bread is free from rocks." Leaning in, she whispered, "I need that woman—her name is Keela—in here before you leave with your cook. Yours needs to show Keela the best way to prepare food for a castle."

Donovan reluctantly smiled. "Nick doesn't know, does he?"

Brianagh wrinkled her nose. "Well, he would, if he were ever around. Because he isn't, I've made the decision for him. Will you take me to the village? The guardsman will let me pass with you as an escort."

"Aye, I'll take you." Donovan nodded. "But we'll take a guard with us. Can't be too careful with the lady of the clan."

"I don't like the sound of that," Bri said nervously, visions of Burke's pit dancing across her mind.

"I don't think you'd like the outcome, were I to let you outside castle gates without one," Donovan replied over his shoulder as he trotted down the hall. "Gather your cloak and meet me at the stables."

A half hour later, she mounted her horse, and with Donovan leading and a bunch of large men surrounding them, the guardsman at the portcullis finally let her through.

They crossed the drawbridge, and a moment later, Donovan reigned in next to her. "'Tis dangerous outside castle walls. The forest to our north—" he jerked his head to the left, where, about a mile out, a thick crop of trees stood, "—holds beasties and enemies. The village is to the south, this way. It's protected by the sea to one side, and the castle on its other… but Nick will have your head on his gates if you venture forth without a guard."

"Beasties?"

Donovan slid her a look. "Aye. Animals with sharp antlers, or those with unworldly roots."

Brianagh blinked in surprise. Reilly always told her Irish myths, and a beast of some sort was usually present, but he never mentioned people fully believed them.

Instead of voicing her thoughts, Bri turned her horse south to match Donovan's. "So the village is in between the castle and the sea? I thought castles were supposed to overlook the ocean, not turn away from it."

"'Tis difficult to see enemies approach from land if one's gazing at the water." Donovan smiled kindly at her. "I believe your solar lies in the east wing of the castle. 'Tis no wonder you haven't seen the village, or the sea. You should ask Nick to change the room. Erin claims there's no sunset in all of Eire like the MacWilliam sunset." They meandered away from the gates, staying close to the outer castle wall. "Which cottage does your Keela live in?"

Brianagh shrugged. "The women in the kitchens say she lives in the white cottage on the edge of the village."

Donovan frowned. "The village is large, with many white cottages."

"How large?"

He raised his brow. "One of the largest in Ireland." At her

surprised look, he smiled. "Your husband is one of the most powerful lairds on this isle. The English crown is forever after him, trying to buy his allegiance. I'm surprised you weren't aware of how much your country covets his land."

"I'm not from England," she laughed, but stopped abruptly as they rounded the castle.

Brianagh's breath caught. Spread before her in varying shades of green despite the winter chill were patches of farmland marked with low stone walls and dotted with sheep and cattle. The village itself sprawled to the right of the it, with a grassy village center filled with people. Row upon row of small cottages were arranged around the village center like spokes on a wheel. And beyond all that beauty lay the sea, sparkling in the late afternoon sun, small boats bobbing peacefully.

"Wow," she whispered, halting her horse. Something shifted in Brianagh. She suspected it might be her soul, sighing with content. This was a view she could look at forever.

"Surely, you've seen such villages in France."

"I've never been to France," she replied, still awed by the spectacular view, thus missing the skeptical look that passed over Donovan's face.

"So if you're not from England, nor from France, I must wonder where you spent your childhood. Your Gaelic is uncommonly good."

"I'm from an insignificant country on the continent," she replied uncomfortably, giving her horse a nudge. "I've, ah, never met a person who's heard of it, so its name is of no matter. And my cousin, Reilly, taught me Gaelic from a very young age."

Suspicions raised, Donovan drew his brows together but followed her down the sloping hill with his tongue held.

When they reached the village, the first thing Bri noticed was the smell of peat fire. It permeated the air, enveloping her in a sweet, familiar comfort. Reilly always had peat fires in his Irish cottage, back home. She noticed the men returning from the direction of the field, and people gathering in the center.

"What's going on?" Brianagh asked as they neared the crowd. They were the only ones on horseback, so she slid off hers and held tightly to the reins. "You weren't kidding. This is a lot of people."

"'Tis almost the pagan new year," Donovan explained, removing himself from his own horse. "Nick sees no harm in allowing his people to celebrate however they wish, even if celebrating a new year at the end of next month is seen as heathen."

"Why would it be considered heathen?" Bri asked. "Next month is December, and January first is the new year…right?"

Donovan shrugged. "Depends on who you ask. English crown thinks it's mid-March—that's what their religious tome indicates."

"The Bible?"

His eyebrows nearly fell off his face in surprise. "Aye! How would you know about the Bible? Have you seen it?"

Prevaricating, Brianagh shrugged, unsure as to her answer. Books probably weren't all that common in the 1400s—she had yet to see one in the castle, although there was plenty of parchment and ink.

"We do things differently here," Donovan said mildly, although Brianagh could feel his eyes boring into her. She continued walking without answering. He went on. "If others found out, the MacWilliam clan may have difficulty in explaining their actions."

Brianagh lifted her own eyebrow at him. "Laird Maguire, I assure you that I have no interest in what *other* clans may or may not celebrate. I just want to find Keela, ask her my question, and return home."

Strange words, strange accent, and strange joy at seeing a

village. Donovan thought it might be time to talk with his closest ally about his new wife.

~

"YOU HAVE TO WOO HER."

Nioclas, to his credit, didn't miss a step. He merely continued on his way, content to let Erin badger him in a way only she could.

"Nick, listen to me! Bri is going crazy in there. She's not used to our way of life, and you haven't done much to convince her that you're an amiable husband."

He did stop then and turned to her, his stomach sinking slightly. Keeping his face impassive, he raised a supercilious brow. "Are you so sure?" he drawled, letting his meaning crystallize. If the clan didn't think he had consummated the marriage, it wasn't going to go well for him when Brianagh left.

He felt the relief course through his body as Erin's face drained of color.

"Well…um, I don't know about that. But outside of your closed doors." She nodded briskly. "Aye. Outside of closed doors, she's quite miserable."

Nioclas paused. Brianagh had seemed fine to him, but he really wasn't near her during the day all that much. He'd seen small changes in the castle—his castle did appear much cleaner when he ate his supper, and the general chaos he encountered in the moments before it was served had disappeared. He figured she'd been keeping herself busy somehow.

"I might remind you that you have a reputation to consider," Erin added, the blush rising to her cheeks.

He choked. "What? How do you—"

"I'm not deaf!" she exclaimed. "And I'll remind you I'm a married woman now."

"You've been married for half a year," Nioclas pointed out, "and that does not make you the most knowledgeable in this area."

Nioclas couldn't believe he was having this conversation with Erin, of all people. She was like a little sister to him, and while he certainly wasn't against her and Donovan together, he had no wish to think about it anymore than he had to.

Which was never.

Besides, he'd already determined that, while he wanted Brianagh in his bed, getting her there was a bad idea indeed. If she carried his child, even more complications would arise, and he'd never be able to bring her back to her home, which would mean he'd have to break a vow. He never broke vows.

Unless, of course, the person to whom he made the vow asked him to.

"I like her, Nick," Erin said firmly. "She's clever and capable of running this whole clan if she's just shown our ways. I think she's going to make an excellent lady for the MacWilliams, but don't forget that we all know you. We all know of your, um, prowess. And we all have eyes. We can see that you stay away from each other, and that you don't share a room, even though you're newly wed."

Nioclas had to concede the point. Erin was the most outspoken among the clan—and he had a very outspoken clan—and she would be the only one brave enough to tell him the truth.

And the truth was, after one week of marriage, the ruse wasn't exactly convincing.

If his clan leaders thought him to be unhappily married and then his wife disappeared after only a few short months, they would never believe him to be so in love with her that he could never attempt marriage again. He needed a plan, and he needed one quickly. "Where is she now?"

"She went to the village."

Nioclas's jaw clenched. "Who let her out of the gates?"

"She went with Donovan and some others," Erin replied. "She tried to find you all morning but was unsuccessful, so she asked Donovan to take her."

"Is he a fool?" Nioclas asked angrily. "He knows what is out there!"

"You do Donovan a dishonor by thinking he wouldn't keep your wife safe."

"I stole a woman from my sire's pathetic excuse of a dungeon. When it comes to Burke, honor has nothing to do with it. You best of all know that."

Erin swallowed visibly. "Donovan took seven men. His personal guard."

Nioclas blew out a breath. "You said it yourself, Erin. She's not used to our way of life. She may have little knowledge of the dangers."

Erin nodded. "She has asked me some rather interesting questions about everyday life. I believe she was sheltered by her cousin. I doubt she's seen battle or wars."

"If she's never seen bloodshed, I do hope her first experience with it isn't with your husband skewered on my sword," Nioclas muttered, his mind racing.

"Nick!" Erin exclaimed as he spun on his heel and took off across the hall. "Where are you going?"

He didn't bother answering. He could not afford to lose Brianagh. *Well, lose her before I've a chance to convince the clan we're a love match,* he hastily amended. And he couldn't take the chance she'd be killed by his fool of a father, either. No lass deserved that kind of an end. His jaw set in a determined line, he motioned to his own personal guards, then saddled his mount and rode out of the castle gates.

CHAPTER 12

As they rode back to the castle, Brianagh couldn't stop smiling. Keela had been overjoyed to come to the castle. Brianagh still had the unenviable task of firing the current cook, but that had to wait until after dinner. She didn't want that man to spit on her food.

"I believe we're late for the meal," Donovan commented as they rode through the portcullis and spied Nioclas standing on the step, his arms crossed and his face forbidding.

Brianagh gulped audibly.

"Oh, he's not that bad," Donovan said, urging his horse forward. "Especially when he finds out what you were about."

Nioclas waited approximately three seconds from when she dismounted to stalk over to her. "What do you think you were doing in the village, unattended?"

"Unattended?" she repeated. "Seven men plus Laird Maguire is *unattended*?"

"Where was your personal guard?"

Brianagh's brows drew together. "My what?"

"Your personal guard, Brianagh!"

She exchanged a glance with Donovan. "I wasn't aware I had a personal anything."

"The guards who brought you back here. I'm certain I informed you not to go anywhere without them," Nioclas replied tersely, his patience wearing thin.

"Oh? When would that have been? I've been looking for you since—"

"When I saw you in the village with naught but a handful of men, I rode back to the castle to summon your personal guard. However, I wonder if perhaps I should have simply hauled you back myself and saved the men the aggravation of your presence!"

Brianagh gasped, outraged. "You were spying on me?"

"Perhaps you ought to take this conversation to a more private chamber," Donovan interrupted. Meeting Nioclas's eyes, he raised a brow, then murmured something in his ear before going inside.

"You. My solar," Nioclas growled before he stomped off.

She stomped after him. He wanted a fight? She was more than ready. She was seething. He'd left her alone in a castle full of strange people for an entire week, and he was angry at her for leaving with his most trusted friend and seven heavily-armed men?

Oh, she didn't think so.

Slamming the solar door behind her, Brianagh threw her hands on her hips. "Might I remind you that you are not my keeper?" She took a step closer. "You offer me refuge and abandon me to the walls of your castle. Then, because my teeth hurt, I search for you for hours so I can fire your cook and get someone in here who knows what she's doing."

"Teeth? Fire a cook?"

"Don't play word games with me right now," she snarled. He blinked and took a step back; she closed the gap. Poking him in the chest, she continued. "You're ensuring that I live in absolute hell for three months, and you think you can treat me like I'm one of your servants?" She glared at him, spitting fire and fury. "I am not your servant, or one of your clansmen you can order about. I am a means to an end—and you aren't making any effort to show your clan that we're anything but mortal enemies!"

Nioclas wanted to listen, truly, but her face, flush with color and passion, snagged his attention more than her words. He was fascinated by the fullness of her bottom lip.

She continued to raise her voice angrily at him, her eyes flashing and her color rising even further.

He could well understand her anger, however misplaced it was. His own fury was nearly palpable when he learned Donovan had taken her from the castle walls with such inadequate protection.

Her voice brought him back to his dreams. Her tirade continued, each word accented by her small finger in his chest, and he felt more and more drawn to her lips.

Without warning, without even knowing what he was doing, Nioclas cradled her head, dug his hands into her hair, and covered her mouth with his.

And his soul sighed as if it had come home.

Melting against him, the fight left Bri's body as her arms lifted, settling on his shoulders as he continued his ruthless assault. He angled her head, deepening the kiss. She moaned into his mouth, and he felt a flare of triumph at her acquiescence.

NIOCLAS BACKED HER AGAINST THE COLD STONE WALL, BUT BRI only felt heat. Fisting her hands in his hair, she kissed him back, shocked at the feelings he awakened. His hands skimmed down her bodice—every touch burned through the fabric, seared her skin, forced her even higher in her response.

Nioclas trailed kisses down her neck, breathing in her

scent as he freed the ties of her gown and slid a hand onto her smooth back. She gasped, and then her lips found his again as he moved his hand to her front.

"We are not enemies," he said softly against her lips, dropping feathered kisses across them. Moving across her jaw and up to her ear, he whispered each word with a kiss. "You. Are. Not. My. Enemy."

She shivered.

He ran his tongue over her neck while trailing his fingers up her skirts. Her answer was incoherent; she felt his smile against her neck. Distantly, she heard a bang, then another.

"Nioclas," she managed before his lips claimed hers again.

The banging grew more insistent.

"I shall kill whomever it is with my hands," he growled into her mouth. Reluctantly releasing her, he helped her tie her gown, then smoky-gray eyes met sapphire blue ones. "We will finish this." Nioclas flung open the door. "What?" he barked.

"We need to speak with you immediately."

"Who?"

"Your brother and I."

Brianagh sneaked a peak around the door and sighed heavily when she saw Donovan and Aidan. They didn't look like they were going anywhere, but that was probably a good thing. She lost all her senses when Nioclas touched her, and she reminded herself that she really didn't want to go down that path with him.

Really. She was sure of it.

"I have to talk to Cook, anyway," she said as she tried to walk out the door.

Nioclas caught her by the arm, and his stormy eyes burned into hers. "We will finish our discussion tonight," he said evenly, but the promise was clear.

She wrenched herself free and stormed out of the

chamber, trying—unsuccessfully—to slam the door behind her. She sagged against the cool stone of the hallway.

What was that? she thought, covering her face with her hands and letting out a shudder. She choked back a sob as she tried to calm herself. Why did he have to kiss even better in real life? He was absolutely irresistible in her dreams, and he was frighteningly seductive outside of them.

Nioclas was the only man who ever stoked a response like that from her. She'd thought herself incapable of passion for her entire life. Now, with just a few kisses and touches... Brianagh was in serious trouble.

She couldn't stay in medieval Ireland, but when her head was fogged with passion, she had a difficult time remembering why.

~

"The morning after your wedding, I sent for O'Malley," Donovan said flatly.

"Why?" Nioclas asked. "I have no alliance with the O'Malleys."

"I believe it's time to know more about your lady-wife."

Aidan almost spit his ale across the table. Nioclas merely raised a brow. He figured Donovan would come to him sooner or later. They worked together in all things, from battle to clan settlements. He would be suspicious had Donovan not raised concerns, but his timing was, as ever, awful.

"You interrupted my wife and me because you wish to know her better?" Nioclas asked mildly.

"Dammit, Nick, she's not who she says she is! You told me you thought her from France. She says she's never been. Her accent is strange, and though she speaks Gaelic, she also speaks the peasant's English! When I took her to the village today, she used a curious mix, and I don't think she knew she was doing it. She used words like *kidding*, but I couldn't understand the reference to goats at all."

"So," Reilly drawled from the door, a bored look gracing his features and his arms crossed. "You're upset because she isn't from France and made an obscure reference to goats. You had me travel all the way across Ireland, in November, just because you don't have enough information about a lass?"

Donovan ignored him and directed his attention to Nioclas. "The English crown wants your allegiance. Burke wants you dead, as do many lairds, including Kildare, Clanricard, MacDermott, Cavan…the list is endless. Yet you marry an unknown lass, with an unknown history, on the word of an O'Rourke. It doesn't make sense, Nick. *She* doesn't make sense." He turned to Reilly. "You owe us answers."

Reilly closed the door and stood by the fire, warming himself. "Ask," came the reply as Reilly blew on his hands. "But get me something hot to drink. It's freezing out there."

"Where is she from?" Donovan demanded.

"America."

"I've never heard of it."

"You aren't as well-traveled as some," Reilly stated flatly. When Donovan reached for his sword, Reilly shook his head. "I'm not in the mood for your swordplay, Maguire. Ask me your questions so I can go to sleep. I'll need a chamber," he added, casting a glance at Nioclas. "I'm not sleeping on the floor of your great hall when so many rooms are unused."

Nioclas merely raised a brow and silently crossed his arms.

"What clan does she claim?" Donovan pressed.

"O'Rourke."

"How old is she?"

"Twenty-nine."

"Why does she look younger?"

"Because America is a nice place."

Nioclas smiled into his cup; he could actually hear Donovan's teeth grinding.

"What are you smiling about, you fool? Don't you see she could take your clan down?"

Nioclas leaned forward, his eyes hardening. "She is harmless. I agreed to marry her a very long time ago. She was on the continent—in America—for safety. She is here now. She's an O'Rourke, my obligation is filled, and she poses no threat to me. She is but a woman, who herself admits to not having much of a relationship with her clan."

"What about the Frenchman?" Aidan asked quietly. At Nioclas's glare, he shook his head. "It's important to know, Nick."

"Frenchman?" Donovan asked suspiciously.

"Matthew de Burgh." Nioclas's face hardened.

Reilly nodded sagely. "Ah, de Burgh."

Nioclas's chest tightened. Even though he suspected it to be true, a small part of him had hoped she created him as a falsehood to keep him at arm's length.

Reilly shrugged. "I'm surprised she even mentioned him. Truly, he means nothing to her. He can't come here. His distance is too great." He shot a meaningful look at Nioclas. "*Much* too great."

Nioclas scoffed. He could believe the lass was from a country he'd never heard of, and he could believe that country was a great distance away. But O'Malley's insinuation that de Burgh lived in a month or year not the same as now…well, he could only believe so much before sensibilities took control.

O'Malley claimed to be her protector, and though he'd used the same phrase Nioclas's mother used when she visited Nioclas's dreams, 'twas most likely happenstance.

Aidan blew out a breath. "So, Lady Brianagh MacWilliam, formerly O'Rourke, is a twenty-nine-year-old woman who can speak the peasant's English as well as Gaelic—"

"And French, as well as some Spanish," Reilly added. "She can also read all of it frighteningly well."

"—and she has no ties to anyone except you," Aidan finished.

"She also has a keen mind, owned her own trade in America, and made enough money to pay her workers and create a comfortable life." Reilly folded his arms. "She is what we call a force of nature. Are we done here?"

"Trade?" Nioclas looked at him skeptically.

"Aye."

Nioclas frowned. Well, that bit of knowledge would have been of aid before he spewed insulting words about it on their wedding night.

"Pray tell, what did she sell?" Donovan asked scornfully.

"You'll have to ask Brianagh that. Where is she now? As I was tossed from the castle before speaking with her after her vows, I want to ensure she's doing well."

"She mentioned something about our cook," Nioclas said to Aidan. "Did you see her when you went to the kitchens?"

Aidan shook his head. "Nay."

"Shall I go look for her?" Reilly asked, draining his ale.

Nioclas shot him a glare. "Not without escort."

"You're more clever than I gave you credit for," Reilly replied, standing. "Trusting me could really ruin your day."

THEY HEARD THE SHOUTING BEFORE THEY EVEN ENTERED THE kitchen. Reilly held up a hand, then whispered to Nioclas, "Watch your lady-wife and see how she handles herself. She's had to release workers before. However, you can bet all your gold the person she's chosen to replace him will serve you well."

Donovan, Aidan, and Nioclas all watched from the side door of the kitchen. Brianagh and the cook were facing off.

Her hands were placidly folded in front of her and she seemed resolved. The cook, however, was slamming things around as he cleaned up from the evening meal's preparations.

"A few rocks won't kill anybody!"

"I can appreciate how difficult your duty is here," Brianagh said calmly, resting her hip on the work table. "Truly, Fergus, your skills with the livestock are impressive. I've seen the way you cut the meat. You're so quick, and you do know the choice bits so well."

"Aye," Fergus replied sourly. "But then, I don't know what I'm supposed to do with it."

"What we really need," Brianagh said thoughtfully, "is a butcher. Someone who can humanely—that is, nicely—kill the animals and remove the parts we don't eat. Then, the butcher would take those parts, like the fur"—Nioclas saw her shudder—"and give it to the right person so we can make coverlets out of them. That sort of thing."

Fergus looked intrigued.

"The problem is, I'm not sure what all those parts can be used for," Brianagh explained, sounding apologetic. She let out a little gasp. "But, Fergus—you do! You could be our castle butcher! Oh, please say you'll do it!"

He looked a bit taken aback. "But who will cook the laird's meals?"

"Oh, don't worry about that. I'll find someone. But I know that Laird MacWilliam has said that no one else is allowed to put a knife to any beast unless you're right there. He doesn't want it to be spoiled." She gave a conspiring nod to Fergus, whose chest puffed with pride.

"I said nothing of the sort," Nioclas grumbled.

Aidan hushed him with a wave of his hand.

"Well, my lady, since you've asked, of course I can help. As you said, I'm mighty fine with a knife and a beast!" Fergus stated proudly.

"Wonderful! Thank you, Fergus. Why don't you take the rest of the day off? You've certainly earned it, doing the work of two people. Enjoy your wife, and do tell her I say hello. I met her days ago when she was hanging the washing. The woman is amazing at getting linens clean."

"I'll tell her you said so," Fergus replied, a bit of awe in his voice.

Brianagh smiled. "Such a lovely woman. Go on, enjoy her company. Have a nice night, Fergus!"

"You too, my lady!" He bowed and scraped his way out of the kitchen. She turned and yelped at the sight of the four men standing at the side door.

"Holy cow, you scared the daylights out of me!" she exclaimed, placing a hand on her heart. Then her eyes landed on Reilly and her face lit up. "Ry!" She catapulted herself at him, and he caught her up easily, giving her a tight hug. "How are you? How did you get back?"

"Oh, don't worry about that. How are *you*? I see you haven't cleaved this bastard's head in two yet. That's promising." He held her out, inspecting her.

"I don't think we should speak in English," she whispered.

"It's all right. These fools don't speak it. We're fine." He grinned when he caught sight of the fury in Nioclas's eyes. Reilly pulled Brianagh under his arm. "How's married life?"

She drew her brows together. "Well…"

"Ah," he said knowingly. "Still holding out on him. That's good. Make him earn it."

"Reilly!" she exclaimed.

"Just so you know, I told him what you didn't."

"Can we discuss this later?" she asked, uncomfortable with the stares she was receiving from the other three still standing in the doorway.

"If you value your life, you will remove your hands from her," Nioclas said in a low voice.

Reilly kissed the top of her head and released her. "You've got yourself a jealous one." Reilly snorted, amused, as Nioclas moved his hand to the hilt of his sword menacingly.

Brianagh didn't know what to say to that, so she turned to Nioclas instead, saying in Gaelic, "I hope you don't mind that I released your cook."

"I believe I understand your reference about your teeth earlier," Nioclas replied, allowing a small smile to escape. "Did no one warn you to avoid the bread?"

"Unfortunately, *no one* did. I've brought in a woman from the village. She's probably already arrived, and she comes highly recommended by the other women in the castle. I'll have her to come to the kitchens immediately once she's settled."

"I'd recommend a taster," Donovan muttered darkly.

Brianagh bristled, but Reilly laid a hand on her arm, ignoring Nioclas's twitchy fingers. "I'll do it."

"You will?" Bri asked.

"Aye. It's probably the only way I'll be offered a meal."

Brianagh burst out laughing. "Please tell me you're staying?"

"That's up to the laird." Reilly grinned, meeting Nioclas's stony face. "I'd need a chamber too." Reilly's face quickly darkened when Nioclas's face didn't change. "I see what you're thinking, MacWilliam. Put me in your dungeon, and I promise I'll get out."

"Is that a threat?" Nioclas asked as Aidan placed a hand on his own hilt.

"Absolutely not." Reilly smiled. "More of a vow."

"Okay, enough," Brianagh said, placing her hand on both Nioclas's and Reilly's arms. "Reilly, you will have a room, and if you really want to taste the food, feel free. But you'll get a meal regardless. But you have to stop goading Laird MacWilliam, else I'll kick you out myself." She looked at the young kitchen maid in the corner, who chopped the food on the wooden board in front of her without taking her eyes off the four enormous men standing in the kitchen. Bri informed her, "Our new cook, Keela, and the Maguire cook will be along soon. If you could help acquaint Keela with the kitchen, I'd be grateful."

"Aye, my lady," the woman said with a quick bob. "Keela's well-known to me."

Reilly watched Nioclas observe Brianagh, then grinned. In English, he turned to her and held his arm out. "Take me to my room and tell me about this new cook you found. Nice job on letting Fergus go, by the way."

"Thanks." She laughed, leading him out of the kitchens. "Remember when I had to let Shelly Waters go? That was awful. She was so mad she spit on me."

"Well, she couldn't match anyone to save her life," Reilly replied. "She tried to match Colin with her brother. And neither were interested in that sort of match." He laughed at the memory of Colin's shocked face when Shelly told him she found his perfect mate, and his name was John.

"Have you seen Colin?" Bri asked suddenly.

"Nay." He turned serious. "I haven't been back."

Her face paled. "Can you not get back?"

He shrugged noncommittally. "I needed to make sure you're all right. Even though it seems like I just dropped you here, I haven't been far."

"I still want to go back," she said softly.

"To what? You're meant to be here, Bri."

She lowered her voice further. "My life is six hundred years in the future, Ry."

"We're not having this argument again." Resolved, he quickened his pace.

She hastened to keep up, noticing Nioclas was only a few feet behind them. The bailey was mostly empty, as the meal bell had already rung. She flashed him a nervous smile, then said to Reilly, "He's agreed to let me return home after three months."

Reilly stopped dead in his tracks, then turned and glared at Nioclas before shaking his head. "You won't want to."

"Yes, I will," she replied, although she sounded less certain of herself than usual.

"Must you always have the last word?" Reilly exploded, facing her. "I'm not taking you back!"

She spun toward him and threw her hands on her hips. "Yes, you will!"

"God, would you listen to yourself? You sound like a three-year-old who didn't get a toy from the toy store!" Reilly shouted.

"And you sound as though you truly want to spend the night in my dungeon," Nioclas answered in English, his sword suddenly at Reilly's throat.

"Nioclas, please don't," Brianagh gasped. "Truly, we fight like this all the time. It's harmless."

"Shout at my wife again, and I don't care what kind of vows you make, you won't see the light of day until summer." Nioclas's face was deadly serious. After a charged moment, he removed his sword. "And you will take her home in three months, if she wishes it."

Reilly shot a look of pure disgust at him. "You realize that if you send her away, you're signing thousands of death certificates."

"What are you saying?" Aidan asked in Gaelic. "Nick, do I slay him here, or would you prefer satisfaction in the lists?"

Nioclas dropped his sword, and without taking his eyes off Reilly, replied to Aidan in Gaelic, "Neither. Have a chamber readied for him on the opposite side of the castle." Nioclas took Brianagh's arm and steered her away from Reilly. "Nay," he warned when she opened her mouth.

She promptly closed her mouth, then glanced back at Reilly to see his satisfied smile. She stuck her tongue out at him with all the immaturity she could muster as Nioclas dragged her away.

But her stomach sank at the realization that her husband had heard —and understood—every word of her conversation with Reilly.

CHAPTER 13

Nioclas steered Bri into her solar instead of the great hall, and firmly closed, then bolted, the door.

He studied her for a moment. "You believe you lived…in a time not now." It was more of a statement than a question.

Bri was trapped. Though he understood the words she and Reilly exchanged outside, did he really understand what they were talking about? She had no idea. His expression gave nothing away.

"Do *you* believe I came from a different time?" she asked evasively, leaning against the alcove in her solar, which looked quite nice now that she and Erin had managed to procure some tapestries for the walls and a few embroidered pillows for the stools.

His smile wasn't friendly when he responded. "I won't play your games. Since you did not balk when I even mentioned such an idea, I can only conclude that you do believe it."

Bri started to feel the sweat form on her back. She hoped he didn't think her to be a witch. Witchcraft was an offense punishable by death. She wasn't exactly sure what Ireland did to witches in the thirteen hundreds, but she had a feeling it involved the medieval version of s'mores and camp songs in Gaelic.

"The O'Rourke legacy isn't a secret, but it isn't truth, either."

Gathering her courage in one hand and her stupidity in the other, she countered, "Are you so certain?"

Nioclas folded his arms across his chest. She could almost feel the barely leashed intensity he radiated.

He glowered. "I see you've been told you're the heiress to this tale. A man cannot travel to times not his own. 'Tis unnatural."

She nodded. "I know."

"Yet still, you believe it."

"What do you do to witches?" she blurted out.

Her fear must've shown on her face, because he immediately relaxed his stance. "Witches? I've yet to see any poor soul do anything to warrant the name." He stepped closer to her, assessing. "Do you believe yourself to be a witch, Brianagh?"

"No," she reassured him quickly, pressing herself against the alcove. "I just don't want anyone else thinking I'm one. I'm not a fan of bonfires."

"The MacWilliams do not burn witches, suspected or otherwise," Nioclas said firmly. "However, there are other clans who do, so be wary with your words."

"You mean, don't spread it around that I'm from six hundred years from now? I have no intention of ever mentioning that to anyone. I don't want to be burned at a stake."

"Six hundred years?" he asked. His expression showed incredulity; he believed her to be daft. "You won't be burned. You're protected by my name," Nioclas replied, and Brianagh could sense his patience was nearing its end.

"Thanks for that. Um, anyway, we should probably make sure Reilly's all set, and I have to tell Keela—"

"Do you ever stop?" he interrupted her. At her confusion, he clarified. "Ever since your arrival, you haven't stopped working. You are the Lady MacWilliam. In times of peace, you aren't required to do anything."

She shook her head, grateful he let the subject of the future drop. "I have to do something. Since you've given me the protection of your name and promised to get me back home, the least I can do is earn some of that."

"All I ask is that you act like my wife," he muttered.

"I'm trying. I've never been a wife, so I'm not really sure what I'm doing."

"Tell me what you did before you came to Ireland." Nioclas placed his large hand over her twisting ones to still them. "O'Malley told me you had your own trade."

She felt a flash of irritation toward Reilly. If he intended to bring her to medieval Ireland, the least he could have done was prepare her better. Although, in fairness, she did rebuff any attempted lessons at Irish history he tried to teach her. She was much more interested in the island's love stories than it's medieval history. Especially the love story of William Butler Yeats and Maud Gonne; she felt she could've found Yeats someone much more suited to him who would actually accept a proposal.

Hindsight was 20/20, she supposed. Although she wasn't really sure if "hind" was the right term, being as she was presently lingering in the past.

Before giving herself a headache, she said, "My trade is in love. I match people together so they can enter happy marriages." *Mostly,* she amended silently. There were quite a few clients who wanted one-nighters, but she always dropped them when she proved it to be true. She was in the business of happily-ever-after, not happily-right-now.

Nioclas didn't stifle his skepticism. "Lairds decide who is best suited, based on alliances."

"In Ireland, right now, they do," she agreed.

"But not in America." At her surprise, Nioclas said, "O'Malley gave me some information. I'd like the rest from you."

"Maybe later," she placated as she slipped by him. "As your wife, it's important that I ensure our new cook is settled in her kitchen."

"And who, may I ask, is the new MacWilliam cook?" Nioclas asked pointedly.

She blushed. "I've already told you. And in my defense, I tried to find you for a long time before I finally made that decision."

"Answer the question, Brianagh."

"Keela, from the village," she finally said.

Nioclas's face didn't change. "You are obviously very new to clan ways. She is a poor choice. As cook, Keela must live here, yet she cares for her aging mother. Who will take care of—"

"Aoife?" Brianagh interrupted. "I've set that up as well. No need to worry. As we speak, I have two men from the castle helping her gather her belongings. She's moving into the castle with her daughter, who will make an excellent cook."

"I will not have an old woman sleeping on my floor!" Nioclas exclaimed.

Brianagh threw him a look as though he was the one who was daft. "Of course you won't. Aoife and Keela will be sharing a chamber nearest the exit to the kitchens."

"I don't have a bed for her," he pointed out—rather triumphantly, if Brianagh heard it right.

"That's why I sent the men," Bri replied smugly. "So they could gather her belongings. That includes the bed."

Nioclas looked taken aback for a moment. "Oh. That was well done of you."

"I thought so. Now, truly, I have to see if Keela is set in the kitchen. Donovan's cook arrived yesterday and I must ensure they get along right from the start. How long are the Maguires staying?"

"As long as he pleases. There is no limit to our hospitality with the Maguires," Nioclas replied, looking somewhat bewildered.

"Excellent. I do enjoy Erin's company, and I'm sure their cook will have much to add to Keela's already superb knowledge of food preparation. I'll see you at dinner, perhaps?" With a wave, she was out the door.

Nioclas stood in the middle of the empty solar, feeling a bit winded, and suddenly noticed the small throw pillows.

He shook his head. O'Malley was right. His wife was a force of nature, indeed.

~

"IS SHE IN LOVE WITH THE MAN?"

Reilly didn't look up from the leather satchel he was digging in. "Nay."

"Are you so sure?"

Reilly groaned. "MacWilliam, you married the lass. She belongs to you. You need not release her to anyone, especially a man as worthless as de Burgh."

"I made a vow."

Reilly stood and faced Nioclas. "Were I you, I'd stop making so many foolish vows."

Nioclas didn't blink. "I could have you killed."

"You could try."

A charged moment passed, and Nioclas slowly uncrossed his arms. "I have no need for a wife who would throw herself from my parapet."

Reilly frowned. "Throw herself?"

MacWilliam frowned harder. "Her happiness, O'Malley. Will she be unhappy to remain here? Was her life so perfect before?"

Understanding dawned. Reilly crossed his own arms and widened his stance. "I will not speak for her happiness here, MacWilliam. That's in your hands. But her life before you? Aye, 'twas a good one. Full of family and happiness. But *not* with de Burgh."

"Your tales make no sense. She was happy, she procured wealth by trade in marriages, and yet she agreed to wed someone to whom she holds no love?" he asked, skeptical. He narrowed his eyes. "I have no reason to believe you."

"Yet you have reason to want to," Reilly surmised. At the look of surprise that crossed Nioclas's face, he continued, "Whatever that reason is, believe in *that*. Things that cannot be explained fully are known to happen in this land. Perhaps 'tis time for you to decide whether or not that vow you made is one worth breaking." His jaw tightened. "I am fully certain that while she may be missing many things from her life before you, Matthew de Burgh is not one of them."

"If you tell falsehoods, you will pay dearly."

"You'd have to find me first," Reilly replied with a smirk. "And if you believe nothing else, believe when I tell you there's no way you could follow me to where I'd go. But it's a moot point, MacWilliam. They have no love for each other."

"Was it an arranged match, her and the Frenchman?"

"He's American, and nay."

"Then why did she agree to marry him?" Nioclas asked.

Reilly shrugged, then reached again into the satchel once more. "Only she can answer that." He pulled out a dirk and grinned at it. "Huh. Thought I lost this one in my last battle." He tucked it into his boot, then gave Nioclas a pointed look. "Surprising what we find when we take a closer look, aye?"

~

When Nioclas found her the next day, Brianagh was directing the activity in the great hall. Tables were pushed against the wall, and women everywhere swept the rushes into manageable piles. The tapestries that lined the walls were carefully removed and taken outside, and men hauled buckets of ashes from the large fireplaces at either end of the hall.

"Come and walk with me, Brianagh?" Nioclas asked as he approached her.

She turned to one of the women near her. "Mary, would you please ensure the tapestries are free of any dirt before they are hung again? I'm going for a walk with Laird MacWilliam."

"Aye, Lady MacWilliam." Mary bobbed, then continued her duties as Nioclas sent someone to fetch his wife's cloak.

"No training today?" Bri asked Nioclas.

"I've finished for the afternoon and thought to take some time in your company," he replied easily.

Brianagh's warning flags rose. From everything she'd heard at the castle, on his training days, Nioclas never finished training before dark unless there was a battle. And from everything she'd seen, that was the truth—he never put his sword down while there was still some semblance of sunlight.

Suspicious.

He helped her fasten her cloak, then led her away from the door, outside of which men were beating the soot from the tapestries. Brianagh quickly advised the men to cover their mouths and noses so as to not breathe it in; they did so immediately and continued on with their work.

"The clan certainly seems to listen well to you," he noted approvingly.

"They respect my title. But soon they'll respect me as

well," she replied, side-stepping a muddy puddle in the dirt.

"Sensible. What was your home like?"

Bri paused in mid-step. "Um…comfortable."

"Comfortable in what way? Safe? Loved?"

She had a sinking feeling her Second Inquisition had started. "I felt safe and loved."

"Your sire told me you stayed with an uncle. How did he put food on your table?"

Brianagh watched the blacksmith pound something at his anvil, marveled briefly at his strength, and contemplated her answer. Connor worked for a major passenger train company. She wasn't sure how to translate that into medieval-speak. Finally, she just said, "Connor ensured we got to and from different places safely."

"As a guardsman? A stable master, perhaps?"

Biting her lip, Brianagh replied, "He made sure the horsepower was safe and well-cared for."

Nioclas frowned, not entirely satisfied with her answer, but he seemed to let it go for the moment. He peppered her with more questions as they continued their walk through the castle grounds, past the women beating the laundry with sticks, through the gardens that looked as though they'd be overflowing in spring and summer, and up to the battlements.

They reached the top of the stairs and immediately Brianagh was hit with an icy wind. She shivered as it went right through her cloak and crept into her bones. The walkway was narrow, about two-and–a-half people wide. The walls were low, measuring at just below her hip, and they were at least three stories above the ground. Risking a glance over the wall, Bri looked straight down into the moat and jumped back as she felt a tug on her cloak.

Nioclas was standing with his legs braced, one hand fisted in her cloak. He flashed her a wry smile. "Don't think to escape my questions that way, lass."

She rolled her eyes. "I'm not that desperate."

"You might be when I'm through."

In response, she gave him her back, then promptly forgot all about him as she caught her first glimpse of the land in front of her. The view was all-encompassing and went on for miles. Even in the middle of winter, the varying shades of green were breathtaking. The different fields, separated by low stone walls or even low-lying bushes, were clearly and neatly laid in front of the bustling village directly between the castle and the sea, which sparkled in the distance. Within the castle walls, people led horses to the stables while others practiced their swordplay in the lists. In the village, smoke rose from the small holes in the tops of the white thatched cottages, and she could see people in its center—some looked like children, running and chasing each other, while others looked like adults in conversations.

She wondered briefly what the concerns of a medieval peasant were like, then immediately wished she didn't. She was certain she didn't want to know. She didn't want to get too involved. Another blast of icy air swept over her and she shivered violently.

"We can go back." Nioclas nodded to a guard as she eased away from the edge.

"No," she said quickly, tightening her cloak around her. "I have been stuck in there for days. I need a break."

"You can go outside when it's raining. All that will happen is you'll get a bit wet."

"Yes, I know," she snapped. "But raining is much different than a deluge."

Nioclas shrugged nonchalantly. "In Ireland, it's all the same. It's called winter."

"I'm well aware of the Irish seasons," she replied waspishly, then immediately regretted her outburst as his eyebrow shot up.

"You said earlier that you'd never been here."

"I've never been to the MacWilliam lands," she prevaricated. Instead of pressing her further, Nioclas suddenly grasped her cold hand and pulled her back to the stairs leading down to the bailey. She followed—she wasn't given much choice, really—and once they arrived safely at the bottom, Nioclas glanced around. Noting there was no one but them, he narrowed his eyes, assessing her. "You seem to have vague answers for such simple questions, Brianagh."

She shrugged, and he closed in on her, trapping her between the wall and the heat of his body. He placed his hands on either side of her, effectively blocking her way out, and then leaned forward so their noses were almost touching.

Brianagh imagined that, to an outside observer, they looked like lovers.

"You will eventually tell me all your secrets, Lady MacWilliam."

Instinctively, Bri shot back, "You'll have to make me."

His eyes burned into hers, their intensity so overwhelming that Brianagh almost closed her eyes in response but held fast and stared back mutinously.

He kissed her suddenly, hard, and she recognized it as a kind of branding. She wanted to refuse him, but her traitorous body leapt to life and responded in spite of her resolve.

He pulled back. "You will tell me," he said evenly, in a low voice that reverberated in her chest, "not because I demand it, but because you want to."

She shoved him away and glared at him.

Nioclas *could* make her want to tell him all her secrets and probably those of everyone she knew. She was in serious trouble, and he knew it.

She strode back towards the castle, not bothering to wait for him, and strengthened her resolve.

CHAPTER 14

"That was..." Nioclas said, trying to find the right words for the dinner he'd just consumed. The delicately roasted chicken and vegetable soup had the entire garrison humming in satisfaction.

"Delicious?" Brianagh asked, trying unsuccessfully to hide her triumph. Ever since Keela had been installed in the kitchens, the food had been so good the clansfolk had been coming up to her all day to comment on it. Bri sent all compliments Keela's way and let the new cook bask in the glow of her own success.

Nioclas held up his rock-free bread. "I don't understand how you knew to choose that woman." He took a bite, then shrugged. "But I must admit, I'm grateful you did."

Bri couldn't help the grin that burst out. "I simply listened to what your clansmen—"

"Our clansmen," he reminded her.

"—our clansmen had to say." Brianagh took a sip of her wine. "The women in this clan know just about everything that goes on in the village, whether they live there or in the castle. The information they have is invaluable to me."

Swirling the drink in her cup, she asked, "Where does this wine come from? It's really good."

"Perhaps you'd care to see the cellars," Nioclas offered, though he wondered why she'd be surprised. He was a powerful, wealthy laird. Why wouldn't his drink be excellent quality? Perhaps she'd been told Ireland was a rough land with rougher drink. He'd find out eventually; he always did.

"You have cellars?"

"Aye, we do." He stood and held out his hand, which she took after a moment's hesitation. "'Tis a well-kept secret that we trade with those from the continent."

"Really?" Bri asked, eyes wide. She'd never thought about trade before. She got the impression the MacWilliams were an isolated bunch, content to live with whatever the land gave them.

Bri didn't realize she'd spoken her thoughts out loud until Nioclas replied. "I don't know why you'd think that. We are on the sea, and this is a very important trade route. Spanish, French, even the Italians dock their ships at this port. We offer them our goods in return."

"What kind of goods?"

Out of the great hall, Nioclas led her down a hallway, then pulled a wooden door open and grabbed a torch from the wall sconce. He led her down the steps, and the air grew damper and colder as they descended. They didn't go far, but when she reached the bottom of the stairs, she sucked in a breath.

Boxes upon boxes of wine were stacked against the stone walls. The front of the boxes were removed so the bottles were visible. All were labeled with parchment, with different names. She'd never seen so many varieties. While not a knowledgeable wine drinker by any stretch of the imagination, she immediately realized why she hadn't had any troubles drinking here.

She was standing in a wine room that held more fine wine than any restaurant she'd ever seen.

"Everything is organized first by my personal preference, then by type, then by age," Nioclas said quietly. The torchlight danced in his hair, drawing Brianagh's eye. She froze as she realized how close he'd come to her while she was studying the wine. "Very few people know about this."

Looking up into his eyes, she swallowed. She could feel that pull again—the air crackled with heat as his gaze bore into hers.

Not going to get involved.

"They give us the best because we give them Ireland's best."

"What's Ireland's best?" she half-whispered, licking her lips.

He lowered his lips so they were a fraction of an inch away from her own. "It depends to whom you speak," he said in a low voice, his eyes still searching hers. "For the MacWilliams, Ireland's best used to be our wool and linen."

"And what is it now?" Her heart thudded madly in her chest.

"Now," he replied, lowering his eyes to her lips, "'tis the lady of my castle."

Brianagh's eyes widened in surprise. She couldn't hear over the thunder in her ears. Why was she having this reaction to him? They were just words, after all.

She froze as he leaned closer, his lips a hairbreadth away from her own. She hitched her breath, cursing herself for staying still, but physically unable to move away. A half-second later, he slowly pulled back, a bottle of wine in his hand.

"If you enjoyed what we serve at dinner, I'll be sure to select some varieties for you to enjoy in your—our—bedchamber, if you'd like."

"*Our* bedchamber?"

They'd been sleeping in adjoining rooms, though the door between them remained firmly shut and locked. Bri thought the arrangement was perfect.

"It's been brought to my attention that the clan suspects we are not..."

"Getting along," Bri supplied. "Erin said as much to me the other day."

"I believe the time has come to let everyone know we've gotten past our initial disagreements, my lady." He offered her the bottle. "Perhaps we ought to begin tonight."

She swallowed hard. "Well, that was the deal we made."

"Aye."

She pushed out a hard breath. "All right. Let's do this."

He cocked his head slightly, a small frown marring his face.

"What?" she asked, patting her hair. "Is something wrong?"

Slowly, he reached for a pin in her hair and gently wriggled it loose. "If a man were to abscond with his lady wife to the cellars, how would one expect her to look upon their return?"

Brianagh swallowed. "Um...mussed up?"

"Aye." He slowly loosened another pin, then frowned again. "I'm afraid I am not mussing you enough. May I?" he asked with a vague gesture.

Well, it was only hair, she reasoned with herself. She gave him a brief nod, and he took the wine from her and placed it on the crate nearest him.

And, she continued to reason, it would certainly help convince everyone that she and Nioclas were past whatever differences they all thought the two of them had—

Her thoughts scattered as his lips descended on hers, gently at first, then with increased urgency. Desire welled up, and her arms snaked their way up his strong arms and over his shoulders. Her hands tangled in his hair, and she grazed her nails against his head; he made a noise and she responded as he swept his tongue inside her mouth. Though the kiss was unhurried, Brianagh felt a rush of adrenaline spike through her, and pressed herself more fully into his body. He wrapped both arms around her, lifting her slightly, and she deepened the kiss. He growled into her mouth, then gently bit her lip as he pulled back.

He held her at his eye level, both of them breathing hard, for a moment. He slid her down the length of his body, but before she could step away, he grasped her face in both of his hands, tilted her head, and slanted his mouth over hers once more. She immediately opened to him, and their tongues danced together.

She couldn't get enough, and at the moment, she didn't care. He broke the kiss, but as she whimpered, he feathered kisses down her neck, sucking gently. He came to the top of her bodice and ran his tongue across the top of her breasts; she sucked in a breath, and pulled back.

She was on fire. She burned. She needed more, and she craved the feeling of desire.

Colin might've been right all along, she thought, dazed. *Maybe passion does count for something.*

"You look properly mussed now."

She snapped back to the present. *Colin.* Her family. Her life back in the future.

She had to get back. And losing herself to this man, to this desire, was not the way to do it.

~

"THINGS LOOKED LIKE THEY WENT WELL FOR YOU LAST NIGHT during dinner, when you and MacWilliam disappeared for awhile."

Brianagh stabbed her needle into the pillow, glaring at the

brightly colored thread, and it landed nowhere near where she intended. "What is his game?"

Reilly carefully sharpened his sword at one of the tables in the great hall as she attempted some needlework. Erin suggested she practice her sewing on a pillow rather than clothing because, as she put it, "It's less expensive to reuse the same pillow than to make the entire garrison new tunics."

Bri conceded her point.

"I believe his goal is to ensure the good folks of this clan believe the two of you to be in love," Reilly replied, holding his sword into the shaft of sunlight. It glinted satisfactorily. "Wasn't that the point of your little bargain?"

"Yes." Bri sulked. "But he kissed me like he meant it."

"You said yourself that it's a game," Reilly said languidly, slanting her a look. "Don't tell me you're falling for him."

"No!" Brianagh exclaimed. "Definitely not! It's just that when I agreed to this, I didn't think it would require kissing."

Reilly placed the blade on the table and gave it a loving pat. "Oh, Bri, come on. Use your brain a bit here. You ran a *matchmaking business*. How many of the couples you successfully matched didn't so much as kiss in public?" At her consternation, he said, "You can tell when people are in love and when they're not. It's one of a woman's best intuitions."

She let out a gusty sigh. "Yeah…I know. I just didn't think it'd be this hard."

He took the pillow from her. "Oh my God, this is awful."

"Oh, shut it," she snapped, grabbing it back. "See? I'm not meant to stay here."

"Why? Because you can't sew a stitch?" Reilly guffawed. "Please. I know you better than that. You've been here almost two weeks. So tell me, who are you thinking of matching up?"

She shook her head loftily. "No one."

"Really?" Reilly gave her an assessing look. "No one here is giving off the lonely vibe? That seems highly unlikely."

"Well, the new cook, Keela..."

"Aha! What's her story?"

"She's been living in the village, caring for her elderly mother. She's quite young and very pretty and can do great things with the food."

Reilly nodded. "Trust me when I say, a person with her skills in the kitchen is almost unheard of in these times. She's a keeper, so don't let another clan try to steal her away."

"Noted. And she is wonderful. But she has never thought of herself as anything other than her mother's caretaker. But now that she's at the castle, and with my realignment of resources available to help with her mom—"

Reilly's laugh made her stop short. "Oh, Bri, I knew you wouldn't be content to sit around and ruin poor, unsuspecting warriors' shirts all day!"

"They told you I messed up their tunics?" she asked glumly, looking at the mess that was her pillow.

"Let's just say I was warned by about a hundred or so men. But look. You've already come up with a plan for this place, haven't you?"

She remained mute.

"Brianagh MacWilliam. I knew you had it in you," Reilly said, applauding her.

She started at the use of her married name, then sniffed and stabbed the pillow again. "Brianagh *O'Rourke*. And I don't know what you're talking about."

"Yes you do. In the time you've been here, you've created a business plan for the castle to run more efficiently and are thinking of potential matches for your new cook."

"I hate you," she muttered.

Reilly burst into laughter. "I know you better than you know yourself," he crowed. "Go on. Admit it."

"Never."

"Never say never," Reilly said gleefully. "I love this. I truly do. At some point, you will thank me for bringing you here."

"Because it'll sharpen my business focus when I return," Brianagh replied firmly. "Make me appreciate what I have more than ever."

"Sure." He chuckled. "If that's going to help you sleep at night, you tell yourself that. But I'm betting if you let your guard down a little, MacWilliam will ensure you sleep even *better* at night."

She threw the pillow at him.

BRIANAGH PROMISED HERSELF SHE WAS GOING TO DRAW REILLY'S sword from his side and run him through with it. And she'd kick him in the shin for good measure.

"Although she hasn't found the right one yet, you just watch. There will be a wedding soon," Reilly was saying, an unholy light of mischief in his eyes. They sat at supper, Reilly to her right and Nioclas to her left, leaving her in the middle of two men keen on discussing her matchmaking abilities.

"You are an ass," she hissed at Reilly.

"I'll agree with that," Nioclas said, "but I still want you to promise that if you find her a suitable mate, she won't leave this castle." As the serving women refilled their platter with another helping of beef, he added, "Ever."

"I don't have anyone in mind for her!" Brianagh exclaimed.

"Pfft," Reilly replied, adding more meat to his trencher. "You always have a plan."

"Always?" Nioclas asked.

"I think she'd be great for Aidan," Erin piped up from a bit farther down the table, causing Aidan to choke on his wine.

"Absolutely not," Aidan replied firmly. "She's a maiden. I

don't want anything to do with a maiden. I'm not looking for a wife."

Donovan laughed into his cup but didn't say anything at Aidan's dark look.

"I'm certain that statement will turn on you," Erin replied sweetly. "Fate is, after all, a woman. An *experienced* woman."

Brianagh snorted and tried to smother her laugh.

"Perhaps Brian? He's usually up on the battlements during the wee hours of the morning," Erin suggested. "At least, he used to be."

"He still is," Nioclas confirmed.

"He might be a bit rough for our sweet cook," Aidan replied thoughtfully.

"Our sweet cook?" Brianagh snorted. "How do you know she's sweet?"

Aidan spread his hands across the table. "She has to be sweet. All angels are, and this food is certainly sent from above."

"Here," Reilly said, holding out a small dirk, hilt-first, to Aidan.

"What's this?" He raised a brow.

"It's your manhood. I'm returning it to you in hopes that you can find a way to silence the drivel that just spouted from your lips," Reilly replied dryly.

Erin sprayed her wine all over the table in front of her as Donovan and Nioclas leaned back and laughed heartily, drawing stares from the rest of the clan, who crowded around various tables set throughout the great hall.

"See?" Brianagh said, leaning over Reilly to meet Aidan's eyes. "An ass."

Aidan nodded in agreement.

"I wonder if she could do it," Reilly mused aloud.

"Do what?" Erin asked.

Brianagh, however, was alarmed. The look on Reilly's face was a cross between thoughtful and sly, and Bri's experience with it told her she should not, under any circumstances, agree to whatever Reilly said next.

"Match the cook."

"Reilly," Brianagh said, a warning note in her voice.

"I wager she can't," Reilly said with a nod. "She did a fair job of it before on the continent, but she's in new territory now."

"I think she could," Erin replied loyally. "She's changed things here already, and I, for one, believe this castle is better off for it." She, Aidan, and Donovan began discussing what the wager terms would be, as Brianagh vehemently shook her head.

"Let's not wager," Brianagh suggested helplessly. "I don't think this is a good idea."

Nioclas gave her a wink.

A wink!

She tried to interject again, but no one listened. They simply continued the discussion around her as if she wasn't sitting at the table with them. She glanced around the great hall, but no one was paying any attention to them. Brianagh fervently hoped the clans folk had too much to drink to remember the discussion.

"I believe you could do it," Nioclas murmured, leaning close. She blinked at him, and he smiled slyly. "Perhaps, if we work together, we could win their wager. And your Keela could have a nice wedding—'tis high time she married, after all."

"Nioclas, this is a woman's love life they want to wager on," Bri replied, shaking her head.

"Nay, we're wagering on your ability to find her an acceptable match," Reilly said, interrupting himself as he and Erin haggled over the terms of the wager.

"Matching someone simply to win a bet is cruel," she retorted.

"But matching someone simply to see them happy?"

Nioclas asked seriously. "In truth, the Irish do not tease about love. We believe, among all else, that a soul is only half of itself. When you find love, the two halves make each person whole." He gave her a small smile. "I can't say I ever fully believed it, but perhaps I have reason to now."

She gaped at him.

Romantic Nioclas? Surreptitiously, she fanned herself. It was rather hot in the great hall all of a sudden.

He smiled lazily at her, then went back to his meal.

"I'll do it," she said suddenly, turning to the others. "I'll find Keela her other half, if she agrees to it."

"I'll help," Erin volunteered.

I'll need it, Bri thought, sneaking a glance at Nioclas. But she didn't miss the self-satisfied smile that crossed Reilly's features.

CHAPTER 15

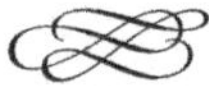

Brianagh was ready. She'd felt the small thrill of excitement course through her once her mind was made up, and she reminded herself to slow down. The first meeting with a client was an evaluation of her commitment to the process, interest in marriage and partnership, and what she expected out of the matchmaker. Bri felt she could accomplish all that without scaring the poor girl.

Marrying for clan alliance, Brianagh had learned, was usually reserved for lairds and clan elders. But everyone else in the clan was fair game, and she was thrilled to learn Keela had only been to the castle a few times before, when the laird called the village in for battles or extreme cold, and had shown interest in the man Erin suggested at dinner a few nights ago. Due to her mother's declining health, Keela had been a dutiful daughter and concentrated on ensuring her mother's comfort. But now that they were both ensconced in the castle walls with a room and two servants of their own, things had become a whole lot easier for Keela to focus on herself.

That was the tack Brianagh planned to use, anyway.

Entering the kitchens, Brianagh halted when she noticed

Nioclas sitting at one of the work benches, the kitchen maids all scurrying to do his bidding. She hadn't anticipated seeing him until the evening meal, but she joined him and put her plans for the cook aside momentarily.

"What are you doing in here, my laird?" she asked. He should've been out training, as was the norm. In fact, she and Erin had plans for the afternoon to sneak down to the lists and ogle. It had quickly become one of her favorite pastimes.

"I'd planned to surprise you, but since you're here…" Nioclas smiled encouragingly at her. "I thought we might picnic."

Bri looked at him in shock. "Picnic?"

"Aye, your cousin told me about the tradition," he said with confidence, "and I've had our kitchen lasses prepare us a midday meal we can eat together."

"A picnic." Bri was dumbfounded. Why would Reilly encourage Nioclas to take her on a picnic? Unless… She took a sharp breath. Unless he wanted them to fall in love and was giving Nioclas pointers.

She tried to dismiss the thought, but once lodged, it wasn't budging from her mind. Reilly was so insistent that she make a life here, when her life was so clearly set in the future…

Her eyes met Nioclas's, and she temporarily lost her train of thought. He truly was beautiful. He was not like his elders with their long, unkempt beards; he believed a beard to be more a hindrance in battle than a help in weather and was shaved most mornings. Today, he had the perfect amount of stubble to make her knees weaken. His eyelashes were long and dark, framing the clear, intelligent gray eyes so unlike the rest of his clan. His lips were absolutely sinful—not too lush, not too thin, as though they were made to fit over her own.

Stop! she commanded herself sternly. But she knew she couldn't. Every woman in a five-mile radius drooled over him, with the exception of Erin, who was so blindly in love with her husband she had eyes for no one else.

Also, Nioclas had put a frog down her dress when she was thirteen. Bri recognized the futility of ever finding a man sexy after that.

"Was that an aye?" Nioclas asked softly, taking her hand.

The electricity zinged up her arm, causing her heart to beat faster, and she nodded.

"Oh," Keela sighed, interrupting them as she placed a satchel on the table in front of Nioclas. "I do envy your happiness, my lady."

"We are indeed happy," Nioclas murmured.

Suddenly, she realized Nioclas was playing the game. This was one more move to convince his clan he loved her.

Hollowly, Bri nodded with a smile. Despite the fact that she agreed to the entire sham, the realization stung. She didn't understand why; she had no interest in staying.

Right?

No. No interest. But it would be nice if someone, just once, looked at her like he was and actually meant it. Matthew certainly never had, although his eyes had been adoring when the cameras were trained on them. But the intensity and even the raw lust Nioclas managed in his gaze, false as it was, had never been thrown her way.

The clan was Nioclas's camera. The thought was sobering.

"Let's be off," Nioclas said, leading her out of the kitchens to the stables while handing her a cloak. "I thought it best if we took a journey to the sea before it becomes too cold to do so."

As Brianagh's usual state was just above freezing, she didn't ask what he meant by "too cold." She merely followed him dutifully and allowed him to help her onto the mare he'd readied for her, hoping he'd packed blankets.

Tightening the cloak, she followed him out the gates, and about twenty-five heavily armed men followed them both.

"Who are they?" she asked, pulling her mare alongside his mount.

"Our personal guard." His face darkened momentarily. "The ones who should've been with you when you left the castle with Maguire."

She angled a look back. "I recognize some of them," she said suddenly. "They were in the village when I was there, although not on horseback."

"Once I learned you'd left with only a handful of men, I ensured your safety. They"—he jerked his head back to indicate the troupe following them at a not-so-far distance—"protected you whilst you were securing our cook."

Bri looked at him in surprise. "Truly? Were you there too, then?" Brianagh couldn't be sure, but she thought he flushed.

"The dangers are great, especially for my wife," Nioclas replied, sounding slightly embarrassed.

"Thank you." She smiled softly at him. "I admit that I don't know very much about the dangers here. I thought I'd be safe enough with Donovan and his men."

"Not safe enough for my preference," Nioclas replied, then snapped his mouth shut.

Brianagh looked back and noticed the guardsmen were doing everything they could not to listen, but it was obvious they could hear every word. Her heart plummeted farther. Nioclas really *was* skilled at his game.

She tried to stiffen her spine. She had no business letting her heart soften toward this man. In just a couple months, she'd never see him again.

The thought was more painful than she liked to admit.

~

"Tell me about your plans for Keela."

Nioclas and Bri were sitting between two large rocks, somewhat protected from the winds off the Atlantic. Bri still had two blankets wrapped around herself and was struggling not to shiver, but it was still nice to be out of the castle.

Nioclas was funny. She'd seen flashes of it while spying on him in the lists and in conversations with Aidan, but he'd never truly directed it her way. He told her stories of his youth and the scrapes he and Aidan used to get into together. She was laughing so hard, she had tears running down her cheeks.

Poor Erin had figured into many of the boys' adventures.

Bri dusted her hands off and snuggled farther into the blankets, considering. "Hmm. Keela. To start, she has to be willing to find someone. If she's not willing, it won't work."

"Why not?" Nioclas asked. The wind tousled some of the strands free from the ever-present leather strap holding his hair back, but it didn't seem to bother him. Brianagh tried to ignore the overwhelming urge to tuck it back into place and concentrated on his questions instead.

"You can't force love," she said with a shake of her head. "I've seen it done too many times. Some arranged marriages grow into respect and then eventually love. But so many don't. The most successful relationships—marriages—come from two people who start with respect, admiration, and passion for the other. And if all that is present, it can, with work, develop into love. But once the passion cools, it's the respect and admiration that keep the couple strong."

"Passion doesn't cool," Nioclas replied. "I've caught many an elder in a corner kissing his wife senseless." He smiled at the memory.

"Oh, it cools," she replied matter-of-factly. "For most couples, it cools even before the wedding."

"How tragic for them, then."

"Nioclas, do you ever want to find love for yourself?" Brianagh asked. "After I'm gone."

He froze. She saw it start in his jaw, and then it was as if his entire body developed a crust of ice.

"Nay."

The vehemence in that word surprised a quick "Why?" from her lips.

"Love will destroy the clan."

It was said so flatly, she didn't doubt he meant what he said. But it didn't make sense to her—how could love destroy anything?

"I don't understand," she finally replied after a few beats of silence.

He let out a sigh, then noticed her blue lips. "By the saints, Brianagh, how cold *are* you?" He quickly moved to her side and opened the blanket, then wrapped them together. "You're shaking! We should go back."

"If you want to," she said, a vague sense of disappointment clouding her. "But I am getting warmer." It was true—the man was better than a furnace. She had no idea how he generated that kind of heat, but she didn't want him to move just yet. She hadn't been this warm since she got out of Reilly's car.

And also, the comfort she felt just by being near him was unlike anything she'd ever felt before. She felt safe.

This is just a game. But I can be warm while we play it, she told herself, snuggling a little closer.

They sat in silence for a few minutes, watching the waves break on the small strand of sand immediately at the water's edge. The sand was quickly replaced by progressively larger rocks, making the shoreline trickier to get to than she'd thought when Nioclas took her to the battlements and she had her first clear view of the water.

"My father will destroy anything he can," Nioclas said suddenly. "He would kill the woman I love without so much as blinking first."

Brianagh's mouth formed a silent O.

"My clan wants me to marry to produce an heir. But Aidan will ensure the line lives on, whether he marries or not.

He has many women in the village who desire him, and he can get any one of them with child if he so chooses. That child would inherit the lairdship by blood."

"Wouldn't Burke go after the child?"

"Aye, if he knew about it. The plan is to send the child away with his mother until he's old enough to come back, or my sire dies, whichever comes first."

"You Irish certainly love to send your kids away," she murmured.

"It's for protection of the clan, Brianagh. Hundreds of people depend on me to protect them in times of war and settle their disputes in times of peace. I have pledged my life for theirs, and they have done the same. In our clan, we've decided that the lairdship will be passed by relation instead of staging a battle between those who desire it. I have no love for bloodshed." Nioclas paused, weighing his next words. "My sire murdered my mother and, I suspect, her entire clan."

Brianagh's heart lodged in her throat.

Nioclas continued. "He thought them to be weak, and therefore, unworthy. When he killed her, something inside me snapped." He stared out at the waves for a moment. "A laird should be a fearsome creature to his enemies and a source of safety to his clan. My sire ruled us for too long as if we were his enemies." He closed his eyes briefly. "I swore that I would be different. 'Tis why we changed the name of this clan from Burke to MacWilliam. And I cannot be married, then send my wife and child off—he'd find and kill them. Any child I have would be considered an heir and in serious danger, moreso than most lairds' children. But if Aidan had a child… Well, it isn't unheard of for an unmarried pregnant lass to leave the clan."

At Brianagh's gasp, his gaze trapped hers. "If it were Aidan's child, she would be more than taken care of,

Brianagh. We would never send her somewhere without protection, coin, and comforts as best we can provide."

Brianagh was quickly getting the picture. He would never love because of the danger posed to the woman, and he would never put a woman in that kind of danger.

"It will not be a surprise to my clans folk when you return to your home, and I claim your death. They will be saddened, of course. But a laird's wife must be protected. She carries the future of the clan in her womb. So when you leave, I will not need to worry about another woman or an heir. I can simply return all of my focus to the clan."

"I guess I came along at the perfect time," she said softly.

He smiled sadly at her. "The Kildare lass—I didn't even know her name, but I knew I'd be the death of her if I wed her. Eventually, he'd find her alone, or worse, with a child… It's best she returned home. Aside from the danger, she's just a child. I have no stomach for that."

"As you've mentioned," Bri replied with a nod. "I can see now why you were so upset when I went to the village with such inadequate protection. Thank you for explaining it to me."

"I can keep you safe, Brianagh."

"I have no doubt." Her heart felt heavy, though she wished it didn't. She wished they were from the same time, without all of the baggage each of them carried.

Their life together could've been so different. So much more.

She gazed out at the rocky beach and noticed the clouds gathering in the distance. "Perhaps we should go back. I think the weather may turn."

He glanced out to the clouds, then kept the blanket wrapped around them as they rose together. He glanced down at her. "I have to leave for a few days. I have business with an ally in the south. I'm taking Aidan but leaving most of my men." He paused, then bestowed a quick smile on her.

"I don't think I've thanked you properly for wedding me under such circumstances."

She forced a bright smile. "Getting me home will be thanks enough."

Nioclas's eyes dropped to her lips, and instinctively she licked them nervously. He leaned in and gently kissed her. "Were our situation different," he murmured before stepping out of the blanket, "I believe we would suit quite well, Lady Brianagh."

"Yes," she agreed quietly. "I believe you're right."

CHAPTER 16

"We really need to find someone suitable, and soon," Erin said a few days later, as she and Brianagh hurried down the stairs together. "Word has gotten out to the men in the village that Keela has agreed to be matched, and that the laird is pleased with her efforts in her new position in the castle."

"So that means they're all suddenly interested in her now?" Bri asked, slightly out of breath as they hurriedly threaded through the various clansmen loitering in the great hall.

"Before coming to the castle, she was just another village girl tied to her ailing mother, and now she's free from that burden because of the women you've chosen to help with Aoife's care. When you add that to what she can do to a slab of beef, it's no wonder the men have been falling all over themselves."

"She's attractive too," Brianagh mused. "I'll need to interview these men and get to know Keela better before we go any further." At Erin's confusion, Bri clarified, "I'll need to speak with the men to determine what they're like off the battlefield."

"Excellent. If you wish, I can help with that."

"Help with what?" Donovan asked, stepping into their path.

"Finding the perfect mate for Keela," Brianagh explained.

"We can stay, aye?" Erin pleaded, placing her hand on his arm. "There's nothing happening at home. I'm happy here for a while yet."

He acquiesced with some grumbling, but it was clear he'd do anything to make Erin happy. Brianagh bit her lip, a stab of jealousy rocking her, and she once again found herself wanting to be the center of someone's world.

She had a strong suspicion that, were circumstances different, she would be the center of Nioclas's world.

She resolved to ignore the hollow ache in her chest and focus on matching Keela, because that was what she loved to do: find someone her happily-ever-after. As it always was with a new client—and then at the subsequent wedding—she had to accept she wasn't destined to have her own happily-ever-after.

As she was debating with herself about the best ways to ignore the disappointment of that depressing reality, Nioclas entered the great hall, handing his cloak to one of the women by the door, and her heart squeezed a tiny bit.

Bri didn't want this complication. She didn't want to be attracted to a medieval man who held more power in his hand than the modern-day Queen of England, but she also didn't want to live without electricity, toilets, or hot showers.

Or Matthew, she reminded herself. *Or my family*.

But for the first time, the reminder didn't ring as strongly as it should have.

When Nioclas joined them and swiftly kissed her hand in greeting, her heart pained her even more and she recognized the truth of it. Despite all its downfalls, medieval Ireland held the one thing the future didn't, and he was currently gazing at her with such intensity her entire body felt as though it had caught on fire.

"Whoa," Erin murmured, looking from Brianagh to Nioclas and back again. "Perhaps we'll discuss this more later, Brianagh?"

"Ah…" Bri faltered, trying unsuccessfully to tear her gaze from Nioclas's.

"Aye, later," he answered for her, then took her hand and nearly dragged her through his clansmen, who either moved swiftly out of his way or thumped him on the back in greeting as he led her back toward the stairs she'd just descended. "Follow me."

For quite possibly the first time in her life, Brianagh felt maybe she ought to follow her heart and see what happened.

So she followed.

NIOCLAS LED HER INTO THE BEDCHAMBER. "I THOUGHT YOU should know of my plans to leave after we dine tonight."

Brianagh, lovely in her MacWilliam colors and flushed from the exertion of him hurrying her to his bedchamber, nodded. "Thank you."

He smiled then, a true smile, and he gestured to his bed. "I've added coverlets to my bed."

She glanced at them and nodded, obviously confused as to why he felt the need to drag her to his bedchamber to display new coverlets.

"I thought, while I was away, that you might keep up the appearance that we're sharing a room, so I ordered extra in case you were cold."

For days, they had left the door between them unlocked and Nioclas had ensured he opened it before any servants came into stoke the fire in his hearth in the mornings. He'd heard his men discussing how their laird wore out the lady of the castle every night, that as she wished for some sleep, she insisted she take to her own bed after their "nightly activities."

His garrison, he came to realize, gossiped more than the elderly women in the village.

But instead of correcting them, he instead was pleased that they believed he and Brianagh were married in truth.

Looking at her now, as she watched him with a hint of a smile playing about her full mouth, he felt his chest tighten.

I could love this woman.

Dangerous, that. But he was never one to deny a truth once it presented itself.

She was certainly the most clever woman he knew and perhaps ever met. She was adapting to the Irish way of life with a speed he never expected, and the loyalty his clansmen offered her was becoming more about who she was rather than her position in his life.

If he could convince her to want to stay, he could envision a future with her. Children, perhaps. Though what he told her was true, he was more powerful than his wastrel of a sire. He could keep his wife safe, and she would never find herself alone with a child, ever. She would have the strongest of his men always protecting her.

She would have him always protecting her.

And at the moment, she looked as though she might be growing fond of him.

"I hope you'll do me the honor of staying?"

"Staying?"

He wondered if she understood he was asking her to stay longer… He wanted her for forever.

Slowly, Nioclas. Woo her slowly.

"Aye. Your chamber is not as warm as mine, and the bed is plenty large enough," he replied.

She looked around the room, taking in the large bed and canopy, the cheery fire, and the scarce furnishings.

"May I…freshen it up?" she asked hesitantly.

Nioclas reigned in his enthusiasm. He folded his arms and leaned back. "Freshen it up?"

"You know, add a small table and chair where Iona can style my hair in the mornings. Maybe bring that screen thing in."

"The privacy screen?" Nioclas repeated. "You would use it?"

She shrugged. "We value our privacy in America…"

"Done," he agreed immediately. "And you may make whatever other changes you feel are necessary."

She gave him a small smile. "Thank you."

"Perhaps a token of your gratitude?" he wondered, presenting his cheek. After a slight hesitation, she quickly pressed her lips against it.

He smiled at her. "That wasn't so terrible, was it?"

Confusion warred with humor in her eyes. "Are you teasing me?"

"If you have to ask, I must redouble my efforts. Alas, I must place that on hold for the moment, though. I must head out to the lists to ensure my men have continued their training in my absence."

"Oh. Okay," she replied uncertainly. She looked around again and bit her lip.

"But first," Nioclas lowered his voice, "perhaps we ought to muss you up a bit. Just so no one suspects I won't miss you as terribly as I will."

Her eyes widened, and he knew she was still unsure if he was teasing her. He stepped closer to her and reveled in her body's response; she swayed towards him, her eyes trained on his mouth. He allowed her to see his seductive smile before he nudged her lips open with his own.

Her reaction was immediate, and she melted into him.

He nipped her bottom lip. "I shall see you at supper, my lady."

The look of astonishment on her face lightened Nioclas's heart.

Aye. There was hope for them yet.

~

THOUGH SHE SPENT THE BETTER PART OF THE AFTERNOON SORTING through the finer details of what her clients had told her in the past—in the future?—Brianagh still couldn't figure out Nioclas's intent. Were they still playing the game? Or was he serious?

A slightly-more-than-tiny part of her wanted to believe he was serious, but she knew such thoughts weren't wise. She didn't want any reason to stay in the Middle Ages; she earned her T-shirt and was ready to go home.

Well, almost ready, she amended, glancing at the large bed. Maybe her reason for going back in time was to see what all the fuss was about that elusive feeling of desire. Perhaps her fate, despite what Reilly continued to insist, was that she needed to learn about those feelings in order to better match her future clients—

"Are you well?"

Brianagh jumped, startled by Erin's appearance. "Me? Oh yes. I'm perfectly well." She glanced at the window in her chamber, noting the lengthening shadows. "I didn't realize how late it's gotten. Is it time for supper?"

Erin nodded and entered the room. "I've said that twice already. Are you certain you're well, Bri? You seem distracted. Is it because Nioclas is going to visit his former lover?"

Brianagh frowned. "What?"

Erin shrugged. "Well, he's not going specifically to see her, I'm sure. He's visiting her sire's stronghold, as he has business with the man." At Bri's raised eyebrows, she hastened to add, "Oh, don't concern yourself about the lass's reputation. Her sire is well aware of her indiscretions, and though he hoped for a match with Nick, he knew such a powerful laird would want someone with more…"

"Discretion?" Bri supplied.

Erin snickered. "Aye. Discretion. The MacDermotts have always hoped to ally with the MacWilliams, but her sire knows such a match is merely a hope."

"Of course," Bri murmured.

"Well, may you never meet Una in the flesh. There's something about her that makes me tuck in a bit tighter to Donovan."

"Where I'm from, that's called women's intuition. It means we can sense that something's not right."

Erin nodded emphatically. "Aye, that's it exactly. But worry not, my lady. Nick is true and honest; he's clearly smitten with you, and during the wedding he did give a vow of chastity to his true love."

"The vows. Right," Brianagh echoed.

A lover.

Of course he would have a lover. Theirs was a game they were playing, so that he wouldn't have to commit to anyone, and she could go home.

The burning sensation in her chest only proved her desperation to return home. She was sure of it.

So sure, in fact, that she took supper in her chamber instead of joining Nioclas, resolved to think on only future things for the remainder of the night.

REILLY WATCHED BRIANAGH STAB AT HER LITTLE PILLOW, marveling at how the thing still managed to stay in one piece with her ruthless assault. She'd been in a bad mood since Nioclas left almost a week ago for the MacDermotts. Reilly hadn't seen her this grouchy since…well, he couldn't think of when. Erin sat with Bri, shooting her puzzled looks as she set up a chessboard.

Bri's sewing reminded Reilly of the voodoo doll she'd created when she'd been stood up for her junior prom. His jaw almost hit the floor as realization dawned. That was the last time she'd been so upset—the day she'd been used for a ticket into the junior prom by a senior. She'd had such a crush on him, and when he didn't show to pick her up, he and Colin went on a recon mission and found the kid making out with another girl in Bri's class.

Bri was heartbroken. The kid sported a broken nose for graduation.

Reilly studied Bri carefully. She didn't direct her anger at any one person. Whenever Erin engaged her in conversation, she replied with a sad sort of smile. When one of the kitchen lasses brought the week's menu to her for approval, she made a change, but was distantly pleasant to them when explaining it. No one else in the hall seemed to notice her, or perhaps they attributed her wrinkled nose and furrowed brow to her obvious hatred of sewing. Or perhaps to her missing her husband while he was away.

When Nioclas walked in with Donovan, the pain flashed so quickly across her face he would've missed it, had he but blinked.

Fortunately for him, he didn't bat an eye.

Nioclas stopped by the table, exchanged some words with Erin, then turned his attention to Brianagh. Her expression softened slightly, and after a moment, he smiled at her and continued on his way. Following him with her gaze, her eyes landed on Reilly as Nioclas passed him on his way to the steps. Bri held up two fingers, then tapped her wrist.

Two months left.

It was her destiny to stay here, but Brianagh had the ability to get back without Reilly, although he was confident she didn't know it. Reilly was certain, however, if she was bent on getting back to the future and thought he was the only one to get her there, she'd move hell and high water to track him down.

He had to make sure he was long gone before that time came. If she was going to mess things up, he didn't want to be anywhere near it when the Fates came knocking at her door.

CHAPTER 17

Brianagh dragged herself up to her chamber, unwilling to watch Donovan and Erin any longer. It was embarrassing how they draped all over each other whenever they were together.

She opened the door to Nioclas's bedchamber and froze at the sight of the steaming tub in the center of the room, with a fire dancing in the fireplace. Glancing around, she saw no one. Taking a tentative step, she called out, but there wasn't any reply.

She closed the door, then walked over and picked up the soft stack of towels by the tub. She inhaled the scent wafting from the water. Lilacs…her favorite. That was strange—who could have procured lilacs in the middle of winter? She wasn't even sure lilacs grew in Ireland. The door opened behind her and she shrieked, the linens flying from her hands as she spun around.

Nioclas held up his hands and took a step back. "I wanted to surprise you."

"You did," she replied, placing a hand over her racing heart. "Do you—?" She waved at the tub.

"I was told you enjoyed bathing with lilac oils," Nioclas

said carefully, gauging her reaction, "so I obtained some for you. This room is the only one big enough for this tub."

"Oh," she murmured taken aback. "Thank you. That was very nice."

"We do many trades with Italy. That's where the oil is made." He rubbed his neck, then paused. "I know you're anxious to return to your home. You seemed upset earlier, and Erin assured me that a bath would soothe you."

Bri bit her lip. "Yes, a bath would be wonderful. Thank you, Nioclas. It was very sweet of you to think of the bath oil."

"Entirely my pleasure, my lady. Enjoy your bath. I'll send Iona in to help with your hair." He bowed and shut the door behind him.

Bri wasted no time stripping and sinking into the bath, worried it might cool. Glancing around at the tapestries, bedding, and what she'd done while Nioclas was gone, Bri had to admit she loved this chamber. The fire was cheery, perhaps because it illuminated the tapestries, which gave so much more color to everything. Her chamber was now all gray—the stone wall, stone floor, and even the bedding.

Depressing.

But this chamber was completely opposite. She had decorated it with comfort in mind, and the small alcove had a window that, when she opened the shutter, let in a cleansing, icy wind. She imagined it would let in a glorious summer breeze off the ocean on just the right kind of day in July or August.

She'd been in the Middle Ages for almost an entire month. She wasn't sure how the time continuum worked, but she hoped when she returned no one would even know she'd been gone.

And despite the overwhelming urge to blame Reilly and his meddling ways—she knew who dropped the bath oil hint in Erin's ear—she knew the blame lay entirely at her own feet.

Her own treacherous heart was not listening to her very rational mind, which continually chanted, *Do not fall for him, it's only a game.*

When Iona entered the chamber, Bri put her thoughts aside and finished her bath.

NIOCLAS COULDN'T HIDE HIS SHOCK. IT SEEMED HIS WIFE HAD been quite busy while he'd been about his business with the MacDermotts.

"All of them?" Aidan asked incredulously.

They walked the perimeter of the outer wall, looking for any weaknesses in the stonework that needed tending. Nioclas had instructed his guardsmen to watch from the battlements rather than follow him around in a giant circle so their conversation wouldn't be overheard. Upon learning that Donovan had news to impart, Nioclas thought it wise to keep all others at bay.

Donovan nodded, rubbing his hand on his forehead. "According to the guards, aye, most of them. The elders who were sleeping in the great hall each have a chamber for him and his wife. The very elderly have rooms all together, and she's given tasks to a small group of women she calls nurses. Those women—the nurses—care for the elderly clansfolk. It's their only duty to the castle."

"By the saints," Nioclas replied, bewildered.

Aidan gave a low whistle. "We never thought to do that, but think of what that could mean! We've always prided ourselves on our respect for the elders, and the elderly. She's ensured their health needs are met, while providing them comfort and protection within the castle walls. Their children will see this and understand that if they leave our clan, they won't find such treatment anywhere else. And instead of looking outside the clan to marry, they'd marry within it. Stay with the clan."

"Grow the clan," Donovan corrected. "It has long-reaching influences. Perhaps her intelligence is even more than O'Malley claims."

"Perhaps," Nioclas murmured, his mind reeling. "I wonder if the clan knows she did this on her own, without my knowledge."

"I don't trust her," Donovan replied, "but if she continues to prove herself worthy of a laird, I could be persuaded to think otherwise."

Nioclas shook his head. "I've told you many times, Maguire. She is no threat to me. She was held in my sire's oubliette. I do not believe any woman would be willing to spend any amount of time in one of those, for any price."

"Perhaps she is just a pawn in a larger game."

"Perhaps."

"Tell me that's why you're allowing O'Malley to stay," Aidan said darkly. "I loathe that man."

"He may be of use to you one day," Nioclas said mildly, squatting to inspect a crack at the foundation of the east wall. He made a note on the parchment he carried. "O'Malley may or may not be the enemy, but Bri trusts him completely. That alone warrants a careful look at his past."

"What have you discovered?" Donovan asked.

"Little," Nioclas admitted. "The MacDermotts had never heard of him, but the O'Malleys are a large clan. I've yet to have any scout return with any information about him. All have returned with the same story—he could be a part of the clan, he could be someone else entirely."

"That's a poorly-run clan," Aidan muttered.

"The O'Malleys certainly won't tell us anything directly," Nioclas pointed out. "We're not exactly allies."

"We're not exactly enemies, either," Aidan shot back, "but *this* O'Malley may just change all that."

"Is there anything else I should be aware of, before we return?" Nioclas asked, turning back to Donovan.

"The nurses are only the start of it. She's appointed almost all the women in the castle to specific tasks, with one woman acting as chief to the task." Donovan shrugged. "I noticed it first with the laundry. Two women gathered the linens and clothing, two different women were washing them, and two more were hanging them to dry in the gardens. All of them informed the same woman of their progress for the day when they'd completed the task."

"Very strange," Nioclas murmured.

"Aye, but the results seem to be positive. I have not one flea in my bed, and my sweet lady wife is enamored with freshly washed linens each day. It seems like a waste of wash water."

"Perhaps not," Aidan replied, considering. "The wash water is poured into the basin each day, no matter if a single pair of hose needs cleaning or an entire castle full of bed linens. By washing all that they can find, that lessens the amount of water used over a longer period of time."

"Fascinating." Donovan shook his head. "How does she know to do these things?"

"I've no idea," Nioclas replied, bemused. "But she did it all without my knowledge."

"Are your wee wife's demands bothering you?" Donovan teased. "To her credit, I haven't seen any clan member just standing in the great hall."

"Everyone seems to be doing something all the time," Aidan agreed. "If you had to be saddled with a woman, you're rather lucky fate saddled you with such as she."

"Very," Nioclas repeated, his thoughts jumbling in his head. A guardsman whistled, and he nodded briskly. "Back to the castle, lads. I've yet to tell you the news from MacDermott, and it involves swords."

"It's been too quiet around here," Aidan said, bouncing on his heels. "I imagined the peace couldn't last forever."

"Nay," Nioclas replied heavily. "It could not."

~

"THE CASTLE IS ALMOST FULLY OCCUPIED NOW, AND THE LAIRD IS clearly taken with her to allow such nonsense."

Burke wasn't looking at the man directly. Instead, he was watching for anyone who may have followed him into the forest. He saw no one but wasn't willing to take unnecessary risks, so he motioned for the fool to be silent, then led him deeper into the trees.

Speaking in hushed tones, Burke urged him to continue.

"She is often left by herself within the castle walls, or accompanied by Lady Maguire." The man's breath came out in icy puffs.

Burke swore. "Maguire stays at the castle?"

The man nodded, his eyes glittering. "Aye, he remains close to the laird. When Maguire is not with his wife, he ensures she's followed by her personal guard, even within the castle. Lady MacWilliam is always with a guard when by herself, and she's allowed to roam the inner bailey at will."

"Has MacWilliam's wife left the castle walls?" Burke demanded.

"Aye. Once, and with only Maguire and seven men," he confirmed.

"Surprising that he'd allow his lady love to wander so unescorted," Burke mused.

"There are thoughts that she may be with child because of her changing moods." He pursed his lips. "Sounds like nonsense to me."

"I pay you for this nonsense," Burke replied, tossing the man a few coins. "So continue."

The man greedily scooped the coins off the damp forest

floor, dropping some through his frozen fingers. When he'd finished gathering them, he grinned a nearly toothless smile. "The laird left for a few days, and the lady seemed to have a hard time with it. Never smiled, which made some of the elders look on her as the laird's true love." The man spat. "She's probably just good in the—"

"And when does the laird plan to leave again?" Burke interrupted.

"Don't know." The man shrugged. "He just up and leaves when he wants, doesn't tell us until he's on his way out the gate."

"And you're just left to defend the castle? Who acts as laird?"

"Well, he left his brother there last week," the man replied, drawing his dark cloak tighter around himself to ward off the chill. "But he's also got someone else in there. O'Malley, he says his name is, but there's something off about the man. He and the lady have fast speech in a tongue I don't know."

Burke felt a flash of triumph. That was what he'd been waiting for, some nugget of information that the woman at the keep was, in fact, the missing O'Rourke daughter. The one with the ability to travel through time.

"This woman—Lady MacWilliam. She came to the castle, married your laird, and began changing your ways. Then, a man arrives, speaking a strange tongue, and he knows the lady?"

The man nodded at Burke's summary. "Aye, all a bit strange. Some think she was put with us to protect her from something, but most of the clan thinks she's a miracle, getting all these changes done and capturing the laird's heart. To hear the women tell it, our laird was never getting himself married for fear that someone might come and kill his wife."

"Oh, I don't think anyone would want to kill her," Burke replied. *Not until she births a son with her same powers,* he added silently. "You've been very helpful. If you provide me with more information when we next meet, your payment doubles. Do you think it possible to bring Lady MacWilliam with you? I'd like to meet this woman who's wrought such change in your castle."

The man's eyes widened. "But if I do that, she's likely to tell MacWilliam we've met!"

Burke slid his dirk out from his belt and flashed it in the moonlight. "Do you want a new laird, lad? One who will give you the battle you crave? Or will you be content to live your sorry life in a wattle-and-daub house, sharpening your sword so that you may throw yourself upon it for shame of your battle skills?"

The man remained silent for so long Burke thought he might have to kill him now, which would throw his entire plan into jeopardy. Instead, he used the last reserves of his patience and said, "Three weeks from tonight, you'll get your chance at battle. But you must get Lady MacWilliam to me, here, before you join with your new clan."

The man nodded. "Tell me what you want me to do, my laird, and it shall be done."

CHAPTER 18

Nioclas mindlessly removed the various weaponry from his belt and boots, placed them in his trunk, and let his shoulders relax. It was good to be home.

The MacDermotts imparted grave news whilst he visited. There were rumors Kildare planned an attack on the MacWilliams for dishonor of his daughter. When passing through the Clanricards' land, Nioclas heard the same rumor; he sent his two fastest men ahead to prepare his clansmen, in case the news proved true.

Nioclas wasn't concerned, as his men were always prepared for battle. Donovan had sent for reinforcements almost immediately upon their return that morning. Nioclas knew even the most loyal of Kildares would turn on their laird if someone better and stronger came along—many had already pledged their loyalty to the English crown and broken away from Kildare and his rule. The man was in trouble. It would've proved a very beneficial alliance to both clans had Nioclas followed through with the wedding. The Kildare clan was high in numbers but low in organization. If they had a laird to inspire them, they'd prove formidable, which is why Nioclas had agreed to the marriage of their daughter before the O'Rourkes dropped Brianagh into his life.

He smiled at the thought. He would be forever grateful to her for making this easier than it should be. Most women would demand much more from him—ribbons, gold, fine clothing. Nioclas had just pulled his tunic off when the chamber door opened and Brianagh entered. Her eyes widening, her hand fluttering to her chest, she let out a tiny gasp of surprise. "Nioclas! I didn't think you'd be here."

He gave her a look. "Where else would I be?"

She blushed. "Of course. This is your room. I'll come back later."

"No need," he replied, sitting on the bed and unlacing his boots. "Stay. I've heard you've made some changes to our home whilst I've been away. Perhaps you want to tell me of them?"

"Are you angry?"

He pulled his boot off and held it for a moment as he considered. Anger wasn't the right word, but he wasn't exactly happy about it, either. He twisted around to face her fully, and was struck mute when he took in her entire appearance.

Much of her hair had escaped its coil at the nape of her neck, and a riot of curls caressed her face and shoulders. Her hands, clutched together in front of her, had smears of dirt mirroring those all over her simple woolen skirt. When she shifted nervously at his silence, he noticed the scuffs on her slippers. Her sleeve looked as though it had been torn but stitched up—and if his men's rumors were true, she'd clearly stitched it herself.

In that instant, he saw the gift he'd been given. Selfish bastard that he was, he wasn't all that sure he wanted to give it back.

"Did you tear your dress?" he asked softly, motioning to her sleeve.

She flushed a deep red. "Well, not on purpose. I was trying to move the table on the raised dais we sit on during dinner, and it got caught on a jagged piece of wood—"

"Why didn't you have one of my men move the table?" Nioclas interrupted.

Her face said it all, but she replied anyway. "I didn't think to ask. They were already so busy."

He pulled his other boot off, then stepped toward her. "Men fear me." At her blank stare, he took another step. "Women fear me as well." She stood still as a stone. "Do you fear me, Brianagh?"

"No," she whispered, searching his eyes.

"Why?"

"I don't know," she whispered again, mesmerized by his gaze.

"You should fear me," he murmured, picking up a lock of her hair. "As my wife, I own you."

His words sent a shiver down her spine, and it had nothing to do with fear. He gently twisted her hair around his hand, then slid his fingers out slowly, watching as she struggled to figure him out.

"Yet you don't complain, you don't demand anything, and you've given this clan your all. You gave me your trust, and I did nothing to earn it." He took her hand in his, inspecting it, noting each scrape, each smudge of dirt, each pinprick. Bringing it to his lips, he gently kissed each fingertip. "Why?" he whispered, bringing his eyes back to hers.

"You saved me," she replied simply.

Aye, but perhaps you saved me as well.

"And you promised to send me back."

A bucket of his moat's water couldn't have dampened his mood faster. He stepped back swiftly. His tone turned icy. "Aye. I did."

A full minute passed in silence. "I don't understand what you're doing," she finally replied.

He closed his eyes. "Nor do I, yet I find I cannot stop."

"You're confusing me. This isn't real, Nioclas. We've been saying that for a month."

He looked closely at her. "You still believe you're from the future."

She nodded.

"And you're willing to give up the protection of my name to return to it." A statement, not a question.

She nodded again.

"Tell me truly," Nioclas said. "Is it because of the Frenchman?"

Bri wanted to say yes. It'd be easiest for them both if it were true. But Nioclas had done more for her in the last month than anyone. He'd not only rescued her from a medieval dungeon, but he hadn't readied the fire for her witch-burning after her confession of when she was from. He also gave her food, clothing, and as he said, protection. And, real or not, he made her feel.

She owed him the truth.

"Nay," she said softly. "It is not."

"Will you return to him?"

She closed her eyes briefly. "No. I don't think I will. You've shown me, through your acting, what a real marriage could be like. I want that."

He stared at her silently for a moment, then gave a slight bow. "That's a balm to my poor self, I suppose. If we're to be serious, I need to know how you expect to return," Nioclas said. "Perhaps you'd best tell me how you…arrived here."

"You still believe I'm daft."

"Perhaps a bit touched in the head, but nothing that would encourage me to share your secret."

"Comforting," she replied dryly. Bri didn't mind that he thought she was slightly off her rocker. The fact was, if the roles were reversed, she would believe he was insane. She didn't think she'd offer him free use of her brownstone in

Boston, but she'd probably buy him something to eat on the way to the mental hospital.

"It's best if you start from the beginning," Nioclas said. "Start with your childhood."

"You want my life story?" she asked dubiously. Absentmindedly, she rubbed her fingers against her gown. Keeping up with his mind was draining her.

"We have all night." He shrugged. "It's best if we talk about your situation."

"Sensible," she murmured. "I do, however, need to change out of this gown. It's a mess."

"What were you doing? Moving a table cannot be so dirty," Nioclas asked as she opened her trunk. She pulled out a long white linen nightgown.

"Do you mind if I wear this? My other two gowns must not be washed yet," she said with a frown, peering into the empty trunk.

"You only have three dresses?"

She blinked at him. "Well, yes. I burned the one I came in —it was covered with whatever was in that awful dungeon." She shuddered at the memory of the moving floor.

"I'll order you more. As the laird's wife, you should have more than three dresses," Nioclas replied, surprised she hadn't ordered them herself.

"There's no need." She twirled her finger in midair to indicate he turn around. "Three is plenty. And I was changing the rushes on the floor of the great hall."

He turned his back to her and said through clenched teeth, "Do I not have an entire *garrison* of men living in this castle?"

"Yes," she replied, taken aback at his change of tone.

"And, pray tell, why could you not have them clear the rushes out of the hall?"

"You can turn around now," she said. "Your garrison is training in the lists all day. Your blacksmith works in his building, creating swords and whatever else it is that he creates. Your stable master works with the horses all day. Your pages are out in the lists with your garrison, trying to earn your respect and, I suspect, a place in your garrison once they are old enough. And the elders are rarely in residence, but when they are, I do not want them doing this kind of work. They've earned a bit of freedom from manual labor, if even half their battle stories are true. I think that covers just about all the men here at the castle."

He just stared at her, his mouth slightly open.

"That left the women and me. Seeing as I'd already tasked all available people to do various things around the castle, it was up to me. And the rushes were disgusting." Brianagh wrinkled her nose. "They smelled awful. They needed to be changed, and Bernie gave me the fresh hay to lay down."

"Bernie?" Nioclas repeated.

"The stable master."

"You called him *Bernie*?" He laughed in amazement. Bernard, his crusty old stable master who was notorious for calming horses with just a touch and scaring children with just a look, did not fit with that name.

"He told me to call him that," she replied defensively. "He's so lonely out there that I insisted he start coming to the castle proper for his meals. He can eat with the garrison in the great hall." He stared at her until she squirmed. "What?"

He grinned. "Impressive, my lady. Bernard is not known for his linguistic skill."

"Oh, he's fine," she replied with a wave. "Anyway, that's how I got so dirty."

"I wonder how you became so good with people," Nioclas mused. "Please. Start at the beginning, and don't leave anything out. I feel as though I'm in for an entertaining evening."

Bri took a deep breath. She really had nothing to lose, so she started at the beginning.

CHAPTER 19

Early the following morning, Nioclas silently dressed so as to not disturb his sleeping wife. He was determined to find out if her words were true. The tales she'd told him had him fascinated into the wee hours of the morning.

She painted a colorful portrait of her life before him. If she were to be believed, Brianagh was even more educated than he. For every question he asked, she had an answer—one she didn't stop to think about—and the answers were cohesive, never contradicting, despite his attempts to get her to misstep. He couldn't find a single loophole in her confessions last night.

But the most convincing—and frightening—evidence she provided were the items she pulled from the trunk.

He felt ill just looking at them.

The first was a satchel. White leather, whiter than any satchel his eyes ever set upon, with blue leather trim. Nioclas knew the world was large, but he never had seen an animal with such pure white skin, or skin of such a distinct shade of sky blue.

"We call it a purse," she explained. "This one is Coach, but there are lots of different ones."

The satchel's clasp made a horrid noise, and though he didn't admit it aloud, the silver teeth tested his bravery. More than once, he reached for his sword, only to be given a sweet look by his wife.

He kept the sword nearby, just in case.

If the satchel hadn't already given him pause, the smaller satchel certainly did. She called it a wristlet, and it was made of a fabric far finer than any he'd encountered from merchants, with the same razor teeth as the larger one.

Once she pulled out its contents, Nioclas nearly forgot about their containers.

"It's a license," Brianagh said softly, holding it out to him. The parchment was stiff, unlike anything he'd ever felt, and had an unnatural shine to it. He carefully rubbed his finger over the portrait of Brianagh. The likeness was more exact than any artist he'd known. The words on the parchment—the license—didn't look like the hand of a person. When he held it in the firelight, an unholy image of sorts flashed across the front, causing him to fling it away, pull a dirk from his boot, and cross himself with alacrity.

"That's a hologram. It's a drawing with a special ink that appears when the light shines upon it." Brianagh slowly retrieved the parchment, chewing her bottom lip. "I'm not a witch, Nioclas."

"I don't believe you to be," Nioclas replied carefully. He preferred the term *sorceress*, but wisely held his tongue.

"Mmm hmm," came the reply. She dug around in the satchel again, unaware of Nioclas's grave fear that the teeth would chew her hand from her wrist, and extracted a tube, made of the same shiny material as the evil parchment. "Lip gloss," she supplied. She twisted the top off and applied it to her lips.

Nioclas blinked in surprise. "You wear face paint?"

She rubbed her lips together, and Nioclas blinked again, this time because her eyes looked a little brighter, and her lips looked even more tempting than they had just a moment prior.

"Not here. But in 2015 I did."

Nioclas resisted the urge to scoff at such an impossibly high number, and imperiously held his hand out. She dropped the tube into it, and he sniffed. "Do men wear such paint?"

She shrugged. "Some. Most don't."

He eyed it warily. "Its scent is not unwelcome."

"It's strawberry scented."

He shook his head and handed it back to her. No strawberry he'd eaten smelled anything like that.

"Tissues, a pen, an appointment card... Oops. I had a dentist appointment. I hope they don't charge me for a no-show," she grumbled, pulling out more foreign items. Suddenly, she froze. "Oh boy."

Nioclas hefted his sword, nearing the end of his limits. "My lady, perhaps we ought to consign these items to the fire. For our safety, and the safety of our clan." *And my reputation,* he thought, swallowing past the fear at so many unfamiliar objects strewn about his chamber floor.

Brianagh's eyes never left her hand, which remained inside the satchel.

Nioclas grew more alarmed. "Brianagh, are you entangled in the coach's teeth?!"

She shook her head suddenly, as though clearing it, and let out a breath. "No. But this...If this doesn't convince you that I'm not from this time, I don't know what will."

"Show me at once," he demanded.

"Put the sword down, Nioclas," she replied, exasperated. "None of these items will harm you. Unless you're stabbed by the pen. But that would be merely a flesh wound. I don't think anyone's ever died of a pen attack."

He eyed the quill warily.

"I'm not taking this out until you put the sword away."

Nioclas did a swift, silent count. Two more dirks on his person, a sword strapped to the wall inside of the small alcove, a bow and arrow hidden in his trunk.

He reluctantly propped his sword against the wall.

"Come sit by me," she said quietly. "I vow, this cannot hurt you. It isn't alive."

"What is it, then?"

Her blue eyes shone as she pulled it out. "It's a tool I used every day. It's called a phone."

The black rectangle lay, unassuming, in her hand.

"Tell me of its purpose."

Brianagh ran a finger over it. "When I press this button"—she pointed to a small circle—"the screen alights."

"It provides fire?" Nioclas asked skeptically.

She shook her head and thought for a moment before replying. "No. It provides light, which is very different. It also acts as my record keeper, as it holds information about other people, such as their castle location and ways to send missives. But most importantly, it holds portraits."

Nioclas was helplessly confused. How could such a thing *hold* portraits?

"Nioclas? Are you all right?"

He settled his mouth into a firm line. "Aye, my lady, of course. I've seen much worse on the battlefield, as you well know." If she fought a smile, Nioclas was grateful for her discretion.

"Ready?"

He nodded, his body coiled and tensed to spring into action, should they need his skills. A bead of sweat dripped between his shoulder blades, and his breathing shallowed.

Brianagh touched the circle and it began to glow. Nioclas gasped and leapt backwards.

"It's the light I told you about." Brianagh watched him nervously. "It cannot hurt us, Nioclas."

He watched as it glowed, then dimmed, then glowed again…then color as he'd never seen filled her hand.

She rapidly dragged her finger across the colors, despite his warning not to touch the evil thing, and her face instantly softened when the tool changed images yet again. A portrait did indeed sit in her hand, and it was somehow even clearer than the portrait from the strange card she showed him moments ago.

Nioclas wiped the sweat from his face. "By the saints…"

She met his bewildered eyes with her calm ones. "I'm not a witch, Nioclas. This is just an example of the amazing things man has created. Would you like to see what my family looks like?"

"By all that is holy, I don't think I can," he whispered. "If not a witch, are you a sorceress?"

She laughed, the sound bouncing off the walls, and lowered the tool to her lap. "No, Nioclas. I have no magical abilities. Reilly does, though. He's the one who brought me here. He is the one who moved time. I'm just the person who got caught up in this family story that's going around. I'm not the chosen daughter, or whatever the O'Rourkes claimed. I'm just a woman from the future, out of place, and not really sure how to get back."

Nioclas heard the sadness, but her face remained impassive. He studied her. She didn't look different, except that her lips shone more in the firelight because of her face paint. His instincts had never led him astray, and his gut wasn't screaming at him to leave. Instead, a strong curiosity had him move closer to her and lean in to view the object that was now fading slightly.

"Where's it going?" he asked.

She touched it again, and the colors brightened. He jumped.

"They dim, to save energy. It's complicated, and I'll explain it later, if you truly care to hear it. What's important is this. My family. See, here's Colin—he's not nearly this serious in person. James is right here; he's a healer, and a really good one. We're all proud of him. My aunt…"

Hours later, Nioclas watched Brianagh sleep peacefully. His mind attempted to absorb all he heard from her lips, and as dawn broke, he wondered if he'd imagined the night before.

The black rectangle tucked into his chest was proof he had not.

He had to seek out the one person who could either confirm her stories…or deny them.

His wife was either completely daft with an incredible set of sorcery skills, or she was telling the truth—she truly was from a place where people traveled by metal birds in the sky, horses were ridden for pleasure and not transportation, and women had the same rights as men.

Nioclas didn't like that he had to rely on a man such as Reilly O'Malley to verify his wife's tales, but as O'Malley figured prominently throughout them and was in so many of the magical portraits, he didn't see any other option.

As quietly as possible, he made his way to the wall outside O'Malley's chamber.

No one would speak with Reilly until he did—Nioclas wasn't taking any chances.

"Lovely to see you this morning, Laird MacWilliam. I wonder how long you've been waiting for me," Reilly quipped when he swung open his chamber door. He bowed with a sardonic smile. "What an honor."

"My solar." Nioclas motioned for Reilly to precede him. When they entered, Nioclas shut and latched the door.

Reilly made himself comfortable. "This couldn't wait until after I'd broken my fast?"

"You may eat food from my larder once you've answered my questions sufficiently," Nioclas replied curtly. "Tell me of Brianagh's sixteenth birthday."

Reilly stared at him as though he'd lost his mind.

Nioclas sat opposite of him. "What color was her dress?"

"You expect me to remember the color of her dress? I couldn't tell you the color of the dress she wore yesterday!"

Nioclas sat down, leaned back, and folded his arms silently.

After a charged moment, Reilly muttered, "Yellow."

"What is the name of her university?"

"Which one?" Reilly asked.

Nioclas's eyes narrowed. "All of them."

"Boston University was undergrad. Tufts University was graduate. Bri also did a year at Trinity here in Ireland, on exchange."

"What did she study?"

"Undergraduate degree is in business management, graduate degree in marketing of some sort."

Nioclas let out a breath. "What is marketing?"

Reilly did pause then. "It's the promotion of goods or services. More or less."

The questions continued, hard and fast. Reilly answered all of them in much the same way Brianagh did—openly, without much hesitation, and continued clarification. At some point, Nioclas sent for food. They ate together as Nioclas relentlessly probed further into Brianagh's tales.

Hours later, Nioclas knew, as implausible as it seemed, his wife was telling the truth. He paced, unable to sit still any longer as the ramifications crystallized in his head. He rubbed his forehead and looked out his window at the land before him. Snow had fallen during the night; the sparkle was blinding in the mid-morning sun. Nioclas stared at it, turning the facts over in his mind.

"Brianagh is the key to the O'Rourke legacy," Nioclas said, almost unable to utter the words.

Reilly shook his head. "Not quite."

"Speak plainly," Nioclas said wearily. "I find my mind is at the end of its sanity."

Reilly smiled grimly. "Brianagh isn't the *key* to the legacy. She *is* the legacy." He leaned forward. "Why do you think I've been pushing her so hard to stay here? She can't return—doing so would erase an entire line of time travelers seeking to protect history."

"How can I ask her to stay, when she has so much in the future?"

"She has nothing in the future if she doesn't stay. None of you do."

"How do you fit in? Are you truly an O'Malley?"

Reilly's face shuttered. "I'm the original O'Rourke protector."

"So you're an O'Rourke," Nioclas pressed.

Reilly stood suddenly, slamming his hands on the table and leaning over it, his face inches from Nioclas. "It doesn't matter from whom I hail. All that matters is that I exist to ensure that Brianagh O'Rourke is brought here, to this time, to you…and to ensure she *stays*."

Nioclas narrowed his eyes. "Why me?"

Reilly barked out a laugh and slumped back in his chair. "You're the one from her dreams, MacWilliam. And she's the one from yours, even if you've tried to forget about them."

"What sort of magic is this?" Nioclas demanded, grabbing his sword.

"Powerful magic. I know more about you than even your brother. Do you honestly believe I'd put Brianagh into your arms without knowing everything about you?"

Nioclas's shock hung between them. He slowly re-sheathed his sword.

Reilly stood. "I've given you your answers. It's up to you whether or not to believe what Brianagh and I have told you. Keep her away from the monolithic structures in the east—yes, MacWilliam, the same one from the legacy you can't seem to accept. And know this: if you do somehow get her back to where she claims she wants to be, you will not only destroy her direct line, you'll destroy your own."

"Aidan will carry—"

Reilly shook his head. "No, MacWilliam. Aidan isn't a true bloodline. He has his own destiny, in his own time…and it is not that of a MacWilliam. Keep her away from the structures in the east."

With that, Reilly gave him a bow, then exited the solar, leaving Nioclas gaping after him.

Brianagh found Nioclas in his solar, rubbing something as he stared at it, lost in thought. She knocked hesitantly, and he immediately locked eyes with her.

"Come in. Please, latch the door."

Brianagh stepped in nervously. "When I woke up and saw you weren't in the chamber, I thought…" She paused, then shrugged helplessly. "I didn't know what to think."

"I had to speak with O'Malley."

She bit her lip. "Of course. You verified everything, didn't you?" When he nodded, she wrapped her arms around herself. "Did he also tell you, as he's been telling me, that my destiny is here?"

Nioclas didn't reply. He absentmindedly smoothed his fingers over the object. "Where did you get this?"

The brooch.

"My aunt." A stab of pain lanced her heart as she thought

of her aunt and uncle. "Evelyn. She gave it to me when I accepted Matthew's marriage proposal. She said it was something O'Rourke women wore on their wedding day." Her eyes brimmed with tears at the memory. It felt as though it were a lifetime ago. Corralling her emotions, she swiped an errant tear. "I miss her. I miss them all."

It was true.

"O'Malley is the only family you have left?"

She nodded. "Yes. He and I were always the closest, though. Ry is very protective, like a big brother. He used to threaten any boy who came within ten feet of me—it was awful. But I know he did it out of love."

"To protect you," Nioclas murmured.

"Yes, to protect me." A moment passed as she recognized the truth of it. "I'm not part of a legacy, Nioclas, no matter what Reilly believes."

He didn't respond. "The mark on your arm…"

"Coincidence," she replied firmly, hugging herself even tighter.

Nioclas steepled his fingers, then placed them against his chin. "What about the dreams?"

Bri lost her breath. Of everything she'd told Nioclas, not once did she mention her dreams of him. No one knew, not even Reilly. She blindly groped for the table, needing to sit lest her legs gave out.

She hadn't had a dream of Nioclas since she'd stayed in Reilly's little cottage on the edge of the sea…since she'd arrived in Nioclas's time.

"Dreams?" she managed.

Nioclas picked up the brooch again, running his fingers over the engraved hawk. "We were sitting in the grass by a dark lake. The sun was shining, it was warm, and we had just finished a swim. Our clothes were wet, and we had laid them out to dry." She let out a strangled cry, but he pressed on. "A bird flew overhead. I told you it was a falcon, but you laughed. You told me it was a hawk." He raised his eyes, gray meeting blue. "When I said hawks were malevolent, you shook your head. The sun caught your hair and it seemed as though it were glowing. You looked like a goddess of the sun." He smiled at the memory, but it faded. "You told me that the bird had no markings on its chest—a falcon would have stripes. You said the hawk had markings only on its wings."

Immediately, Brianagh recalled Nioclas in the lists. His chest had no markings…but his arms did. Her gaze flew to his biceps, covered with the sleeves of his tunic.

"Aye. To resemble a hawk."

Her eyes were so wide, she was certain they were going to fall out at any moment. She couldn't catch her breath. The dream he described was the last of what she took to calling "the originals." The lake dream was the last one in a string of repeated dreams. She despaired over dreaming something different, but the ones she did have were sweet enough to last a lifetime. Until the night she dreamed she lost him.

"Nioclas," she started, but he wasn't done.

"I had the brooch made to take with me into battle," he continued, "as a favor, of sorts. I thought if I had you near me, it would protect me from death. I never felt more alive than I did in those dreams."

"I thought I was crazy," she whispered. "When I saw you for the first time, I thought I'd lost my mind."

"Nay." Nioclas sighed. "You did not. I thought I'd lost mine when I had those dreams, and after I'd had this brooch fashioned, I told Aidan that our new clan would bear a hawk on our crest. After a goodly bit of ale"—he laughed humorlessly—"I confessed the dreams. I told him all. Aidan, to his credit, believed you were a sign sent from our mother, to help ease the burden of lairdship." Nioclas looked at her.

"Do you think that's what it was?" she asked softly.

"I don't know. Perhaps." He rubbed his hands over his

face. "Do you understand why O'Malley is so adamant that you remain here with me?"

"He thinks we'll mess up history."

"He believes *you're* the legacy, Brianagh. That you're the one who will pass the ability to move time to your children, and them to theirs."

"He's wrong," she replied stubbornly.

"What if he isn't? There are no coincidences in life, Brianagh. Everything happens for a reason."

"He's wrong," she insisted.

"After all you told me about your family last night, after all you've shown me, I urge you to consider what may happen to them if you are, in fact, the legacy," Nioclas said. "They wouldn't exist, Brianagh."

The reality hit her, but she refused to believe it. "I'm not responsible for generations of people! I'm a matchmaker. That's it. I'm not a legacy!"

"Regardless of whether you are or not, my lady...you have my sword at your feet." Nioclas slid the brooch to her and stood. "For however long you may need it."

CHAPTER 20

Brianagh sat as still as a stone on the battlements, silently staring at the sea. When Erin eventually found her, she'd been there for hours, numb from both her thoughts and the cold.

"Brianagh, you should come inside," Erin said gently, placing a hand on her arm. "It's freezing out here, and you'll catch your death."

"I miss my family," Bri whispered.

Erin sat down next to her, linked her arm through Bri's, and rested her head on her shoulder. "Aye, I know the feeling well. When I married Donovan, I had to leave my clan behind. The first few weeks were wonderful. I had my love. I thought that was enough." She smiled, a faraway look in her eyes. "But by the end of the first month, I missed my daily chats with Mama. I wanted to go back to visit, but Donovan couldn't go, and it's too dangerous to travel that distance without him."

"Have you seen her since you've been back?" Bri asked.

Erin wiped a tear from her cheek. "She died two months after I married." She gave a watery smile. "Nioclas came to tell me himself. He's a good man, Brianagh. You're very lucky to have him as your own."

"He is a good man," Bri replied softly. "That's the trouble."

"If you care to discuss your troubles, I'm right here. And, despite what the heathen brothers think, I can keep a secret better than either of them." They shared a giggle, then sobered. Erin continued. "Really, Bri. You've been so out of sorts lately, but then I see Nick give you the same kind of looks Donovan gives me, and I don't understand. Is it because you miss your family? Are you so far from them?"

"Oh, Erin, you have no idea." Erin rested her head on Bri's shoulder, and Bri sighed, resting her head on top of her friend's. "I wonder if I'll ever see them again. And they don't know what happened to me."

"Did O'Malley take you from them?" Erin asked, concern etching her words.

"No, I went with him on my own." Bri's eyes misted. "But I didn't think I was leaving forever."

"Nick is a very wealthy man, Bri. In times of peace, such as this, he can afford to travel. He's not tight on his purse strings. He keeps his castle simple so as to not draw attention to the clan. Just like he keeps the prosperity of our village to himself—he doesn't want any problems to arise from greedy lairds, or worse, the English crown."

"You don't need to defend him to me, Erin. I think he's one of the very best men I've ever met," Bri replied sadly.

"Then what grieves you, Brianagh? You have a wealthy husband who loves you—"

"He doesn't, Erin."

Erin pulled away and looked at Bri. "I've seen the way he looks at you, Brianagh. He certainly feels something."

Bri shook her head. "Believe me when I tell you he doesn't love me."

Contemplating her, Erin asked, "Do you *want* him to love you?"

Therein was the crux of her problem. As Brianagh had sat on the battlements and let her thoughts wander, that question had come up repeatedly. Did she want the love of any man? What if Matthew was in love with her—could she ever learn to love him back now that her heart belonged to another?

Perhaps that was the cruelest joke of all. While pretending to be in love, she'd actually fallen, and by convincing everyone they were a love match, she secured her ticket home to her family.

Bri started to cry softly. She drew her knees up and buried her face in her arms, then felt Erin's arms around her.

"When my mother died," Erin said quietly as Bri wept, "I felt as though I'd made a mistake in marrying Donovan, because it took me from her. She'd been sick, but no one believed it to be serious. My father died when I was little, and it was just Mama and me most of my life. She cried at my wedding but refused Donovan's offer to come to the Maguire clan. Claimed she was a MacWilliam through and through." She sniffed. "But I see now that she didn't want me to see her suffering. It was selfless and selfish and a million other things I haven't yet found the words for, and may not ever find. But I am comforted in the fact that when I had her, she loved me very much and wanted only the best for me in my life. When she realized I had a love match in Donovan, she pushed Nioclas to secure his hand. She was the best of mothers."

Bri wiped her eyes and took a deep breath, then blew it out slowly. "I'm so sorry, Erin. She sounds like she was a wonderful woman."

"She was. And she always told me to follow my heart first. Perhaps," Erin said after a moment, "if you love him enough, he'll love you in return. Nioclas has had a very difficult life. He needs time and encouragement from a woman who loves him. If your love could be enough until then, I don't think you'll regret it. Eventually, he'll return it threefold, and word of your happiness might reach your family. They would know that you are safe and well-loved. The MacWilliam clan respects you very much—they want you to be one of them. Go to their festivals, hold their babies, dance when minstrels visit the castle. They want that from you, Brianagh, because you are the woman Nioclas chose to wed. And maybe you can find a measure of peace believing that your family will hear of the MacWilliams, who are living a happy, loving life on the edge of the sea in the most beautiful land in the world."

Bri sniffed and put her head on Erin's shoulder, and they sat together, staring at the sea in silence, each lost in her own thoughts.

~

WHEN BRIANAGH AND ERIN RETURNED TO THE CASTLE, THEY were greeted by a very flustered lass running from the kitchens to flag them down.

"What's wrong, Deirdre?" Bri asked, hurrying over.

"There's a line of men waiting to speak with Keela, and she's trying to fix the evening meal!" Deirdre exclaimed. "They won't leave, though. They've demanded to see her, claiming the need to spout poetry or some such nonsense." She wrinkled her nose. "It's out of hand now. They're crowding the kitchens, and we're about to take a knife to them so we can get dinner done!"

Bri and Erin exchanged a look, and then Bri nodded firmly. "Right. I'll handle this. Deirdre, lead the way."

It was worse than Deirdre claimed. The line of men was actually a large cluster, all blocking the way in and out of the kitchen, clamoring to be heard over one other. Bri stifled a laugh. Poor Keela.

"Excuse me," Bri said, tapping the nearest man, who

looked to be somewhere in his sixties.

"Oh, Lady MacWilliam! Of course, aye, aye," he said, elbowing men out of the way. "The lady of the castle wants to get through, move out of the way. Lady of the castle."

Bri felt a little like he was calling, "Watch out, hot coffee!" No one listened.

She placed two fingers in her mouth and whistled once, loud and sharp. Their heads snapped around so fast, Erin let out a giggle.

"Impressive," Erin murmured. "Teach me how to do that?"

Bri grinned at her, then looked at the men. "I'd like to get inside the kitchens, please." They parted like the Red Sea, and she swept through them, Erin following closely behind. "Good sir," Bri called out to one of the men holding a bunch of dead tree branches, "do be so kind as to close the kitchen door behind you."

"I've come to woo the cook," he replied. "I'm not leaving until she agrees to marry me."

The other men began protesting and jostling each other again. Bri gave another whistle, followed by a sweet smile. "Tomorrow, you shall all come to the great hall after the midday meal. There, you will talk with me and answer a series of questions, and Keela will have final choice." She held up her hand at their grumbles. "Be away with you now, if you have any desire to eat whatever that delicious smell is coming from."

The crowd dispersed and the door was shut, albeit reluctantly.

Bri turned to Keela, who was clutching her spoon like a weapon, and gave her a pitying laugh. "Oh, Keela, we have our work cut out for us with that crowd."

Keela shook her head in wonder. "I thought you and the laird would choose a mate for me, my lady. I didn't expect to have to make the decision myself!"

Bri smiled, then got down to business. "Now, Keela, we have a few answers to sort out before we start this process. I need to know where you want to be in the next few years."

Keela's face scrunched up. "Well, here, my lady. In the kitchens of this castle, cooking you and the laird tasty meals. I love it."

Bri nodded, then asked for a piece of parchment and some ink. Her client interview had begun.

~

Awkward.

That was the only word Bri could come up with for her interaction with Nioclas at dinner. She'd hoped he would skip it, but as he was a man who ate as much as he could as often as possible, perhaps missing a meal was a bit of a stretch, even for her hopes.

Luckily, she had Erin to keep the conversation from stalling.

"Nick, we really need to find some musical entertainment tomorrow night," Erin said, reaching for her cup. "It's important—we need dancing and merriment."

"Merriment?" he replied. "Where do you expect me to find a minstrel, Erin?"

She shrugged. "I don't know. You know more people than I do, and you'd be paying them, so I think it's best if you find some."

Nioclas shook his head in resignation. "Truly, this is your life every day," he said to Donovan. "Willingly."

"Aye," Donovan replied cheerfully.

Aidan shook his head in disgust. "You two are perfect for each other."

"Thanks." Erin beamed.

"Do you mind if I invite minstrels to the castle?" Nioclas asked Bri quietly.

"Oh, of course not," she replied quickly. "We need them to help Keela decide who she's interested in marrying."

He looked at her as if she'd gone mad. "I don't think I care to know the details."

"Probably not, as it involved about fifty men from the clan standing around the door of the kitchens." Erin smiled at him. "But don't worry, Nick. Bri cleared them all out so Keela could continue to make our supper, and she got a lot of questions answered about what Keela wants from her husband, so we have plenty with which to work. It's going to be so fun."

"Fun?" he asked.

"Aye. Bri taught me the word. It means full of cheer."

"Fascinating." Nioclas turned his eyes on Brianagh. She blushed. "I look forward to this fun. I'll see to your minstrels, Erin, and perhaps a juggler or two for sport."

Erin clapped her hands together. "Thank you, Nick! Donovan, you'll dance with me?"

"I'll be the only one to dance with you," he growled playfully.

She giggled, and Bri smiled wistfully at them. It was so cute to watch a grizzled warrior such as Donovan act so in love and not bat an eye at it.

"Is Reilly planning to join us?" Brianagh asked to no one in particular.

"He's making preparations to leave on the morrow," Aidan replied with a self-satisfied grin. "I think he's stayed long enough, myself."

Brianagh's eyes widened, and she grabbed Nioclas's arm. "Did you send him away?"

He shook his head. "Nay, Lady Brianagh. He made this decision himself."

"Do excuse me," she said hastily, standing up. "I must go find him."

"I'll escort you." Nioclas rose after her.

Bri walked silently beside him. The only sounds once they left the great hall were those of his boots and her slippers on the stone. She felt she should say something, but words escaped her. Nioclas, for his part, remained silent as well.

Knocking on Reilly's chamber door, Nioclas opened it at his call and brought Brianagh inside.

"Were you planning to say goodbye?" she asked without preamble.

Reilly shoved his hands through his hair. "Brianagh, I can't stay. I have to go back."

She narrowed her eyes. "Back where, Reilly? Back to where I came from? Or another time?"

Reilly shoved the last of his belongings into a satchel on his mattress. "Bri, my duty is done, and no matter how much I wish to see you every day, I can't. That's not my destiny." He glanced at Nioclas. "What I'm about to give her must remain locked in a trunk, never to be seen by any but you and Brianagh. It will get you killed."

Nioclas peered at the object. It was a shiny portrait of Brianagh, Reilly, another woman, and three grown men. The garb was most unusual—Brianagh had a skirt that displayed her calves, and deadly looking shoes with spikes. Her arms were also bare.

He handed it over to her accusingly, and after just a look, she burst into tears.

"What is the meaning of this?" Nioclas demanded.

"You see why you can't show this to anyone," Reilly replied dryly. "Aside from the fact that your wife's legs are showing…that's a photograph. A portrait from the future."

"See? This is my aunt Evelyn, and my uncle Connor. And that's Colin, and James, and of course Reilly," Brianagh managed through her sobs. "I miss them so much."

"How many portrait painters do you have in the future?" Nioclas wondered aloud. He glanced at his sniffling wife, then sighed. "I'll let you say your goodbyes in peace." When the chamber door shut, Reilly grabbed her in a bear hug. "Bri, I'll explain everything to them. They'll understand—well, Evelyn will, anyway. And they'll see it in the history books how well you fared."

She couldn't see through her tears, but as she was pressed against Reilly's chest, it didn't really matter. "Please don't leave me."

Reilly's eyes were suspiciously wet. "Bri, I can't promise I'll see you again. But if the Fates allow it, I'll be back sometime in your future."

"I don't want to stay," she mumbled into his chest.

"I know," Reilly whispered, "and it's killing me to leave you. But I can't stay, Brianagh. I can't."

She wept into him for a while longer, then finally pulled back, her nose red and her eyes puffy. "I love you, Ry. But please take me back. I don't belong here."

"I love you too, Bri." He kissed her forehead. "This is your home—you *do* belong here. Make the bastard admit his love for you so I don't have to come back and skewer him on the business end of my sword."

"Keep practicing in your garden," she said with a half-hearted laugh.

"You knew?" he asked incredulously.

She nodded, then stepped back. "Of course. I know more than you give me credit for!"

"As do I, Bri." He kissed her one more time before opening the door.

"I'll find my way back home," she warned him, wiping the tears from her cheeks.

"I can't be a part of that."

"Then I'll do it without you."

He opened the door and ushered her out. "I pray you do not. Goodbye, Brianagh."

She stared at the door as hopelessness enveloped her.

CHAPTER 21

It was snowing.

Brianagh wondered how long the snow would stay on the ground. She had only a month and a half left before Nioclas would take her to Dowth. Would he travel all the way across the country if there was snow on the ground? What kind of danger would she put him and his guard in, if they were to get sick in weather like this?

Concerns aside, it was a beautiful sight, the untouched sea of white. What already covered the ground sparkled, and the flakes drifting lazily from the sky reminded her of a painting she saw in Dublin on her first trip to Ireland, when she was just a young girl.

Bri sat at the alcove window, dressed in her nightgown but wrapped tightly in her fur-lined cloak, the shutters thrown wide. Idly, she wondered if medieval Ireland celebrated Christmas. Surely not in the same way she was used to—presents, Santa Claus, the crowds at the mall—but did they have anything to mark the passing of the holiday? She didn't even know what the precise date was. All she knew was that it was late December 1457.

Suddenly, she very much wanted to know the exact date.

Had her days become so blended that she couldn't keep track? She missed the feeling of productivity. Although she certainly had figured out how to keep herself busy, she hadn't gotten that same euphoria she experienced after a dedicated search and placing two perfectly matched souls together.

Happy sighs. That's what she was missing.

Stretching, Brianagh closed the shutters and shucked the cloak. She had a chance at both the happy sighs and the productivity today with Keela's upcoming screening. Phase two of matching: the significant other. Bri opened her trunk to pull out her dress, but what she pulled out was something entirely unexpected.

The long gown made of deep blue and gold silk rustled as she shook it out. Gold braids lined the seams, and the sleeves were sheer from elbow to wrist. It looked like something Erin wore from her trunk of a thousand dresses. Bri teased her about it almost daily.

A note fluttered to the ground. Picking up the parchment, she read:

B – Your sleeves were torn in your old dress, and the hem on another. The third was simply ugly, so I had them all placed in the rag bin. You should dress beautifully every day. – N

She touched the fabric again. It was well-made, with strong fabric. She smiled, grateful for his thoughts of her comfort.

Bri slipped the dress over her head and ran her hands over the gown. It was beautiful on the outside, but the skirt had a light fur lining—deliciously warm and perfect for a snowy day. She pulled out the new shoes and slid them on. They were sturdier than her old slippers, and much warmer too. They also had a fur lining.

For the first time in a long time, Brianagh felt warm from head to toe. It was a heady feeling.

Opening the door, she found Nioclas leaning against the

wall. He smiled when he saw her, then gave a little bow. "I see you found your new wardrobe."

"It's beautiful." She grinned, spinning. "But even more, it's warm. Thank you!"

"Entirely my pleasure," Nioclas replied. "I ordered them a few weeks ago, but just received them last night. I'd hoped they would cheer you."

"Them? You mean there's more than one?"

"Aye, the seamstresses should be bringing them to the castle this morning. I've had a few made in colors I thought would suit you. Do they suit?"

Smiling, she nodded her head. "Absolutely, thank you. It's very kind of you, but I admit, I'd be worried about moving tables around in this!"

"I am glad to hear it," Nioclas said with a smile. "Shall we eat? I find I'm eager to hear of your plans for the men who are taking up space in my great hall."

"Taking up space?" Bri echoed.

"Aye. O'Malley said it to Aidan last week, before he left. I thought it fitting for what's happening in my castle."

Nioclas wasn't joking. The men were crowded in the great hall, talking loudly in groups. Some were relaxed, others seemed to be practicing verses of poetry—and all turned to them as they descended the stairs.

"Carry on." Nioclas waved at them. He winked at Bri. "We aren't going to eat here. I've set us a table in a much quieter locale."

Bri was still trying to recover from the wink when he led her outside into the falling snow. She turned her face up and caught a snowflake on her tongue, then blushed when she caught Nioclas staring.

"I used to do it when I was a girl," she explained sheepishly. "The first snow of the season, and Colin, James, and I would run outside to see who could catch the first one. Force of habit."

"We will need to have speech about that," Nioclas said quietly, steering her toward the kitchens, "but perhaps not until tomorrow. Today, you have your matching to accomplish."

"Matchmaking," she corrected him. "And yes, you're right. Did you—"

"Aye, there were minstrels about last night, and I managed to procure them for an evening of..." Nioclas trailed off, trying to remember the word.

"Fun," Bri supplied.

"Aye. An evening of fun. And tomorrow, we shall have speech."

"Thank you," she said softly. At his bemused look, she said, "For giving me today. Speaking of, do you know the day of the month?"

"It's two days before the solstice," he replied, ushering her into the kitchen, where the prep table was set for them.

About a week until Christmas, then.

She hoped her family would celebrate. She hoped they weren't so worried about her that they couldn't enjoy the season - it was Evelyn's favorite time of the year.

Bri breathed in the scent of freshly baked bread and forced her shoulders to relax. She caught sight of Keela and immediately smiled at her frazzled countenance.

Squaring her shoulders, Bri sat down and began to outline their plan of attack.

ERIN SAT NEXT TO BRIANAGH ON THE RAISED DAIS, LOOKING OVER the fifty-seven candidates they were preparing to question. "This is a wonder," she whispered. "I can't believe how many men are here."

Bri shuffled her parchment, then smiled. "Keela is young, pretty, and can fill a man's belly with the best-tasting food in

Ireland. The only thing that surprises me is that there aren't more."

Bri already went through the initial list with Keela, who had agreed for the selected ones today to be interviewed. Brianagh called the first man—she decided to call them alphabetically by first name, to ensure everyone had their chance. She explained to Erin that she would first ask a standard set of questions; then, if she thought he might be a potential match, another, smaller set of more personal questions.

Back home, Bri also explained that this was her cousin Colin's job. She claimed he was talented at figuring out how genuine a person was in his or her desire to find a soul mate. Ironic, she had laughed, that he couldn't ever seem to find someone of his own. Brianagh thought his standards might be impossibly high, but he claimed otherwise.

After hearing about how many women were interested in Sir Colin, Erin tended to agree with Brianagh.

Bri began to question Annan. Four questions in, Erin realized he was more interested in finding a mother for his seven children than love. Understandable, but not for Keela. Bri must have agreed, for she quickly concluded his interview and moved on to the next.

Erin watched with fascination. She listened as Brianagh asked questions, sized them up, then made decisions based on she-only-knew what. Some men were looking for a good meal, some were looking for the status Keela would bring his family as the laird's cook, and still others were looking to start a family of their own. Brianagh treated them all with the same kind, patient smile that would form when a suitor asked her if he was one of the chosen ones. She refused to give any indication as to who would be in what she called her Top Five, but Erin had a good idea, based upon the amount of writing Brianagh made on her parchment.

At one point, Erin leaned over and asked, "Did you learn to write in a convent?"

"No," Bri whispered back, scribbling furiously. "Kindergarten."

Erin nodded as if she understood. Kindergarten sounded like a place of learning. She'd have to see about Donovan taking her there. Erin had never met any woman in Ireland who could read, much less write, as quickly as Brianagh was at the moment. Perhaps Kindergarten was the name of Brianagh's homeland. She was very tight-lipped about it, but Erin figured it caused too much pain for her to speak of it, so she didn't ask.

Two very long hours later, Brianagh declared them finished and thanked the last man in line. He bowed, then joined the other men at the far end of the great hall.

"I shall announce the five men we've selected tonight at dinner. Those five men will be allowed to dance with our fair Keela during the evening's entertainments."

"When will we find out if we get to marry her?" one of them called out.

"When Keela determines which one of you she'll have," Erin said loftily. "It is, after all, her choice to make. We're simply aiding her."

The silence in the room was deafening, then a loud burst of laughter broke out. Brianagh scanned the men and quickly wrote some more. She glanced up at Erin. "Clever."

"What?"

Bri gathered the parchment again and stepped down from the dais. "Those who laughed clearly don't see her as her own person. More like property."

"You realize that we are just that," Erin pointed out. At Bri's exasperated stare, she said, "What? It's true. We're sold much like cattle, only we are given a single owner. A husband can beat his wife if he so chooses and none could save her."

Bri shuddered at that thought. "I thought you had Brehon law?"

"We do, but it's only enforced if the laird allows it. So you see, it could always be worse," Erin chirped, holding the door of the solar open. "Let's ensure Keela doesn't suffer a fate like that."

"I don't believe the laird would allow it," Bri growled.

"Well, as you'll be there to ensure it, I believe you," Erin replied with a grin.

CHAPTER 22

"My lady, I don't mean to sound ungrateful..." Keela began, wincing as the minstrel's voice cracked mid-note.

"No," Brianagh replied. "I understand. Truly." She searched out Nioclas and saw him holding up the back wall with Donovan and Aidan. She gave him a pleading look, and after saying something to the others, he pushed off and strolled to the minstrel. A moment later, the minstrel snapped his mouth shut, bowed deferentially to Nioclas, and moved into the crowd. Brianagh was certain she wasn't the only one who breathed an audible sigh of relief.

"How are we to encourage dancing if there's no music?" Erin asked, patting Keela's hand but shooting a worried look to Bri.

Bri was watching her husband speak to one of the other minstrels. She smiled as she saw what he was about. Turning to Erin and Keela, she replied, "I don't think we need to worry very much. Our laird is taking care of it now."

They watched as a small harp was brought to the center of the floor, and a man carried a stool to it. He sat down, cracked his knuckles, and placed his fingers on the strings. A hauntingly beautiful sound immediately silenced the room.

Brianagh was so lost in the music she didn't notice Nioclas come up behind her on the dais, and she nearly jumped out of her skin when he placed his hands on her shoulders. He was every inch the respected laird. He stood tall, his bearing regal, and he watched the musician without expression.

But then he glanced down at Bri, caught her staring at him, and bestowed a quick, soft smile for her alone that sent her heart into double-time and parched her throat. She smiled weakly back at him before turning back to the harpist—and realized they were on display for the entire clan.

The game. Of course. She pasted a smile on her face.

Once the song ended, the singing minstrel joined the harpist, but thankfully with a lute in hand. They began another song, and people began to crowd the space, forming lines and couples in a semblance of a dance. One of Keela's suitors asked her to dance, and she allowed him to lead her to the makeshift dance floor.

"Care you to dance, my lady?" Nioclas asked, his voice low in her ear so only she could hear.

"No thank you," Brianagh replied, irrationally hurt that he didn't really care for her, that he was still just putting on a show.

She was actually irritating herself with her twisted logic. She didn't want to stay, but she wanted the man to fall in love with her. That was all kinds of not okay, and she needed to check herself, stat.

He leaned down and, into her ear, whispered, "Was the minstrel so terrible that he ruined your good humor, my lady?"

The man's nearness was a danger to her health. Her heart was pounding, and she couldn't catch a proper breath.

Why must I react this way to him? she lamented, hopelessly confused as to what she wanted.

"No. I don't know the steps," she finally said, her eyes never leaving the dancers.

"Allow me to teach you?" Without waiting for a response, he tugged her up and led her onto the floor. The tempo was quick, and all around her, people were dancing and laughing.

Merriment.

Bri let herself be led into the slightly chaotic dance, apologizing when she stepped on or bumped into someone and enjoying the fact that no one seemed to care if she had any rhythm. One of the clan elders spun her away from Nioclas, and she was passed from person to person. She attempted to learn each clansman's own way of dancing, and they loved that she was allowing them to teach her. Nioclas retreated to the outskirts of the dancers, watching her with amusement.

Brianagh tripped and landed in the arms of Aidan, who was smirking at her breathlessness.

Any residual irritation faded at his laughing green eyes. "I believe it's my turn to show you how an Irishman dances," he said, his eyes twinkling as the minstrels changed songs. The tempo was slightly faster, and Aidan led her back to the center of the dancers. The crowd made room for the two of them, and Aidan grinned at her. "As his brother, you realize that my most important duty is to annoy our laird," he explained. He grabbed her by the hands, spun her in a little circle, then proceeded to dance with her without removing his hands from her own. He urged her to go faster, then slower, then faster again, to the claps and cheers from the clan around them.

Aidan spun her once more, then started laughing as he bumped into Nioclas. "My laird," he said with a barely contained grin.

"I believe my wife has had enough of your dancing," Nioclas replied, unruffled, as he held out his hand to Brianagh.

She took it without thinking. "I think I've had enough dancing in general," she said. "I need a drink!"

"Then a drink you shall have," Nioclas replied, his own smile tugging at the corner of his lips. "Come, my lady, and let us get you some wine."

"Wine makes me hot."

He pulled her close so he could whisper in her ear. "I believe I have something in the cellars that may cool you…or make you burn even more. I'll leave the decision to you."

Brianagh stared at him, open-mouthed. Just when she convinced herself to stop with all the feelings, he whispered things to her. Things that no one could hear, for her ears only.

She didn't understand what he was doing, and just like that, she was twisted up again.

"But," Nioclas continued slowly, unaware of her inner turmoil, "not until later, perhaps. For now, you should sit, and I'll ensure you have refreshment brought over." He thoughtfully rolled his lip between his thumb and forefinger.

"O-okay," she stuttered, distracted by what his thumb was doing to his lip. Back, forth, back, forth, back—

"Brianagh," Nioclas said, dipping his head to capture her eyes with his. "Go. Sit."

"Oh! Right." She gave her head a little shake, and while walking back to the high table, she realized he'd done the lip thing on purpose and found herself cursing him again. If he was playing the game for his clansmen, he was winning at it.

Bri wasn't competitive by nature, but she didn't like to lose. And, as she certainly wasn't on the winning team at the moment…

She cast a glance over her shoulder and caught the smoldering look Nioclas was casting her. She bit her lip seductively, winked at him, then basked in his surprise.

Two were supposed to play at this game.

~

BRIANAGH DRAGGED HERSELF UPSTAIRS, CONGRATULATING herself on a night well done. Keela had the time of her life, and even her mother, who sat and watched from the side, had herself a good time. Although Aoife couldn't dance, Kane MacWilliam paid much attention to her. He flirted with the old woman, made her laugh, and fetched her drinks as though she were a queen.

Impressive. Kane was observant enough of Keela to notice her life revolved around her mother, and that earned bonus points in Bri's book. And it was a clever move. By paying attention to her mother, he was guaranteed Keela's attention without having to fight for it. Double points for him.

Bri latched the door shut, then turned—and nearly jumped out of her skin when she saw Nioclas sitting by the hearth.

"That was a very long night," he said by way of greeting.

She let out a breath, then smiled proudly. "It was, wasn't it? In the very best way, though. I think Kane will be wonderful for Keela."

"He is one of my most loyal guardsmen," Nioclas agreed, "and he is one of our best warriors. It will make it easier for them, as they both live on castle grounds now."

Bri wrinkled her forehead. "I didn't think of where they're going to live."

Nioclas laughed. "Brianagh, must you be the one to figure it all out?"

She shrugged and joined him in front of the fire. "Usually, yes."

"Not this time," Nioclas promised. "As it's my castle, I'll find a place for Keela and her husband, whoever he turns out to be. After reading those"—he pointed to the sheaves of parchment by the alcove—"I am more inclined to lean toward your matching all my men!"

"Why do you say that?" Bri asked, not bothering to fight her smile.

"Donovan said something quite interesting tonight while we were listening to that poor soul attempt to sing."

Bri winced in memory. "He was terrible, wasn't he? I felt so badly for him. He wanted to make such a good impression on you."

"He should have started with the lute," Nioclas said, rubbing his ear absently.

"And stayed with it," Bri laughed.

"Absolutely." Nioclas chuckled. Turning serious, he added, "Do you ever wonder why men battle?"

"Well," Bri replied, thinking. "I've always thought it was for power. Then gold, then land."

"Perhaps those are the reasons men attack. But why do men who have none of those fight?" Nioclas asked. Before Bri could respond, he answered his own question. "Donovan believes it's for a man's own home and a good woman to share it with. And I think…I think I fight to protect my clan's right to that. But lately, Brianagh, I've been wanting more. I've been wanting that for myself." He paused, then gently touched her cheek. "I am not a man who wants what others have. I've worked for everything because of my clan, because they trusted in me when I was very young, and to repay them, I've dedicated my life to their happiness, their peace."

Brianagh closed her eyes against the prick of tears.

"But I've found that their happiness doesn't lead me to a full life," he whispered. "I watch Erin and Donovan—he isn't less of a laird because of her. He's more. He's better because he has an even stronger reason to protect what's his."

Brianagh nodded. "I think you're right."

"Aye. It took me my entire life to realize what that means." Nioclas paused, gently brushing her cheek with the back of his scarred hand. "I think you might be my more, Brianagh." He gently kissed away the tears on her cheeks and whispered, "End this game, Brianagh. It's become too real. Consider staying here, with me. Don't answer me now. I know I ask a lot, perhaps I ask more than I even understand. Just let me show you…"

And then his lips were on hers, and she was kissing him back. He responded, pulling her closer, his hands tightening on her waist, then removing the pins from her hair. He combed it with his fingers, his mouth never leaving hers. He deepened the kiss, tangling their tongues. Breathless moments later, he pulled his head back and silently searched her eyes, imploring wordlessly.

She closed her own again and kissed him with every ounce of passion in her soul.

Nioclas swept Brianagh into his arms and carried her to the bed, where he followed her down onto the feather mattress. As they helped each other out of their clothes, there was no need for words. They explored each other by firelight, with small sighs and intense kisses.

And when Nioclas finally entered into her and made her his, and he hers, he knew he would give up everything for her. He could only hope she would be willing to give up everything for him.

CHAPTER 23

Late the next afternoon, Brianagh found herself on the battlements again. It was the most private place she could go to think. Not many people liked the dizzying heights, and the guards stayed clear of her. She'd been dogged all morning by her personal guard, and while she understood Nioclas wanted to protect her, she wasn't able to go more than a few steps without everyone following her.

It was frustrating. She needed some time to process what happened.

She'd slept with Nioclas.

The realization was sobering in the light of day. But, she readily admitted to herself, she wouldn't take it back. It was the most amazing night of her life, but it was also the most complicated. She loved him—it physically hurt her chest to think of leaving. But it hurt to think of staying, too. She'd have to give up everything. Losing her family would be the hardest. Being forced to fully give up her family in order to gain her love was more than unfair.

But the hard truth was that Brianagh knew if she lost Nioclas, she would lose herself too. He was a part of her soul. She knew it all the way to her bones.

It was a lot to digest.

"My lady, I'm so glad I found you! One of the women in the village needs you immediately!"

Bri jolted out of her revelations and found one of the guardsmen making his way up the battlement steps. "What's the matter, Odhran?"

"A childbirth is not going well. Lady Maguire is in the village with the woman now, but has asked for you."

"Lady Maguire?" Bri asked, standing carefully. "What's she doing there?"

Odhran shrugged, helping her down the narrow stairs. "I'm not certain, my lady. But Lady Maguire did say it was urgent that you join her immediately."

"Laird MacWilliam said I'm not to leave the castle without the rest of the guard."

"No time, my lady!" Odhran said sharply, then quickly bowed his head. "Forgive me. The villagers are superstitious. If the babe dies and Lady Maguire is thought to have cursed it, she'll be drowned before the laird is any wiser. If you are there, you can dispute any claims, and your word is law."

Brianagh's eyes nearly popped out of her head and she urged him forward. "Let's go, Odhran," she replied firmly. "Erin will not be accused of anything if I have anything to say about it."

They hurried through the bailey, and when they reached the outer gate, the guardsman refused to let them out. "Strict orders not to let Lady MacWilliam out without the entire personal guard!" he shouted down apologetically.

Brianagh threw her hands on her hips. "I command you to open this gate at once!" she called back. "This is an emergency, and I need to get to the village immediately!"

The man looked skeptical.

Brianagh almost stamped her foot in frustration. Erin was probably with the poor woman now, comforting her in her last moments and worrying about being burned to a crisp if someone claims she killed the woman.

"Sir, look here! I'm with Odhran. He is one of my guardsmen, and he will be enough until the others can catch up. Open the gate!"

Something in her voice must have tipped the gatekeeper off, that she truly was heading into an emergency, and he reluctantly opened the gate and lowered the drawbridge. She hurried through and turned toward the village, but stopped when Odhran put his arm on hers.

"Nay, my lady, we must take a safer route, as it is just me to protect you. We'll go around, through the forest," Odhran said, casting glances around them.

"If you think that's best," Bri replied uncertainly. She looked over at the forest, which was covered in fresh snow from last night. "It's getting dark. Let's hurry."

She followed him into a thick copse of trees, carefully picking her way over tree roots and fallen branches. After a few minutes, she looked around. She had a terrible sense of direction, but even she knew they weren't headed toward the village. "Odhran, I think this is the wrong way!"

He caught her by the arm as she lost her footing, then righted her…but didn't let go. "Nay, we are not."

Her heart lodged in her throat and she tried to shake him off her arm, but he tightened his grip and drew his sword. "Do not fight, or scream." The sword glinted in the dying light of day. "Just come with me, and I won't have to hurt you."

"Odhran, what are you doing?" she whispered, her voice shaking.

"By morning, your husband will be dead. I'm ensuring you get to the new laird before that happens," he replied, dragging her deeper into the forest.

"Dead?" Her heart plummeted to her knees. All around her, night was falling fast. She had to release herself from his grasp and somehow run fast enough to get away from him. She could follow their footprints back to the castle, if she could see them.

Odhran stopped suddenly, then cocked his head. "We wait here."

"Please, Odhran, just bring me back. I won't tell Nioclas, I promise," she babbled, trying to work her arm free. She was going to have a huge bruise there; his grip was overly tight. "He'll come looking for me, you know!"

"I'll gag you, if you don't stop talking," Odhran growled. "He can't look for you if he's dead."

Brianagh recoiled and tried to control her breathing as they waited for whatever—or whomever—they were there to meet. Reilly was right—she really was too trusting of people. She vowed that would stop once she was free.

If she ever was freed.

"You've done as I've asked," said a voice from her right.

Brianagh whipped her head around, and her heart started hammering.

A short, stocky man with beady eyes appeared from nowhere. His balding head shone in the moonlight, and his beard covered most of his face. Brianagh couldn't make out his features very well, but all the hair on her neck stood up.

"Give her to me."

"Not until I get my gold," Odhran replied.

The man chuckled. "Your payment. Of course." He withdrew a small bag and dropped it into Odhran's outstretched hand. "You'll do well in our new clan." The man grabbed Brianagh by her other arm, and Odhran let her go.

Bile rose in her throat as she realized she'd just been sold.

"Please let me go," she whispered. "My husband will give you anything you want, I promise!"

"Stop talking," the man said curtly. "Odhran, the battle has started." Odhran nodded, then turned away. The man clucked his tongue. "Pity you won't be there to see it." In a flash, he buried a sword into Odhran's back. Brianagh covered her mouth and watched in horror as the snow around him turned red.

"Move," the man commanded.

She bit her lip to keep from crying out and stumbled when he pushed her in front of him. She regained her footing, and kept moving. The bloody sword in the man's hand left her no choice in the matter.

~

"We're under attack!" Aidan exclaimed, bursting into Nioclas's solar. "I see Kildare colors…and Burke's."

Nioclas swore. "I should've known he would ally himself with Kildare."

Donovan skidded up to Aidan, panting. "Erin is locked in her chamber with the other women, but Brianagh left the castle."

Nioclas's stomach dropped. "What do you mean left the castle?"

"She's gone. Many people told me she left with Odhran for the village, about an hour ago, and no one has seen her since."

Nioclas slammed his fists onto the table, causing the inkwell to tip onto a stack of parchment. "Just Odhran? Did the gatekeeper let her out?"

"He's dead," Donovan said.

Nioclas swore again. Battle cries floated up to the chamber, and he grabbed his sword. "Burke came for Brianagh—secure the stairs!" Nioclas called to Donovan as he and Aidan ran from the room. They charged down the steps, directly into a full-fledged attack. Releasing a battle cry, they jumped into the fray, Nioclas shouting orders as he fought to get through the great hall.

He had to find Brianagh before Burke did, but if he knew

his sire, he probably already had her.

"Kildare, put down your sword!" Nioclas called out, spying the laird near the front door, clearly waiting for him. "You're losing your men in a wasted battle!"

"Never!" Kildare spat. "You've ruined my daughter! Our honor is lost!"

If he wasn't so busy fending off two Kildares bent on killing him, Nioclas would've shaken his head. He'd seen men go to war for less, but he felt compelled to yell, "I didn't ruin your daughter. She will make a perfectly good wife to someone else. I offered you alliance—wasn't that enough?"

"How can we ally with one who would steal his own sire's bride while being promised to another?" Kildare sneered as Nioclas finished off both men with a clean swipe across their bellies.

"My sire has no bride."

"Oh, he does. The O'Rourke lass, MacWilliam—you stole her from his bedroom!"

Nioclas's eyes narrowed. "You are a fool, Kildare. I offered you alliance, and you chose to listen to a murderer instead. 'Tis truly a bad decision…and I rescued her from his oubliette. Which," he said as he crossed blades with the man, "is a far less dangerous place than his bed."

"When I am laird of your people," Kildare said as he leapt backward to avoid Nioclas's lethal swing, "I will ensure they know what a treacherous man you are!"

"Treachery?" Nioclas barked out a laugh. "If you need to know about treachery, look no further than my sire. Pray tell, where is he while your men die all around you?"

"Rescuing his bride from the likes of you," Kildare replied smugly.

Nioclas felt his first true fear since he held a sword to his father's throat twenty-two years ago.

"I do not want to kill you," Nioclas warned, "but you've

put my wife into danger. I suggest you pull your men out of my castle and go home with your tails between your legs."

Kildare narrowed his eyes. "We stay until I can carry your head back to put on my spike."

Nioclas smiled grimly and with renewed purpose. "Not the right answer."

~

HOURS LATER, DONOVAN MET NIOCLAS IN THE STABLES. BOTH were covered in blood. Wearily, they looked out over the bailey. Bodies lay strewn about the courtyard, as they did in the great hall. They were lucky that only a dozen MacWilliams were lost. Kildare and Nioclas's sire did not realize how prepared his men were to jump into battle.

With Kildare dead, there was only one soul left that needed dispatching to avenge his clansmen's deaths and his wife's kidnapping. Nioclas wiped his sword on the dirt.

"Where do you think he took her?" Donovan asked, resting his head against one of the stalls.

"What I'm about to tell you goes no farther than this building," Nioclas said, "and I tell you because I trust you more than any other, save my brother." He took a deep breath. "Brianagh is the O'Rourke legacy—she's from the future. She and O'Malley lived there until the day she was thrown into my sire's dungeon. I have proof of it, but I cannot show you. You must trust my word. According to O'Malley, Brianagh can move time, although he's not sure if she knows that. What she knows is that her children will have the ability, and that I'm the fated one to give her those children. They traveled here using an ancient structure in the east—and that is where Burke laid in wait for them. He knew where to find her—I don't know how. I believe he'll try to take her back there, then try to get her to move time to return to a time when he could easily kill me."

Donovan was staring at Nioclas as though he'd lost his mind. "Nioclas, did you take a blow to your head?"

Nioclas closed his eyes. "I wish I did," he replied quietly. "But nay. I did not."

"A structure," Donovan echoed. "In the east."

Nioclas shot him a glare. "Yes, Maguire. In the east."

"You think she's the one!" Disbelief was written all over Donovan's face. "The key to the O'Rourke legacy?"

Nioclas looked him in the eye. "She's not the key to the legacy, Donovan. She *is* the legacy." At Donovan's stare, he groaned. "For the love of all that is holy, are you going to help me get her back or not?"

"Of course," Donovan replied. "And then we'll attempt to locate your mind."

"Arse," Nioclas muttered as Aidan came bounding into the stables.

"It's over, Nick, and we've lost thirteen—seven guards, six villagers. The others are cleaning up and I'll have all the Kildares and Burkes brought back to the Kildare land. They'll bring Kildare first."

"His wife will be relieved at his death," Donovan said quietly.

"As will his daughter," Nioclas agreed. "Perhaps they can breathe easier, knowing he's dead. Let's go get Brianagh before our sire does her serious harm."

Aidan shook his head. "Nick, he probably doesn't know about her."

"Never underestimate that man," Nioclas replied darkly. "He knows. And I think he's taking her east."

"Didn't O'Malley tell you to keep her away from there?" Aidan asked cautiously.

"Aye, and I'm worried." He quickly outlined his thoughts to Aidan. "We can't let him change history."

"Nay," Aidan agreed, opening the stall for his own horse and mounting it. "We cannot."

"Donovan, travel southwest, toward Burke's lands. I need to cover every part of this country. Leave Bri's guard with Erin and take your men. If you find Burke, don't hesitate. Just kill him where he stands and bring the body back here." Nioclas swung around to his brother. "Aidan, you'll travel east with me. With seven less guardsmen, I'll need you guarding my back against him."

"We meet back here in a sennight," Donovan said, "or send a messenger with news. Godspeed, MacWilliams."

Aidan grasped Donovan's hand, then turned to Nioclas. "Eastward. Lead on."

CHAPTER 24

Brianagh had no idea where she was headed, but she had a suspicion she was being held for ransom.

It was the only logical explanation she could come up with for the events of the last twenty-four hours. When she gathered the courage to ask what her kidnapper wanted from her, he merely smiled and drew his sword across her upper arm.

As far as fear tactics went, it was highly successful. She did little more than breathe from that point on. At some point during the night, three men on horseback joined them, closing ranks around her and her captor.

His guard.

Her arm stopped bleeding a few hours after he sliced her. It ached abominably, but she knew it was not as deep as it felt. He'd merely scratched her to prove he was serious and scare her into silence. She hated that it worked, but she thought he really might kill her.

From the small snippets of conversations the men had, one of them finally said her captor's name.

Burke.

A whole new wave of fear shook her. Burke—the same man who threw her into his dungeon—apparently had some issue with her that she couldn't quite figure out. But when they finally dismounted and he tied her wrists together with a rope, she realized she didn't have to.

"We will sleep here tonight. These men here have their orders. If you try to run, they will not kill you." Burke yanked her against him, putting his face inches from hers. "They will hold you down and take turns having their way with you. And when they're done, I'll have my turn, and you'll wish it was them again."

He leaned back and grinned, taking a deep breath in. "I love the smell of your fear, Lady O'Rourke. Or do you prefer Lady MacWilliam? That's not truly a clan name, anyway. I removed them when the woman I married proved inept." He leaned forward once more, his beady eyes glittering in the moonlight. "I hope you don't prove to be inept."

She shook her head frantically, and he shoved her to the ground. "Sleep there," he barked, "and don't make any noise." He indicated to one of the other men. "We camp here for a few hours, then move again. You'll take first watch." Burke made himself a bed of blankets he pulled from the saddlebags and laid down. Blowing her a kiss, he whispered, "Sleep well, my lady. Tomorrow, we ride for Dublin."

Brianagh dozed but never fully slept. Each time she opened her eyes, Burke was smiling at her. Her stomach roiled at the sight and sweat trickled down her back. She had to figure out a way to get away from him. If she had to die, she wanted it to be trying to get back to Nioclas and not at the hands of his deranged enemy.

As dawn broke, Brianagh was back on the horse. Her wrists were chafed raw from the bindings. When his horse couldn't run as fast as he wanted, Burke decided it was time for a new horse. He redirected them to a village where he very pleasantly stole a new horse—after reminding her of his skill with a sword and of her fate if she were to run.

She was allowed to place her hands inside her cloak during the half hour it took for him to purchase the horse with a bag of gold coins. And after he checked the inside of her cloak for anything she may have picked up in the village, he allowed her to keep her hands inside.

The man's changeability was as frightening as his sword.

Two days into their ride, Brianagh was at the end of her rope—literally. She'd worked her fingernails to the quick scratching at the fibers, and she was nearly through them. She hadn't a clue as to her whereabouts, but as Burke repeatedly stroked his sword in a loving way, she thought it best to get away from him as soon as possible.

She'd been devising ways for two and a half days, but the man was vigilant in his watch. He even watched her go to the bathroom in a cold, calculated way.

She was tired of being frightened. It was exhausting.

Bri thought if he was going to kill her, he would've done so already. Also, if he was going to use her as bait to get to Nioclas and *then* kill her, he'd be going much slower so Nioclas could catch up.

All her self-defense classes were useless—they were taught with modern-day amenities. She didn't have her car keys to jab in his eye, she didn't have any heels to slam into his foot, and she didn't have a can of Mace, although that would've been the most handy.

Unfortunately, Burke clammed up every time one of his men so much as questioned their destination, so she was fairly certain he wasn't going to blab his evil master plan to her. As the third night fell, she was still deciding how to go about it when she recognized where they were.

Dowth.

And suddenly, Brianagh knew exactly what Burke's plans for her entailed.

"OPEN THE TIME GATE, BRIANAGH O'ROURKE."

They stood by the raised mound of Dowth, the same place she stood with Reilly all those weeks ago.

Brianagh stared at Burke, open-mouthed. "I-I can't!"

His sword was against her throat in a split second. "You can, and you will. Open the gate!" he growled.

Brianagh's mind raced. If he needed her to bend time, then he wasn't going to kill her if he thought she could do it. Immediately and with a confidence she didn't really feel, she took a step away from the sword. "Put that away. I can't travel through time now because it only works at sunrise. I can't control when it's effective." She sat against a partially-buried kerbstone, then leveled a stare at him. "And you have to cut my rope—I need both hands." She was quaking inside, but her voice didn't hint at it.

Burke gave her a long look, then looked at the sky. The moon was brilliantly full. All around them the trees were bathed in the bluish light, casting long shadows across the open field where they stood. Dowth's kerbstone felt strangely comforting against her back.

Brianagh drew her strength from it. "When sunrise comes, you will see if I can open this or not. But I cannot open it without the first rays of the sun." She was babbling, making stuff up, but she needed the extra time to figure out what her next step was. She knew she couldn't open it herself. "I'll, ah, also need to know where you want to go," she added.

It seemed like a good thing to say. Reilly apparently knew how to bend time to his will. Perhaps she could make it bend to hers as well. Say, to wherever Reilly was resting his head. He'd be helpful in getting her back to Nioclas.

Brianagh stopped short and realized what she'd just thought.

If she really did have the ability to time-travel, she could go back to her family through this very ancient site. She could leave it all behind and live out the rest of her days in comfort: electricity, hot water, showers. Chocolate.

But the reality of leaving Nioclas—of never seeing him again, nor feeling his arms around her, or feeling his presence…no.

She couldn't leave him. She didn't want to leave him, because she loved him with every bit of herself.

She loved him.

"We stay here until sunrise, then," Burke snarled. "With any luck, MacWilliam is lying cold in his grave. He can't sneak up on us here."

One of the men called Burke over, and he dragged Brianagh with him, apparently not willing to have her more than an arm's length away.

"We found these tracks in the snow," the guard said, squatting down next to them. In the light of the moon, Brianagh saw Burke frown. She strained to see what they were looking at, then had to bite the palm of her hand to stop her gasp.

She'd know those tracks anywhere. Doc Martens.

Colin.

Brianagh didn't dare look around. She had no idea where he was, if he was alone, or how he ended up here, but all the guards agreed the track was new. There were other footprints, but they were much less distinguishable. They couldn't tell if it was just one other set, or if there were more than just the one person, nor could they determine what kind of boots they were.

She cleared a spot on the ground, brushing away the snow, and gathered her cloak underneath her as a barrier, as she'd done each night since her capture. Carefully, she lay down, facing the small opening of the monolithic structure, scanning it for any indication of her cousin.

She saw nothing, but she knew he was somewhere close, patiently waiting for his chance.

An hour or so after she laid down, she felt the ground tremble. Sitting up quickly, Bri realized it wasn't an earthquake—it was hooves. And the riders were getting closer, fast.

Burke was on his feet with lightning speed. His three guards stood at attention, waiting for the riders to burst through the copse of trees. Brianagh was pulled behind Burke, placed between him and the opening of the structure.

"Do not open that without me," he snarled. "If you do, I will go to the Maguire clan next and take care of your friend. And I'll erase her new clan too." His eyes held the promise of a determined madman.

"Burke." Nioclas walked out of the forest, and Brianagh's heart flipped in her chest.

He had come for her.

The horses they'd heard were nowhere to be seen, but Burke didn't seem to notice. "I see Kildare didn't finish you," he said, his voice flat. "What a waste. At least I got what I came for, though…and, because you can't see her where she stands—" He pulled her in front of him and placed a wicked-looking dagger at her throat. "—she's right here. Safe as can be…unless you walk closer."

"Release her," Nioclas growled. "She can't do what you think she can."

"She's already admitted it to me," Burke snapped. "If I die, she dies with me, and it's my understanding that your line dies out when she does, so truly…if you kill me, you accomplish what I want, anyway."

"I thought you wanted your power and your clan back," Nioclas challenged.

"I want your death more," Burke replied, hatred and

hysteria lacing his words. "Tell whatever other men you brought with you to stand back, or I'll kill her right now." He tightened his grip on the dagger. "I have very little to lose, lad."

Nioclas put his hands up. "My men will not move unless I give them leave to do so."

"Well-trained pups, are they?" Burke sneered. "All the more foolish for you."

"Perhaps," Nioclas agreed. Brianagh couldn't see his eyes—he was too far away—but she never took her eyes off him. If she had to have a last look, she wanted her final vision to be of her love, ready to defend her in the predawn mist.

A movement to their right distracted Burke. Using all she'd learned at her self-defense class, she kicked backward and up as hard as she could, pushing his arm away from her neck. She twisted out of his grasp, then gasped as she saw Aidan, like an avenging angel, standing over them. He grabbed her by her wrists and yanked her behind him, then staggered back as the dagger that was at her throat not a moment before landed in his right shoulder.

Nioclas rushed in, calling out for his men, and suddenly there were men everywhere. Brianagh clutched at Aidan, screaming his name. There was so much blood, and she needed to staunch it. She was grabbed by the shoulders, but she shook off whoever it was as she tried to pull Aidan away from the battle.

A pair of arms went around Aidan's waist, and Brianagh glanced up into Colin's eyes.

"Hands on rock," he said urgently. She placed both hands on the rock, and Colin, in the same voice she'd heard only once before in her life, said, *"Le cumhacht na bhFáithe, ordaím duit oscailt don mháthair."*

"With the power of the Fates, I command you to open to the Mother."

The rock widened and she stumbled inside, Colin

following her as he dragged Aidan in with them. The wall closed immediately, and she felt her way along the wall to the small passageway.

"Colin, how d-did y-you..." she stuttered. "This is Aidan. We need to stop the bleeding! And we need to get to Nioclas! He's outside, we have to let him in!"

Colin placed a hand on her arm. "Slow down, Bri. Your friend here has passed out. And sunrise is just about here." He carefully worked the dagger free and laid it on the ground. Ripping his shirt into pieces, he quickly made a tourniquet. "We can't see the light from this side, but it still works the same," Colin explained in a rush. "Lie against your friend and hold onto him. I'll hold onto you, and we'll make it back. James is there and he will help."

"But Nioclas..."

"This is all I'm allowed to do," Colin implored. "Hold onto him!"

Bri laid against Aidan's chest, wrapping her arms around him, ignoring the pain in her wrists and arm. Without warning, the world around her exploded into shards of light, and her only coherent thought was, *Please let them live.*

CHAPTER 25

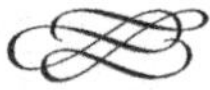

"He doesn't look so good."

Colin's voice floated to her as if he were very far away. Slowly, Brianagh came to. She was lying down on someone, her face skyward. Arms were around her. She struggled to sit up but couldn't move her limbs very well. Whoever was holding her helped her into an upright position, then steadied her as she clutched her spinning head. Blinking in the light, Brianagh dimly realized she was sitting with Colin on the ground.

"Col?"

"Go slow, Bri. James and Reilly are stabilizing your friend so we can get a move on, before we get caught here," Colin said, steadying her.

"I'm bleeding," she said numbly, looking at her dress. "A lot."

"That's your friend's blood," Colin replied, "and we'll get you cleaned up. Don't worry. We've got this. Just relax."

Bri saw James and Reilly leaning over Aidan. His eyes were closed, and she couldn't tell if he was breathing. When asked, Colin reassured her that he was alive, just unconscious. She let out a shaky breath, then paused.

She'd time-traveled again.

"Colin?" she asked, twisting in sudden surprise. "You're a time-traveler?"

"Direct descendant of a well-kept family secret," he replied with a cheeky grin.

She just stared at him in shock before turning back to the scene in front of her. James was in full doctor-mode, checking all sorts of things on Aidan. Reilly kneeled in the dirt and handed James whatever he requested. And Colin, dressed in full medieval garb minus his Doc Martens, still held on to her.

"Is this really happening?" she whispered, her eyes filling with tears. "Without Nioclas?"

"Keep it together," Colin said quietly. "We'll figure it out, Bri."

At James's nod, James and Reilly hefted Aidan and began to haul him toward the SUV parked nearby.

"Come on. We've got to move before anyone sees us," Colin said, helping her stand. She stared at him in shock, then looked over to James, and finally to Reilly, who rolled his eyes at her, then winked.

"You'd think you'd be used to this by now," Reilly said with a smirk.

His teasing had the desired effect; she let out a quick breath and assessed the situation. "O'Malley," she called sharply. His head swung around in surprise. "I'll need answers, but first, we need to get his shoulder fixed. Where are we taking him?"

"We're going to bring him back to Reilly's house," James replied briskly as he and Reilly carefully loaded Aidan into the SUV, "and see what we can do from there. We can't bring him to a hospital. They'll throw him in a mental hospital when he eventually wakes up."

Brianagh stopped paying attention. She'd caught sight of what they'd set up inside the vehicle. The back seats were laid flat, and everything from IV bags to bandages was stocked inside of long white bins they'd attached to the sides.

"It's a makeshift ambulance," Colin explained.

"Answers later," she said firmly, snapping her mouth shut and clambering in once James settled Aidan. Colin hopped into the front seat, and Reilly took off as the sun rose in the distance.

"He's lost a lot of blood," Bri said nervously. "And he's not waking up, James."

"Relax, Bri. I'm an ER physician. I know what to do," he replied calmly as he started an IV in Aidan's arm and began checking all sorts of things. "He's not going to wake up for a while yet. I'm giving him some pretty strong pain meds so he won't wake up in the car and freak out."

"He's not going to know what all this is," she said, unable to keep the worry from her voice. "When he wakes up, he's going to be so confused and pretty angry. Especially if he sees Reilly."

"No clan love between the O'Rourkes and the O'Malleys?" Colin asked.

"Actually, he's a MacWilliam," Bri replied. She met Reilly's eyes in the rearview mirror. "His name is Aidan…and he's my brother-in-law."

James paused in his ministrations, and Colin simply froze in the front seat. Silence reigned.

Reilly smiled.

BRIANAGH STOOD IN REILLY'S BATHROOM, STARING AT HERSELF IN the mirror. She looked much the same, but so much had changed in the two months she'd been gone.

Colin and James both informed her Matthew flew to Ireland after two weeks. He'd led the search groups and pleaded for her safe return on television, both in Ireland and in the States. He'd kept up the effort until last week, when he produced a document claiming she'd given him all rights to her business prior to her trip.

Somehow, she wasn't terribly shocked.

Brianagh ran her fingers through her hair, inspecting her reflection. She'd almost forgotten what she looked like. Her eyes were a deeper blue than she remembered, and her hair—still wet from her shower—looked longer, darker, and wavier than before. She glanced at her arm and grimaced. She needed to see James about that sooner rather than later. The cut was deeper than she thought, and very red. Bri had no doubt it was infected. Medieval swords probably had more germs than she cared to admit.

She finished drying off, luxuriating in the softness of the warm towel, and dressed in her jeans and one of Reilly's T-shirts, feeling out of place and uncomfortable. She found herself wishing for a long, fur-lined dress. Or, better yet, her husband.

Brianagh found James on the couch downstairs, holding a beer against his forehead, his eyes closed.

"How's the patient?" she asked, sitting beside him.

James didn't open his eyes. "If he lives, it'll be a miracle. He should have a blood transfusion, I think, but Reilly said no."

"I agree with Reilly," Brianagh replied softly. "James, I need you to take a look at something." Pulling the sleeve of her shirt up, she showed him her wound. "I can't raise my arm very high, and it aches something fierce."

"Jesus, Brianagh," James exclaimed. "This is, what? Four inches long?"

"And pretty deep," she admitted, wincing as he inspected it.

"How old is it?" He led her to the kitchen and pulled down supplies from one of the cabinets.

"A few days..."

"Do I even want to know?" he asked, squirting some antiseptic on her.

She bit her lip against the sting.

"Whoa! What happened?" Reilly asked, walking into the kitchen as James scrubbed his hands at the sink. Reilly's eyes narrowed. "Don't tell me. Burke."

"And his sword," Bri confirmed. "He was making a point."

"I'll kill him myself," Reilly growled.

"I'm rather hoping Nioclas got to him first," she said. "Colin pulled me away, and I don't know what happened. I have to get back to him as soon as possible."

Reilly and James exchanged a look.

"What?" she demanded, instantly suspicious. "What do you know that I don't? He's not dead," she added forcefully.

A heartbeat passed, then another. "Bri…" Reilly finally spoke, his eyes troubled. "We don't think you *can* get back."

Brianagh narrowed her eyes. "Come again?"

James prepped a syringe, then stuck her arm with it. She didn't even flinch.

Reilly sat down at the table with her and massaged his temples. "We can't just time-travel whenever the mood suits us," he explained. "It has to be in protection of the line. Your line. Colin was able to go back because you would've died had he not pulled you out. But *you* were the one who pulled him and Aidan forward."

"Really?" she whispered, the color draining from her face.

"Aye," he said seriously. "You must be protected at all costs, Bri. You're important. Your child, and your child's children, will be important to history in ways you can't even imagine."

"Nioclas will protect me." Bri took a fortifying breath. "He will. I just have to get back to him!"

Reilly swallowed visibly. "Nay, Bri…he won't."

"He will!" she cried indignantly. "He promised. He never breaks his promises!"

Colin entered the kitchen from the garden, looking cautious. "Whoa! What the hell happened to your arm?"

"Colin, you have to take me back to Nioclas," Brianagh said, her voice catching. "You have to. Please, Colin—"

"I can't bend time myself," Colin said quietly. "I'm just sent where I'm needed, to protect the line."

Reilly left the room as James prepared the stitches.

Brianagh's desperation turned to anger. She turned to James. "James, can you…?"

"Nope. It seems that only one descendant in each generation has the time-travel gene. I, thankfully, am not that descendant." He began to stitch her numb arm. "Colin's the lucky man."

"Can't you just try?" she snapped.

James shook his head. "I can't, Brianagh."

"I don't understand." She seethed as Reilly came back, a large book in hand. She shot daggers at him with her eyes. "You did this to me! You let me believe I was from here—from now!—and then you threw me into Nioclas's arms without even a how-do-you-do. And now, after all this, after I've fallen in love with him, you force me back here!" She choked on her tears. "How could you do that to me, Reilly?" She swept them all with a glare as James finished her stitches. "How could any of you do that to me? We're *family*." She swiped angrily at her tears. "At least, I thought we were!"

Reilly opened the book and slid it across the table. "This is why we can't bring you back," he said, his sadness almost palpable. "I'm sorry, Bri."

She wiped the tears away and scanned the text in front of her, then stopped cold.

On the first day of 1458, the Lady of the MacWilliam clan (Brianagh, formerly O'Rourke, 1428–unknown) disappeared. Her death was never confirmed. The Laird of the MacWilliam clan

(Nioclas, formerly Burke, 1423–circa 1458) was rumored to be killed in a battle with his father, Richard Burke, who regained control of the MacWilliams.

Under his lairdship, the MacWilliams died quickly—all clan elders were tried and hung for treason against their laird, and any women who could not bear his children were also killed. Any MacWilliams who tried to leave the clan were hunted, then killed publicly as a warning to other clans.

The MacWilliam line died out fifteen years after Richard Burke regained control. Causes of death included brutal murder, starvation, and torture. Laird MacWilliam's body was never fou—

Her heart shattered, Brianagh pushed the book away. Her tears made it too difficult to see the words on the page.

REILLY GLANCED OUT THE WINDOW, WATCHING BRIANAGH AS SHE sat on the low stone wall in the back garden. "The Fates are an evil entity."

Colin placed his hand on Reilly's shoulder. "You know that's not true. But I wish we could help her."

Reilly sighed. "I know." He stared at her for another moment.

Brianagh hadn't moved for almost three hours. She sat in the bitter cold, her face expressionless.

"My entire purpose was to keep her safe," Reilly exploded, slamming his fist into the wall directly above the hole he'd punched in it an hour earlier. "I keep every man who could possibly throw a wrench into their plans away from her for her entire life. You think the Fates maybe could have given Brianagh her love for more than it took to get her pregnant? MacWilliam was a good man, damn it. He would've died for her—hell, he *did* die for her."

"Wait a second—Bri's pregnant?" Colin echoed, completely confused. "How?"

Reilly leveled a stare at him. "The normal way, I suspect."

Colin looked back at Brianagh. "How do you know?"

"You're still here, aren't you?"

Colin's eyes grew wide. "So, Bri has a child, then—what? The child is sent back—"

"To his proper time, just like Bri was, aye," Reilly said darkly. "That's what I figure."

"Does she know?"

James joined them at the window. "I don't think she does," he said solemnly. "Do you think she'd be sitting out in the cold if she knew she was carrying the love of her life's child?"

"How's MacWilliam?" Colin asked.

"I think he'll be ready to come out of it soon," James said. "You'll need to be the only one with him, Ry. Even as hurt as he is, he's incredibly powerful." Turning his cheek, he displayed the bruise on his jaw.

"He punched you?" Reilly asked in surprise. He thought Aidan to be weakened from the loss of blood, but clearly, he had something left.

"Sure did. Started mumbling in Gaelic. I caught *dungeon* and *father*." James rubbed his jaw carefully. "I wouldn't want to be on the receiving end of his full-strength blow."

Reilly paused. "Wait a minute…Aidan is here."

Colin looked at him pityingly. "Yes, Ry. Aidan is here."

Reilly shoved Colin out of his way. "I've not lost my mind, you fool. But if Aidan is here, you can bet that Burke never stopped looking for him. He was the one man who could rally the clan, and take it back from Burke!"

"I don't follow. Do you follow?" Colin asked James, who just shook his head and focused on Reilly as he flipped frantically through the *Ireland Through the Ages: Powerful Clans of the 14th and 15th Centuries* book.

He found his page, leaned over, and scanned the words. He flipped a few more pages…and froze.

"Here," he said, and read aloud, "Richard Burke had another son—*Aidan MacWilliam, formerly Burke, 1426 to unknown*—who allied with Laird MacWilliam. Burke spent much of his gold attempting to locate his second son. However, those efforts proved unsuccessful. Missives found in recent excavations from other local clans—*Maguire, Clanricard*—wrote of the second son, verifying his existence. His death was never recorded."

"If he thought Aidan was a threat," Brianagh said from the doorway, "Burke would use anything he could to lure him back, so he could kill him."

"Aye," Reilly agreed. "Anything."

"Again, I'm not following," Colin cut in. "Could you two speak English, please?"

Brianagh locked eyes with Colin. "I don't think that's a good idea. You need to brush up on your Gaelic."

"Why?" James asked, curious.

"Because," Reilly said with a reluctant smile, "he'll be needing it, where we're going."

Colin frowned.

"I'll be the first to admit that I will grab at any hope that Nioclas is alive," Brianagh stated, appearing at the doorway. "But I'll also be the first to tell you that Burke would take great pleasure in torturing my husband for as long as he could before killing him." She fought the tears that threatened. "If Burke believes Nioclas knows where Aidan is, you can bet your life that he's holding him in a dungeon somewhere—either his castle, or mine."

"Aren't we possessive?" Reilly said, a hint of pride creeping into his voice.

"For the first—and possibly last—time, I think you might be right, Reilly." Brianagh straightened her shoulders. "My destiny is not here. I think it's about time I take it back."

"Good lass," he said approvingly.

"You mean I have to go back there?" Colin groaned.

"Aye," Bri and Reilly chimed together.

"Let's take a couple days to prepare," Reilly said. "Bri, you research everything you can about what happened, or didn't happen. Colin, you and I need to work on your swordplay more. And James—"

"I can't go. I'd just get in your way, with my lack of sword skill and poor Gaelic." He shook his head. "I'm much better suited to staying here, cleaning up any mess you've left behind. Especially Bri. I'll handle Mom and Dad, as well as the press and, if necessary, her death certificate."

Brianagh swallowed. "Because I won't be coming back?"

"With any luck," James agreed, somber.

They were interrupted by a banging at the front door.

CHAPTER 26

Colin joined Reilly at the door and folded his arms. Brianagh could feel the combined fury of them both, and seeing them stand together, appearing outwardly relaxed…even she was a little frightened of them.

And they were on her side.

Reilly and Colin waited patiently as the silence drew out.

Finally, Matthew de Burgh said, "Just sign the damn papers, O'Rourke. She left it all to me."

Colin looked down at the papers Matthew shoved under his nose, then glanced back up. "No."

"All you're doing is delaying the inevitable," Matthew sneered. "You don't want to sign? Fine. All that does is create more paperwork for me. And let me just point something out. Money talks. Reputation talks. And she agreed to be my wife in a very public way. Everyone knew she was crazy about me. It's not so far-fetched that she'd leave me—a very capable businessman—in charge of her business. You fighting me for it just drags your name through the mud."

"So this is why you took the trouble to propose?" Colin replied. "Clever."

"Sign the papers, O'Rourke."

"How about this," Colin responded. "You answer my questions, and I'll sign your papers."

"Games?" Matthew smirked. "I thought you were above that."

"I'm not," Colin growled. "Was the entire reason for dating Bri just to get her company?"

"It sure as hell wasn't to get her into bed," Matthew replied with a snort. "She isn't exactly what I would call *eager*. She hasn't a responsive bone in her body." He laughed.

Reilly tensed, but Colin stayed him.

"Okay. Question two," Colin continued evenly. "If you wanted the company so badly, why not just offer for it?"

"A hostile takeover of a matchmaking company?" The frustration was evident in Matthew's voice. "It's a PR disaster. No person paying the kind of fees Brianagh charged would want to be involved in a company bound by red tape."

"All right," Colin said slowly. "Question three. How many women were you with during your time with Bri?"

"I don't know. It doesn't matter. What she doesn't know won't hurt her, not that it matters now. So if I were you, I wouldn't say anything, to save her feelings…if you ever find her, that is."

Brianagh ducked between Reilly and Colin. "Hello, Matthew. How kind of you to search for me."

Matthew's jaw dropped.

"I know," she continued. "As you can see, I'm very much alive. And very much willing to tell everyone how I've never—and will never—sign anything over to you."

"Brianagh, it's not what you think," he started.

Brianagh looked him up and down, then shook her head. "I don't know what I was thinking." Looking over her shoulder, she asked, "If Nioclas ever met Matthew, I don't see how it would end well."

"Who's Nioclas?"

"My husband. He's a very jealous man, and a very strong one. Irish warrior and all that."

"You're married?" Matthew asked. "But you're engaged to me!"

"Well," she mused, "I *was*."

"BRIANAGH MACWILLIAM!"

"The medicine wore off," James called from the kitchen.

Bri gave Matthew a quick smile. "That'd be him. He gets a bit...*passionate* when I'm not there. Gotta go. Good luck with the hostile takeover."

Two hours later, Brianagh and Reilly finally had Aidan calmed down enough to explain what was happening. He looked shell-shocked.

"Please let James put the IV back in," Brianagh asked patiently. "It is giving you good medicine, Aidan. You'll heal faster with it."

"Your healer has some powerful magic," Aidan replied forcefully. "My head feels as though it's separated from my body!"

"That's the pain medication," she explained. Glancing at Reilly, she continued. "Aidan, we need you to be as strong as possible. We think Nioclas is in grave danger."

"How so?"

Reilly gave him the abridged version of their suspicions.

Aidan nodded. "Aye, I can see Burke doing exactly that. If he subdued Nick and was able to take him alive without threat of being overthrown again, he'd take it."

"I don't know where the dungeons are in the castle," Brianagh said. "We need your wits and your sword."

"So I really am somewhere in the future?" Aidan asked.

"Yes," Brianagh exclaimed. "You could believe it when we were in the fifteenth century just fine, why not now?"

"It's hard for a mind to wrap itself around," Reilly said in understanding. "Perhaps you can see me as less of an enemy and more of an ally, now that you know the full truth of it?"

Aidan snorted. "I still think you're an arse."

"So do I," Brianagh confessed, "but he's the best kind of arse."

Aidan let out a sigh. "Do you swear to me that your healer won't attempt to poison me?"

Brianagh clasped his hand in her own. "Aidan, I vow it." She looked into his eyes. "I love your brother, more than anything or anyone. I need you to help me save him. Please."

"Aye," Aidan grumbled, giving in. "Let your healer at me. But no devil sticks. And no leeches."

"We don't do leeches anymore," James said in broken Gaelic, from the doorway where he'd been waiting during the exchange. "They've been proven ineffective."

"Aye, and your devil sticks are effective?"

"It's just a tiny needle," Reilly scoffed. "A warrior such as yourself, afraid of the tiniest stitching needle known to mankind?"

Aidan glared at him. "I don't know why anyone likes you."

"I'm a paragon of human empathy," Reilly extolled. "A giver to mankind. I save people from themselves, and—"

"You forgot 'arse,'" Brianagh cut in. "James, please make him better."

"Sure thing, boss." He walked up to Aidan and held out his hand. "I'm James, Brianagh's…well, grandson, many generations removed."

"Weird," Brianagh muttered.

"Very," James agreed. "I'm going to explain everything as I go along, all right? Let me know if you can't understand me, and I'll have Brianagh translate."

"Your Gaelic is very poor," Aidan agreed.

"And your English sucks," James replied pleasantly.

"Perhaps we can teach each other. As you can see, I've stitched up your wound..."

"Well, someone should tell her..." Reilly looked to Colin.

"Oh, hell no," Colin replied, holding his hands up and backing away. "No way."

"Well, don't look at me." Reilly shook his head. "I want nothing to do with it."

Aidan finished his beer and made a face. "This is the worst ale I've ever had the misfortune to drink."

"Try a Guinness," Reilly suggested. "You'd like that. In fact, I'll get you one. You can take it with you when you tell Brianagh her news."

"What news?" Brianagh asked as she walked in the front door. All four men were sitting in the living room, holding a beer—or, in Aidan's case, an empty bottle. Brianagh placed her grocery bags down and threw her hands on her hips. "You sent me out for groceries so you could figure out who would be telling me something?" she accused. "Spill." When no one made eye contact with her, Brianagh tapped her foot.

"James is the doctor. He should be the one," Colin offered helpfully.

"Oh, aye," Aidan and Reilly agreed quickly, nodding.

"You three are pathetic," she snapped. "James. Just tell me already."

He shrugged. "Okay. You're pregnant. And Aidan, you should ease up on the alcohol, I don't want any interactions with the medications."

Brianagh blinked at him. She was positive she didn't hear him correctly.

"It's true," James said to her calmly as he took a pull from his beer. "I can give you a test to prove it, but Colin wouldn't have been able to pull you away unless the line was in danger. That's the way we think the legacy works."

"I can see the legacy working that way," Colin agreed.

"I am not having four men—who have no children of their own—tell me I'm pregnant." Brianagh shook her head, stunned. "This cannot be happening."

"Well, you *are* married," Reilly replied.

"Not that!" Bri exclaimed, coloring. "I mean the four of you knowing before I do! I don't feel any different. So I might not be."

"Figure out the math, then get back to us," James replied.

"It's too soon to know," Brianagh argued.

"I'll give you a blood test," James said with a shrug. "But I'll need another beer. Anyone need another?"

"Another beer before you stab me with a needle? Really, James?" She glared at him. "And *if* I was pregnant, it's none of your business anyway."

"Oh, I disagree," Aidan replied seriously. "It's very much our business. That's the laird's heir you're carrying. And I'll try that Guinness. It has to be better than this." He tossed the empty beer bottle onto the table with disgust.

"That's also my great-great-many-extra-greats grandparent," Colin chimed in.

"And the reason I've dedicated my life to protecting yours," Reilly added quietly.

Oh. When put that way, Brianagh understood their point.

"You four are going to become overbearing, aren't you?" She sighed heavily, but she gave them a small smile.

Family.

FOUR DAYS LATER, BRIANAGH, COLIN, REILLY, AND AIDAN WERE dressed in their medieval clothing. Aidan had a bottle of antibiotics stashed somewhere on himself, Colin had tubes of first-aid cream tucked into various pockets Bri had sewn—successfully—into his tunic, and Reilly carried a satchel with food and water. Brianagh was supposed to carry nothing, in case she had to make a run for it. Despite that, she snuck a few Cadbury chocolate bars into her pocket on the inside of her own tunic. She glanced down at herself. As the dress she was wearing when she arrived was ruined, she was wearing some of Reilly's clothes.

She wondered what Nioclas would say when he saw her dressed as a man. Erin would no doubt be green with envy when she found out.

"Remember to boil the water before you drink it," James warned as they approached Dowth.

"Can I handle this beast?" Aidan asked for the umpteenth time.

"No!" Reilly and Colin chorused, again.

"Brianagh, be sure any meat is cooked all the way through, you don't want to poison the baby," James continued over them.

"I would tame it, and it would call me its master," Aidan said with confidence.

"If you shut up about it, I'll give you one of your very own someday," Reilly promised, fully aggravated. No one drove his Range Rover.

Ever.

"I'll take care of Matthew. With the papers signed and verified by the Irish government, we shouldn't have any issues with Celtic Connections," James assured Brianagh. "Colin will take care of everything."

"You wouldn't be able to handle this," Reilly scoffed, talking over James. "You can barely handle your own horse."

"My horse has never thrown me," Aidan pointed out smugly.

"Mine was shot with an arrow!" Reilly exclaimed indignantly. "As was I!"

"Which I stitched for you," James cut in before continuing his lecture to Bri.

"Are they going to argue like this the entire time?" Colin asked Brianagh.

She shrugged, amused.

"...and really, Bri, once you get into the second trimester, stay off any horses," James advised.

"This is the most ridiculous ride I've ever taken," Brianagh announced.

"...sometimes morning sickness returns in the third trimester, but it should be temporary."

"My horse has the good sense to keep me on his back until we arrive at a safe place!" Aidan exclaimed.

"Is anyone else hungry?" Colin asked.

Brianagh hoped one of them had brought aspirin. It was going to be a long journey—and she didn't mean the time travel.

Eventually, they piled out of the car like clowns in a circus and James immediately wrapped Bri in a bear hug. "Be safe." He smiled at her, then ruffled her hair. "More importantly, be happy."

She felt the tears threaten.

"First trimester emotion," James said knowingly. She smacked him on the shoulder, and he grinned. He kissed her, promised to send her love to his parents, then said his goodbyes to the others.

Brianagh made her way to the rocks for what she hoped to be her last time. She was ready to save Nioclas and get on with the rest of her life. She wanted that happily-ever-after.

CHAPTER 27

Donovan's men were waiting for them when Bri, Aidan, Colin, and Reilly made their way toward the MacWilliam castle. After a grueling two days of travel on foot, the horses and additional men provided not only relief, but speed. Instead of going to the MacWilliam hold, however, they turned to the Maguire one.

Brianagh was grateful for both, but she was anxious to get to Nioclas. She paced Donovan's hall, listening intently as the four men discussed the events. After a few minutes, Erin joined her silently, linking her arm through Brianagh's.

"Burke is focused on finding Brianagh." Donovan scratched his chin. "I believe he thinks Nick knows but isn't talking."

"You think he's torturing him?" Colin asked.

"Without a doubt," Aidan replied grimly. "If Burke's had him for the two weeks we've been gone, I'm unsure as to how we'll find Nick. He'll be alive but perhaps not for long."

Reilly held up his hands. "Let's not get ahead of ourselves. Start at the beginning, Maguire, and tell us what you know."

"When I first returned to the MacWilliam castle, I realized no one had heard from Aidan or Nick," Donovan said. "I knew you were in some trouble then, if you hadn't been able to send a missive. Erin and I made haste for here so I could gather my men to retaliate. But then I received word that Burke arrived at the MacWilliam castle more than a week ago, with Nick bound and gagged. Burke claims he had all Nick's guardsmen killed, and as we haven't seen them, despite our scouting, he may be telling the truth." Donovan shook his head in disgust. "Burke claims he left the bodies where they fell because there was no clan to send them to, as the MacWilliams were now Burkes."

"Let me guess," Reilly said. "He then made the remainder of the clan swear fealty or die?"

Donovan nodded. "Most of the elders are dead for that reason. Some of the villagers as well."

"Bloody business," Colin muttered. "So what's in it for him? Why is he so bent on getting Brianagh, now that he has his power and clan back?"

Donovan shrugged. "Burke is not a stupid man. Everything he does is for a reason—but he may well be the only one who knows what it is."

"I know what he wants." Brianagh swallowed hard and stopped pacing. "He wants the power of the legacy. He wants control not only over a clan, but over time itself."

"The havoc he would wreak upon history..." Colin said. "That would be the ultimate power, wouldn't it?"

"He knows that I can move time," she continued. "If he only knew that I couldn't do it unless it was to save the line, to save my future children...well, perhaps it's a good thing that he believes that. It might be the only thing keeping Nioclas alive."

"You don't know?" Erin asked suddenly. She turned accusing eyes on Reilly. "She doesn't know?"

"Know what?" Aidan and Brianagh chorused.

"How would *you* know?" Reilly asked suspiciously.

Erin gulped. "I-I saw the missive."

Brianagh didn't bother to hide her exasperation. "Erin, explain what you're talking about. What missive? What don't I know?"

"Reilly wrote a missive to Nick—it was definitely in some sort of code, but being as I'd already overheard Reilly and Nick discussing how you're truly the O'Rourke legacy, I figured out the rest quickly. Bri, not only can you travel through time, but you can actually bend it to your will."

"He was supposed to burn that," Reilly said darkly. "If that got into the wrong hands—"

"Oh, I'm sure he did burn it," Erin replied quickly. "I just got to it before him."

"Your curiosity knows no bounds," Aidan said, slightly awed.

Brianagh walked up to Reilly and pinched his arm as hard as she could.

"Ow! What the—"

"Tell me everything. Now, Reilly." She put her face within inches of his. "Everything. Now."

Reilly rubbed his arm and pouted. "Well, yeah, I mean, sure you have the ability to do it…"

"You opened the wall," Colin reminded her. "Remember? When I was dragging MacWilliam, my hands weren't free. When you placed your hands on the wall, you gave it the power to go where you wanted."

"I just wanted to get to Reilly," she replied.

"And Reilly knew that, which is why he had the Range Rover ready and James knew what was going on," Colin explained.

"The pieces fit, but you led me to believe that I was stuck in the future! Without any way to get back to Nioclas!"

"I didn't want you to put the baby at risk by doing something colossally stupid," Reilly shot back. "I know you better than you know yourself!"

"Wait—baby?" Erin gasped. "Bri, you're with child?"

She gave an impatient nod. "Yes, but just barely."

Donovan held up his hands to silence them. "I don't understand much of what you're saying, but what I'm gathering is that Lady Brianagh can move time to her will, and she's carrying the future MacWilliam laird."

"This is insane," Brianagh muttered, beginning to pace again.

"We've wasted enough time," Aidan said in agreement. "All this can wait until after we rescue my brother. It shouldn't be too difficult, right? I mean, Burke doesn't have many who are loyal to him."

"He has the Kildares," Donovan cut in. "He and Kildare made a binding agreement that, in the event Kildare died during battle, Burke would assume control of the clan until a battle for the lairdship could be arranged."

"Clever bastard," Aidan growled. "The Kildares will swear loyalty to anyone for the right price."

"Any price," Donovan agreed. "They're no better than mercenaries. Right now, there's at least two score of Kildare men at the castle."

"Then we'd best figure out how to get past them and rescue my husband, don't you think?" Brianagh arched a brow.

"Aye," Donovan replied. "Let's plan our attack."

Dawn's light filtered through the small window Nioclas himself built, two stories above his head. He cursed himself and his foresight to create an inescapable dungeon.

The heavy locks on the gate that led up the stairs to the lists were forged by his own blacksmith not two years ago. The key, once upon his own belt, now rested with his insane father, whose daily joy had become torturing Nioclas for information about Aidan and Brianagh's whereabouts.

Nioclas didn't know for certain where his wife and brother went, but he did hope they were safe. Burke claimed he was still looking for them, but Nioclas couldn't know for certain. His sire enjoyed nothing more than instilling fear in his prisoners—or his clansmen.

Looking over at the latest to join him, Nioclas sighed. Kane's nose would never be the same and he may never walk the same again, either.

"My laird," Kane began, looking up at the small window, "if I am to die this day, I ask a favor."

"Of course."

"If you are able, tell Keela that I love her."

"You'll be able to tell her yourself," Nioclas replied, ignoring the pain that sliced across his ribs when he breathed too deeply. "We'll make it through this, clansman."

Kane shook his head. "I'll be lucky—I'll die a swift death by sword. You, however—he's killing you slowly. We all know it, my laird. He's brought in the villagers and already killed five of them for speaking out against him. He's placed men around the gates to keep us from escaping. Any attempt is met with immediate death." Kane shuddered. "I fear for the women most, though."

Nioclas felt the familiar rage and the ensuing helplessness. He was chained to the wall, wrists hung above his head, feet shackled to posts in the floor. Kane had already tried to free him, but the shackles were padlocked. Nioclas's own nose was broken from his sire's fist, and his back was torn apart by his whip.

"My biggest mistake was to underestimate the number of men Burke gathered," Nioclas said, venom in his voice. "He's no doubt paying them from my coffers."

"No doubt," Kane agreed. "If I had just fought harder…"

"Not a good road to travel, my friend," Nioclas said. "Be brave, and if you must die, do it as a warrior without regret."

Kane dropped his chin to his chest. "He threatened to kill

her if I didn't put my sword down." His tortured expression nearly broke Nioclas.

"You must protect what is yours…at all costs."

"Forgive me," Kane whispered.

"There's nothing to forgive," Nioclas replied heavily. "If I were in your position, I'd have done the same. There is no shame in protecting those we love."

They fell silent as the light from the lists filtered down the stairs through the locked gate. And, as he had every morning since Burke's forty men overpowered him and his guard, Nioclas hoped Aidan and Brianagh were as far away from the castle as possible.

A shadow appeared from the stairs. Tensing, Kane and Nioclas watched it come closer, then silently eyed the hooded, cloaked man as he toyed with, then popped open the padlock.

He eased the gate open quietly, then stepped into the dungeon and removed the hood of his cloak—and both men stared in shock.

"Saints above, Brianagh, what are you wearing?" Nioclas choked out.

"You've been stuck in here for two weeks and that's the first thing you come up with?" she asked. She rushed over to him and inspected the shackles around his wrists. "I can't wait to tell Erin. Do you think Donovan would mind her in clothes like this?"

His gaze raked her from head to toe. From what he could see, she was dressed as a man, her leggings hugging the lines of her shapely legs. His mouth dried as she reached up to test the chains, and the cloak slipped down her shoulder as the fastening loosened.

She caught sight of his expression and she let out a laugh. "If you're having wicked thoughts, then I have no doubt of your recovery from whatever damage Burke's inflicted. Kane, I need your help."

"Anything, my lady," he said quickly, at her side in an instant.

"I need you to get on your hands and knees so I can climb onto your back, and use it as a step, I can't reach the locks to break them," she explained. The words were barely out of her mouth before he complied.

Stepping on him carefully, she balanced herself, then pulled a long pin from her coil of hair and went to work on Nioclas's right wrist.

"Where did you learn such a skill?" Nioclas demanded.

Brianagh shot him a smile. "I'll let you guess, my laird."

"Remind me to thank her," he replied as she freed his wrist, then started in on the other.

"Sure." Brianagh concentrated on the lock. When it, too, popped effortlessly, she hopped off Kane and went to work on the chains at his feet. "I think Erin would be very pleased to hear you grovel."

"I wouldn't go quite that far," Nioclas replied, rubbing his wrists. Pain shot to his shoulders as the blood began to flow again. "Is there a plan?"

"Yes," she said, handing Kane a dagger from inside her cloak. "Here, you'll need this until you can get your sword back." To Nioclas, she said, "We weren't sure what state we'd find you in, so you're not exactly a part of the plans. There is someone at the top of the stairs that you won't recognize—his name is Colin."

"Your cousin?" Nioclas asked, bewildered. "But that would mean—"

"Yes," she said hurriedly, "it does. He's guarding the gate while I free you, and Donovan has his men attacking the Kildares—or Burkes, or whomever—any second now. So let's get out of here!"

"Wait," Nioclas said. He grabbed her and kissed her, hard. "Thank you."

"You're welcome," she replied, smiling up at him. "And if

I don't get a chance to say it later…I love you. More than anyone, or anything."

His eyes searched hers, and he kissed her again, but it was interrupted by her cry of pain. He released her. "What is it?"

"My arm," she managed. "I think I tore my stitches when I was breaking your wrist locks. Burke cut me with his sword before you came to save me. It's been healing, but I think I just did some damage to it."

"My laird, I hear the sound of battle," Kane interrupted.

Nioclas nodded once, then followed him up the stairs, keeping Brianagh close to his back, and allowed his fury to overcome any pain.

Burke would pay for many things this day.

CHAPTER 28

Colin handed Nioclas and Kane swords as soon as they ascended, and the four of them made it halfway across the lists before they were charged.

"Aidan and Donovan are in the great hall," Colin said quickly. "You're too weak to fight right now, Laird MacWilliam." He pushed Bri and Nioclas behind him, then drew his sword. "Go! We'll meet you there!"

Colin and Kane clashed swords with the two Kildares who still stood, and Nioclas and Bri ran for the wall. Slipping inside, he took her hand and together they ran the length of it, passing the crack where Erin and Bri had first spied on their husbands. Further down, the wall turned sharply left and narrowed. Slowing to accommodate the darkness, Nioclas gripped his sword and motioned for silence.

Brianagh followed him as they made their way closer to the castle proper. The wall began to widen slightly again, and they came to a halt at the end of the passageway, where they reached a stone wall.

"Dead end," Bri whispered, her heart sinking.

Nioclas shook his head slightly, then gave a careful push. The wall opened a fraction.

Bri watched in amazement as Nioclas inched it open silently until he had enough space to see through the crack. He gave a mighty shove and pulled Brianagh into an empty chamber.

"I need to get you to safety," Nioclas said in a low voice.

"Burke is after me," she replied. "This is my battle, too."

"Must you always argue with me?"

"Reilly asks me the same thing, all the time," she replied pertly. "I know the plan, Nioclas. Trust me."

"I do, but I don't want you dead."

"That's good," she said, "because I don't want me dead, either. Let's go finish this so we can finally get to living, okay?"

Nioclas kissed her hand, then tucked her behind him as he peeked out the chamber door. "All clear. Where to, my lady?"

"I've heard all great battles take place in the great hall," she responded matter-of-factly, ignoring the sweat on her temple and fear in her heart.

"Then, by all means," he replied grimly, "I shall go to the great hall. But I cannot fight with fear that you are not safe. Please, Brianagh. Do not follow me."

Her eyes filled with tears. "But you're weakened, Nick…"

"I have much to fight for, my love. Please."

Hearing her strong warrior beg for anything caused her tears to overflow. She nodded wordlessly, then kissed him with every ounce of love in her soul.

"We run for the upstairs chamber with the strongest door. Once there, barricade the door, Brianagh, and let no one but me in, do you understand?"

She nodded, and they darted into the hall and up the stairs. The sounds of battle cries and men dying came from all sides.

"I must find Burke," Nioclas said quietly. "This doesn't end until he dies."

She nodded wordlessly. He kissed her once more, then was gone.

She barricaded the door and set to pacing.

BRIANAGH HAD NO IDEA HOW LONG SHE STAYED IN THE CHAMBER. The battle cries had died down long ago, and still she paced, alone, unsure as to what she should do next. Nioclas hadn't yet come for her, and every noise she heard made her jump. The afternoon light was beginning to fade. There wasn't much daylight in the winter, and she knew firsthand how cold it would become. She had no kindling for a fire, and the shutters in the chamber had broken in a few places, allowing the cold air to seep into her bones.

She wrapped her arms about herself and plodded to the window to look out across the bailey. A heavy mist had rolled in from the sea, enveloping the castle in its embrace. It clung to the battlements, shrouding the castle from the village beyond. Brianagh felt as though she were suspended in a castle atop a cloud.

Brianagh avoided looking down. The number of dead bodies strewn across the bailey made her nauseous. The smell of blood wasn't helping, either. But mostly, her fear as to why Nioclas hadn't come for her yet had her wishing for a stronger stomach.

A sudden, insistent banging had her spinning to the door, her heart in her throat.

"Open up, Brianagh!" Nioclas called.

She ran to the door and fumbled with the latch and the large piece of wood she'd laid across the bars on either side. With it finally unlocked, she threw the door open and lunged into her husband's arms.

"Easy," he said soothingly, running a blood-caked hand over her hair. "We're safe. The castle is ours again."

"Is he dead?" she asked, her voice shaking.

"We can't find him," Aidan said from behind Nioclas. "We think he ran, the coward."

She glanced around Nioclas and saw all of them—Aidan, Donovan, Reilly, and Colin—standing in the hallway, battle-weary warriors. She was profoundly grateful for each of them.

They walked downstairs together. Brianagh covered her mouth and tried to quiet her stomach at the dead men around them.

"Mostly Kildares," Nioclas said with a sigh. "If he had but taken my alliance…"

"He was a fool, and his people suffered for it," Colin said with a grimace, walking to the only table left in the hall. Leaning on the wall next to the hearth, he rubbed his face with his hands. "These are difficult times, MacWilliam."

"We need to find him," Aidan said, his voice low and insistent. "He won't stop until we are both dead, and Brianagh is his to control."

"Aye," Nioclas agreed, pulling Brianagh in front of him and wrapping his arms around her protectively. He watched as his surviving clansmen began to drag the bodies out of the hall. "I should send scouts out—"

"Send me," Aidan cut in.

Nioclas dropped his arms from Bri. "Nay. I thought I'd lost you once before and I could barely stand it. I cannot afford to lose you again."

Aidan grabbed Nioclas's arm and gave him a hard shake. "I must find him," he said fiercely. "He will not stop, Nick. He'll find more men to attack us—you, me, Brianagh, our clan. And what about your children? He'll come after them as well."

Nioclas remained silent, acknowledging the truth of it.

"Only I can do this," Aidan said, hardening his resolve. "You must send me—our clan needs you here."

Nioclas closed his eyes briefly, and when he opened them a moment later, they were hard chips of granite. "Cian!" he called out to an older man who joined them by the hearth. Turning to Aidan, Nioclas placed a hand on his shoulder. "You will take the utmost care."

"Aye," Aidan replied, his voice strong.

"My laird?" Cian asked, giving a quick bow.

"How many elders are alive?"

"Five, and I hope you know our loyalty still lays, and always has, with you."

"I know," Nioclas replied, placing his hand on the elder's shoulder. "I only wish the others had given their oath so as to save their lives."

"Clan before self," Cian said, a touch of sorrow in his words. "We thought the best way to help the clan was to stay alive so we could fight this battle. The others…didn't."

"I know," Nioclas repeated, his voice like steel. "That is why I'm giving you the most important duty I've ever given since the day we rode against Burke over twenty years ago." Nioclas raised his voice so all in the hall could hear him. "Cian MacWilliam, I charge you to go forth with my brother, Aidan MacWilliam. Your purpose is to find Burke—and kill him on first sight."

"You do not want the honor?" Cian asked.

"Honor has nothing to do with it," Nioclas stated firmly. "He is a threat to us." Raising his voice again, he continued. "Burke will gather more men and attack us again. When those men lose to us, as they will, he will run from battle—again—and continue the cycle until he has killed me and my brother and taken my wife for his own. Aidan will be your laird in my place. You shall honor him as such and do as he asks."

"Aye, my laird," Cian replied, bowing. "When do we depart?"

"Soon," Aidan said. "Say your goodbyes, then meet me in the stables."

"My wife died last year, and there were no children. I am ready to leave immediately, my laird."

Aidan nodded, then turned to Nioclas and embraced him carefully.

"Bring him back dead," Nioclas said.

Brianagh threw her arms around Aidan, finally letting her dam burst. "Please take care," she pleaded through her tears. "I can never thank you enough."

"If I don't return, you can name the little one after me," Aidan whispered, then threw her a lascivious wink.

She laughed, then swatted him on his uninjured arm. "Don't," she laughed, then sniffed. "Ry, Col, are you staying?"

"For a bit," Reilly replied. "But not long. We'll help clean up here, then be on our way."

Aidan turned before leaving the castle, giving her a quick wave and blowing her a kiss. She pretended to catch it, then smiled sadly as he disappeared down the steps.

"I hope he finds him," she said, staring at the empty spot in the doorway.

"He'll find what he's looking for," Reilly whispered in her ear. Straightening, he said, "Perhaps it's time you get your husband up to his chamber and take care of his wounds?" He handed her the satchel they'd originally stuffed with food, now filled with the supplies James insisted they take.

She took the bag, then looked over at Nioclas. He was in discussion with Donovan about something, and she nodded. "Yes, of course."

"I'll have someone send up hot water," Reilly said, catching her arm. "Be sure to wash everything before applying any of that to him."

She nodded, then wrangled her husband away from Donovan and herded him upstairs.

~

After allowing his wife to fuss over him before, during, and after his bath, Nioclas admitted to himself that he liked the feeling of being cherished. She refused to allow him to bathe himself; she'd insisted upon washing every inch of him.

He complied with haste.

She carefully dried him, then had him lay face down on the mattress naked so she could apply a salve of some sort to his back. She attended to each whip mark gently, packing them with a poultice she made with her mysterious satchel of supplies.

Her feather-light touch was leading him to madness. With more patience than any saint he knew of, Nioclas sat still while she wrapped a stiff cloth around his back and chest. When she finally stood back and pronounced him finished, he grabbed her and flipped her onto the bed.

"Nioclas!" she exclaimed breathlessly. "Your back!"

"And my ribs," he said as he trailed his tongue up her neck, "and my wrists." He nipped her jaw. "And my heart."

Her breath caught as he reached her ear. His tongue did wonderful things that made her close her eyes and moan softly.

"You're the one to heal me," he whispered, blowing gently on the spot he'd just kissed. "Just you…"

"Maybe," she said slowly, "more than just me."

He kissed the sensitive spot behind her ear, and she shivered. "Brianagh, I don't know what Erin Donovan told you about that MacDermott lass," he murmured, "but since the day I dragged you up from that hole in the stables, it's only been you."

She took his hand and guided it to her belly. "No, Nick. I mean…more than just me," she said again softly. His eyes widened at his hand lying on her flat stomach.

Then his eyes flew to hers, surprised and amazed.

She nodded. "Once was enough, I suppose," she said with a small smile.

His gaze intensified as he stared into her eyes. "Once will never be enough," he said. "Forever will never"—he kissed the corner of her lips—"be"—he kissed the other corner —"enough." He slid his tongue between her lips, and she sighed, giving him greater access. He deepened the kiss, his hand never leaving her stomach.

"NICK!"

"The man has the worst timing known to mankind," Nioclas said against her lips.

She laughed, then wrapped her arms around Nioclas's neck. "Can we ignore him and hope he goes away? That's what my aunt always told me to do when someone was particularly annoying."

Nioclas growled playfully. "If anyone bother you here, they'll have to deal with me. I don't, unfortunately, ignore annoyances." He kissed her hard on the mouth, then rolled off the bed and stalked to the door. "What?" he snapped to Donovan and Reilly.

"We think Burke is still in the castle somewhere." Donovan glanced down. "You might want to get dressed for this one."

Brianagh sat up, her eyes wide. "What?"

Donovan nodded. "His horse is tethered—we found it in the forest not an hour ago."

Nioclas swore, then grabbed his léine and began wrapping it around himself. "He could've left on foot."

"Not likely," Reilly replied, appearing at the door. "We also found this."

Nioclas took the scroll from Reilly and unrolled it. His jaw set as he read it. "Cavan."

"What's Cavan?" Brianagh asked, waving them all into the room and shutting the door behind them.

"Who," Reilly corrected her. "He's a MacWilliam ally."

"Or was," Nioclas said. He handed the scroll to her. "He looks to be the next clan Burke wishes to bring against us."

"This is a contract that if the other dies in a battle with the MacWilliam clan, the other is to assume lairdship until the battle for true laird can take place," Brianagh said. She looked up. "I'm confused."

"It's the same agreement he had with Kildare," Donovan said angrily. "He sends the laird and his men in to die, then assumes control of the clan once the dirty work is done. It's his strategy for acquiring his own clan again."

"Very bold," Reilly agreed. "But effective. With the laird's signature and seal, there's no contesting this."

"Which is why we think he's still on castle grounds," Donovan added. "He has nothing without this parchment."

"Well, no time like the present to find the bastard," Nioclas said. He shot a look at Brianagh. "We will finish what we started, my lady. I vow it."

"I know how seriously you take your vows," she replied with a small smile.

"And I know how foolish they are," Reilly said pointedly.

Nioclas's face turned to granite as he laced up his boots. "Not this time, O'Malley."

CHAPTER 29

Brianagh sat in the kitchen, chopping vegetables to keep busy. Keela was working alongside her silently, and Kane guarded the door after he'd barricaded the other. Twenty other men guarded the kitchen area in various form. Despite Brianagh's complaints, Nioclas refused to move on his stance. She was carrying his child and she would be protected at all costs.

She gave an extra oomph to the poor vegetable in front of her, then put her knife down and sighed.

"I understand the feeling, my lady," Keela said, wiping her hands on the front of her apron. "But we must feed these men to keep their strength up. If we concentrate on that, it'll pass the time."

Bri nodded. Keela was right—it was something to do while they waited. She was pretty tired of waiting, though. She couldn't believe she'd freed Nioclas from the dungeon just that morning.

His stamina was incredible. If the positions were reversed, she would've had at least a small nap by now. But, as she was learning, a laird's duties never truly ended.

Nor a laird's wife's, she thought, looking over the table of vegetables she'd chopped. "I think it's time to start the soup," she said, digging in the woodpile. "It looks like we're out of kindling, though."

"I just stocked it this morning," Keela said, pointing with her knife to the small buttery in the corner. "Check in there."

"I'll check," Nioclas said as he entered the kitchen. "I don't want you lifting anything."

"I'm not made of glass," Bri called to him as he rummaged in the buttery. "Don't get all overprotective of the little things, Nioclas."

He emerged with an armful of kindling and added it to the small fire in the hearth. He brushed his hands off, then turned to Brianagh. "Walk with me."

She followed him outside and to the gardens behind the kitchen. It would be lovely to plant something there in the spring, she thought as she glanced around. Fresh herbs, some tomatoes if they could get them, perhaps even a flowering plant of some kind to add a bit of color. She smiled in anticipation.

Nioclas led her to the same alcove where they'd discussed their marriage, and the memory brought another smile to her face. So much had changed since then, and she wouldn't trade it for the world.

"I'd like to stand," she said when Nioclas motioned for her to sit. "I'm feeling restless."

Nioclas didn't say anything for a long minute. "O'Malley did everything he could to keep you safe."

"I understand that," she replied, curious.

"He brought you to a place where you had family to care for you and medicines to bring a man back from the dead."

"Were you digging around in my satchel again?" she asked with a grin.

Nioclas gave a half-smile. "My duty, as your laird, but also as your husband, is to provide you with that same kind of safety."

Her chest tightened as a feeling of dread enveloped her. "Wh-what?"

"We've decided it's for the best of the clan," he added heavily.

"What's best for the clan?"

"As you have the ability to return to a safer time, I give you the order to return to your home, and you are to leave posthaste. A full guard stands ready to accompany you back to the east."

Her heart pounded in her chest. "No. No no no, Nioclas, I don't want to—"

"This is an order from your laird!" Nioclas barked. He immediately softened his tone. "We cannot find him. He will never stop hunting you, Bri. He'll hunt our children. It's not safe here. You must go back." He bowed his head, determination evident in his countenance. His hand rested lightly on his sword, the sapphire shining dully in the thick mist. He looked older…older than even two hours before when he'd left her in the kitchens with Keela and his strict instructions. She could feel the tension radiating from him.

"We've done what was needed to ensure the clan lives on, but you must return with your cousins." He was stoic. Serious. "Clan first, Lady MacWilliam."

"No," she replied firmly. "I won't go. You can't make me. I love you!"

His expression shuttered, and Nioclas shook his head. "You deserve to be loved in return, Brianagh. You can find that in another time…and perhaps with another man."

The breath left her body in a whoosh, and she stared at him in shock, her heart shattering. "You don't mean that," she whispered.

He nodded once.

And suddenly, Brianagh saw her dream:

…his head was bowed, his determination evident from his countenance. His hand rested lightly on his enormous sword, which

held but a single sapphire in its hilt. He'd shown it proudly to Brianagh the day his clan leaders had presented it to him. He looked older than he'd ever appeared to her before, and she could feel the tension radiating from him. He was stoic. Serious.

The last time she had dreamed of him, he had loved her sweetly. He was relaxed, happy, as in love with her as she him. She watched as he nodded once, and it was done.

He grasped her hand and placed...

He slid the brooch into her hand, and she saw the flash of a sword, swinging in an arc from behind him.

"No!" Brianagh screamed, grabbing his tunic and pulling him as hard as she could toward her. "No, no! Behind—"

He landed on the ground, gaping up at her. "What the—"

"My men didn't beat you enough," Burke snarled, standing just outside the alcove where Nioclas had been standing.

Nioclas's guardsmen came running into the garden, and Burke grabbed Brianagh. She struggled until he put his sword against her belly and she froze.

"Clever little wall you have here," Burke said conversationally. "Keeps the wind and rain out nicely."

"What do you want?" Nioclas growled.

"You had it right," Burke replied. "I want your wife. And her control of time."

The guardsmen looked to Nioclas in concern. He ignored them and focused on the sword at Brianagh's belly. One false move and Burke would kill her.

"I've nothing to lose by killing her," Burke said as if he'd read Nioclas's thoughts. "I'll be dead before moving an inch, with all your guardsmen here. But I think you want the lady to live, so you're going to call off your guard."

"Guards, leave us," Nioclas said without hesitation. When they balked, he shot them a glare. "I command you to leave us!"

They backed up until Nioclas, Burke, and Brianagh stood alone.

"Let her go free, and you can have me," Nioclas said in a low voice. "You can kill me and take the clan for your own."

"Just so your woman can travel back and kill me before I have a chance to kill you? I don't think so," Burke replied with a sneer.

"It doesn't work that way," Brianagh ventured. "I can't time-travel."

"Shut up," Burke growled, wrapping his fist in her hair and pulling her head back. "I know you can. I've seen you do it."

"No," she choked. "You've seen Reilly do it. And Colin… but not me."

Burke's eyes narrowed.

"Enough," Nioclas said in warning to Brianagh. Nioclas tossed his sword to the ground, then removed his daggers. When finished, he stood with his arms outstretched, completely unprotected. "She can't help you, Burke, so take what I offer. My life, for hers."

Burke didn't loosen his hold on Brianagh, but he inched them closer to Nioclas. "Lay on the ground."

"Not until you release my wife," Nioclas replied calmly.

"Nick, please, don't do it," Bri cried. "Please—"

"Release her, and you may kill me. Claim the babe as your own, have your clan back. All of it is yours, Burke…but only if she lives."

Burke tightened his grip in Bri's hair, then rubbed his jaw along her neck. He smiled. "I love the unwilling ones," he said. She shuddered, digging her fists into her skirts.

Nioclas took a menacing step forward, and Burke twisted Bri's head away from his and tightened his grip on his sword.

"I think the revenge is best if I just kill her, then you," Burke said with a smirk.

Nioclas shook his head in disgust. "Coward."

Burke's eyes narrowed to slits, and he pushed Brianagh away. He rushed at Nioclas, his sword pointed at Nioclas's chest.

Burke's face suddenly contorted, and he halted, then staggered. He dropped to his knees, his eyes wide, as Brianagh stood behind him, her face colorless and her arm extended.

A knife protruded from Burke's back, buried to the hilt.

Nioclas wasted no time. He grabbed his sword and leapt to his writhing sire.

"She's the devil!" Burke choked. "Witch!"

"You will not speak of my wife as such," Nioclas snarled. "Go to hell, Burke," he said and drove his sword into Burke's belly.

Wrenching the sword free, he barked out to his guard to ensure his sire died—and to ensure his wife lived.

"I'll be fine, Nioclas," Brianagh said, placing the cold cloth on her eyes. She took a deep breath.

"I can't believe you hid a knife against your leg," Colin said with admiration. "Brilliant, Bri. Just brilliant."

Nioclas looked at Colin. "And you're certain she'll be all right?"

"Absolutely. She's in shock, but eventually she'll be back to her old self," Colin said confidently.

"Why did you risk your life like that, Brianagh?" Nioclas asked, his face still twisted with worry.

"Because, I was tired of being the victim." She pulled the cloth off and sat up, still a little shaky. "I decided that death by Burke was not how my life was going to end, so I made an executive decision."

"You and the damn executive decisions." Colin sighed. "You were almost skewered on the end of that sword!"

Nioclas exclaimed. He broke out in a sweat again just thinking about it.

"But I wasn't," she replied calmly. "I have a barely nicked finger. That's all."

"We need to address the issue of your guardsmen," Colin said seriously. "They heard what Burke said, and they saw his face after you killed him. And they saw Brianagh's eyes too."

Bri bit her lip. "You're sure they won't want to burn me at the stake?"

He grimaced as what Colin said struck home. He knew his guardsmen heard everything Burke said about Brianagh's time-traveling. They crossed themselves and murmured to each other, but they did not hesitate to follow his orders to dispose of Burke's body and locate her cousins.

His cousins.

His grandchildren?

Nioclas rubbed his forehead. This was all too complicated after the day he'd just lived.

Brianagh was nodding at him from her bed. "My family can be overwhelming," she said knowingly.

He put his head in his hands and laughed.

Donovan knocked on the open door, then entered and raised his eyebrows at Nioclas. "Has he gone daft?"

"We think so," Reilly affirmed. "He does seem a bit overcome."

"Distressed," Colin agreed.

"The MacWilliam does not get distressed," Nioclas announced through his hands.

"Uh oh," Bri murmured. "He's begun to refer to himself in the third person. That's never a good sign." She watched her husband through blurry vision, then brightened when she looked at Donovan. "Hey! When I squint a little and turn my head just so, you look like a Viking!"

He gaped at her for a moment. "The herbs you doused Burke with…did they addle your mind as well, my lady?"

"Herbs?" Reilly asked.

"Aye. The guardsmen said Burke spoke such nonsense, that he must've eaten some sort of herb to produce such alarming thoughts." He gave her a conspiratorial wink.

"Well, I think that solves the question of what to tell them," Nioclas said with a smile.

"They're powerfully fond of you," Donovan said to Brianagh. "They're all hovering like small lasses, waiting for word. May I tell them you are well-recovered?"

"Please," she replied happily. "That's just so nice of them."

"You've turned my guard into a bunch of simpering fools, and you think that's *nice*?" Nioclas snorted, but inwardly, he was more than pleased. It was a good day after all.

A FEW DAYS LATER, COLIN AND REILLY STOOD IN THE BAILEY, shaking hands with Nioclas and Donovan. Brianagh stood by their horses, gently stroking their noses and holding back her tears.

She hated goodbyes.

"Hey," Colin said, joining her. "You promise he's what you want?"

She tried to smile, but she was pretty sure it looked as though she'd just received a shot of Novocain. "I'm sure," she said, her voice strong. "I'm going to miss you, Col."

"I'll miss you, too." His eyes were suspiciously wet. He sniffled as manfully as possible. "I love you, cuz. Don't worry —I'll keep the business afloat. You need to work on this branch of it, though. With just one successful match in two and a half months, you're falling behind schedule."

She slid something into his hand, and he glanced down at it, surprised.

"It's got everything you'll need on it. I took the password

off," she offered, as Colin shielded the phone from anyone's view.

They both looked down at it, and he swiped the screen. It lit up, then blinked twice.

"The battery's about to die," Bri said, swallowing hard. She looked into Colin's brown eyes, nearly undone at the understanding in them. They both looked back down and watched silently as the screen dimmed to black.

"I'll make it even better than you can imagine," Colin promised. "We'll be the best in the business. Smashing success. I'll make it global."

Brianagh placed her hand on his arm. "I hope so, Colin. If for no other reason than I want you as happy as I am—"

Colin coughed. "We'll see what the Fates have in store for me. Don't hold your breath."

"I always hold my breath," she murmured. "It's the only way to have that happily-ever-after sigh."

They both looked at Keela and Kane, who were clasping hands and watching the goodbyes together. "The weddings are always the best part of a match," she murmured.

"Keep it up," Colin said, giving her a bear hug. She buried her face in his tunic and breathed him in. His laugh rumbled in his chest. "And just so you know, I'm moving from your couch to your bed."

"Remember to change the sheets," she said. "No, seriously. Dirty sheets are disgusting."

"How dirty can they get?" he asked with a cheeky smile.

She made a face. "I'm absolutely certain I do not want to know the answer to that question." She kissed him on his cheek, then smiled wistfully. "Stay safe, Col. Don't time-travel unless you have to."

"I don't plan on it, but then again, it's not really up to me, is it?"

She smiled sadly. "No, I don't suppose it is."

Reilly walked over to her and held his arms open. Colin released her, and she fell into Reilly, tears pricking her eyes.

"He'll take good care of you," he whispered.

"And I'll take good care of him," she whispered back. "Ry…thank you."

He kissed the top of her head. "I knew you'd see it my way. Eventually."

"You're an ass." Brianagh smacked his shoulder. "Be safe. And if you can swing a visit now and again, you'll always be welcome here. You won't even have to be the taster."

"It wouldn't hurt to keep my chamber ready, just in case," he said with a wink. "Who knows what the Fates have in store for me next?"

Nioclas approached them and handed Reilly a piece of parchment. "If you come across Aidan and Cian, please give them this."

Reilly nodded and tucked it into the leather pouch at his hip. "Trust me yet, MacWilliam?"

"Not even a little," Nioclas replied. "But my friends call me Nick."

Reilly inclined his head, then gave Bri one last squeeze. "Take care of yourself, and your family."

"Always," she said, unable to see his face through her tears. "Clan first."

Nioclas wrapped his arms around her as Reilly and Colin mounted their horses and rode across the bailey, then over the drawbridge, disappearing into the forest.

"No regrets," he murmured.

"No regrets," she echoed.

"I do wonder," he said as they walked up the castle steps, "if my clan believes I love you."

Her breath hitched, and she looked up at him in surprise. "Um…"

"Clan MacWilliam!" he boomed across the bailey. Heads turned, children stopped playing, and the general daily chaos died down. He grasped Bri's hand, brought it to his lips, and kissed the inside of her wrist. Her lips parted in surprise—and something deeper.

Nioclas grinned wickedly at her, then turned back to their clan. "I am grateful for the peace we've earned this day. I'm grateful for your loyalty, which is the strongest in our beautiful Ireland. But most importantly, I'm grateful that Lady Brianagh chose me for her husband." He smiled at her. "She found me through the mist, and my soul has found its mate. May you all be as lucky in love as I."

He kissed her, and she melted into him. He pulled back and gave her another wink.

"Take me to bed already," she said with a grin.

He swept her up to the cheers of their clansmen. "I live to serve," he replied, his own grin mirroring hers, and carried her over the threshold.

EPILOGUE

Ireland, 1465

Brianagh MacWilliam whole-heartedly believed in happily-ever-afters. Hers was currently standing at the water's edge, holding the hand of their two-year-old toddler.

The sounds of children's laughter joined with the call of seagulls. Brianagh hugged her knees and watched as Claire and Nioclas cautiously approach the water's edge. The day had been unseasonably warm for May in Ireland.

The water came crashing back to shore, and a moment later, the toddler stood in the sand, soaking wet, and let out a wail.

"Poor Claire," Nioclas said with a laugh as he brought the crying toddler to Brianagh. She held out a piece of linen and Claire snuggled in. Nioclas dropped onto the blanket next to them.

"Sire, please have speech with Rian," Austin, their five-year-old son, whined as he trudged over. "He told me the water beasties will get me in my sleep, but *I* say I'll slay them before they even cross the drawbridge!"

"Our peace and quiet lasted longer than I thought it would," Brianagh said as Austin elbowed her out of the way to get closer to his father. Brianagh waved their eldest son over to deal with the latest round of teasing.

As he often did, Nioclas watched his son amble to his mother, a look of complete innocence etched on his face. He felt the familiar pang in his chest. He and his own brother had often used that same look as they attempted to deny whatever Erin claimed they'd done to her.

"Go on and slay the water beasties together," she said, ushering them from the blanket. "We've only a few more minutes until we must leave. A storm is coming." She pointed to the gathering clouds over the sea, and the boys ran off, friends again.

Nioclas watched them wistfully.

"I miss him too."

Nioclas glanced down at his wife. Brianagh knew his thoughts better than he himself. Aidan had never returned from the mission Nioclas sent him on eight-and-a-half years prior. It still haunted him, but the pain of his brother's loss lessened with each passing year.

"Aye," Nioclas said, tousling Claire's hair. She smiled beatifically at him, then popped her thumb in her mouth and closed her eyes.

"Perhaps a visit to Aunt Erin and Uncle Donovan's is in order," Bri suggested. "We haven't met their newest child yet, and I know the boys love to play with Katriona."

"Mmm, aye. But does Kat like to play with the lads?"

"If you and Aidan did even half of what ours do to that poor child, then you truly were the Devil's spawn." She laughed.

"They haven't hit their prime yet," Nioclas replied, scratching his chin thoughtfully. "Just wait until Austin is a bit older and can climb trees as well as Rian. Then they'll discover the beauty in a well-placed bucket of worms."

Brianagh shrugged. "Remember who Kat's mother is, my love."

"There is that," Nioclas agreed.

"Let's visit sooner rather than later," Bri said softly. She smiled her secret smile. "I don't think I want to be riding in about three more months."

Nioclas threw back his head and laughed. "Another bairn?" he exclaimed. He gave her a smacking kiss on the lips, then smiled softly, his eyes full of love. "If this one's a lad..."

"I think we should name him Aidan." Lightning struck in the distance over the water, and Brianagh placed her forehead against her husband's.

"I love you, Brianagh MacWilliam," Nioclas whispered.

"And I love you," she whispered in return. Their lips met, and Brianagh's soul breathed in contentment.

She was home.

~

THE END

BONUS SCENE

February 14, 1459

Brianagh MacWilliam carefully adjusted the elbow-length veil. She smoothed the ribbon-lined edges into place, and then blew out a satisfied breath.

Taking a final, critical look, Bri allowed the joy to overcome her. This moment was almost a year in the making. A radiant bride, a proud groom, and the love that surrounded them both.

It was, by far, her favorite wedding to date.

"You look beautiful," Aoife said quietly, holding her daughter's hand tightly. "Kane is a lucky man, to be your chosen love."

"I'm the lucky one, Mami. He was willing to die for me," Keela replied, the awe of his commitment lacing her words.

"He *is* willing to die for you," Aoife corrected. She ran a weathered hand over Keela's dark blue wedding dress. "He's loved you for years. Ever since you were children."

Brianagh smiled. "He has?"

"I didn't know," Keela explained. "He told me directly following the hand tying ceremony last year. He said I've always been the one for him. Of course, we grew up together in the village, but didn't speak much once he left for his guard training here at the castle." She turned to her mother, a dreamy smile gracing her face. "His sire was so proud that day, remember?"

"Aye, he was, and with good reason. I believe he wanted this match between you two very much," Aoife mused. "He was quite pleased when the clan was told of your choice."

Bri smiled. "The Fates work in mysterious ways."

"This feeling…it must be what you felt when you wed Laird MacWilliam, aye? Where you felt as though you were so full of happiness, that you might float away on a cloud?"

Brianagh thought back to her wedding day, only a year earlier, a small smile on her lips. Scared, worried, uncertain… not exactly floating on a cloud. But if Bri knew anything, she knew brides—and she did, no matter the century—so she merely murmured, "I imagine so. Come, Keela. It's time to get you wed."

Her smile was radiant. "*Finally.*"

As winter weather had fully embraced Ireland, the ceremony was held in the great hall, with a blazing fire in the large hearth that kept the chill at bay. Keela and Kane faced each other as the clan priest—Brianagh still didn't know if he practiced Christianity or the old ways, as she never quite got up the nerve to ask him, and she *still* didn't understand Latin —recited his verses in front of the couple.

Nioclas leaned back and draped his arm around her shoulders. He pulled her close, and her joy once again filled her soul. She snuggled into him.

"I believe your Latin is as terrible as it was when we wed. Shall I translate for you, my love?" he whispered, his breath tickling her ear.

She laughed lightly and nodded. "Yes, please."

He cocked his head as though listening deeply to the priest. "Aye, he's getting to the good part." He cleared his throat, then placed his mouth against her ear, his voice low and quiet. "Had I known then what kind of deep love awaited me in your arms, I would have continued to wait, up to and past eternity, to call you my own. Your presence in my life has made me a better man than I ever thought possible. My sword will always be at your feet, my heart forever in your hands."

Brianagh pulled away from him, her eyes misting. "That's not what he's saying."

Nioclas placed his thumb and forefinger on her chin and turned her head forward again. He placed his lips back to her ear, smiling against it when she shivered.

"Ssh. My sweet lady wife, you trust me with the care of your heart, and I vow to ensure you will never regret that choice, nor your decision to stay with me. My love for you is more legendary than any tale told by any clan in Ireland, even those with fantastical tales of travel through time."

She choked on her laugh.

"As the bearer of such love, 'tis my honor to make it known to all people in this land that I am the most blessed man to ever walk these green shores. Our children will feel the safety of our love. Our clan will know the strength of it. And history will understand that there never was, nor never shall be again, a love as true as mine for you."

Brianagh closed her eyes, tears on her cheeks, and Nioclas gently turned her head back to his own. "You, my lady Brianagh, are my forever. I love you with the entirety of my soul."

"I love you," she whispered, and pressed her lips to his.

The clan cheered, and Bri broke their kiss to see Keela and Kane locked in their own.

"This life is not always easy." She smiled ruefully. "But the hard times are what make these happy days so beautiful." Wiping her tears, she gazed into the gray eyes she loved so much. "For years, I truly thought love was something for everyone but me. You proved me wrong, and I am so grateful for it. In the darkest of these cold days, you are my warmth and my light. I never wish to be without you. You, my winter laird, are my happily-ever-after. "

He kissed her again, wrapping his arms around her and pulling her onto his lap.

As the clan cheered again, she smiled against his lips. In the end, it worked out.

It always did.

A NOTE FROM THE AUTHOR

THANK YOU SO MUCH FOR READING AND SUPPORTING AN INDIE AUTHOR!

I hope you enjoyed *The Winter Laird.* If so, please consider writing a quick review wherever you purchased this copy. Every review is important to authors, and helps readers find us so we can continue writing the stories you enjoy.

Please join my mailing list for updates, news, and general good times. (No spamming, ever.)
www.nancyscanlonbooks.com

Drop me a note — reader email feeds the soul!
nancy@nancyscanlonbooks.com

AN EXCERPT FROM AN ENCHANTED SPRING (MISTS OF FATE BOOK TWO)

Chapter 1

Colin O'Rourke watched his cousin-in-law, many times removed, absently roll a pencil between his fingers. They were closer than brothers, and had been for the better part of eight years. Over that time, Colin had observed, helpless, as Aidan MacWilliam's countenance slowly changed from easygoing to aloof. But most worrisome was this latest visit.

Colin's voice was quiet. "It may be time to accept that your future lies here."

The pencil froze mid-roll, and Aidan's sharp green eyes pierced Colin's dark brown ones. "I will never accept that. I *will* get back, or I'll die trying."

Colin wisely held his tongue. Despite his refusal to accept that he'd been brought forward in time for good, Aidan had become immensely successful. He had more money than he knew what to do with and an extended family who understood clan loyalties.

But Colin knew that wasn't enough for a fifteenth-century Irish warrior. Aidan needed something to live for, something to spark his interest in life again. "Aidan, what's left to try? You've exhausted all possibilities."

Aidan angrily flicked the pencil onto the desk and stood. "I know there's a time gate somewhere. All manner of strange folk traipse through O'Malley's garden—they're coming from somewhere, without the aid of anyone. So there's something out there that will get me back." His tone turned surly. "I simply haven't found it yet."

Colin held back a frown and changed the subject. "Well, if you need a distraction, I could use your aid."

Aidan reluctantly sat back down. "Aye?"

It was becoming harder to simply sit by and watch someone he loved creep ever closer to a dark precipice that was neither acknowledged nor denied. Colin knew that if Aidan didn't find a way home soon, he might tumble headfirst into that abyss and never return.

"I'm expanding Celtic Connections into the UK and Ireland."

Aidan nodded. "The LA office doing well, then?"

Colin's elite matchmaking service had had such success in Boston, he had opened two other offices in Toronto and Los Angeles. Both were fully booked with an impressive clientele list.

"Sure is. But with so many offices, I need a new department for publicity and public relations. European expansion isn't something I'm ready to make public yet, and I need someone to handle the department setup."

Aidan shrugged. "Sorry, mate. I don't know anyone in that field."

"I realize that. What I need is for you to do some recon."

Aidan sat forward slightly though his face remained impassive. "Recon," he echoed.

"Yes." Colin watched him carefully. "The sword you brought with you, when you arrived in this time—it's on the auction block."

"What?"

Colin nodded. "One of our clients is facilitating the auction, which has loads of medieval artifacts up for grabs. Your sword is one of them." He flipped open a binder to a marked page, then handed it to Aidan. "Looks like the owner died suddenly, and he left all his relics to his son. Luckily for us, the son has zero interest in medieval history, but he seems awfully interested in the money it could fetch."

The curses that flew from Aidan's mouth were inventive, and Colin barked out a laugh. "The auction is in a few days, in New York City. Which is exactly where the person I'm looking to hire is located. This would kill two birds with one stone. You'd get your sword, and I'd get my PR person. So —you in?"

Aidan nodded curtly. "You know it. I've been tracking down that damn sword for years."

"Well, here's your chance to get it back," Colin replied. *And,* he added silently, *I'm talking about much more than the sword...*

~

To: Emmaline MacDermott

Emmaline Perkins stared in apprehension at the large envelope on her desk. The red CONFIDENTIAL stamp seemed to stare back at her, challenging her to break the seal. But that wasn't what held her back.

It was addressed to Emmaline MacDermott.

Even now, seven months later, Emma shuddered at what would've been her surname, had fate not intervened.

She took a closer look and noticed the seal was already broken. That explained why her bullying, brown-nosing coworker had so gleefully dropped the envelope into her lap earlier. Heidi Swanson was only gleeful when someone was about to fall hard on her face.

Emma was on her way to the top at Price Publicity. Her A-list client roster grew weekly, and her boss had hinted that she was up for a promotion. Her hard work and dedication to being the best publicist possible wasn't going unnoticed by the movers and shakers of New York City. Her job was to calm down, smooth over, and cover up any situation before people found out there was something to find out.

Heidi *hated* her for it.

Her talents weren't limited to her professional life, either. She was quite successful in ensuring no one knew anything about her cheating ex-fiancé, or his threats against her.

She gave her head a small shake to dislodge the bubble of fear, and her sleek, dark blond ponytail swung gently against her neck. She reminded herself that she was sitting in her office, perfectly safe. Benjamin MacDermott was currently hanging out in a ten-by-ten cell on an aggravated assault conviction. The attack on a bouncer in a nightclub was just one of many things she hadn't been aware he was capable of…but she knew not to underestimate him anymore. Despite the fact that he'd been behind bars for five months, a shiver of dread raced up her spine whenever she saw, heard, or even *thought* his name.

And now, she thought with that same shiver, *here it is, staring me in the face.* She looked at the envelope again and blew out a slow, shaky breath.

To: Emmaline MacDermott.

Whoever sent this envelope to her was playing a sick joke, to be sure.

Emma peeked inside the folder, and she had to swallow the bile back. Her heart sank. She grabbed the envelope and headed for the nearest conference room, her phone to her ear, giving the appearance of leaving to take an important client call. She carefully closed the door and drew the blinds, then dumped the contents onto the polished wood table.

She drew a sharp breath.

Her ex-fiancé, dressed in some very inventive bondage gear, was tied to a bed. A red-haired woman, dressed in a similar getup, was mid-strike with a whip and a ferocious look on her gorgeous features.

In a detached way, Emma thought the woman rather looked like something out of a movie. Perfectly placed action shot...Emma understood how the woman was such a huge star.

Emma would understand, of course, since the woman in the pictures was her biggest and most demanding client, Jenny Kincaid. The same Jenny Kincaid who had a romantic comedy releasing this week. A romantic comedy, it seemed prudent to remind herself, that costarred Jenny's husband of ten years.

Not Emma's ex.

Emma squinted at his face and couldn't suppress the now-familiar shudder up her spine. Emma had long suspected Ben of cheating, but she always rationalized that she had no real proof. They were so far into the wedding plans. They'd been together for so long. They had been college sweethearts.

Her list of excuses seemed endless.

But almost seven months ago, Emma had arrived at the office only to realize she'd left some important papers behind. She texted Ben, hoping he hadn't left for work, but it was close to ten in the morning and he didn't respond, so she headed back to their apartment. She opened the door to see Ben and Jenny engaged in some very...*experimental* positions.

What ensued was a mess. Jenny didn't even bat an eye. In fact, she asked Ben if they could meet at her hotel later, to finish the job, to which he agreed, and Jenny gave Emma a sickening girlfriend-to-girlfriend smile before reminding her of client confidentiality.

Emma was too shocked to respond. But, when she finally was able to react (and Ben had put some clothing on), Emma threw him out of the apartment. He accepted it with minimal fuss.

Or so she thought.

A couple of weeks later, Ben was waiting for her when she got home.

"How did you get in here?" she demanded, stepping into the apartment.

"I can't get my deposits for the wedding back."

His voice was so controlled. Emma felt a frisson of fear, but this was Ben. She'd known him forever. He wouldn't hurt her. Physically, anyway.

"Consider it payment for breaking my heart. Get out." She held the door open and gestured at him to leave.

He casually walked toward her, then slammed the door shut and pinned her against it, making her cry out in surprise.

"I don't think you heard me, Emmaline. *I. Can't. Get. My. Money. Back.*" His eyes, once so warm and loving, were brittle and hard.

"You're hurting me!" she squeaked, trying to twist from his grasp. He held firm.

"Don't pretend you don't know, Emmaline. I need that money. It's mine. And I owe some very big people—very *important* people—a lot of cash. Now, because you were so"—he slammed her against the door—"damn"—he slammed her again—"stingy"—another crash against the door—"with your bank accounts, I can't pay them back. And they'll kill me, Emmaline."

Emma couldn't breathe. This was Ben! He was an insurance agent, for crying out loud! Who could be trying to kill him?

He released her suddenly, then stepped back. "You're going to give me the money. I want twenty thousand by Thursday."

She gasped. "Ben, I don't have—"

He was back on her in an instant, crushing her. "You have

a very nice life insurance payout," he sneered, his lips inches from hers. "Remember? I set it up myself. And I know I'm still your beneficiary, Emma." His eyes turned to ice. "I'll use it if I have to."

Emma felt the threat all the way to her soul, and she choked back a sob. This was not the Ben she'd known, the Ben she'd loved for so long.

This was a monster.

She nodded, unable to form words, and he pushed her to the floor, where she fell in a heap. He opened the door and stepped over her, then turned and looked down at her in disgust. In a low voice, he added, "You've made things very difficult, Emmaline. If you run, I will find you. And it will be deemed an accident. I'll make sure the payout happens quickly and efficiently." He smiled coldly. "You'll have a lovely funeral. Not that anyone would show up. I'm all you ever had."

He pulled the door shut, and Emma lost her stomach.

Emma was shocked back to the present when someone knocked on the conference room door. "I have this booked for a client meeting!" a voice called apologetically.

Emma swallowed hard and stuffed the incriminating images back into the envelope. She would get them to the shredder immediately.

Ben had been sentenced to a year and some months in jail, and Emma had hoped when he came out she'd have a plan.

A glance at the unexpected envelope in her shaky hand had her wondering if she might want to start planning.

At some point, her wineglass emptied itself.

Emma gave it a small frown. It had been doing that all night, but she refused to be bothered by it. She just refilled it from the bottle that was sitting obediently next to her on the small table on her tiny little terrace, in her tiny little corner of New York City.

She squinted at the bottle before she put it down. It was mostly empty—when did that happen? She must've swigged —er, *sipped*—more than she thought. She couldn't bring herself to care, though. After the day she'd had, coupled with not taking a night off in forever, she deserved some down time.

Her clients' social lives had replaced her own years ago. She put every ounce of herself into being a great publicist. She could smooth over any situation her clients found themselves in. Her years of dedication (okay, not taking a vacation or a full weekend in the entire seven years she'd been at Price Publicity) gave her contacts all over the city—reporters, journalists, magazine editors, restaurant owners—but her biggest successes came from social media. Her coworkers always turned to her for the best ways to spin something in 140 characters or less, inventive hashtags to offset negative press, and clever social media statuses that made light of serious situations. And she also possessed a good ear for warning bells, which helped her notice the bad vibes before a disaster struck.

However, as she sat on her little terrace, looking out over the crowded street below, she wished she were anywhere else, for the first time since she had arrived in the city years ago. It was a never-ending barrage of busy lives, all colliding in a few square miles. And her job never let her go—"regular business hours" was code only for one's physical presence within the Price building, because the clientele at Price Publicity tended to make rather serious mistakes at all hours of the night.

She took another swig of wine as her phone rang.

"'Lo?" she answered, peering into the wineglass.

"Emma—we have a crisis."

Emma took another swallow of her wine before

answering. Her tongue felt a little fuzzy. "Josh, I'm not working tonight."

"Are you drunk?" her boss asked. Emma could almost see his brow furrow, as if he couldn't possibly fathom the prim and proper Emma Perkins getting drunk. By herself.

On a Wednesday night.

"Nooo," Emma snorted.

"Oh my God. You *are* drunk."

"Why are you calling me, Josh?"

"Because you need to be in the office tomorrow morning at seven. I was checking my email—"

"You really do work too much," Emma interrupted.

"So says the pot to the kettle," Josh snickered. "Listen, a hi-pri came into our inboxes almost an hour ago. We've all been waiting for your response."

Emma's fuzzy brain tried to snap to attention at the mention of a high-priority email, but it just wasn't working right. "From who?" The only client who would warrant a high-priority email was the one in the incriminating photos.

She took another large sip to block out the memory.

Josh's voice was serious. "Mr. Price."

Emma stood up quickly, choking on her wine. Putting a hand over her eyes to stop the spinning, she managed, "Mr. Price, as in, Mr. Price, the CEO?"

"That's the one."

She swallowed hard. Mr. Price gave everyone a smartphone loaded with at least two email apps so he wouldn't have to call them. In his opinion, every employee at his firm was on call for him all day, every day, through email. He reserved the phone calls for his clients.

Josh continued, "Emma, stop drinking and get yourself together. Mr. Price wants to see us in his office at seven tomorrow morning. There's a potential new client—Mr. MacWilliam—he's so wealthy he eats money for breakfast.

He's demanded you and only you, and he's refusing to deal with anyone else...even Mr. Price."

"Oh, God," Emma groaned.

"Exactly."

Mr. Price loathed when clients refused to deal with him directly. Especially the exceptionally wealthy ones. And if they requested someone outside the top tier of management, Price wanted detailed, in-person reports three times per week for the length of the contract. If she didn't deliver results in the form of a contract extension, there would be hell to pay.

Who was she kidding? Her life was already a living hell; it wasn't like it could get much worse.

"Okay, respond to that email for me? I'll be there. Tell him I'm with a client right now or something."

"Done," Josh replied, the *tap-tap-tap* of a keyboard audible over the line. "I'll meet you outside the office at six thirty."

"Okay," Emma said with a sigh, ruefully pouring the contents of her wineglass into the plastic potted palm on the terrace. "I hope I'm not hung over tomorrow."

"Tonight, take two aspirin and drink an entire glass of water before you go to bed," Josh instructed. "I need you alert, Perkins. In the morning, you're going to drink a small glass of orange juice. No coffee."

"What?!"

"Trust me, Emma. Keep it simple, right?"

Emma smiled a little. That was her mantra for her clients—keep it simple. Simple press releases, simple statements, simple truths—or lies, as the case warranted.

If only real life worked like that.

"Good night, Josh. I'll see you in the morning."

"Six thirty, Emma."

Emma hung up, morose. Work always came first; everyone always needed something from her. But that was how her world worked—she gave, everyone took, and she was paid for it. Emma squared her shoulders and reminded herself that she didn't need anything else from anyone. She had herself, and that was enough. It had been that way for years before Ben, and she was committed to being that way for years to come. She had her job, her health, and her true passion.

When Emma was small, maybe seven or eight, her father had given her a giant toy castle. It was enormous, one of the spectacular dollhouses they sold in department stores, and it sparked her imagination like no other toy. Her mother gave her a tiny princess doll, and an entire garrison of knights to protect it. Emma usually made the princess rescue the knights, which made her mother laugh. The tinkling sound was full of joy; she always said how proud she was that her daughter was willing to save herself from any evil princes.

It was Emma's clearest memory from her childhood, aside from the day her teacher led her into the principal's office, where a police officer told her that her parents had been killed in a car accident.

When the time came for her to move into her grandparents' house, she left the castle and the toys behind.

But in college, something propelled her to take a medieval studies class, and in it, she found peace and a rediscovered love of knights in shining armor, which led to a major in Medieval Thought and Antiquities. It was her passion, and even though her job was demanding, she made time every month to write an article or two for various obscure publications. Articles that she told no one about, and even wrote under a pseudonym. It was her last shred of that girlhood dream, and she didn't want reality to ever intrude.

She blinked back the prick of tears. Her reality was anything but valiant knights. No, hers only included the evil princes. She was grateful her mother wasn't alive to see how the princess rescued such underserving knaves instead of knights.

Emma shook herself from the direction of her thoughts,

refusing to start a pity party that would no doubt have her reaching for another bottle of wine. She couldn't go down that path, not when she had an important meeting in the morning about some hotshot client. She looked up at the sky, wishing she could see the stars, but in the city, all she ever saw was the kind of star who demanded more and more of her.

Her phone buzzed with a text from Josh, reminding her to take the aspirin. Emma headed inside the empty apartment, trying to ignore the loneliness that threatened to overwhelm her.

~

An Enchanted Spring (Mists of Fate Book 2) is available now.

ALSO BY NANCY SCANLON

THE WINTER LAIRD

(MISTS OF FATE BOOK ONE)

Modern-day matchmaker Brianagh O'Rourke needs a break.

Medieval Irish laird Nioclas MacWilliam needs a bride.

When their worlds collide, they must work together to save his clan…and her life.

~

AN ENCHANTED SPRING

(MISTS OF FATE BOOK TWO)

Aidan MacWilliam is an out-of-time warrior.

Emmaline Perkins is an out-of-luck publicist.

He'll show her a world she can't believe…and she'll show him a world he didn't believe in.

~

ONCE UPON A SUMMER NIGHT

(MISTS OF FATE BOOK THREE)

Colin O'Rourke is taking his matchmaking business global.

The only thing standing in his way?

His soul mate…

ALSO BY NANCY SCANLON

FALLING THROUGH TIME
(MISTS OF FATE BOOK FOUR)

Gwendolyn Allen is done waiting.

Reilly O'Malley waited too long.

When the Fates step out, can love step in?

ACKNOWLEDGMENTS

I'm very blessed with the people who helped me to realize my dreams. First, my husband, Sean, who (for years!) read the back of my romance novels in a deep, dramatic voice just to hear me laugh. I love you and wouldn't want to be on this journey with anyone else. I'm thankful for my children, who ate cereal for dinner in the final month of the writing of this book (they didn't complain…).

Thanks to Mom and Dad for ensuring that, growing up, I always had a book or twenty to read, and to my sisters for trying hard not to tease me about my bookworm ways. (It was perhaps the only thing you didn't tease me about!)

Jill Buckley, Lindsey Miller and Laurie Silvia—your early feedback helped me to see where my story shined, and where it needed some polishing. My humble thanks for your love of these characters!

To you, dear reader—thank you for taking a chance on me. I hope you enjoyed every second of this book, and will continue on this amazing journey with me.

Last but certainly not least, I need to thank my Nana Miller. At the vulnerable age of 16, I poured my teenage soul into a novel. When she read it, instead of saying anything, she gave me a proud smile. Her unspoken belief in me gave me much-needed confidence, and I knew then that I would be an author someday.

Nana, someday is here, and I know that it wouldn't be Heaven for you without a book in your hand—and here's mine. I love you and miss you. This first book is for you. xoxo

ABOUT THE AUTHOR

Nancy Scanlon is the author of the Mists of Fate series. When she's not writing, she spends her days parenting two kids, playing with her two huge lapdogs, and trying to get her husband to laugh at corny jokes. She adores all things misty, caffeinated, chocolate, and grammatically correct.

facebook.com/NancyScanlonBooks
twitter.com/NancyScanlon1
instagram.com/NancyScanlon.1
goodreads.com/NancyScanlon

Made in the USA
Las Vegas, NV
11 May 2024